THE PRIVATE LIFE OF
JANE MAXWELL

By Jenn Gott

The Beacon Campaigns
The Lady of Souls
Fixing Fate
Heart's Blood

Hopefuls
The Private Life of Jane Maxwell

THE PRIVATE LIFE OF
JANE MAXWELL

JENN GOTT

HOPEFULS
#1

THE PRIVATE LIFE OF JANE MAXWELL

Cover design by Jenn and Graeme Gott
Cover images: woman © lassedesignen/Shutterstock;
pigeon © Daniel Ruyter/Unsplash;
cityscape © Nirzar Pangarkar/Unsplash;
jumping feet © Dan Carlson/Unsplash;
taxis © Andrew Ruiz/Unsplash

ISBN 978-0-692-73150-5
eBook ISBN 978-0-9908914-4-4

To the creative teams behind the DC "Arrowverse" and the MCU—thank you for getting me hooked on superheroes and never letting me go.

&

To all of the forgotten women who've helped shape the world of comic books since the art form first began. Ladies, this one's for you.

THE DAY THAT DOCTOR DEMOLITION FINALLY MANAGED TO
seize control of Grand City Capital Bank, the Heroes of Hope
were meeting to plan his capture in an underground parking
garage, and Jane Maxwell was fired from her job.

She stood in her boss's office, staring down at him like the
dumbass that he was.

"Wait . . . You're *firing* me?"

Her boss—weedy, thin faced, poor posture and poorer skin—
nodded as if he was in the row of bobbleheads that lined the
edge of his desk. "Effective immediately."

Jane threw her arms wide, as if she couldn't possibly accept
the enormity of the stupidity before her. Which she couldn't.
"Because I dared to stand up for myself?"

"Because you insulted our *readers*."

"*One* reader," Jane said. "Well . . . and all the trolls he brought
along for the ride, but—"

"You called him a fuckface, Jane."

"He *is* a fuckface!"

Her boss shrugged. "And that's why you're out."

"I don't believe this," Jane said. She put her hands on her hips and began to pace the office like a caged animal, that was how much she didn't believe this.

All around the room, framed posters of heroes and villains towered over her. City skylines at night, valiant protectors standing tall as they surveyed their domain, rubble flipping through the air in the wake of a furious explosion. Jane caught flashes of enormously flexing muscles, and women in skintight catsuits twisted up in impossible poses.

She stopped in front of one in particular, a cover shot of six people: the Heroes of Hope, each striking their signature pose. Windforce, covered head-to-toe in blue spandex, hovers several inches off the ground as his skydiving wingsuit flares around him. Granite Girl, petite but oh-so-deadly, her skin hardened as she throws one of her lethal punches. Rip-Shift, in cyberpunk black and mirrored sunglasses, steps out of a rip in the fabric of reality, the world parting around him like a curtain. Pixie Beats, grinning in her masquerade mask, her punk-rock-meets-ballerina styling bright even in miniature, is shrunk down and standing on Mindsight's upturned palm. Jane's eyes, as usual these days, avoided looking at Mindsight too directly, though the image of her filled Jane's mind: the film-noir aesthetic of trench coat, fedora, and shingle bob, the mask obscuring her face, the fingerless gloves. Finally, in the middle of it all, gazing heroically beyond the camera, the leader of the group. Muscles run tautly beneath the sleeves of an armored suit drawn in what Jane called "Hero Red." Light gleams around his fingertips, outstretched toward the sky. A red mask obscures only his eyes, leaving a chiseled chin and a blinding smile fit for a toothpaste ad.

In the corner of the frame was a set of autographs in silver ink. Jane stared at hers, the familiar scrawl.

She turned back. "I *gave* you Captain Lumen."

"Yes, and we're all very grateful for your work—"

"Fuck you, Eddie. If you were grateful, I wouldn't be out of a job. If you were *grateful*, QZero would stand up for me."

Eddie pinched his lips. Through the skylight of his office, the sun was hitting him in just the right way to accentuate his bald spot. Jane took note of the way the shadows divided his face, her brain already chewing on an idea for the way she'd design Doctor Demolition's new statue of himself, when she realized with a jolt that she'd never *get* to design it.

She stormed out of the office. Eddie was midsentence, something about the reputation of QZero, about Jane being a public figure now, about not letting herself get dragged into mud fights—as if it had been *her* fault that some knuckle-dragger had started sending death threats to her office. All Jane had done was talk about what was happening. The "fuckface" remark wasn't even in her first blog post, wasn't even directed at her stalker. It was only after forty-eight hours of being flooded with comments, of needing to shut down the flamewar now raging on her blog, of being a trending hashtag on Twitter, that she'd finally snapped.

Jane cut a sharp path through Quantum Zero Comics. In her mind, she saw the panels perfectly: a view from above, lines across the image as if it's being seen through a security camera. The hall is empty save for a silhouette in the distance. A close-up of clenched teeth, another of clenched fists held fast beside her body. Her finger, pressing the elevator button, the thick lines of her ring drawn in loose, bold strokes. On the next page, a series of employees scattering at the sight of her, ducking into cubicles or back into the restroom.

She didn't look at anybody as she stalked through the jungle of desks and drawing tables. A bank of enormous windows looked out over the city, and Jane marched straight to her own table, right in front of them. The best view in the house—or at least, in this department. Pieces of her reflection caught the bright sunlight: the yellow of her plaid shirt and the shine of her glasses.

In comics, you always get a nice file box to carry your stuff outside; Jane mashed everything that she could fit into her messenger bag and the pockets of the jacket that had been hanging across the back of her chair ever since it had finally warmed up in April. An umbrella hung off her wrist and banged against her thigh as she lugged an armload of reference books out the door.

Twenty minutes later, her stuff was piled on the table around her as she fired off a series of angry texts from the corner of her favorite Starbucks. Her phone jerked underneath the mash of her thumbs, her whole body curling over the table in frustration.

I mean, where's the loyalty??? Like I haven't given them fucking EVERYTHING.

I'm sorry, Janie, her mother texted back. *I know it's rough.*

Rough?? It's OBSCENE. I should sue them. I wonder if I can sue them.

You want me to ask your father?

Jane shook her head, an automatic response. She pulled up the emoji menu, trying to find one that would express her feelings on *that* idea, when someone came up beside her.

"Jane?" he asked. "You okay?"

Jane jerked, startled out of her little bubble. Her thumb struck a picture of a pair of red ladies' shoes, and then slid over to "send" before she realized. She looked up, already frowning. "You really don't want to ask me that today, Cal."

Cal gave her a sympathetic smile as he took off his sunglasses. "That bad?" he asked, pulling out the empty chair beside her.

"You could say that. I—Oh. Sorry, one second." Jane's phone chirruped in her hand, her mother sending back, *I don't understand—is that a yes or a no?*

No, Jane typed. *Later, mom, GG. Love you.*

"I hope that I'm not catching you at a bad time, then," Cal said as Jane put her phone facedown on the gritty tabletop.

Jane slumped back in her chair. "You did, but I'm kind of grateful for the distraction. What's up? You back in town for long?"

Cal hesitated, just long enough for Jane to notice. He shrugged. "I don't know yet. Listen, though, um . . . I was hoping that you'd have time for something tonight. Can you meet me? Say, at seven?"

"This is all very mysterious." Despite herself, Jane almost laughed. "What's the deal?"

"No deal . . . nothing I want to talk about here, at any rate."

Cal glanced around the Starbucks, at the baristas chatting as they made drinks, the bored trail of customers yawning and glancing irritably at their phones, the group of old ladies with their knitting, the one pretentious arty type that had set herself up with a laptop and a chipped mug from home. He seemed to be scoping the place out, and when his attention returned to Jane, finally, there was a tiny frown wrinkling his forehead.

"Can you do it? Seven o'clock? I'll meet you back here?"

Jane raised an eyebrow. There was something . . . different, about Cal today. Beyond his behavior, beyond this shadowy "meeting" that he was insisting on. Jane's artist eye trailed him up and down: he was good-looking in a movie star sort of way, his blond hair mussed just so, his jeans and t-shirt perfectly tailored, a leather jacket that was exactly the right amount of broken-in. There was a reason that Jane had modeled Captain Lumen after him, and not just because QZero had refused the scripts where Jane had written her as a woman.

Jane shook herself—she must have been imagining it. "Yeah, whatever." It's not like she had plans anymore. "Seven is fine."

Cal let out a breath. "Thank you." He stood up to go, tapping his phone against hers. "My new number," he added. "In case . . . in case you run into trouble between now and then. You let me know, all right?"

"Sure." Jane frowned as she turned her phone over. *New contact*, it said. "I'll do th—"

But when she looked back up, Cal was already gone. Jane craned her neck, then leaned over in her chair to get a better look at the door, out the window, up at the counter. Despite a clear view of the street, there was no sign of him.

Jane scowled. "You're seeing things, woman," she muttered, as she pulled up her Twitter feed to see if news of her departure had broken yet.

WHEN JANE WAS FIFTEEN, SHE ALMOST DIED.

This isn't an exaggeration. It wasn't that she was caught doing something and that her mom was going to, like, *literally*, kill her for it—no, this was actual, life-and-death death, and it had come so close that Jane had felt the coldness of its jaws against her skin.

Only six other people knew the truth of this story, and those only because they were right alongside her when it happened.

It wasn't as exciting as it should have been. Jane was out with her friends: Cal and Devin and Keisha and Marie and Tony . . . and Clair. Always Clair. This was the night of Tony's sixteenth birthday, and he was pissed because his parents hadn't let him schedule his driving test yet. Everyone agreed that this was vastly unfair. He was the oldest, and they'd been counting on him to be their ride. Now they'd have to wait *who knows* how long—God, maybe all the way until *December*, when Keisha would be next.

For seven teenagers stuck in the outermost stretches of the suburbs, this was as good as death.

They rode their bikes out, then, since *fine*, they didn't have a *car*. Like a bunch of dumb kids. Tony wanted to do something different, so they were out hunting new hotspots to meet up. That's what they called it, "hotspots," like if they started hanging out there, then obviously all the cool kids would follow. Never mind that it had never worked before. Tony had heard of an abandoned building on the far edge of town, a chemical factory that had been empty since the eighties. This seemed the ultimate height of cool, so they'd peddled out farther than they'd ever gone, the night sky stretching out endlessly above them. They roved as a pack, whooping it up and cruising down the middle line of the road or even into the oncoming traffic lane—feeling like total badasses—until they'd see headlights in the far, far distance, and then they'd all scramble not to collide as they jerked out of the way.

Years later, when Jane drew the version of this that didn't happen, the infinitely cooler one that needed to appeal to the all-important 18–25 demographic, she'd crammed them all into a bumblebee yellow-and-black Camaro from 1973. There was beer in the backseat, and the hint that maybe someone had a joint hidden away for later. But in real life, they were on Schwinns and Walmart specials, helmets safely strapped to their heads, Pepsi and Snickers bars crammed into Cal's backpack.

It took ages to reach the factory. Long enough that their legs were aching, that their shirts clung to their sweaty backs. Long enough that they'd started to talk about turning around. But then the building rose up out of the horizon like some kind of apparition, the castle finally coming into view at the end of a long and grueling quest, and that had been enough to refuel their enthusiasm.

They ditched their bikes at the chain-link fence that edged the property, and made the rest of the trip on foot. Dry grass came up to their knees, *shushing* as they trampled through it. Jane had tied her jacket around her waist, letting the cold air pour against her. Clair's arm kept bumping against Jane's, though it was hard to say if she was doing it on purpose, or if the ground underfoot was just so uneven that in their haste she hadn't noticed. This was after they'd come out to each other, but well before they dared to tell anyone else, and so Jane didn't take Clair's hand, even though she desperately wanted to.

When they got to the factory, the door was locked. Tony and Cal tried to bust the lock, and even Keisha went over and gave the door a good kick because her legs were so strong from ballet, but it refused to open. They tried looking for another one, or maybe a window they could break—but this was the only door, and the windows, if there were any, were so high that they disappeared into the dark.

"This *sucks*!" Tony said, a sentiment that was quickly agreed upon by all. But, with nothing to do about it, they began to shuffle back toward the road, grumbling and mumbling about how nothing cool ever happens around here, anyway.

That was when they spotted it.

Well, Clair spotted it. She'd always had sharp eyes, wide and observant. Plus, she was taking one last look back. "Look!" she'd shouted, and she pointed to a spot behind them. A large piece of equipment lay rusting out on the lawn, a box that might have been a generator or something. Just beyond it, they could see the faintest glow, haloing it as if it was a mission point in a video game.

They all ran over it.

This is where their stories differed. The others, in an unspoken agreement, concluded that someone must have accidentally snagged on a power cable leading up to it, which for some reason hadn't been shut down properly. The cable made contact with the generator, sending out a jolt of electricity that threw them all back, and scrambled their heads for a good ten minutes or so. That was the reasonable explanation, and despite the group's collective love of science fiction, they also prided themselves on being so *rational* and scientific. Cold, hard logic was their mistress, and any hesitation there might have been at accepting this obvious explanation was quickly swept aside.

For a long time, even Jane accepted this. Even once she started telling her story, she framed it as a great jump-off point for an RPG that Devin was trying to develop, modeled after Dungeons & Dragons but more *sciencey*. What if that *wasn't* what had happened to them, she said? I mean, obviously it was—but just for the sake of the game, let's use this as the backstory.

But little by little, she'd started to remember more, or maybe she just imagined it. It was hard to say. So little by little, she'd started to write it down. A strange device, sitting just behind the generator. A mechanical base with a green orb pulsating in it, wires and cables hooking it directly to the generator of the abandoned factory. "*Do you think it's aliens?*" they asked in the comics, years later, when the issue hit the stands. "*Maybe a government conspiracy.*" By this point, the RPG was long since shelved, and so Jane was free to use her tale in a different medium.

And so the Heroes of Hope were born: transformed by the radiation of the alien/government device, each with unique abilities that allowed them to band together and fight crime wherever it may arise. And in the real world, the seven of them woke up with wicked headaches and a mad thirst. They chugged down all of Cal's Pepsi, and raced back to the main streets to buy some pizza or something, laughing at how close they'd come to death, because everyone knew what happened when you touched a downed power line. They collectively swore to never tell their parents, and that, it seemed, was that.

CAL WAS LATE, AND WHEN HE DID SHOW UP, HE WAS OUT OF BREATH.

"Come on," he said, instead of "hi." He grabbed Jane's hand, dragging her into the street.

"Where are we going?" Jane asked as she trailed behind him like a puppy on a leash. Her Converse caught on the sidewalk, and she tripped against his back.

She was in no mood for mysteries and surprises today: the latest issue of *Hopefuls* was out, but the reviews were getting buried beneath the news of her firing. Maybe Jane should have been pleased by that—let those bastards at QZero burn, let the beginning of their most epic story arc get swept away and ignored under the onslaught of a headline that would flare and then die out like a flashbang—but her heart ached over it just the same. This was *her* story, and it was getting ignored by a mess of her own creation.

Cal didn't answer her question. He hailed a taxi at the corner of State Street and Bellwood Boulevard, ushering Jane inside as if she was Us Weekly's favorite popstar of the month and the paparazzi were hot on her tail. Jane fell into the cab, her elbow clonking against the opposite door as she scooted over to make room. Cal leaned forward, whispering directions to the cab driver, and when he sat back, he wouldn't look at Jane. His attention kept flying to the passing rooftops, the deepening shadows of every alley. Jane saw their little cab as if from outside, the yellow of the roof drawn as the only splash of color in an otherwise dark panel of black and gray and off-white cars packed thickly around them. You'd see Cal's alert face through the window next, though Jane would have added a smattering of raindrops on the glass to throw just enough shadow on his perfect cheekbones.

For the first time, Jane wondered what she was even doing here. There were so many things that she should be taking care of right now. All afternoon, she'd poured over spreadsheets of her finances, trying to figure out how to make things work until she could get a new job lined up. Or maybe she should try her hand at freelancing again? Though that idea left a sick knot in her stomach—the uncertainty of her next paycheck, the demands of fussy clients. She'd done it before, and been so happy to shed that life when she landed her job at QZero. *Maybe* she could try Kickstarter or Patreon, but honestly she had no idea where to even *start* with those. Plus, her greatest ideas didn't belong to her anymore, legally. Jane frowned, adjusting her glasses as she stared absently out the window of the cab.

They stopped in the heart of midtown. Tall buildings crowded thick around them, like Jane was a mouse standing underneath the trees of an ancient forest. She stood in the dying sunlight, reflected yellow-orange off the building in front of her, and pushed up the already rolled sleeves of her shirt. Jane had been wearing the same style for so long that it had gone out of fashion and come back around again: plain jeans, slightly baggy through the legs, a camisole or graphic tee with an open plaid shirt layered like a jacket over it. In the world of artists, she blended in fine, but here in the financial distinct, the difference was as strong as good scotch.

Cal came around, taking her by the elbow. "This way." He led her through a sea of monochromatic suits, sharp lines and sharper glares. Everything here was reflective: the buildings, the black sports cars, the leather handbags, the phones and smartwatches winking at them from every direction.

They entered a high-rise that Jane had never been to before. It turned out to be a hotel, the lobby full of lawyers and execubots, of brokers and investors. Jane groaned inwardly. Cal's favorite place to pick up women was a hotel bar—why bother with the local flavor, he liked to say, when you could have the continental breakfast?—and now it all made sense to her. The mystery, the secrecy; Jane would never have agreed to come with him, not if he had told her the truth.

Jane stopped walking, but Cal's grip on her arm jerked her forward. "Cal," Jane said. She kept trying to backstep, to get him to slow down. "Cal, come on. I'm not in the mood for this."

Cal stopped, but only because they'd reached the elevators. He raised an eyebrow at her. "'This'?"

"Yeah," Jane said, pushing her glasses up her nose. "I mean, I know you guys think you're being helpful, and everyone keeps telling me that I need to get back out there and meet new people, but it's just ... I'm not ..." She paused, taking a shuddered breath. God, this really wasn't the day for their meddling. "I'm not ready. I don't know if I'll ever be ready."

Cal was just looking at her, his face steady. Jane couldn't meet his eyes. She kept looking, instead, at his sunglasses, folded up and hooked on the breast pocket of his leather jacket. Her own reflection gazed back at her, distorted like a fun-house mirror. Why did everyone insist that she had to *move on*? It had only been a year. And a half.

Cal's hand slid from where he'd been holding her elbow, up to a comforting grip on her shoulder. He gave her a light squeeze. "Hey, Main Jane. I promise you, that's not what this is about."

Jane made herself nod. "Okay," she said, the most that she could get through her closed-up throat. She was hugging herself without meaning to. A suit came to stand beside them, and a flare of self-consciousness burned through Jane. Her face was warm, probably a little blotchy. She turned away from the suit as the elevator doors clunked softly open.

People shuffled out, people shuffled in. Cal had released his hold on her, but he still kept her close as they settled in. He pressed the button for the top floor, and Jane raised her eyebrows at this, but said nothing.

At the twenty-third floor, the last of the other passengers got off. A blond woman in a flawlessly tight white dress, her killer stilettos clicking in the marble hallway. She cast a curious glance backward at them—at Jane, really, because Cal had at least finally nailed his cool-guy aesthetic. He gave the blond a wicked grin as the doors slid shut. He could have been a secret agent on Casual Friday, or a superhero in his alter-ego garb.

At that thought, Jane's stomach gave a lurch that had nothing to do with the elevator setting off once more. She didn't have long to dwell in discomfort, however, because almost as soon as the doors had closed, Cal moved over to stand in front of the floor buttons. He pulled out his phone, swiping it awake. The elevator panel had a screen showing their current location, inching up one floor at a time. Cal laid his phone across it, similar to how he'd tapped his number into Jane's phone earlier.

"What are you doing?" Jane asked, but Cal only shook his head. He had some kind of app open, a keypad that he hurriedly typed a long string of numbers into. After a moment, his screen turned green, and the elevator chimed twice as if they were preparing to arrive at their floor.

Only they hadn't. Instead, the elevator lurched as it sped up. Jane stepped to the side, steadying herself against the wall. Cal was tucking his phone into his jacket, and pulling his sunglasses out. He slid them into place as the elevator finally came to a halt.

The doors opened.

Dying daylight poured in. Jane threw her hand across her face, temporarily blinded by the setting sun. Cal guided her forward, the wind whipping her ponytail and the trailing ends of her shirt.

They were on the roof, and they were not alone. When Jane lowered her hand, the Heroes of Hope were waiting for her.

"OKAY, GUYS, THIS REALLY ISN'T FUNNY."

They were standing in a loose semicircle, each of them looking at Jane with surprise and a twist of distaste. Technically, it wasn't even the entire team: just Tony and Marie and Devin. And Cal, obviously, still standing tall beside her. But the three of them had donned actual *costumes*, matching the designs that they'd dreamed up when they were fifteen, when they were all picking which superpowers they'd have gotten in the accident, what their names were, and arguing over stats for the RPG. Jane had changed some of it, when she'd adapted them for QZero, but much of the original essence of the characters remained.

She turned to Cal. "Please tell me that this is some kind of joke. I would hate to think that you guys decided to get all nostalgic and start LARPing."

"Oh my *god*," Marie/Granite Girl said. "The only joke here is on us. What *happened* to you?"

She was motioning at Jane as if there was something obvious for Jane to notice—but when Jane looked down, it was just her, just normal. Marie, on the other hand, was fully decked out in Granite Girl's original costume, army pants and a black tank top, thick combat boots stomping against the gravel. A classic black mask obscured all but her scowl. Marie's supertoned arms flexed, far more defined than Jane remembered from the last time they'd talked.

"Cal," Marie said, incredulous, "this is never going to work."

"We'll have to make it work." Cal cut across the roof, reaching behind an air duct and retrieving a black utility bag. From the depths of it, he pulled out a handful of bulky wrist cuffs, and tossed them in turn to Devin and Tony and Marie—dressed as Windforce, Rip-Shift, and Granite Girl. Jane watched in silence as they strapped the cuffs on. The devices covered nearly half a forearm, thick black straps lashing them in place. Screens along the top came to life, and rows of white LEDs ran loops around their wrists like light-up bracelets over the cuff.

"Oh, no," Jane said, as Cal approached her next. A cuff was in his outstretched hand, already glowing in the rapid descent of dusk. "No, this has gone far enough. You know, you all picked a really terrible day for a prank."

Cal frowned. "This is no prank, Jane, I assure you. I realize now that things are . . . different for you here, but you have to believe me when I say that we need you. The city *needs* you."

"I'm not listening to this." Jane turned, ready to storm back into the elevator, when a sharp whistle cut the air. She froze, the hair on the back of her neck standing on end. She had never heard the sound before, not for real, though she had imagined it a hundred thousand times. In the comics, she'd always written it as a long *SKREEEEEE*, tiny letters at a slant, the color of the text nearly identical to that of the background to indicate that it was just on the edge of hearing.

The Shadow Raptors.

"Look out!"

She was knocked down before she realized what was happening. The tar of the roof bit into Jane's hands and cheek, the heavy pressure of Cal's body as he huddled protectively over her. Her glasses were knocked askew, and as Cal leaped to his feet, Jane scrambled to get them back in place. She rolled onto her back, just in time to see the perfect shot, a frame that she'd end an issue on.

A Shadow Raptor, caught in midair as it careened toward her. Time seemed to freeze, hanging this image for study. It looked exactly as she'd always pictured them. Half man and half monster, the raptor had body-builder muscles covered in deep green scales. Its legs and head were dinosaur, a mouth full of flashing needles—with feet tipped by talons sharp enough to cut through steel. In its human hands were a pair of obsidian daggers, currently pointed right for Jane's heart. Its tail whipped out behind it, heavy as a tree trunk, ready to strike down anything that might try to sneak up on the beast.

Jane didn't even have time to scream. She gasped in a huge lungful of air, but in the instant that she would have released it in a shriek of terror, a fierce gust of wind tore across the rooftop. A whirl of vibrant blue and white careened into the Shadow Raptor's side, sending the beast flying toward the edge of the building. The wind cut away as fast as it had sprung up, the flaps of Devin's wingsuit dropping to his side. He turned to Jane, his face completely obscured by a spandex mask. A gloved hand extended in Jane's direction, but Jane could only boggle.

It wasn't possible. Devin didn't *really* control the wind, using it to thrust himself forward at high speeds, or lift himself as he glided over the city. That was Windforce, and Windforce *did not exist*, no matter how much Devin may have wished it so when they were teenagers.

There was no time to sort it out. More Shadow Raptors were pouring onto the roof all around them, scaling the sides of the building like it was nothing.

"Go!" Devin, or rather Windforce, shouted, and Jane didn't question him. She scrambled onto shaky legs, her Converse slipping gracelessly over loose tar.

Only there was nowhere for her to run. All around her, Shadow Raptors spread like vicious dogs, snarling and lunging at the Heroes of Hope. Granite Girl was battling against two of them, her mottled gray arms ripping whole limbs from their bodies, her followup punches quite literally rock solid. Rip-Shift sliced his hand through the air, first in front of him and then to the side, and twinned shimmering lines split the surface of the world; the glimmering lines reflected in his sunglasses as he leaped through one, the Shadow Raptor fast on his heels, and then they both tumbled out of the other. His long black coat, everything leather like something out of *The Matrix*, flicked behind him as he teetered on the edge of the rooftop, watching the Shadow Raptor fall. Windforce was back in the thick of things already, lifting the Shadow Raptors and slamming them into the roof with deadly force.

All Jane could do was stand and stare. The fight had a surreal edge to it, as if she was inside one of her own drawings. Everywhere she looked was a panel of her comics: knives flashing in the dying light; the rippling of the world as Rip-Shift parted gaps between two points; blood spurting in an elegant arc as Granite Girl ripped a fistful of scales from a Shadow Raptor's back. A darkened rooftop, the glow of the city switching on behind them. It was *terrifying*, obviously it was terrifying, and yet it was also so completely impossible that it did not feel as if Jane could be hurt by it.

Until a thousand points of pain flared in her shoulder. Jane cried out, turning in time to see that a Shadow Raptor had grazed her with the edge of its kick. Its claws had sliced through both shirt and flesh, and Jane clamped her hand across the wound, blood pouring freely through her fingers. She started screaming.

The Shadow Raptor turned its head at the sound. Narrow nostrils flared as it huffed in twice, catching the scent of her blood. Its teeth were dripping with red, and it clearly *wanted* to lunge forward and make her its next meal, but then Granite Girl was right on top of it, riding it like a horse. She snapped its neck with a sickening twist.

"Jane!"

Jane whirled. Cal was racing toward her. A cut ran artfully down his temple—just enough to show the readers that this fight was serious, without posing any actual danger to the hero. He ducked beneath a Shadow Raptor as it flew out of one of the rips Rip-Shift had torn in the world.

"Here," Cal said. He thrust the cuff back into her hands. He was already wearing one himself, and he had his phone out again, an app with a single large, green button flashing through the night. "Put this on, quickly. There's no time."

What else could Jane do? She hastily slapped the device on her wrist, wincing as she raised her arm to show Cal that it was in place. A fast glance around the rooftop showed more Shadow Raptors clawing their way over the lip of the building. The Heroes of Hope regrouped around Jane, breathing fast, their arms raised defensively at the encroaching circle of Shadow Raptors.

"I'm sorry," Cal said, throwing a heavy look in Jane's direction. "I didn't want it to be like this."

"Like—?"

"Just *go!*" Granite Girl shouted, and Cal pressed the button on his app.

The world around them wavered. Vertigo pressed in thick and fast, drawing bile up Jane's throat. Light flickered in and out, reducing her vision to an extremely low frame-rate movie. The Shadow Raptors were still closing in, closer and closer, and Jane wanted to scream but had no breath. The roof beneath her feet disappeared, and for one heart-stopping moment Jane was in free-fall—then they tumbled forward, the whole group of them, landing on an identical rooftop.

Not quite identical: the Shadow Raptors were gone. The sky was darker, a thick layer of clouds pressing down across them and shrouding the building in smog. Jane coughed, the taste of metal laying heavily on her tongue.

"Don't breathe it in," Marie said, her mouth already covered by a handkerchief that muffled her words.

But it was too late: Jane's lungs burned, her eyes stinging against the smog. Her head spun, and she collapsed onto her knees, even as Marie and the others were crowding fast around her.

"*Told* you this one was an idiot," Jane heard Marie saying, as blackness narrowed her vision down, knocking her out cold.

* * *

CLAIR'S VOICE CAME TO JANE IN HER DREAMS.

Of course it would. In dreams, anything is possible. People can fly, or breathe fire. Rooms can rearrange themselves while you're in them. Time can pass slowly or quickly. Accidents can be avoided.

The dead can be alive.

In her dream, they're outside behind Jane's parents' house. Jane grew up in the last house on the street, the last house in town. Beyond the tiny square of lawn that Jane's father tended to every Saturday, a wide expanse of nothing stretched into infinity. Weeds swayed beneath the deep blue sky, an ocean of wildflowers and untamed rabbits. But if you followed this one path, worn down by so many pairs of feet tramping through it over and over again, eventually the ground would slope down, and you'd find yourself at a river tumbling serenely through like a snake in the grass. The river was shaded by the boughs of a giant oak tree, so big that you could see the top of it all the way from Jane's bedroom window, and from the tree there hung a tire swing.

Jane's head was full of memories of that tire swing. Sometimes it seemed as if everything that was ever worth happening, had happened there.

Which is why she hadn't been there in a year and a half, although she returned now. Her dream spun time back and played it forward again, different from how it had really gone. Like unraveling a sweater to correct a mistake. Jane stood in the tire swing, her toes hooked on the rough rubber lip, her fingers stiff from holding the rope for so long. Clair was opposite her, their collective bodyweights canceling out the tilt, more or less. They huddled around the rope, clinging on tight as Jane would dip her body, sending the swing veering off in one direction or another. Clair squealed the way she had when she was eleven, the summer after she'd fallen off of it and broken her wrist, the summer she'd been so afraid to get back up again.

"No, no, no, don't make it spin!" Clair said, her eyes screwed up tight, though there was an edge of giddy laughter in her voice. Jane whipped her body to the side, encouraging the tire to start whirling around, and because it was a dream, she didn't have to put in any effort at all. They tumbled around and around, the world blurring to ribbons beyond them, and Jane watched the flashes of color shift from green to brown to silver-blue to brown to green. She counted the rotations, one, two, three, and threw herself from the tire swing at just the right moment to plunge into the freezing river. She broke the surface just as Clair was flying in after her, nearly belly-flopping in her attempt.

"You are the worst jumper ever," Jane said, paddling against the current. She brushed Clair's bangs out of her face as they drew near, wrapping their arms around each other.

Clair leaned in, planting a gentle kiss on Jane's wet forehead. "Maybe that's what you could do next: become a professional tire-swing jumper."

Jane smiled. "It could be my superpower."

"Aw, but what about Captain Lumen? She'd be out of a job!"

A tiny bit of happiness broke off Jane, drifting away down the river. She shook her head. "The world doesn't need Captain Lumen these days," she said. "And anyway, I'm not her anymore, remember? *She's* not even herself anymore."

"That's where you're wrong." Clair cupped Jane's face, both of their heads just barely out of the water as they floated lazily downstream. "You're so needed, Jane. Everyone needs you. The *city* needs you."

The city needs you. Jane blinked, trying to chase away the faint trace of memory—but it had already taken hold. The idyllic summer afternoon collapsed around them, plunging into night. Jane lunged forward, wrapping her arms tightly around Clair, some part of her already aware of what was happening. The faintest whistle was rippling through the grass around them: *SKREEEEEE.*

She woke up with a start. Jane squeezed her eyes shut, trying desperately to hold on to the world she'd had a moment ago: just her and Clair, the feeling of Clair's skin against her own. But the sensation was already gone, fading like the dream that it was. Loss flared in Jane's chest, like a shrapnel fragment lodged forever between her ribs.

Faint and steady beeping drew her eyes open: a hospital monitor. The sound brought a fresh wave of heartbreak to the surface, and Jane threw the blanket off her and shot to her feet before she'd gotten a sense of her surroundings—desperate to get away from it. That sound had haunted her for *months* after Clair's death; sometimes, in the middle of the night, she still woke up thinking that she heard it, amid the background of the heater, the thumping bass of passing cars, the shuffle of footsteps in the stairwell near her empty bedroom. Jane would lay there, heart racing, staring at the ceiling. Counting the minutes until the feeling passed.

The beeping was louder this time, solid and real in a tangible way that those phantom nights had lacked. Her bedroom was gone, and in its place she found herself somewhere sterile and impassive. Jane's feet hit smooth floor, neither cold enough for tile nor warm enough for wood. The room was dark around her, illuminated only by strips of blue and the softest white. A single monitor, indeed showing vital signs—*her* vital signs?— was molded into the wall by the corner. The heart rate on the monitor spiked as Jane looked down at herself: hospital gown, pale blue by the looks of it, her skin wired up with sensors.

She should have recognized it sooner, but sleep and panic had dulled her senses. And besides, this room was usually drawn in the light.

As if sensing the disparity, panels above Jane's head snapped on full bright. Jane was halfway through ripping all of the sensors off of her body, and she only just avoided screaming in shock. Her head whipped up. She spun in place, trying to see who had turned on the lights, and this is when the sense of familiarity crept up her spine.

Smooth white seams along the gentle slope of the room's walls. An inset with a mirror over it, slim drawers underneath to create a built-in dresser—though they were so small, one was often forced to wonder what sorts of things you could keep in there. A ficus tree in the corner. Jane knew without turning around that the bed behind her would be narrow and covered in blue fabrics, a curling sort of canopy hanging over the head of it. From the perspective of a patient, lying down, the underside of the canopy displayed a variety of nature scenes, intended to soothe and promote healing.

A rejuvenation pod.

Jane threw the last handful of sensors aside, slapping a panel to shut off the disconnection alarms. She pulled back the neck of her hospital gown. The room was silent now, but as she looked at the smoothed-over skin of her shoulder—just the faintest trace of lines, the smallest scar, which would disappear by tomorrow—Jane almost wished that she hadn't disconnected the sensors. The sound of her vitals was the one trace of *real*, the one trace of *normal* that she could grab hold of, however horrid it was for her to listen to.

She spun around. There was a chair in the opposite corner, white with blond wood feet that curled underneath like a rocker (though it wasn't). Jane had modeled it after something she'd seen in an IKEA catalog, when she'd drawn it for the comic. Her clothes were piled neatly on the seat, her Converse high-tops tucked underneath.

Jane changed as quickly as she could. Her shirts still had a tear along the shoulder, but they'd been cleaned of blood (they smelled of laundry detergent, nothing that Jane ever used herself). She held her shoes against her chest, thinking that socked feet were even quieter than sneakers, as she approached the door.

It hissed open just before she reached it. God, that hiss was exactly as she used to imagine it. She saw the way that the panel would look, as she eased into the hallway: the picture drawn low to the floor, just her Doctor Who socks as her foot stretches gingerly out of the room, toe first. A close-up of her face, eyeing first to the left and then to the right. The hallway stretched white and empty in both directions, the curved walls forming a tunnel around her.

She ran.

Her socks slipped and slid in ice-skater lines down the smooth floor, one hand stretched out for balance, the other mashing her high-tops against her chest. She followed the line of the hall as it made a gentle curve to the left. She was still too foggy-headed to have a conscious plan, so she ran on instinct. Left and then right, another right. She told herself that she didn't know where she was going, that she hadn't mapped out every part of this building. Lair. Hideout.

The Heroes of Hope's secret headquarters.

Except not, because that was impossible.

Right?

Around the curve, the hallway ended abruptly. Jane spilled out into a darkened lounge: low-slung white couches and a curved bar, an elaborate fish tank along one wall. The outside edge of the room held a bank of windows, currently blocked with automated shades.

The Heroes of Hope were assembled inside. Some of them.

Rather, Marie and Tony and Cal were. Devin had disappeared somewhere, and Jane still hadn't seen Keisha anywhere in this nightmare. Jane skidded to a halt, sliding into the back of one of the couches as Marie—standing near the fish tank, gesticulating wildly—finished saying, ". . . turns out that it's *not even her*! Face it, Cal: the plan *failed*."

At the sound of Jane's entrance, everyone turned. They had changed out of their superhero costumes, but even in normal clothes, there was nothing normal about them. They looked like movie versions of themselves: Marie, her blond hair styled for once, her clothes free of the usual smears of flour, chocolate, and children's finger paint; Tony, dark hair slicked back, tanned and buff like he'd only ever dreamed of in his youth, his bushy hipster beard shaved off. Even Cal, now that she looked—since when could he afford designer jeans?

Cal stepped forward, softness on his face. He'd been leaning against the closed windows, and as he moved toward her he said, "Jane. You shouldn't be up yet."

"I'm fine," Jane said. It was the furthest thing from the truth, but in terms of her *physical* condition at least, she was all right for now. She knew that much.

Jane sidestepped as Cal approached, because it looked like he was starting to reach out toward her. She hugged her Converse tighter against her chest.

"Does someone want to start telling me what the *hell* is going on here?"

Marie and Tony and Cal all looked at each other. Marie rolled her eyes, tipping her head back with exaggeration. It was a move that she'd started doing when she was seventeen, as if the weight of the world was far too stupid to bear.

"Don't look at me, man," Tony said to Cal. "You're the one that brought her here." He leaned back in the couch, crossing one leg over the other. He was holding an expensive-looking drink, and now he took a pull of it, ice cubes clinking.

Cal rubbed the back of his neck, like a boy trying to work up the courage to ask someone to the prom. "Technically, we *all* agreed—"

"Only because you told us that their world was exactly like ours," Marie cut in. "That we were *all* there. But this"—she threw her arm in Jane's direction—"is not the Jane I know."

Jane flinched back under the burst of attention, everyone sneaking in a quick glance, sizing her up. It was clear from their expressions that they did not like what they saw. Well . . . Cal, maybe, had some faith in her, or at least wanted to. But that was all.

She felt disconnected from herself, seeing the lounge from a distance. She was small, blending into the edges. The light fell in the middle of the room, at Tony on the couch with his bright amber drink; at Marie in her monochrome of gray slacks and white sweater, her hair stained florescent by the light of the aquarium. Even Cal, in dark jeans and a muted t-shirt, seemed to gleam from his teeth and his sun-blond hair. Here, in this setting, they felt larger than themselves. They felt like *symbols*, of justice and liberty. Of hope.

Jane was the cloud of doom. The dark shading that threatened to creep in and snuff them out.

Finally, Cal sighed. "It might be easier to show you," he said, as he tapped a space just beside the bank of windows.

Drawing this transition always used to frustrate Jane. The windows appeared as a solid wall when the "blinds" were shut, but melted away upon touch: first breaking into neat, slim panels, like slats of a white picket fence; then pieces would begin to break off, shimmering as they broke into smaller and smaller bits of dust, before fading into the depths of what was now clear and perfect glass.

The city spread out beyond, as familiar as the back of Jane's hand. The view from their headquarters had been lifted directly from the QZero offices: the one that Jane was looking at now was how it would appear from the break room. Jane had sat at a table and sketched this panorama a hundred times: the sharp peaks of City Hall, stained orange in the setting sun; Regent Park, a three-block square cut right out of the heart of the metropolis; the river, flirting in and out of view in the distance.

Jane approached the window with caution. Night had blanketed the city. A thousand lights winked through a shifting haze of smog, muddying the familiar landscape, but it was still enough. The park, City Hall, the skyline that she'd committed to both memory and paper so many times over.

Only one piece was different: a gap, like a missing tooth, in the heart of downtown. Several key buildings were just *gone*, leaving nothing but twisted, blackened metal that rose like skeletal trees after a wildfire. Jane touched the window, the glass cool beneath her fingers, as she traced their lines.

"What *happened*?"

"Doctor Demolition happened." Cal had come to stand behind her, his reflection hovering past her shoulder. "I don't know how to tell you this, Jane, but . . . you're on a parallel world. Three weeks ago, Doctor Demolition developed a deadly weapon, one with the power to destroy a whole city block. We tried to stop him. We finally discovered where he was keeping it, but when we got there—"

"He'd already moved it," Jane said. She was still staring out at the cityscape, her eyes instinctively seeking out the major landmarks. Along the edge of the gap, she spotted it. She pointed, her finger pressed against the glass. "To there: the top of Woolfolk Tower."

It wasn't much of a tower anymore—half melted, nothing but a handful of twisted girders.

Jane sought out Cal's eyes in the reflection. "I'm right, aren't I?"

Cal nodded. Shock was written plain on his face. "You're right. How did you—?"

"Because I *wrote* it." Jane turned around, putting the view to her back. "Or . . . I was *going* to write it, anyway. That's the start of the Spectral Wars storyline. The first issue just came out."

This time it was everyone else's turn to look confused and incredulous. Marie pushed herself off the aquarium. "You think this is some kind of *game*?"

"Not a *game*," Jane said. "A story. My story."

Our story, she corrected herself in her head, but that wasn't worth getting into right now. Besides, Clair had never liked to claim credit, even in private. Even when the best ideas were hers.

Spectral Wars was hers. The beginning of it, anyway—Jane never did get to learn Clair's ending. She swallowed down the lump of remorse that had risen in her throat.

Cal held up his hand, cutting off Marie before she could start up again. "Well, it's *real* here. Doctor Demolition is *real*, and so is the damage he's done."

Jane couldn't help it—she laughed. Just once, just enough to get a death glare from Marie. "Sure it is. And I suppose that now you're going to tell me that you're *really* Captain Lumen."

A wave of confusion crossed Cal's model-perfect face. "No, Jane . . . You are."

"Riiiiight." Jane nodded along, slowly, like this was all making perfect sense.

It's true that Captain Lumen used to belong to her, before QZero insisted that no one would buy the comics with a woman at the helm of the team. Cal had never gotten into the PRG as teenagers, never chosen a superhero identity for himself, and so Jane had given up her powers to him, booting "herself" to a support role off on the sidelines, rarely seen.

Even so . . . *Jane*, as a true and proper hero?

"Right," Jane repeated. "Okay, well—good talk. Thank you, this has really helped to clarify things for me."

Cal frowned. "Jane—"

"No, I mean it," she said. "I finally understand: I have completely fucking lost my marbles."

"She's not wrong," Marie muttered.

Jane laughed again. Not because it was funny—it wasn't funny, none of it was funny—but because if she didn't laugh, she was either going to scream or cry. She fell back against the windows, still laughing, her head *clonking* the glass.

"Jane," Cal tried again. His hand approached her shoulder.

"Don't touch me!" Jane's laughter cut off as quickly as it had started, as she staggered away from him. She kept backing up, as if putting distance between herself and Cal would somehow change the situation. "Seriously," Jane continued, "just—just don't. I admit it, okay, this is really convincing. I mean, like, *really* convincing—you almost had me. But whatever it is you're playing at, can we please *drop it now*, because I am seriously starting to get freaked out!"

Her voice was constricting, rising steadily as she talked. She had backed up until she was pressed against the aquarium herself. She heard Marie scoff, stomp off to another part of the room.

"*This* is the woman that you think can save us all?" Marie muttered, no doubt to Cal, as she passed.

"Jane," Cal started, "I want to help you, I really do. What can I say? How can I prove this to you?"

Jane let out a strangled laugh. "You can't. I'm sorry, but this . . . it's all too much. Parallel worlds? *Supervillains?* Come on. This stuff makes fantastic stories, but *it's not real*. And to try to prove to me that it *is* would take . . . ," Jane trailed off, considering this. *Was* there anything that would convince her? They had already done everything they needed to, if she was willing to be convinced.

She looked at the cityscape again, the view that should have come from QZero. Unease crept up her spine as she went back over to the window. It really was the *exact* same view, she was sure of that now. Which meant that this building, whatever it was, occupied the same space as her old office.

You're in a parallel world. Jane shook her head. But at what point did skepticism become denial?

"I don't know," Jane said finally, as the cheerful *ding!* of an elevator cut through the lounge. "I don't know what it would take. Something *extraordinary*. Something . . ."

The elevator doors whispered open behind her. Jane was still looking out the window, so her first view of the person that entered was just a hazy reflection, bathed in the light of the elevator. She shimmered like a ghost.

She *was* a ghost.

Jane could not breathe, could not speak. In the reflection, Jane watched her rush into the room, this impossible apparition. "I came as soon as I could," a voice said. The only voice in the world.

Clair's voice.

The prospect of turning to face her was harder than it should have been. In Jane's mind, she spun around immediately, took in the sight of her, then threw her arms wide and tackled Clair in a hug. The panels unfolded: the light from the elevator, pouring in from behind to illuminate Clair like the magical gift that she was; Jane's face, full of shock and pain and delight, a single speech bubble with a tentative, "Clair?"; a blur as Jane shot forward. There would be a full-page panel of their kiss.

In the real world, Jane's Converse fell from her hands with two heavy *thuds*. She steadied herself against the window, desperate to turn, but frozen in place. She heard Clair enter the lounge, heard various greetings exchanged. Heard the silence that followed, heavy with anticipation.

"Hi," Clair said, somewhere behind Jane. "Um, I assume that you're Jane? I'm—"

Jane turned. "Clair."

Oh God, it really was Clair. Jane's heart twisted, sharp as a knife. Clair, with her lopsided smile and the beauty mark just underneath her right eye. Clair, with her crisp, Roaring-Twenties bob that always made Mindsight's panels so much fun to draw. Clair, the only face that Jane had wanted to see in a year and a half. Perfect Clair. Her Clair.

"Um, actually, it's Amy?" Clair said. She tucked her hair back, the point of her bob curling below her earlobe like an accent shadow. "It's nice to meet you." She stuck out her hand.

"You hate the name 'Amy,'" Jane said automatically. Clair had abandoned it in the sixth grade, trimming down her last name, "Sinclair," instead.

Clair flushed. "Oh, it's . . . it's not that bad. I tried to change it once, but that was . . . that was ages ago, and . . . you didn't— that is, Jane didn't—well, not just Jane, nobody liked it much." She shrugged it off, smiling. "Amy's fine. I'm used to it."

She was still holding out her hand. Jane stared at it. The manicured nails, painted yellow. The soft pads of Clair's—Amy's—

fingers. She was wearing fingerless gloves, a trademark sign of Mindsight. Jane swallowed around a dry lump in her throat as she accepted Amy's handshake.

So . . . not Clair. And yet, the grip of Amy's hand, the traces of restoration solvent and perfume drifting off of her, the steady hold of her eyes, never once shying back . . .

Clair.

Not Clair.

But the closest thing that Jane was ever going to get.

There really was only one question left, anymore. "Why me?" Jane asked.

Amy's face softened. "Because our Jane is gone."

THIS IS HOW THE SPECTRAL WARS BEGAN: WITH A SINGLE PIGEON DYING.

That was the first panel, the entire first page. It was a beautiful sketch, far more realistic than the typical style found inside the pages of *Hopefuls*, more like something from a naturalist's journal. Jane had fought hard to keep it that way. Her editor had fought her. Her boss had fought her. The other artists, the colorists, the inkers, had questioned her choice when they'd seen the first storyboards. The drawing was straight out of Jane's sketchbook, a watercolor that she'd carefully torn from the binding and tacked up onto the wall of the meeting room that first morning, when the Spectral Wars was born.

"This is the first page," she'd said to them, and a trill of laughter had circled the room. They thought that she was joking.

She wasn't joking.

The pigeon had a purpose in the narrative, of course it had a purpose in the narrative, but that wasn't the real reason why the issue opened with it. The real reason is that the pigeon was the first thing that Jane had drawn after Clair's death.

It was three months, exactly, since the funeral. Jane hadn't touched her pencils, her pens, her sketchbooks or drawing tablet, since the day that she'd gotten the phone call from the hospital, because she'd been drawing when the call came in. She was still holding the pencil when she swiped the call, tapping the speakerphone symbol so as not to interrupt her work. "Hello?" Jane answered it the old-fashioned way, because she did not recognize the number.

A moment later, her pencil crashed against the sheet that she'd been working on. It had broken the tip, the collision leaving a burst of unintended scribble across the face of Doctor Demolition like a scar.

In the weeks that followed, the sketch had gotten covered up by all the accumulated debris that follows a death. Piled-up mail, mountains of sympathy cards. Hospital bills. Insurance bills. Takeout menus.

The morning that she started drawing again, three months later, her sketchbook was still buried. Jane ignored it as she made herself breakfast. It was actually *morning*, for once, and Jane was actually *cooking*, for once. Her mother had threatened to move in with Jane if she didn't start taking better care of herself, so here Jane was: robotically going through the motions. Toast. Coffee. An apple, the one fruit that was still good (sort of) from the mountain of rotten fruit baskets that littered her fridge. Jane ate at the counter, her plate on the papers that covered her sketchbook. She didn't remember where she'd left it, didn't care.

A shower. Showers would keep her mother from moving in. Jane let the glass fog up good and thick so that she wouldn't have to look at her reflection in the mirror across the way. The hot water was already gone by the time she stepped in. She kept her gaze unfixed, the better to avoid looking at the bottles of Clair's shampoo and bodywash, her pink razor in the soap dish. Jane hadn't thrown anything out, not yet.

Dressed. Clothes that more or less passed the sniff test, and to hell with whether they matched. While she'd been making breakfast, she'd noticed that she'd run out of milk sometime, somewhere, and she decided that she should go out and get some. Barefoot, damp-haired, Jane passed through her kitchen like a ghost. Did she need bread? Eggs? Everything felt distant, like she'd forgotten how to be a grownup. She knew, intellectually, that she and Clair used to go shopping together once a week, always spending more than they'd like, always running out of things, but for the life of her, Jane could not imagine what it was that they'd bought.

Milk, then. Start small. Jane had no idea what she'd use the milk *for*—she didn't like drinking it straight—but it seemed wrong, not to have milk in the fridge. She stuffed her feet into her shoes, and though she heard her mother's voice in her head admonishing her for going out with wet hair, she ignored it. She remembered her phone, and her keys, barely, pushing the door back open at the last second before it slammed shut.

Outside, the world shuffled on. It was a gloomy February day, but Jane thought that it was surprisingly warm. The snow that they'd gotten two weeks ago was melting, slowly, reduced to patches along the front of buildings, and a narrowing strip in the street gutters. Jane zipped up her jacket, and as she looked down to navigate the front steps, she spotted it.

There was a dead pigeon on the stairs.

It had probably been left there by a neighbor's cat, "gifted" to whoever filled its food bowl. The bird's neck was bent at an awkward angle, its beak slightly open. Glassy eyes stared at nothing. A few feathers were ruffled out of place along its wing and its belly, but other than that, it was surprisingly peaceful. To look at it, you might almost think that it had laid down for a nap, or simply grown weary of flying, and these were the closest steps to sit and rest on.

Jane looked up and down the street. People were out walking, ignoring her as they hurried by. Nobody else had noticed the bird yet. Its passing had gone quietly, humbly, with none of the fuss that accompanied the death of a person.

It's hard to say exactly why Jane had rushed back to her apartment, why she'd thrown papers around in a whirlwind as she tried to find where she'd left her sketchbook. Sure, Clair had liked pigeons—despite the fact that they were a nuisance, despite being called vermin by everyone else. It still made no particular sense to Jane that morning, as she finally located her sketchbook and tore it from the counter—empty Chinese food cartons flying as she yanked it out from underneath them. She raced back down the stairs, terrified that someone would have spotted the pigeon by then and thrown it away. But it was still there.

Jane sat down on the top step. The stonework was freezing through her yoga pants, numbing her ass. Jane ignored it. She ignored the people glancing curiously at her, as they squeezed by on their way in or out of the apartment building. She sketched the bird, over and over again, whole pages of its broken body. The curl of its tiny feet, as if clinging to the memory of a favorite branch. The chip along its beak, which Jane assumed was from an older injury that it had learned to live with. The tiny patch of blood underneath it, which she only spotted when she crouched down low enough so that she was almost nose-to-nose with the dead bird. The smell of it filled her face as she sketched the shadows underneath its useless wings, musty and already rotten.

"Jane," her mother had said to her over Skype, two days later when Jane was showing her the rough storyboard of the first several pages of the Spectral Wars, "it's not that I'm not glad to see that you're back at work . . . but are you sure that you shouldn't be talking to someone?"

Jane shook her head, tucking her hair behind her ear. "I'm fine," she said, and at the time she believed it. Look: in the past two days, she'd done more art than she had even in the last few weeks *before* Clair's death. Jane had written out the plot for the Spectral Wars arc, everything—the beginning, which Clair had dreamed up and told her about just days before the accident, and the middle and ending that she'd had to come up with all on her own. And it was so *good*. It was *perfect*. It was heartbreaking.

On the screen, Jane could see her mother's skepticism. In the pull of her lips, a clear "hrmph" face turning her mouth into a slash. In the way she tapped her coffee cup, the one that Jane had bought her for her last birthday: her manicured nails tap-tapping against the athletic stretch of the letters that spelled out "café o' pilate." Jane's mother was in her office, bright and sunlit, tasteful art prints of famous paintings hanging on the wall behind her. Jane's own apartment, seen in miniature through the smaller square in the corner, was dark and even more cluttered than it had been before, but that didn't matter. She'd be going back to QZero soon, pitching her story soon. Clair's story.

It was the only thing that mattered anymore. Let the rest of Jane's life fall by the wayside; she hadn't ended up buying the milk after all. The *work* would continue. The *work* would get out there. Clair's brilliance would shine on forever, her last and greatest idea brought to life. Jane would get this story published, dammit, or die trying.

"WE FIRST NOTICED SOMETHING WAS WRONG WHEN THE PIGEONS STARTED DYING," AMY SAID.

"You mean *you* noticed," Jane said.

Amy flushed. "Well, yes. But that's not the point."

Maybe not, but it was important to Jane. In the comics, she'd modeled the Heroes of Hope physically after her friends, but she'd given them different names, different lives. Instead of becoming an accountant and then running for the city council, comics-Tony was a policeman. Instead of marrying rich and moving to the affluent suburbs, having three kids, becoming a food blogger, comics-Marie was a technology genius who ran a multimillion-dollar startup company. Instead of pursuing restoration science and eventually branching out to become the assistant curator of the Grand City Museum of Fine Arts, comics-Clair worked as a nurse in a children's hospital.

"You realize that I could make you a doctor, right?" Jane had asked her once, at the beginning of her stint at QZero, when she was just starting to pitch *Hopefuls* to her boss. *"You could be Chief of Staff, and run the entire place if you wanted to."*

Clair had smiled. She had just cut her hair short, and Jane was sitting on the couch sideways beside her, sketching the new lines of her bangs, the curl at the end of her bob.

"Doctors are great," Clair had said, *"but nurses are the ones who are there all the time, helping inch children toward their recovery. I want to be there for someone."*

A nurse it was, then. With the same face, but a different name. Different home, different habits, different hobbies. Except for one: when Jane started writing the Spectral Wars storyline, she gave comics-Clair an interest in birding. She'd written it in as a side interest, fairly new, but to Jane's delight and surprise, when she went back and reviewed some old issues, there were already a few hints that comics-Clair might be fascinated by birds. It was a seamless retcon, and it had allowed comics-Clair to be the one to first raise the alarm.

It mattered.

Because without it, they never would have discovered Doctor Demolition's plan in time.

Jane listened to the story all over again. Clair's voice—Amy's voice—washed over her. They had eventually sat, on opposite sides of the curling couch that Tony had abandoned when he realized that the next twenty minutes were going to be nothing but exposition and backstory. He and Marie left the room, retreating to the other parts of the headquarters, but Cal had stayed. He positioned himself on the couch between Jane and Amy, and he kept leaping into the recitation at the most inconvenient times, as if Amy didn't know her own tale.

Except, no, Jane tried to remind herself. *It's* Clair's *story, but it's just been* Amy's *life.*

She wasn't ready to begin processing what that might mean. For now, she just sat and listened.

To Jane's relief, a few of the details were different. She didn't think that she could take it, to listen to Clair's story again, in Clair's voice again, and have it be exactly the same. As if time had folded back on itself, as if they were lying in bed, unwilling to shut up and actually *go to sleep, goddammit*, and instead were hashing out different plot lines, different possibilities. Laughing and getting sidetracked, saying goodnight and then starting up again five minutes later when a thought occurred to one of them.

She listened. She listened as Amy described their discovery, the process of tracking Doctor Demolition down. How the team had divided, one group pursuing Doctor Demolition to the top of Woolfolk Tower, one group following a seemingly unrelated investigation into a set of caves that they'd found beneath the city. The two storylines played out in tandem, as they slowly revealed themselves to be more closely interwoven than it at first appeared. Two epic fights, sprawling across the pages. The dramatic reveal at the end, right before they'd defeated Doctor Demolition at the last possible second: that Doctor Demolition was not, in fact, the mastermind that they'd always assumed. That he was a puppet supervillain, answering to a shadowy figure known to him only as UltraViolet.

This is where Amy's story diverged. This is also as far as Clair's storyline had taken her. Jane had built the rest of it up on her own, one painful step at a time as she realized that plotting was not anywhere near as much fun by herself.

In Jane's version: the Heroes defeated Doctor Demolition, incarcerating him in the Vault, a specially designed cell in the basement of their headquarters. The superweapon was dismantled, and the team began to pursue a line of logic to attempt to unravel the mystery of UltraViolet's identity. The Spectral Wars began to unfold, a massive effort on UltraViolet's part to seize control of the city for herself.

In Amy's version: the weapon went off. Though the Heroes did manage to capture Doctor Demolition, and did currently have him locked away in their basement, a hole now existed in the heart of downtown. Thousands of lives were lost. Gas from the superweapon had plumed up, blocking out the sun, poisoning the populace. Panic had ripped through the streets. The police were trying to keep hold of a frightened city, but crime was running rampant. They hadn't had the *time* to try to find UltraViolet.

And now Captain Lumen went missing. *Jane* went missing.

This hit Jane harder than it should have. She did not, after all, know this other version of herself. She didn't even have her own comics to help fill in an imagined version of Jane's "double," the one that actually *was* Captain Lumen. It wasn't until several minutes later when Jane realized that it wasn't that she was concerned for this *other* her—this *other* her only barely existed, in

Jane's mind—but that instead, her chest was hurting just thinking about what *Clair* was going through now.

Or, you know, Amy. Whatever.

And yet, Amy kept herself remarkably composed. Which really shouldn't have come as a surprise to Jane: Clair was always levelheaded, always collected in a crisis. She rarely worried, believing that everything would work itself out in the end; and even when she *did* worry, she always did such a good job of keeping her worry in check that sometimes even *Jane* had a difficult time spotting it.

She tried to spot it now. She couldn't see it at first, and a flare of pain wrenched at her heart—was she already out of practice? But then, there, look: the tiniest pull of Amy's lips, like she wanted to frown but wasn't letting herself. The way that she rubbed at her forehead as she paused for thought.

"The problem *now*," Cal cut in, so abruptly that Jane jumped—she'd almost forgotten that he was there, "is that UltraViolet has stepped up her game. Last night, she raided the mayor's office. Six people are dead, as far as we know, and the rest, including the mayor, are being held hostage. Just after midnight"—Cal paused, as he pulled out his phone and tapped it awake, as he selected something and held it out to Jane—"she issued this."

A video was already playing. A posh office, full of sunlight and modern furniture. In the center of the frame, a figure faded in and out of view. Her face was obscured by a full mask, only her mouth visible, but that wasn't what made her difficult to identify. She kept shifting: purplish gray one moment, invisible the next. It was difficult to keep your eyes fixed on her. Jane's impression came more from what artists call "negative space," the shape that emerged from the edges of the woman's silhouette. She looked even more convincing than Jane had ever managed to draw her.

"To the people of Grand City," UltraViolet said. Her voice filtered out of Cal's phone, already warbled to be unidentifiable via the use of a voice changer. "Let's make this simple, all right? I'm issuing the following demands, in exchange for the safe release of your mayor and his staff: five million dollars in cash; a helicopter, delivered here, plus guaranteed free passage while I cross the border; sixty pounds of bromeric acid; an official state holiday honoring me, to be celebrated every August sixteenth; a dozen crates of the new AF-72 assault rifles . . . and the personal surrender of the so-called 'hero' known as Captain Lumen."

"Is she serious?" Jane asked.

"Shh," Cal said. "Wait."

In the video, UltraViolet continued: "If I do not receive these items, hand-delivered by the unarmed and fully cooperative Captain Lumen, then I promise you that the fate of these sixteen men and women are going to be the least of your worries. And just in case you think I'm not willing to make good on my promises . . ."

The camera panned. A handful of men and women in rumpled business suits huddled in the corner of the office. Most of them were sitting, cross-legged or with their knees drawn up, but one was sprawled out in a prone position on a pristine white throw rug. Someone had rested his head on a swiped couch pillow, while his suit jacket laid over him, the best substitute for a blanket that they could manage. His shoes were off, and at first Jane thought that someone had left his socks on—but then she realized, as the camera drew closer, that his feet had turned the deepest shade of forest green.

Jane's stomach did a backflip. The camera moved along him, letting the audience take in the thick sweat that stuck his clothes against his body, the subtle tremble that never seemed to stop, the way that his hands (also turning green, albeit slower) kept clenching and unclenching. When the camera finally reached his face, he looked so ill that it was hard to even recognize him, especially since his was not the face that Jane had been expecting. She'd assumed that the mayor here would be the same as the one on "her" world: a portly little man with a habit of blinking far too often for Jane's taste, and half-moon glasses like he was some kind of wizard. She hadn't voted for him, and hadn't been terribly concerned to learn about the hostage situation.

But his wasn't the face that she saw, struggling for breath, his lips blue and purple as they whispered something over and over to himself like a silent prayer. Instead, she saw one that she knew as well as her own reflection. She did, after all, have his nose.

The face was her father's.

The camera turned abruptly away now, UltraViolet once again filling the frame.

"Your precious mayor has until five o'clock Thursday evening before the antidote can no longer be administered in time. However, I've already distributed my virus in a diluted form around the rest of the city—I'd guess that the rest of you have about a week before people start dying." UltraViolet leaned in. Her lips, painted purple, curled into a smirk that sent a wave of panic straight down Jane's spine. "The choice is yours, Captain Lumen. You've always said that you'll do anything to save this city . . . I wonder if you mean it."

"YOUR FATHER WANTS TO COME TO THE WEDDING,"
Jane's mother said. It was five years before Jane was fired from
QZero—the opposite end of the spectrum, in fact, because Jane
had just gotten her job the week before. Things could not have
been going better for Jane: she'd been hired to work on the team
for one of QZero's older franchises, a set of characters going back
to the forties, storylines that were old and stale and musty, but
Jane had ideas. She was putting together a sample issue, in her
spare time, of a new cast of heroes. A new voice in the industry.

It was a Saturday, and Jane was home working, until her
mother called. Jane was not at all happy to be pulled aside from
it, and especially not for the *hell* of dress shopping with her
mother, but her mother had insisted.

"Why do you want my opinion?" Jane had asked over the
phone. "You have better taste than I do."

"Because it's your *wedding*."

"But it's your *dress*."

"You know, most brides are happy to choose the dresses that will be in their wedding photos for the next sixty years."

"Most brides don't have a co-bride that they can foist all that girly crap off onto," Jane said. "Why don't you wait until tomorrow? Clair will be available then."

"I don't want *Clair's* opinion, darling, I want *yours*. You're *my daughter*. Humor me, just this once, will you?"

Jane put her pencil down, and pinched the bridge of her nose. Her glasses slid up her face, as she reached underneath them to rub at her eyes. "All right, all right. When do you want to go?"

"I'm outside now. Look out the window."

Sure enough: Jane turned, pushing the sheer curtain beside her out of the way. On the street below, her mother's familiar black town car glinted like a beetle in the sunshine.

Forty-five long and grueling minutes later, Jane was slumped in a padded chair that looked like something from a Victorian grandmother's parlor, while her mother stepped out from behind a curtain in a gown fit for walking down the red carpet.

"Too much," Jane said, but a salesgirl was already whirling up to stand beside Jane's mother.

"Oh, Ms. Holloway, how gorgeous!" the salesgirl gushed. She had her tape measure out already, as if this was all much more important than it really was, and there was not a second to waste.

Jane's mother took a middle approach: she regarded herself carefully in the three-way mirror beside Jane's chair, ready to be pleased, but not yet convinced. As she turned this way and that, raising and lowering her arms to see how the dress "moved," she dropped the bomb. She wasn't even looking at Jane. "Your father wants to come to the wedding."

Jane snorted. "Good. It'll hurt that much more when he can't."

Jane's mother clucked her tongue. "Jane. You know that he has no objections to your lifestyle, don't you?" She turned to the salesgirl, who was hovering just behind her with a slightly confused expression. "My daughter is a lesbian."

"Mom!"

"What?" Jane's mother shrugged. "I'm proud of you—every part of you. So is your father."

"Oh, it's fine," the salesgirl said hurriedly. She gave a broad smile to Jane, like they were suddenly best friends. "Congratulations on the ruling."

"Thanks," Jane muttered. As if she had anything to do with the state congress's decision to allow gay marriage, as if she hadn't already been living with Clair since forever. Jane was looking forward to the legal benefits they'd now share, of course, but the way that *other people* reacted to it . . .

Jane's mother, in particular, had been *beaming* since the vote went through. You'd think that she was the one to be recognized as equal under the law, from the joy that filled her voice whenever she spoke of it.

"There, you see?" her mother said now. "It's *normal* now."

Jane rolled her eyes. She wasn't going to argue, especially not in public, in front of a salesgirl that she didn't know at all, though Jane could think of a hundred arguments that she could make to that naïve assessment of society.

"So if that's what's holding you back from asking him to come—"

"I'm going to pretend that you didn't just suggest that his potential bigotry is the only reason I wouldn't want him there," Jane said.

"You have to forgive him sometime, Janie."

"Since when?"

"You know what, you're right," Jane's mother said, apropos of nothing, "this dress *is* a bit much. Let's try the blue Sophia that I was looking at earlier, shall we?"

The salesgirl nodded. She turned and all but dashed out of the room with the eagerness of a puppy.

Jane leaned back in her chair. High above her, broad windows let in light to bounce off a sloped white ceiling. The room was too warm for March, and Jane was dressed for the bitter winds that had been lingering in the city all week.

"He's *trying*," Jane's mother said. She hadn't moved, hadn't stepped back through the curtains yet. "You have to at least give him that."

"I don't *have* to do anything."

"Sweetie, people get divorced. That's *life*."

This was exactly the sort of zen-minded thinking that Jane had come to expect from her mother. In the six months immediately following the divorce, she'd been just as bitter and angry as Jane had been, even going so far as to file the papers to change her name back as soon as Mr. Maxwell moved out—but then, in the span of three weeks, she'd gotten a therapist, a life coach, and a yoga instructor, and ever since then she walked around talking about life giving you what you needed, following your courage, and espousing the value of kale-and-protein smoothies at every opportunity.

It's not that Jane didn't appreciate her mother's position. If anything, she had more reason to feel spurned than Jane did. But it wasn't just her father's poor timing—walking out at the start of Jane's senior year of high school, putting her college fund into a financial tug of war. It wasn't just that he'd announced his decision the *day after* Jane and Clair had finally come clean about the nature of their relationship to both of their families— something that they agonized over for nearly two whole years before finally building up the courage to do it. It wasn't just the fact that he'd cheated on Jane's mother. It wasn't just the move to the heart of the city, abandoning his career as a family lawyer in a small suburb and going full-corporate for a mega-firm that protected CEOs from having to pay taxes. That was enough to keep Jane bitter for a year, maybe two. After a while, Jane had simmered down. Her mother was doing well. Jane's college fund was fully funded. Maybe it was time, Clair had urged her, to reach out. Try to make a connection.

So Jane had gone to his firm, hoping to surprise him for lunch. Only to be denied an appointment because, in the snippy words of his receptionist, "Mr. Maxwell doesn't *have* children. I would know."

He'd sent Jane a text after that—a *text!*—that read only: *Sry 2 have missed u. Mayb call 1st nxt time?*

Jane didn't respond, and he didn't follow up.

"You're really going to hold that against him forever?" her mother asked her now, still standing there in the too-much dress. Jane hadn't spoken, but her mother had always been good at sussing out her thoughts. She used to claim, when Jane was little, that this was her superpower: that she would always know what Jane was thinking.

"He's not invited," Jane said.

"And what am I supposed to tell him, when he asks me why not?"

Jane stood up from the stiff, Victorian-grandmother chair. She collected her coat from where she'd draped it over the back. "Tell him that if he doesn't have children, then I clearly don't have a father to invite," Jane said. The salesgirl swept back into the room, carrying a pale-blue number draped over both of her arms. Jane fingered the gossamer overlay. The dress had an empire waist and reminded Jane of the sixties, for reasons that she couldn't quite place. It would look gorgeous on her mother, with her corn-silk blond hair and dimpled cheeks still bright with the false youth of an expensive beauty regime. It would make her look like a hippie, her arms raised high, waving a sign with *Make Love, Not War* written in cheap paint. Jane's mother had been both too young and too responsible to have ever actually been a part of that lifestyle, but Jane liked the idea of it.

"I like this one," Jane said, as she dropped the fabric and moved toward the door. "Wear it with flowers in your hair."

Jane's mother frowned. "Flowers?"

Jane shrugged. "You wanted my opinion, I gave you my opinion. That dress. Flowers. Do it or don't, it's up to you. Now, if you'll excuse me," Jane said, "I have a comic to finish."

THE FORCE OF JANE'S INDIFFERENCE SURPRISED EVEN HER.

She just sat there for a moment, looking at Cal's phone. The video had frozen on the last frame, UltraViolet blurred half in and half out of existence. A circular *Replay* button blocked most of her head from view. Jane could still see a bit of her father in the background behind her, the outline of a prone figure as captured through the mist of UltraViolet's disappearing form.

Was it just that this wasn't really *her* father, when you got down to it? It had been years since Jane had ever wished her real father active harm, after all, and she imagined that if the situation was happening on her own world, that she would feel at least some concern for his well-being. She hoped that she would, anyway. She didn't like to think of herself as heartless.

"So . . . that's it?" Jane asked after a moment. "You want to just hand me over to be slaughtered by this woman?"

"*No*," Amy said, while Cal offered, "There's no guarantee that she wants Captain Lumen's death."

"Oh, that's a comfort," Jane said. "Thanks a lot, Cal."

Cal winced. "That's not what I meant. Of *course* we're not going to hand you over. We wouldn't hand over our Jane, and we're not handing over you. But do you see why we need you, now? Whatever we decide to do to counter UltraViolet's scheme, it's not going to work unless we have a Captain Lumen to distract her."

"Wait, so you don't even *have* a plan yet?"

"No, there's a plan," Cal said quickly. He nodded, with great confidence.

Too much confidence.

Amy, meanwhile, raised an eyebrow.

It was all Jane needed to know. She pulled her glasses off, massaging her brow.

There was too much to process, too many emotional bombs exploding all around her. The mere shock of what they were telling her at all—that she was in a parallel universe, that her comics were somehow *real*—would have been enough to warrant a week off to hide in bed and eat gallons of black raspberry ice cream. But now: Clair/Amy, and her *father* who wasn't her father, and a city already laced with poison. A threat from a supervillain that Jane didn't even really know or understand yet. The weight of it all, pressing down on her shoulders.

She couldn't do it.

That was the simple truth. Whatever, exactly, this team of heroes wanted from her, whatever role they would ultimately expect her to play . . . Jane couldn't. She *wrote* about heroes; she was not one herself. She had never wanted to be. Even as the teenage versions of themselves sat around in Keisha's basement or sprawled in the grass beside Devin's above-ground pool, tracing out maps and listing stats and abilities, teasing each other about their chosen superpowers and arguing about the various strengths and implications of each, Jane had never *wanted* that imagined life. Not really. The idea of being powerful and glorious held a certain appeal, of course it did, but that was the beauty of art and comics and games: they allowed Jane to step into those roles for as long as she felt comfortable there, to revel in the fantasy of it without actually risking her personal safety; and then, they allowed her to *leave*.

When she put her glasses back on, she made herself look at Cal, not Amy. She could handle his disappointment, his judgment. "And if I refuse?"

A muscle twitched along Cal's temple. In the comics, this was a sign that he was stressed, and when he got stressed, there was the potential that his superpowers—that Captain Lumen's superpowers—might prove harder to control. Jane had written it this way to give the character some flaws, and it had helped a plot point of an early issue. But in this reality, he was just Cal—no superpowers, not that Jane knew of, anyway—and his irritation was insubstantial and nonthreatening. It blew across Jane's awareness as nothing more than a hot breeze.

Before he could answer, however, an alarm started blaring. Jane saw a panel of Cal looking up, his expectant face bathed in red light from strips that had blinked on near the ceiling.

And then Captain Lumen sprang into action.

Or that's how it would be in the actual comics, anyway. Jane forcibly reminded herself that Cal was *not* Captain Lumen here, though it was hard to accept it as he leapt to his feet, his stance wide and commanding, his perfect blond hair catching the red warning lights.

The doors to the elevator slid open; Tony was back, Devin and Keisha in tow. Free of his mask, Devin's hair sprang out from his head in a proud 'fro, a symbol of his mixed heritage. He ran his hand through it now, nervously tugging at the base of his curls. Keisha, the only alternate version that Jane hadn't met yet, took her in with barely a glance. She looked a lot like the Keisha in Jane's own world, her dancer's muscles taut and toned, though her skin was at least two shades deeper brown. Also, her hair was longer, twisted and bunned at the back of her head, and her pumps, jeans, and blue silk blouse were far more conservative than Keisha's usual vibrant style.

It still felt unreal. Despite the panic, and all physical and sensory evidence to the contrary, it still felt more like some bizarre dream than an actual sequence of actual events, and as such, at times it was hard for Jane to concentrate on the seriousness of what was unfolding around her.

Like another Shadow Raptor attack.

Jane's attention snapped back fully at the mention of these beasts. Lingering fear crawled up her skin as Keisha and Devin and Tony presented the facts: an attack on Wilson Labs, at least two dozen Shadow Raptors swarming the building. GCPD had been dispatched, but—

"They'll never be able to fend off that kind of attack!" Cal snapped. "What's Captain Daniels *thinking*? He has to pull them out of there!"

Tony snorted. "Yeah, *you* want to try telling him that?"

Cal shook his head. He and the rest of the team were already moving, already packing themselves into the sleek white elevator. Jane stood in the middle of the lounge, gawping, nothing but the fish to keep her company as she watched these real-life versions of the same familiar heroes. It seemed for a moment as if Jane had been forgotten (even Amy was absorbed in formulating their plan of attack), until at last Cal glanced up, just as the elevator doors were beginning to close. He stuck his hand out, halting them for a moment.

"Jane," he said, and everyone that was chattering around him fell silent and looked out. A flash of panic coursed through Jane, convinced that he was going to ask her to come with them, to fight side by side. But all that he said was, "Stay here." He let the doors fall shut before Jane could answer.

Jane tried to tell herself that she didn't feel small and insignificant, standing in their wake in the empty lounge. She hugged herself to keep from shaking as all the panic and shock swept over her again. She did not want to go with them, no, that much was true—but neither did she relish the idea of being the one to stay behind. This was not her comics; she could not control the fight that they were about to enter, could not guarantee their safe return. Cal, Devin, Tony, Marie, Keisha—Clair. Not-Clair, but . . . Clair. Jane's stomach twisted up. She should have argued with them, should have begged them not to go, but even as she felt this, she knew it would have been a futile exercise.

She turned, heading back to the hallway that she'd come in from. There was nothing that she could do to change their minds, no way to protect them, no—but she'd be damned if she just sat around waiting for news of their return. Jane knew this building: every inch of it, every detail, every security measure.

She knew where their command room was.

"WELCOME, JANE."

Jane held her breath as she crossed the threshold. The buttery-smooth computer voice, normally typed in a font just a little different from the usual handwritten dialog, filtered down from above. To get inside the command room required a retinal scan, voiceprint, and six-digit PIN. The retinal scan and voiceprint were instantly recognized as this world's Jane Maxwell, of course, but at the instruction to enter the PIN, Jane had hesitated. She didn't exist in the comics world, not really. Her character was a minor scientist that occasionally showed up to dispense relevant technobabble, and did not have her own access to the various levels of the headquarters. Jane stared at the screen, blue digits counting down as it awaited input, and punched in the first series of numbers that popped into her head: 091600. The date of her first kiss.

The doors slid shut behind her, and a soft *hiss* indicated that they'd successfully resealed. Jane stood just inside of the room for a while, taking the view in.

Located in the very center of the building, the command room was a perfect circle. One half of it held a crescent-shaped conference table that always had the exact right number of chairs needed. A vibrant, interactive map of the city lit up the curve of the wall to her left, while to her right bloomed a spread of massive screens and computer workstations, far more than they ever had cause to use. The biggest screen was nestled in the middle, and currently it showed, in pieces: a series of police reports; panicked tweets from eyewitnesses; a blurry video on a loop, a Shadow Raptor ripping off the door to Wilson Labs with its bare hands; security footage from outside the Heroes' headquarters, as the team members sped off on motorbikes or in low-slung sports cars. A satellite image of Grand City was tucked in the corner, tiny blips popping into existence as each of the Heroes linked up to the tracking system.

A blue blip appeared: Mindsight, and Jane's strength came back to her. She raced forward, tapping on the audio feed that connected the team.

"—going to take Corsetto Street and approach from the south," Devin was saying. His Puerto Rican accent came in thick over the speakers, a sure sign that he was feeling the adrenaline.

"Fine," Cal said. "Granite Girl, go with him. Windforce and Pixie Beats, stick with me. We'll try to punch our way through the front entrance. Mindsight—"

"Already on it." Amy's voice was steady and strong, the way that Clair used to give presentations at the museum.

Jane watched as Amy's blip began to pull away from the others. All of them separated and regrouped, heading their various directions. Jane let out a breath—at least they were sticking to a pretty standard Heroes of Hope strategy. In a straight-on fight, Amy's empathic superpowers weren't much help, which meant that she often hung back until there was at least one enemy downed. She could swoop in at that point, try to extract information out of the fallen combatant—information on what their plan really was, where their leader was hiding, whatever the plot *needed* her to find, really. Jane had plenty of reservations about using Mindsight like this, but Clair had always insisted that was just how it had to work. When Jane tried to press her on the subject, when she expressed a specific desire to adjust how Clair's empathy worked, Clair would get incredibly defensive. *"That's just how it works, Jane,"* she'd say, as if it was *real*.

A slight chill crept up Jane's spine now, watching Amy's blip as it circled around the far way.

She tried to focus on something else. Cal, Tony, and Keisha were approaching Wilson Labs. Jane leaned in, reading the name off of Cal's blip: Deltaman. She wondered what he was capable of.

The squeal of brakes and the familiar *SKREEEEE* of the Shadow Raptors carried easily across the audio feed. Jane tapped a few places on the screen, and a hacked line to Wilson Labs' security footage rose out of the depths, displacing several other pieces of data. She saw Tony and Keisha leap from their bikes, but it was Cal that really caught Jane's attention, because it was Cal that she had no way of knowing what to expect.

He looked . . . well, kind of like a ripoff Batman, if Jane was being completely honest with herself. She cringed at the visual design of his costume: rubberized body armor sculpted to look like muscles, a sweeping black cape, even a frickin' *utility belt* cinching it all together. Though at least he didn't have the signature cowl, instead obscuring his face with a hood from the cape and dark greasepaint around his eyes. And okay, when he threw his arm straight and flexed his wrist, a variety of darts shot out of what was no doubt a clever deployment system hidden along the length of his sleeve. But *still*.

The Shadow Raptors swarmed, and the team kicked and slashed and fired. Jane glanced at the upper corner of her large display, pleased to see that Devin and Marie had reached the back entrance, and were currently working their way up the side of the building. Two or three heat signatures were approaching their position, however, and so Jane tapped a button on her controls without even thinking. "Windforce, Granite Girl, watch the next level—there's a handful of guards on their way to the windows."

"Jane?" Cal asked, incredulous. Their comms were all inter-

connected, and Jane heard him puff with exertion as he jerked the head of a Shadow Raptor, snapping its long neck. "What are you doing?"

"What, just because I'm stuck back at base, I can't help?" Jane *pfft'd*. "Please, I—behind you, Cal!"

Cal whirled. He ducked, and the Shadow Raptor that was lunging at him toppled across his back. The Shadow Raptor landed hard, already turning, and Cal whipped a gun from his belt and downed it with two deafening *BANGs*.

Jane flinched, though the speakers had muffled the noise somewhat. Even still, her ears rang, and she had to piece together rather than outright hear as Cal asked, "How did you even get *into* the command room?"

"Well, I *am* Jane Maxwell. You think the computer is going to know the difference?"

If Cal had something clever to say to this, Jane didn't hear it. She was still trying to clear the ringing of her ears, and by now the sound of glass shattering was filtering through as Devin and Marie broke into one of the upper windows of the lab. Jane pressed her ears shut a few times, swallowing as if maybe they needed to be popped. A faint whisper caught at her attention, and she could have sworn that she heard the computer say "*Welcome—*" again, so clearly her hearing was still playing tricks on her.

Or not—searing heat blasted beside her, a crackle of energy raising all of the hairs on Jane's body. An energy bolt, like purple lightning, struck the display. Sparks flew, the screen shattered like a dropped phone, and Jane screamed as she ducked to the floor. The conversation and noise of the rest of the Heroes of Hope cut out, leaving nothing but a weighted silence and a deep and growing chuckle.

"Well, well, well," said a heavily digitized voice. "Captain Lumen. I have to admit, I wasn't expecting to run into *you* here."

Jane had thought that her heart was already racing as fast as it could, but at the sound of this voice, it summoned another burst of speed, slamming into Jane's throat. UltraViolet—Jane recognized the sound of her from the video.

Not that this recognition did Jane much good. Fear had struck her paralyzed, glued to the floor in a useless ball of cowering limbs. This close, the floor tiles smelled strongly of disinfectant, souring Jane's already roiling stomach. *UltraViolet, UltraViolet, UltraViolet.* The name kept swirling through Jane's head, piercing her thoughts like a nasty headache as the clack of UltraViolet's boots drew closer.

"Oh, come now," UltraViolet said. "Don't tell me that you're just going to *sit* there and let me kill you. What would the city say, Captain Lumen? Your reputation would die along with you—and we all know how important that is to heroes, don't we?"

This was supposed to goad Jane—goad Captain Lumen—to get to her feet. Jane knew this, but that knowledge did not make strength magically appear in her limbs, nor did it unblock the connection between her brain and her body. She couldn't move, even if she wanted to. And really, she didn't want to. The only movement that Jane was even remotely interested in was *run*, and that . . . really wasn't an option here.

Finally, the boots reached her. Jane had watched their progress, as they came around a table and into the limited view from her spot on the floor. Shifting in and out of visibility, like some kind of projection. Yet Jane knew that this was no projection, that if UltraViolet wanted to plunge a knife into Jane's back, she was wholly solid and capable of doing so.

This was how she was going to die, then. The realization struck Jane, funny and tragic and pathetic and horrible all wrapped into one. Curled on the floor, in a parallel world that by all rights shouldn't exist. Killed by her own imagination. Her father always used to tell Jane that there was no future in comics, and now finally he was right.

UltraViolet reached down, and Jane screamed—but nothing stabbed at Jane's vital organs, no blades pierced her skin. Instead, a gloved hand wrapped itself in the fabric of her shirt and hauled her upward, like grabbing a kitten by the scruff. UltraViolet drew Jane to her feet, and slammed her against the broken display.

The two women stared at each other. They were the same height, roughly (it was hard to tell, with the ridiculously spiked boots that UltraViolet was wearing), and close enough to the same build. Trying to get any more details than that was impossible. Even when UltraViolet wasn't shifted into transparency, there was something . . . *off* about her. Like the light kept bouncing from her at the wrong angles, distorting her image. It made Jane's head hurt to look at her.

UltraViolet, however, had no such difficulties studying Jane. She leaned in, tipping her head to examine Jane in detail. Jane tried to hold herself against the controls behind her, steady and brave and true, but in reality her knees were about ready to give out.

"Wait . . . You're not Captain Lumen," UltraViolet said after a moment, and never had Jane been more relieved for a supervillain to be right about something.

Jane made herself shake her head. "No," she squeaked. "No, I'm not."

But in an instant, Jane knew the revelation had not helped her. UltraViolet leaned back, and those wicked purple lips, the only clear thing about her, curled into a terrifying smile.

"Then there's no reason to keep you alive."

Her hand found Jane's throat before Jane could react. Jane gasped, though only about half of the air made it down before a crushing grip cut off the supply. Heat from UltraViolet's fingers stabbed like knives, radiating out from the point of impact until it felt as if Jane's entire body was on fire. Darkness blotted Jane's vision. She could not move, could not scream. She tried to claw at UltraViolet, but her attempts were feeble at best. The world shifted in and out of existence. Her lungs burned hotter than the rest of her body, desperate for another breath.

She didn't even hear the bullet. All Jane knew was this: that one moment she was on the brink of passing out into an endless sleep, gulping at air that would never come, and that the next moment contained nothing but sweet relief. The pressure on her throat released. Jane collapsed to her knees, sucking in huge lungfuls of air as UltraViolet swore. A blur of motion made Jane look up, in time to see another crackling bolt of purple lightning streak the air—*away* from Jane.

Clair was standing in the open doorway. Rather, Amy. Rather, Mindsight, her vintage pearl-handled revolver held level as she fired again in UltraViolet's direction. UltraViolet veered, and the bullet pinged off a metal support beam and bit deeply into the wall.

A brief struggle followed. Jane screamed, her throat raw, when UltraViolet lunged for Mindsight, although Mindsight was fully prepared for the move; she darted aside in the perfect dodge, twisting so that her trench coat flared like a cape. A simple black mask obscured her eyes, a fedora tilted forward to cast a shadow across all but her blood-red lipstick. The look that she cast at UltraViolet's retreating back should have spit daggers, but Mindsight had to make due for firing off another three rounds from her gun as their enemy disappeared into the hallway.

They let UltraViolet go. Without the rest of the team, their scant numbers were not enough to overpower someone of her skill, and as the door hissed shut in her wake, Jane collapsed against the wall in relief. Tears sprang forth, sobs racking Jane's chest before she could stop herself.

"Shh," Amy said, shedding her persona as easily as the hat and mask that she dropped onto the conference table. She crouched in front of Jane, reaching out to rub her back.

Jane threw her arms around Amy. Her face buried in Amy's shoulder, her fingers dug at Amy's arms. Amy rocked back underneath the force of it. Jane's sobs of shock and fear continued to rip through her, and after a moment, Amy's arms folded protectively around Jane.

"Shh," she said again. "Shh, it's okay. I'm here."

She was, she was. Amy's voice, Clair's voice, one and the same tangling into Jane's hair. Clair's hands on Jane's back, rubbing familiar comforting circles across her spine. Clair's blunt hairline brushing against Jane's cheek. Jane cried as hard and as raw as the day of Clair's funeral, as she leaned against Clair's sturdy body. Alive, whole. Her heartbeat a steady drum in Jane's ear, her breath teasing Jane's hair like a spring breeze.

Clair. And yet . . . not Clair.

Jane pulled herself back, as if she'd been jolted with one of UltraViolet's electrical pulses. Amy looked at her quizzically. Without her mask, there was nothing but Clair's familiar eyes studying Jane's movements.

"I'm . . . I'm sorry," Jane said. She pulled off her crooked glasses and wiped at her eyes with the back of her sleeve.

Amy nodded distractedly. "It's okay. Are you . . . are you all right? She didn't hurt you, did she?"

"No," Jane said as she put her glasses back on. It helped to have something tangible to focus on, simple questions to answer: are you okay, are you hurt. No, no. It was far better than dwelling on the questions swirling like mist around Amy's face. *Who are you? Are you really Clair, somehow? How different is your heart?*

Thankfully, Amy turned away. She got to her feet, examining the room as if looking for clues. "I wonder how she got in?" Her voice was shaky, but that could easily be from simple fear— their security *had* just been breached, after all, and in the worst possible way. A chill swept through Jane, wondering, as she was sure that Amy was as well: If UltraViolet could do it once, what was to stop her from doing it again?

"How did you . . . ?" Jane started, but the words died in her throat.

Amy turned back. She was standing by the conference table, one hand balanced on the smooth edge. "How did I know?"

Jane looked away, but nodded.

"I sensed that you were in danger," Amy said, the words stabbing at Jane's heart. "Shortly before you cut into the comm line, I knew that something was wrong. Mine was malfunctioning, but after you cut back out again, I managed to get a message to the rest of the team. They should be here soon. We agreed—the attack on Wilson Labs was likely a ploy to draw us away."

Jane stared at her own fingers. They were lined with ink, stained so deeply into the crevices around her nails, the whorls of her fingertips, that no amount of scrubbing ever got them clean anymore. She twisted her wedding ring, braided platinum branches, around her finger. "You could have waited for the rest of them. You didn't . . . you didn't have to come back for me."

This statement was met with silence. Jane looked up a moment later, afraid of what she might find. Amy had sat in one of the conference chairs, and was now leaning her elbows on her knees and cradling her head in her hands.

"I waited last time," Amy told her shoes. "When . . . when our Jane disappeared. It was the exact same feeling, like a panic attack squeezing the air out of my chest. I could have gone after her myself, only I didn't know what to do without the rest of the team to back me up. But by the time we got there . . ."

"I'm sorry," Jane said. "Amy. I'm so sorry. This must be so hard on you."

Amy forced a brave smile as she sat up. "It's hard on all of us. Jane's a valuable member of the team. It's . . . not the same without her."

"Well . . . sure, I'm sure that everyone's worried about their teammate," Jane said. "But I mean . . . she's *your* wife."

The stillness radiating off of Amy was so absolute that it rocked Jane back. Jane stared at Amy, both of their eyes growing wide.

"*Isn't* she?"

"We're *married*?" Amy asked.

"We're *not*?"

Amy shook her head. One time, all the way left, then all the way right. She left no room for doubt. "We . . . Well, it's just . . . It's just that my Jane—*our* Jane, this Jane, um . . . She doesn't—"

Jane held up her hand: stop. She couldn't listen, couldn't even imagine. A world in which she didn't love Clair? It was the most impossible of all the impossible things she'd been told today, the one fiction that she couldn't get herself to accept. She drew her knees to her chest, wrapped her arms around them. Felt the bumps of her wedding ring with her thumb.

Amy's eyes caught the motion. The flash of platinum. She made herself look away from it, but Jane had seen.

"Amy—"

The door hissed open. "*Welcome, Cal. Welcome, Devin. Welcome—*"

The rest of the greetings were cut off as a burst of voices started talking all at once.

"What *happened* here?!"—"Are you two all right?"—"I told you that we should have upgraded the system! I told you!"—"Fuck!"—"It was UltraViolet."

This last statement was made by Amy, already to her feet,

and it cut the rest of them off midstride. Only the computer continued, the last "*Welcome, Marie*" trailing off into silence.

"What, *here*?" Cal said.

"Fuck!" Marie said again. She ripped her mask off, throwing it dramatically onto the conference table. Tony placed a steady hand on her shoulder. She was so much shorter than him that he barely had to lift his hand at all.

Cal took a breath. His hood was thrown back, but dark smudges still ran like warpaint across his face. "Okay," he said. It wasn't okay, and everyone knew it, but somehow it felt better to hear the lie aloud. "Okay, so . . . Obviously this is bad, but . . . we're going to be taking her down soon anyway. The deadline is still almost three days away, so all that we need to do—"

"It won't work."

All eyes turned to Jane. She was still sitting against the wall, underneath the broken display. She pulled herself up, refusing to be seen as smaller and weaker than the rest of them.

"UltraViolet saw me. She knows that I'm not Captain Lumen. She's going to see through any attempt that we make to convince her otherwise."

Marie rolled her eyes. Keisha sighed. Devin frowned, Tony winced, the corners of Amy's face turned down in a sad-puppy expression.

Only Cal appeared undaunted.

"No," he said. He drew himself up. "No, this can still work. We can train you—I can train you. I know that we can still do this."

Jane laughed—a broken, bitter sound. "Even if I believed you—which I don't, by the way, because I have a lot more knowledge of my capabilities than you do—but even if I believed you . . . don't you think that she's going to notice when I can't display a *single one* of Captain Lumen's powers?"

Cal shrugged. "It might not be necessary to display them. But also, our Jane didn't start to exhibit her powers until the Rift appeared. Maybe you just haven't been threatened enough in your life to *need* them to come to the surface." He raised an eyebrow. "Until now."

"What's that supposed—?" Jane started to ask, but Cal

glanced pointedly downward. Jane let her gaze be guided, as a hush overtook the room. She raised her hands, staring in disbelief. Her fingers were glowing a golden orange-red, bursts of light all but tearing themselves from her fingertips. Panic shot through Jane, and the glow flared so brightly that everyone had to shield their eyes and look away. When Jane dared to risk another look, the glow was gone, burned out from the force of her release.

But that did not mean that it hadn't been there in the first place. And if it had happened once . . .

Jane's mouth turned dry. She swallowed, trying to bring some of the moisture back.

"Come on," Cal said. He clapped a hand onto Jane's shoulder. "I think it's time we get started . . . Captain Lumen."

6

CAL DROVE. ONE HAND ON THE STEERING WHEEL, HIS thumb tapping to the beat of music playing softly from the speakers, the other hanging out the window. They'd all agreed that their headquarters was unsafe, given the circumstances. So while Keisha and Marie and Tony stayed behind to revamp their security systems and keep an eye on the hostage situation, Jane was in an SUV with Cal and Amy and Devin, heading out of the city. There was really only one place to go: their original headquarters.

Jane remembered it well. The drawings of it, anyway—she'd never been there in real life, and was both surprised and not surprised to learn that the building actually existed. In the comics, it belonged to Captain Lumen's family, and was the house where Cal had grown up. Well, calling it a house wasn't really doing it justice—the place was a *mansion*, a twenty-million-dollar estate on the most prime slip of waterfront property in the region.

Homes here weren't so much bought as inherited, passing down the long family line. Their neighbors were former presidents, and CEOs of multinational corporations. Jane had given Cal a pedigree that he could never live up to. It had endeared him to readers, that he would leave all of that behind to fight crime on the inner streets of Grand City.

She watched the world slip past her window. Jane and Clair had taken a weekend vacation up there five years ago, just so that Jane could capture the feel of the place. It was in the months leading up to their wedding, and Jane's mother had begged them to hold the ceremony up there, on the beach. "Wouldn't it just be *perfect*?" she'd said, more than once, as she pulled up pictures on her laptop and turned it around for both of them to see.

Jane had rejected it outright, though Clair was more polite about it. She smiled, agreeing that it was a lovely place, very nice—but they had a better idea for their venue, assuming that Clair's promotion went through in time. "Besides, Charlotte's Landing is just so expensive," Clair said.

Jane's mother waved off their worry with a deft flick of her wrist. "Let me worry about that." She reached for the laptop, her fine jewelry catching the light as if to make her point for her. Ms. Holloway had hired a top lawyer during the divorce, a personal rival to Jane's dad, and had managed to wrangle an impressive settlement out of her ex-husband. Since then, she'd invested wisely, renewed her real estate license, and started selling only the best properties—properties like you'd find in Charlotte's Landing.

Despite all of that, she had never moved out of the house where Jane had grown up. Jane secretly loved that about her mother—that she'd pawn off multimillion-dollar houses to spoiled city brats and rented high-rises to bankers who would spend most of their time in distant hotels, but never fell prey to the desire to live larger than she needed.

Jane's heart ached as they drove. Her mother took this route all the time. Jane pulled her phone out of her pocket, though even if she could manage to get it connected to a network here, her mother's number in this world likely belonged to someone else. Which meant that somewhere, back in Jane's real life, she'd up and left without so much as a text—and what, exactly, was her mother supposed to think when she found out? How many days would it be before she tried calling? How many more before she showed up at Jane's door? Shit, Jane's rent was due this weekend—if her stodgy old landlord didn't get his check, would he just up and sell Jane's stuff? Cal had insisted that the device he used to bring her here wouldn't recharge enough to use again for another few days. She might get back in time, but if not . . . would Jane even have a home to go back *to*?

Jane tried to put it out of her mind, because there was nothing to be done about it at the moment. She focused on the landscape. Outside of the city, the cloud of gloom from Doctor Demolition's weapon turned to haze as the morning rolled in, then disappeared altogether. Sun beat against the highway, and burned the yellowing grass beside the road. They were in the middle of a drought, Devin had explained when he caught her frowning at it.

"Really?" Jane asked. She had to twist around in her leather seat—Devin was directly behind her, sitting beside Amy. "For how long?"

"Near on two years."

"Seriously?"

"Yeah," Devin said. He brushed his hand over his head, smoothing out the loose curls that had sprung free of the man-bun he'd donned that morning. "Funny thing is, no one can figure out what's caused it. Weather patterns seem fine. They keep predicting rain, but . . . it's just not happening."

"Global warming?" Jane offered.

Devin shrugged. "Maybe. Doesn't seem directly related, but . . . hell, it's all so messed up these days."

Jane turned back to her window, oddly comforted. Not because of the weather, of course—it was just nice to find that some things hadn't changed between worlds. The Devin that Jane knew, the one that had only ever pretended to be a superhero, would have been following this topic, too. Ever since he was a boy, he'd been *obsessed* with all things science. His specific field of interest had rotated on an almost monthly basis, but even after he'd settled on his love for astrophysics, he tried to keep abreast with the major news coming out of all subjects. Weather was a hobby; Devin collected barometric readings and temperature variations the way that some people collect stamps. He particularly liked to make fun of local weathermen. He had an honest-to-god dartboard hanging in his basement, with various weather patterns and percentages across the segments, and he liked to invite people down to throw darts at it and draw up what he guaranteed was a more accurate forecast than you'd find on Channel 7.

He wasn't wrong.

Outside, the world moved on. City gave way to suburbs, suburbs gave way to open stretches of farmland. Dairy cows dotted the hillside. The traffic eased up around them, and Jane pictured the curve of the road from above, a slither of black cutting through struggling green and dying yellow. The contrast of a red barn to set the stage, one hundred percent pure Americana. A close-up of a bored cow's jaw, caught midchew, bits of grass clinging to its wet lips. She'd show the inside of the car next, looking back at it through the windshield: the front full of nothing but Cal's bright face and white smile, overpowering the smaller huddle of Jane herself. Behind them, in the shadows, you'd just be able to see Amy's head, tilted forward as she read a book in her lap, and the closed eyes of Devin as he leaned his too-tall head back and tried unsuccessfully to take a nap.

"So listen," Cal said as he clicked his signal light on. He was shifting lanes, making way for a large white semitruck just getting on from the entrance ramp. "Before we get there, we should probably go over our cover story."

Jane turned. Cal's powder-blue polo shirt and prep-boy shorts were reflecting so brightly that she almost had to shade her eyes just to look at him. "What cover story?"

"I just don't think that it's the best idea to tell your mom that the real Jane's missing. Ow!"—Cal turned, his eyes off of the road for several terrifying heartbeats as he glared at Amy behind him—"What's that for?"

"This Jane is just as *real*," Amy said, which was sweet, though Jane only sort of heard her; she'd grabbed the console in front of her the instant Cal's attention drifted, her knuckles turning white. Jane tried to keep her breathing steady, willing her heart to calm back down.

Though Cal was focused on merging back into the right lane, Amy noticed as Jane pried her fingers free and returned her hands to her lap.

"Are you okay?" Amy asked.

Jane forced a nod, and a shaky smile. "I . . . get nervous in cars."

"Oh," Amy said. "I'm sorry. I didn't know that."

Jane tried to shrug it off, though she couldn't bring herself to look at Amy. "No, well, why would you?" Jane asked. *You're from another world, one where you never fell into a coma after flipping your car in the tunnel coming home.*

"Can we get back to the cover story?" Cal asked. They were cruising straight again, just another gleaming silver fish in a school headed toward the shoreline. "We're going to need some other excuse for bringing Jane home."

"Wait, 'home'?" Jane reached over, abruptly turning off the car's stereo. "I thought that we were going to Charlotte's Landing. The first hideout."

"Um, we are?" Cal said. "I don't know where it is in your world—or, well, your comics, I guess, if we're going to believe that. But here, it's always been in the basement of Captain Lumen's house."

"Captain Lumen," Jane repeated. Her voice was dead, and she leaned back against the seat's headrest with a groan. "God, you don't really mean to tell me that *I* lived there?"

"Don't sound so happy about it," Cal said.

Amy cleared her throat. "It's a lovely place, Jane. Very nice."

"Yeah," Devin said with a snort, "if you like water polo and racism."

Cal rolled his eyes. "You make everything about race."

"Everything *is* about race, White Boy."

"Whatever," Cal muttered. "So does anyone have any suggestions? I don't think that Mrs. Maxwell is going to be thrilled that we're out here rather than dashing out to rescue her husband."

"Don't be so sure," Devin said, chuckling under his breath.

Jane frowned. She caught Devin's eye in the rear-view mirror. "You mean they're still married?"

Devin shrugged. "If you can call it that."

"More important than the cover story," Amy said, leaning forward, "is probably how to handle the . . . well, the fight. *Especially* if Jane's going to be posing as our Jane. It's going to make it harder."

"Mm," Devin said. Cal's mouth set into a hard line, his brow creasing as he stared straight ahead.

Jane looked back and forth between all of them. "Are you really going to make me ask?"

Amy sighed. "Jane hasn't spoken to her mother in over a year."

"Why not?"

"No one knows. She wouldn't talk about it."

"Great," Jane said. She threw her hands up. "That's just great. So basically what you're telling me is that I am supposed to convince my mother—who's not my mother, by the way—that I am her daughter, here to . . . what? Make amends or something? Without even knowing what it is we were fighting about?"

"Sorry," Amy said. "But . . . well, yes. That's more or less it."

Jane turned away from them. She leaned her forehead against the window, her glasses *clanking* and skewing crookedly on her face.

"Hey, but on the plus side," Cal said, with entirely too much cheer, "you're in for some great eats! Juanita makes a *mean* lobster bisque."

Devin snorted. "You know that's not really her name, don't you?"

"What?" Cal said. For a terrifying moment, Jane thought that he was going to turn around to boggle at Devin—but just then a gray sedan with a pile of kayaks strapped to its roof swerved, cutting them off. Jane braced herself, but Cal had the situation well in hand.

"Yeah. That's just what she lets you call her."

Cal frowned. "Nah, man. I visit her all the time when we're up there."

"For the free food."

"No! Well—yeah, sure. It's damn good. But me and 'Nita, dude, we're tight." He took his hand off the wheel, crossing his fingers as he waved them in Devin's direction.

"Uh-huh. Tell me, how many kids does she have?"

"Shit, you can't expect me to remember something like *that*," Cal said. He glanced over his shoulder at the approaching traffic, hopping lanes as he attempted to get back ahead of the kayak-happy sedan, which had greatly reduced its speed now that it was in the lane it wanted.

"Cal!" Amy shouted. "The exit!"

Cal muttered something wordless as he slammed the pedals. The car lurched forward, tires squealing, as he whipped back into their lane just in time to sail down the exit ramp. Jane gripped the door handle and the seatbelt over her chest, so tightly that her knuckles ached. She didn't release her hold until they'd tapered toward a more reasonable speed. Her fingers were radiating golden yellow, and Jane balled her fists as she tried to will the . . . the power, she guessed, back to wherever it had come from.

Luckily, no one else seemed to have noticed. Traffic concerns had overtaken the conversation; at this time of the year, the main thoroughfare into town was jammed with day-trippers seeking a relief from city life. Cal and Amy and Devin bickered lightly about which path to take through town, if there was a parade this weekend, which run of the ferry they were more likely to catch (though Jane didn't see the point of arguing about that one—they ran, apparently, once an hour).

No one paid attention to Jane, so she shut her eyes and tried to focus on her internal sensations: the steady pattern of her breathing, the thrumming of her heart, the subtle vibrations of the car against her legs . . . the tingle in her hands. She wanted to see if she could trace back where, exactly, the power was coming from. Though she'd been pretending it and drawing it and writing about it for roughly half her life by now, Jane was finding that she was still no better equipped to deal with it than the original Captain Lumen had been, back when Jane wrote his origin story in *Hopefuls* #14. It was one thing to understand the science she'd made up—it was another to actually *feel* it. The weight of it as it filled her up, dragging against her like she was swimming with her clothes on. The faint buzz in her head, like her whole body was operating on a different frequency than it used to. The whisper in her mind, a siren song of everything that she was now capable of, how she could manipulate the world around her, control it, bend it, *conquer it*—

Jane wrenched her eyes open. Her heart pounded in her ears, her breath was shaky in her chest. She tried to bring herself back to the present—the car, the chatter, the world outside of her window. The farms were gone. They were inching into town. Narrow streets cut through canyons of buildings, rising tightly on either side of the car. Cafés and art galleries, churches and bed-and-breakfasts. Old New England clapboards were painted white and blue and yellow, cheerful flowerboxes blooming, the brick sidewalks shaded by the branches of elm trees. On the corner, an old house was being renovated, its siding stripped off in a way that made Jane avert her eyes as if it was shameful. Pedestrians ambled along in bright white shorts and designer flipflops, straw purses and cloth shopping bags hanging from their arms. Jane pressed a button to lower the window, and the smell of fried seafood drifted out of a dozen different shopfronts. They stopped at a crosswalk and an old man dressed all in red, white, and blue strolled past, a giant Uncle Sam hat perched atop his head, little American flags stuck in the band. Absolutely everybody outside was white.

She stared at her hand. Was it just her imagination, or was her own pale skin reflecting more sunlight than was normal? Jane focused on it, trying to will it back. A few moments later it did *seem* less pasty, although it was hard to say if she was successful, or if the sun had gone behind a cloud.

One thing was certain: she could no longer just passively go along with whatever the rest of the Heroes of Hope wanted from her. Going home was not an option until she learned to control these new abilities, and the only way that she was going to do *that* . . .

Jane glanced sideways. Cal, in the driver's seat, his thumb still tapping along to music long since shut off. In many ways, he was a spoiled doofus, Jane knew this. But in the comics, he'd always managed to dig down, find the inner strength necessary to conquer problems. He'd learned to control these powers, when he was Captain Lumen. Maybe he really *could* help her do the same.

It couldn't hurt to try.

HOPEFULS #14 WAS THE TURNING POINT OF THE EARLY

series. Jane had waited to introduce the origin story. She wanted to give the readers a chance to know the characters as they were, to begin to form a connection, to have favorites and for ships to begin building in the dry dock of fanfictionland, before she shook things up by showing the "before" pictures of their lives.

The issues came out once a month, so this put the release of *Hopefuls* #14 somewhere near Jane and Clair's third wedding anniversary. It had taken almost a year to convince QZero to sign on to the new series, then months of rewrites before Jane finally had a version that met with approval across all their key demographics. Then production time, and a delay while QZero began a flurry of press releases and media hype. A popular late-night talk show host had gotten wind of the project, and as a favor via a friend of a friend, had been given an early draft— and loved it. His endorsement skyrocketed things to a new level of coverage, and QZero wanted to ride that high as much as they could in the months leading up to the launch date, which now had to be moved to coincide with the theatrical release of a popular movie in one of their main franchises.

The release was a hit, though inflated somewhat by the novelty of a new batch of superheroes. Jane knew that, and accepted the slight decline in readership that followed the end of the first arc of the opening storyline. By the time *Hopefuls* #14 came out, just over a year in, their numbers were still great, sure—but to hear the execubots talk about it, you'd think they were facing the beginning of the end. The pressure was on for Jane to create a triumph.

She knew that just throwing people back to the beginning would bore readers, and that by the time she rolled around to the present again, they might have lost the place of the main plot threads. She had to find a way to tie it all in—the past and the present informing each other, looping together to create an inevitable conclusion that would leave the readers breathless.

"Okay," Clair said, "so what if Doctor Demolition, in his normal alter ego, has been manipulating the Heroes from the beginning? Like, he needed them to have their powers, so that he could harness them for some evil purpose as yet to be determined?"

They were in the living room of their apartment, facing each other on the couch as they ate enormous bowls of homemade mac and cheese. Wednesdays were Binge and Brainstorm Days, where they ate anything they wanted, turned their music up loud enough to annoy the neighbors, and set aside four hours in the morning to stream whatever show they were into at the moment. By now Jane had enough clout and creative discretion to work from home a few days a week, and Clair's job as Assistant Curator meant that her hours, while long, were flexible enough for her to join in often.

Jane lifted a messy forkful of elbow macaroni. Mozzarella cheese, nontraditional but just how Clair liked it, trailed down and clung as a warm string to Jane's chin. Jane wiped it off with her finger, and scraped it against the side of her bowl.

"Isn't that kind of cliché?"

Clair looked up, her eyebrow arched in a withering *really?* expression. "It's comic books, Jane. Everything is cliché at this point. What matters is what kind of personal spin you put on it."

Jane shrugged. "Fair point."

It ended up being a little more complicated than that, but the essence of Clair's idea remained. While the Heroes were exposed to the radiation that triggered their dormant genetic abilities by accident, these powers did not start *emerging* straight away. Cal, tucked away in his parents' estate, did not have the support of the rest of his friends as his abilities began to manifest. He had no idea what had caused them. He had no idea what they meant—did not even fully understand, at the beginning, that the bursts of light springing from his fingertips at random were the beginning of a superpower. He thought he might be going insane. He thought he might have some rare disease. He thought, once, in a panic as he locked himself in the boys' bathroom at his fancy prep school, that maybe he wasn't even *human*. Maybe he was the result of some twisted genetic experiment. Maybe he was an alien, like Superman, crash-landed on Earth as a baby and raised as one of their own. Maybe he was an alien, who they had *then* experimented on, and now men in black were going to come storming in any day and lock him in a secret facility in Montana, and he would never see any of his friends again. He would never see Tracey, the girl he was currently crushing on, again.

A sharp knock rapped on the bathroom door. "Mr. Greenwood?" (In the comics, Jane had given aliases to all of her friends, so Cal Goodman had become Nigel Greenwood. It got a little confusing at times, even to her, but it was something her friends had all insisted upon when they'd agreed to let her use their faces and superhero alter egos.)

Cal/Nigel drew himself to his feet. The bathrooms at Hanover Preparatory Academy were single-occupancy toilets, a half-bath like you'd find at home. "A moment!" he called, as he flushed and washed his hands so that the person on the other side of the door would think that he'd been in there for legitimate purposes. Jane had given the readers a close-up of his forehead, slick with worried sweat, and the pulse fluttering in his neck; you could just see it, over the starched shirt collar and the green-and-gold tie. Cal/Nigel's hand on the doorknob, as he steadied himself.

In the hallway, a man. Always, he is either cast in shadow, or angled so that you cannot see his face. A hint of his suit jacket indicated that he'd dressed as a teacher, but other than that, the perception of him comes from Cal's reactions. On the first page, you saw over the man's shoulder, Cal's face somewhat nervous in the frame of the bathroom door.

"Ah, Mr. Greenwood," the speech bubble said. It oozed in from somewhere out of view. "My name is Arthur Edmunds. I believe that we have something in common."

THE MAXWELLS' PROPERTY WAS LOCATED ON AN ISLAND off of an island, requiring not just one, but two separate ferry trips to get there. On the first ferry (larger, crowded with tourists snapping selfies), the four of them sat in a silent group and watched the sea go by. Cal's sunglasses reflected the brilliant blue of the water, the crisp white of the ship. Amy's hair blew across her face in a perfect angle to highlight her cheekbones. Devin leaned back in his seat, his legs stretched out in front of him, using his phone and pretending not to notice as the other passengers gave him a wide berth.

For the first time since she'd arrived in this world, Jane wished for her sketchbook. The ship was a textbook in character studies, and there was no way that Jane would be able to remember them all. There was a woman with frizzy, flame-red hair and a flowing purple kimono, reciting poetry—either from memory, or making it up as she went. A person of indeterminate gender sat with a parrot on their shoulder, reading a fat fantasy novel. Jane turned, and a frail old couple in matching, out-of-place Hawaiian shirts walked by, their wispy white hair blowing straight up in the breeze, the curve of their scalps in clear view; they were strolling arm-in-bony-arm along the deck, smiling at people and telling anyone who would listen that they were here for their *sixty-third* wedding anniversary—*sixty-three years*, folks! The man grinned, his overlong teeth crossing slightly in the front. "That's a long time," he said to Jane when they passed, and Jane's heart twisted up as she forced herself to nod and agree. "It sure is."

Out of instinct, Jane found her wedding ring with her thumb, familiar grooves rippling underneath her touch.

Amy smiled pleasantly at the couple, wishing them many more years of happiness ("That's what we're planning on!" the old man said with a wink), and waited until they were gone before she leaned over toward Jane.

"By the way," Amy said, keeping her voice low so that only Jane and the sea breeze could hear her, "you might want to consider moving that to your other hand before Mrs. Maxwell sees you."

Jane looked down at the spread of her fingers, resting on her lap. Her wedding ring was nontraditional, crafted by a local artisan to resemble a braid of tree branches. Plenty of people had completely misunderstood the point of it, but if this Mrs. Maxwell was anything like Jane's own mother . . .

Jane slipped it easily from one hand to the other, trying hard not to feel like she was desecrating something sacred. Clair would have told her to do it; she would have been practical, just like Amy was being practical. Amy nodded, approving. Briefly, Jane considered that an even more discreet solution would be to add her own ring to the hidden chain around her neck, where she kept Clair's, but nothing was going to convince her to go quite *that* far. The ring didn't fit as well on Jane's right hand, or maybe Jane just wasn't used to it. She kept balling her fist in a subconscious attempt to keep it from falling off, even though it wasn't going anywhere.

She was still balling her fist as they approached the house. The second ferry captain, the one that would take them across the scant six hundred feet from the larger island to the smaller, had recognized their group on sight. "Miss Maxwell!" she'd said, grinning as she squeezed between several of the other passengers. "It's such a pleasure to see you again!"

Jane glanced at the brass name badge pinned to the captain's starched white shirt. "Captain Ambrose," she said. She accepted the captain's handshake with a false ease. "How have you been?"

Ambrose shrugged, but her grin never left her face. She was a tiny woman, barely up to Jane's chest, weathered and tan. Her blond hair was clamped into a bun on the back of her head, and her face was lined with wrinkles of sun and smiles. She squinted in the sunshine as she said, "Can't complain. We've had ideal weather this season."

"Excellent," Jane said. She let her attention drift to the water, sparkling like champagne. The first tinge of gold was beginning to stain the surface, the light growing weary with the weight of late afternoon.

Ambrose excused herself a moment later, and Amy sidled up to take her place. "That was perfect," Amy said, keeping her voice low. "Keep up that level of haughty disinterest, and you should pass all right."

Jane smirked, though she wasn't sure if she should be pleased or disturbed by her success. They hadn't planned ahead, so Jane hadn't even gotten so much as a crash course on how to play her double—all that she had to go on, really, was the address they were heading toward, and the clothes that she'd been presented with. Before they'd set out from the Heroes' main headquarters, it was decided that Jane's torn shirt would best be replaced. Amy had brought her a change of clothes that Jane hadn't questioned, though she had raised her eyebrows at the designer label inside of the jeans, and it's not like she *normally* wore silk blouses. At the time, Jane had been too distracted from the emergence of her powers to think much about it, but standing on the deck of the ferry, the outfit had settled something in Jane's mind. Like wearing a costume, the clothes had unfolded a personality for Jane to borrow. All that she'd had to do was drape it over her shoulders.

Only now, as Cal turned off of the main road and onto a long driveway of white gravel, Jane's confidence began to falter. It was one thing to pass herself off to a ferry captain—it would be another trick entirely to fool the shrewd eyes of Mrs. Maxwell. *Any* Mrs. Maxwell. Jane glanced down at herself, suddenly self-conscious of the few wrinkles in her blouse from the seatbelt, of the scuffs along the toes of her own Converse.

It was too late to turn back now, though. They followed a bend in the drive, and the trees alongside dropped away. In their place was grass so green that it hurt, the glitter of the ocean far beyond, and the house . . .

Jane's eyes widened, settling on the house. Drawing it several dozen times did not prepare her for the sight of it in real life.

From the styling, it clearly wanted to present itself as modest. The barnlike curves of a cape-style roof were done in humble blue, leading to white clapboard siding. Blue shutters and flower-boxes were perfectly painted, perfectly tended. A sprawling white porch brought to mind images of southern plantations, people sipping lemonade and sitting on wicker chairs. If it was about a quarter of the size, if it didn't make a ninety-degree bend to accommodate a three-car garage, it *might* have successfully passed itself off as any one of the many New England coastal homes they'd passed on their way here.

As it was, though, its true purpose was unmistakable. This was a house dripping with *money*. Jane gawped, taking it in as best as she could: in manageable, panel-sized chunks. White gravel crunching underfoot, somehow spotless despite being both outdoors and driven across regularly. The ocean view in the distance. The idyllic coral-pink sunset, staining a backdrop behind the roof of the house. The spread of pecan cookies and, yes, lemonade, sitting on a glass-topped table along the porch. The front door swinging open before they'd even rung the bell.

Jane was halfway up the steps. She froze midstride, her foot still hovering in the air.

Was this all some kind of elaborate trick? Or had the Heroes of Hope really been so incompetent as to not think to look here?

Jane Maxwell was standing in the doorway.

Oh, different, sure—but that much was to be expected. She did not wear Jane's glasses, and her hair was shorter, expertly curled ends just gracing her shoulders. She wore a pencil skirt and black blazer, pearls, and four-inch spiked heels, like she'd just come from a boardroom; and, dammit, she was better toned than Jane herself was, calf muscles clearly visible underneath her sheer pantyhose. But the face, it was . . . well, almost like staring at a mirror. Jane supposed that any differences were just the result of being from a parallel world, or else something that Jane had never had cause to notice in her own reflection.

This other Jane, the one that wasn't Jane, regarded the group ascending her porch as if she'd just found a collection of road kill.

"Oh, Jane. Would it have really killed you to put on some proper foundation?" she said.

Cal bounded up the steps, extending his hand. "Nice to see you again, Allie." He was all grins and yacht-club smiles.

The other woman—Jane? Not Jane?—narrowed her eyes and crossed her arms to avoid shaking his hand. "Cal. I've asked you not to call me that."

"Allison?" came a voice from inside of the house. "Is that them?"

Allison? Jane thought. *Who the fuck is Allison?*

Allison, the woman that wasn't Jane, turned. "Yes, Mother," she called over her shoulder. "They're here."

A squeal of delight, far too normal and down-to-earth to belong in a house like this, filtered out through the open door.

It grew louder as it approached, heels clacking underneath the constant "ooooh!", until a flurry of color burst outside, knocking Allison out of the way.

Jane's mother—or more accurately, Mrs. Maxwell—rocked to a halt on the porch, taking Jane in. She looked . . . amazing, Jane had to grudgingly admit. Flawless in the glowing way of movie stars. If Jane didn't know what Mrs. Maxwell would have naturally aged like, she never would have suspected plastic surgery—no doubt working in tandem with stylists, dietitians, and fitness coaches. Not that Jane's mother was homely by any stretch of the imagination, but this was something else entirely. Every line had been erased, every blemish buffed away.

A pang struck Jane's chest, a deep longing for her mother's natural elegance.

"Oh, Jane!" Mrs. Maxwell said, clasping her hands together in front of her. "I can't tell you how happy I am that you've decided to come home—especially at a time like this."

Jane glanced to the side. Amy stepped up beside her, and gave Jane's upper arm a brief squeeze of encouragement. Jane forced herself to look Mrs. Maxwell square in the face. She tried a brave smile. "Mom. It's . . . good to be here."

A loud *harrumph* emanated from behind Mrs. Maxwell. Allison stepped back into view. "Gee, Jane. Don't sound so happy about it."

"What does it matter to you?"

"Girls," Mrs. Maxwell chided, "be nice. Allison, your sister just *got* here—and these are trying times for all of us. I think that we can manage to extend each other a bit of compassion and understanding, don't you?"

Allison's mouth pinched flat. She glowered at Jane, her mood darkening the whole porch. She turned without a word, disappearing into the house.

Jane watched the open doorway. An immaculate foyer, large and full of dying light, and a single haughty figure cutting through it on her way toward a curving staircase.

Sister?

The word drummed through Jane's mind, loud and uninvited. She felt small all of a sudden, an ant in the shadow of this massive house. How in the world did the Heroes think that Jane could pass herself off as this world's Jane? That she could fool a mother she did not know, a father she did not like—a *sister* she had never met?

Never mind becoming Captain Lumen, never mind going up against UltraViolet. Jane would be lucky if she even made it to the deadline.

THE POWERS, THEN.

In a basement below the basement, Jane stretched her fingers. She shook out each foot, flapped her hands around to loosen up. Did a series of quick jumping jacks. Rolled her shoulders, tipped her neck side to side.

The squeal and crackle of an intercom broke the silence. "Any time you're ready," Devin's voice said.

Amy's voice jumped in, just before the intercom cut off. "Devin! Stop being—"

Crackle—nothing.

The silence echoed. Jane stared ahead: the long stretch of tunnel, a set of targets set at the far end. The brick walls were painted white, with a wide blue stripe running down the length. The floor was plain concrete, though large swaths of muddy-red padding, like the kind you'd find in a school gymnasium, lined the floor in patches. Back in the sixties, when the house was built, the property had been owned by an arms tycoon who'd gotten rich selling weapons to the military; the subbasement was a bunker, designed to withstand a nuclear blast. This room, so the story goes, was where the man's weapon tests were conducted. Behind Jane, the thick pane of a one-way mirror hid the faces of Cal and Amy and Devin from view.

Jane glanced to the side. Scorch marks and the scar of deep gouges marred the walls, though it was hard to tell if that was from the original owner, or the result of their own youthful experimentation.

She took a deep breath. *Don't think about why you're doing this,* she told herself. *Just . . . see if you can do it. It's like a game.*

Her assurances did little to actually convince her, but these were the lies that needed to be told. She thought of her comics. Of the hours sprawled on her stomach as a teenager, sketching what these abilities looked like.

In the comics, Captain Lumen had the ability to create bursts of light, which could either be highly focused and used as a weapon, or spread broadly for illumination. Years later, he'd discovered the ability to manipulate light in a lower frequency, allowing him to shift his perspective to see in infrared — and then again later, Jane had let his powers dip lower still, to manipulate wireless signals. Nobody expected anywhere near that level of control from Jane now (indeed, it would be dangerous for her to even *try*), but the fact that they were looking for even the bare minimum still scared the shit out of her. What if her powers were a fluke, fading ever since they'd first displayed? Or, perhaps worse: what if she *could* still conjure her powers, but controlling them proved beyond her?

Stop it, Jane thought to herself, shoving the idea firmly aside. *You can do this.*

Another lie, but what did it matter at this point?

Jane thrust her arm forward, straight as a sword. She focused on the ball of her fist, remembering the feeling that she'd had earlier. The power thrumming through her. The thought of it was sharp, and Jane tried to keep from flinching back from it. She remembered the way her hand had started to glow, light radiating from her fingertips down to her palm. *Power, power, power.* Jane bit her lip, feeling silly. Why hadn't she written something simpler? Superspeed, maybe, or flight? At the very least, she could have given Captain Lumen a trigger, a catch phrase that he whispered to himself to switch his abilities on.

Of course, even if she had, there was no guarantee that's how it would work in real life.

Jane snorted. *Real life*, sure. It still felt like half a dream. One of those days when you're so tired that your mind slips, and suddenly nothing is quite *real* anymore—you touch something, say something, and it's like you're watching it from a distance. Jane had walked around like that for months after Clair's death, and the feeling of it now was like being smothered under a thick blanket.

Clair. Jane winced, and shoved the image of her quickly aside. Focus, dammit. Focus.

Another deep breath. She stared at her fist. Her ring, on the wrong hand, felt heavy and off-balance. But there was no sense in pretending: it wasn't working. No power thrummed through her now. Nothing to manipulate, nothing to control.

Jane turned around, watching herself in the one-way mirror. The tunnel loomed massive around her, reducing her to a wisp.

"I can't do it," she said. She spread her arms, to indicate the enormity of everything that she couldn't do.

Crackle. Cal's voice: "You just need to focus, Jane. Focus on what you want to do, not how you want to do it. Try again."

Jane made a face. She saw it in the reflection—childish, petty. The defeat that she'd declared so easily stung her, and she turned around before they could see the flush of embarrassment in her cheeks.

What she wanted to do.

What she wanted to do was go home. However much her life might be in shambles at the moment, at least it was familiar. Her apartment, her bed, her own Grand City. There was a pile of sketches on her coffee table, right at this very moment, half-finished concept art for the next few issues of *Hopefuls*. It didn't matter that Jane wasn't going to get to finish them—she wanted to see them. She wanted to prop her feet up on the coffee table and lean her drawing board against the slope of her legs, spread the pages out in front of her. She wanted to cry over the loss of her job, and spend several hours doodling pictures of dicks on various back issues. She wanted to wrap herself in Clair's old sweaters. The smell of Clair was long since gone from the cashmere, but the *comfort* of it remained, the idea that Clair's arms had slid through those same sleeves, that this exact fabric had kept her warm against the chill of another autumn setting in.

But then . . . even thinking about retreating to these comforts brought the acid of guilt to Jane's stomach. How could she consider walking away, when so many people's lives were at stake? Worse, still: she had no idea how it was that UltraViolet had spread the poison to the rest of Grand City. Though nobody had mentioned it, there was the possibility that even some of the Heroes of Hope were infected. That Amy might be infected.

Fear and rage struck fast, clutching hot at Jane's throat. She threw her arm forward, her fingers spreading open as if tossing confetti to the winds. A burst of light exploded from her open palm, as bright as sunshine. It was wild and chaotic, and so unexpected that Jane actually screamed and leaped back, as if she could separate it from herself. Instinct snapped her hand shut, the power snuffing out like a candle.

A rapid pulse thundered in Jane's ears. Her vision was blotchy, disjointed. She staggered toward the wall, the only solid thing that she could make out. She was so dizzy with surprise at herself that she barely heard the door slam open and then shut, the rapid rain of footsteps rushing toward her.

The smell of Clair assaulted her. Warm arms wrapped around her shoulders, a happy squeal buzzing near her ear. "Jane!" Amy shouted. "You did it!" Amy leaped up and down, jostling Jane in her enthusiasm.

Jane knew that Amy was overreacting—that the minor display of power, while certainly bright, was nothing compared to what Captain Lumen could do. That Jane was supposed to have been trying to focus the beam, direct it toward the targets. That it would take a lot more than a light show to pull off whatever Cal was planning.

And yet. A grin was tugging at Jane's lips, because it was so much like Clair, like Amy, to overcelebrate the first step on a journey. *"First steps are so important, though!"* Clair always insisted, whenever anyone tried to dampen her enthusiasm. *"Nothing else can follow if you don't start!"*

So Jane returned Amy's hug, lavishing in the attention. There was still so much work to do, so much to figure out. But it was true: this, right here, this was where it all begins.

THEY WORKED FOR ALMOST TWO HOURS, UNTIL AMY called it because the Maxwells' dinner would be served soon. "You should probably get a shower in first," she said. "I'll show you to your room."

Her room. Jane didn't know if she was ready for it, but it turned out to be so impersonal that she might as well have been staying in a hotel. Like the rest of the house, it had been decorated in a seaside theme: the bed, spread in pale blue and white, was set underneath a piece of bleached driftwood. A white trunk rested at the foot of her bed, a soft blanket folded on top, a bowl with random bits of seaglass nestled atop that. A magazine lay on the nightstand, but somehow Jane suspected that the decorator, rather than her double, had rested it there. Black-and-white photographs of a beach lined the walls.

Jane showered, and selected the least pretentious pair of shorts from the walk-in closet. She found an actual t-shirt, its logo faded from the start, and then she scooped her hair up into a ponytail. In the bathroom, she poked through cabinets and drawers: some of her familiar products—her toothpaste of choice, the tampons she liked—but mostly skincare brands that she'd never heard of, prescriptions for Xanax, three separate hairdryers. This Jane had an electric toothbrush, a scary-looking hair-removal device, and several packs of contact lenses. Jane opened the box of contacts, looking at the tiny lenses lined up and waiting. She'd never considered switching away from glasses before—the idea of touching her own eyes made her shudder. She put them back and pawed a little deeper. Something pink and disk-shaped caught her eye and she took it out, turned it over. She actually stared at it for several long seconds, awareness knocking at her mind without actually making it through.

Then it did: birth control pills.

"Jesus, Jane!" Jane dropped the pills and slammed the drawer shut. She actually backed away from it, as if somehow proximity to such a thing could make it contagious.

Her skin was still crawling several minutes later, as she padded down the long hallway toward the main staircase. She did not want to think about it—so, naturally, it was the one thing that her mind kept swirling back to. She just kept remembering Amy, her shock at the idea that they were married. Jane shuddered.

There's another explanation, Jane told herself as she walked. *A hormonal issue, perhaps.*

Which was possible, sure—but the idea settled sourly in her stomach. She would have to try to ask Amy about it, somehow, sometime . . .

Her thoughts were scattered a moment later when she found Mrs. Maxwell in the foyer, talking to several people in gray and navy suits. Jane paused at the top of the stairs, uncertain if she should interrupt. There was a *serious* quality in their mannerisms, a feeling that leeched the warmth from the air and made Jane feel like a child who had stumbled upon a pack of grownups. Jane sat on the top step, drawing her knees to her chest as she watched. The foyer was deep from this angle, and the overhead lights cast dark slashes across the figures gathered below.

". . . could be dangerous to delay," one of the men in suits was saying. "If we storm the building now—"

"You'll just give UltraViolet a reason to kill everyone inside," Mrs. Maxwell cut in. "Including my husband. We still have time."

One of the other suits sighed. A woman, short, with mouse-brown hair gathered in a thin ponytail. "That's assuming that UltraViolet is telling the truth. Our own doctors are projecting that it could turn fatal within a matter of *hours*. Please, Mrs. Maxwell—why push it?"

"I will not risk all hell breaking loose just because you want a chance to bring glory to your division, Sylvia," Mrs. Maxwell said. "I'm sure that the Heroes are handling the situation."

The short woman, Sylvia, bristled. "With all due respect, ma'am, there's been no word from the Heroes since shortly after their defeat at Woolfolk Tower. With the chaos they had to deal with in the aftermath . . . We can't even be sure they're all still alive."

"Oh, they're alive—and working on a plan, I can promise you that."

Sylvia smirked. "Can you, now? What makes you so sure?"

"Because UltraViolet is still trying to kill them."

"I see," Sylvia said. "And you'd bet your own husband's life on this?"

There was a slight pause before Mrs. Maxwell answered; the smallest of attached speech bubbles, an ellipsis hanging off the top of her answer. "I would. They've never let us down before."

Sylvia's voice was soft as she said, "I think the people of downtown would disagree."

"Things would have been a lot worse if the Heroes hadn't been there," Mrs. Maxwell said.

Jane shut her eyes. There was something fiercely protective in Mrs. Maxwell's voice, which Jane worried would give the whole thing away. Cal had told Jane that Mrs. Maxwell knew about their powers, knew who they really were. He'd said it to be reassuring, so that at least this was *one* thing that Jane wouldn't have to lie about, but now Jane almost wished that she didn't know. The idea of her mother—not her mother, but still—knowing what they do, knowing the way that they go out and risk their lives, and still being proud enough and brave enough to stand there and defend her daughter against criticism . . .

But there was something more to it, Jane realized as she opened her eyes. Mrs. Maxwell had already pulled out her phone, turning her attention away from the visitors as if they and their concerns didn't warrant the attention. Jane watched, the enormity of what they were doing bubbling up inside of her. It was one thing to accept the crazy circumstances of her situation; it was one thing to begin training, to see the raw strength of her own powers for the first time. It was another thing entirely to realize that people—real *people*, with lives and dreams all their own, with loved ones waiting for them—were depending on her being successful.

God, she was going to be sick.

Sylvia grimaced, taking the hint but not yet willing to yield. The rest of her group was already making motions toward the door; only Sylvia stood her ground. "I hope that you're right, Mrs. Maxwell," she said. "Because if you're not, a lot more people are going to suffer before this is over."

Mrs. Maxwell didn't even look up from her phone. "Don't worry—I am."

There was nothing more for them to say after that. Sylvia nodded stiffly. The others were at the door by now. One of them stood back and opened it for her, his hand at his chest as if he was holding a hat to it like a proper Southern gentleman.

"You shouldn't be eavesdropping."

Jane yelped. The voice was so close, yet she hadn't heard the source of it approach. She whirled, her heart racing, only to find the near-identical copy of her own face glaring down at her.

"Holy *crap*, Allison," Jane snapped as she got to her feet. "You scared the shit out of me."

Allison shrugged, just one indifferent shoulder. "Not my fault you didn't hear me."

"Girls," Mrs. Maxwell called up from the foyer—the commotion must have drawn her attention, "stop dawdling. Come down and have something to eat."

As if this was any other night—as if Jane was still a teenager, and she'd grown up in this house, and everything about it was normal. Jane shot Allison a look, but Allison was already shoving past her, their shoulders knocking as she began to descend the steps.

There was nothing to do but follow.

Mrs. Maxwell had not waited around to see if her instructions were listened to. Jane trailed Allison through a series of living rooms, each decorated with its own seaside theme. When they finally reached the kitchen, Jane found they were the last to arrive. Everyone was gathered loosely around the kitchen island, tumblers of scotch or tall glasses of beer littering their hands.

"No, I'm *telling* you," Cal was saying, "I *saw* her making name-tags for herself one time with the label maker. 'Tia Juanita,' they said. Juanita!"

Devin shook his head. "Dude, those were labels for her salsa.

She buys store-bought and puts them in mason jars to pass it off as her 'Aunt Juanita's' special recipe. *Tía Juanita*. Have you never even taken a Spanish class in your life?"

Cal frowned. "Now you're just talking shit."

"I swear, I'm not. White people can't tell the difference, and she sure as hell isn't going to waste her authentic recipes on you lot."

"But . . . not her special salsa! I love that stuff!"

Devin laughed. "Yeah, I know."

"Here," said a voice beside Jane, drawing her attention away as Cal and Devin continued to argue back and forth. Amy was holding out a drink. "This will help."

Jane accepted it gratefully. "Thanks. I don't know how I'm going to survive this."

Amy grinned and raised her glass. "To family."

"Family," Jane said, tapping her glass to Amy's.

If only hers was actually in attendance.

THE YEAR JANE'S PARENTS WERE GETTING DIVORCED, THEY DIDN'T HAVE A THANKSGIVING DINNER.

"What do you *mean* we're not 'doing Thanksgiving'?" Jane had asked. She was sitting on her rickety dorm bed, on the phone with her mother, when this conversation took place. Through the window at the far end of the room, Jane could see half-dead ivy crawling its way up the brickwork of the student center next door; she was doodling it, in ink, along the edge of her notebook, the recreation pulsing with far more life than the real thing as it worked its way between entries on Jane's "weekly news for Mom" list. Her pen stilled, underneath *Finals, UGGGHH*, and above *Lunch with Jess D and crew—possible new book club??*

Over the phone, Jane heard her mother take a small breath. Clearly, this had been rehearsed.

"I just think it might be nice for us all to take a break this year," Ms. Holloway said. "It's such a headache, you know, and for what? Plus, the house is in no state for it right now."

Jane frowned. Her mother, in the wake of the separation, had taken it upon herself to remodel the kitchen, master suite, and main-floor bathroom—in addition to fresh coats of paint throughout the house, new furniture in almost every room, and repurposing the den into a home office that Jane doubted anyone would ever use. It all seemed a bit *much* by Jane's standards, but now she had to wonder if her mother hadn't timed it this way on purpose.

"What about Grandma?" Jane asked. Jane's mother's mother flew in from Omaha faithfully on the Tuesday leading up to Thanksgiving, and always stayed through the beginning of December. Jane's mother, like Jane, was an only child.

A slight shifting, like Jane's mother was shrugging or adjusting the phone from one shoulder to the other. "She's going to stay with her sister in Fort Lauderdale. She understands."

"Wait, you already *told* her?"

"Yes, Jane," Ms. Holloway said with a sigh. "I'm sorry, but it's settled."

"But . . . ," Jane trailed off, uncertain what kind of argument she could make that wouldn't sound like a little kid. Even though, at the moment, she *felt* like a little kid—and really, she thought, didn't she have every right to? Coming out to her parents, the divorce, moving to college, the remodel—over the past year, it felt as if Jane's entire childhood was being dismantled piece by piece. A certain amount of regression was only to be expected.

"But when will we see her?" Jane settled on finally, after a long, empty stretch of silence. There really weren't a lot of miles between Jane's dorm and her mother's house, but now it felt as if the phone lines between them stretched so far that they could wrap to the moon and back.

Ms. Holloway sighed. "I don't know. Maybe Christmas. Maybe your birthday."

"What's wrong with Thanksgiving?"

"Because I don't *want* to," Ms. Holloway snapped.

Jane jerked back, away from the phone, as if she'd been physically struck. She looked at the phone in her hand: the stubby gray antenna, the buttons already worn down from frequent use. The phone used to belong in the family kitchen, until Jane's mother had replaced it with a newer set that had three handsets instead of just one. Jane liked having a portable phone, rather than the clunky old corded one that had come with the dorm. She liked to stick her head out the window and imagine that she had a fire escape that she could sit on during cool evenings, her legs dangling through the bars as if she was in a romantic comedy.

Now, though, she wanted to throw it across the room. The old clunker from the dorm could probably take it.

"—sorry, sweetie, I didn't mean it like that," Jane's mother was already saying as Jane cautiously put the phone back to her ear. "It's just . . . it's been hard. You know that."

"I do."

"And it's just . . . *Thanksgiving*." She said this with the same weight that someone might say *jury duty*, or *traffic court*. Or *finals*. "And then she'd be all, 'What can I do to help?', and 'Have you been going to church?', and then you'd want to bring *Clair* over, and—"

"Wait, wait," Jane cut in. "What's wrong with Clair?"

There was the slightest pause across the line. "Nothing. Grandma loves Clair, of course. She loves all your friends."

Understanding settled thickly, like drying concrete, through her veins. Jane's free hand clenched into a fist in her lap. "You don't want her to find out that I have a girlfriend."

"Don't be like this, Janie."

The bitter bark of a laugh escaped Jane's chest. "Like what? *Gay?*"

"Stop it. I'm a supportive parent, and you know it."

"Until you actually have to stand up for me, apparently."

"Oh, like you have any *idea* what it's like to defend your daughter's choices constantly."

"My *choices*?" Jane said. "You make it sound like I got a tattoo on my ass. We're talking about *who I am*, Mom, not—"

"Yes, and for*give* me for not wanting to deal with it all on top of everything else right now, all right? I'm getting enough of this crap from the neighbors. I'd rather not bring it into the house when Grandma sees the two of you together." She sighed. "It's just easier to avoid it this year. Don't you see?"

Oh, Jane saw, all right. She sat up in her bed, anger coursing through her. "Fine," she said. "You don't want Thanksgiving this year, that's fine. I'll just stay with Clair's family instead."

Jane could practically *hear* her mother rolling her eyes. "Jane—"

"Goodbye, Mom," Jane said. She had already found the off button with her finger, and she hung up the phone before it was even away from her ear.

STORE-BOUGHT OR FRESH, THE SALSA WAS PRETTY GOOD.

They ate on the back patio—one of the back patios. Stars sparkled above, champagne and Mrs. Maxwell's diamonds sparkled below. Jane sank deeply into the cushion of a wicker chair. In the heart of their semicircle was a table with a fire pit crackling in the middle; the fire served to keep the evening's chill at bay, and their dinner warm. The food was served in a come-as-you-are style, spread around the perimeter of the table so that people could dish up and sit back in their chairs as they saw fit. Despite the circumstances, Jane felt a swell of comfort when she spied the familiar spread of Tex-Mex: steak fajitas; warm tortilla chips with guacamole and salsa; chili con carne, thick and gravy-like in a heavy stoneware bowl. Jane's mother had grown up in the outskirts of Houston, then moved to Seattle, Los Angeles, D.C., and finally Grand City. She'd shed her Texas accent long before Jane was ever born, but always broke out the spices and rich meats of Tex-Mex when she needed to feel like home.

"I guess the vegan stint didn't last long," Allison said. She was standing near Jane, regarding the spread on the table with a critical eye. Her plate was empty—she held it in front of her chest like a shield, her agitated fingers tapping against the back—but she'd glanced pointedly at Jane's as she sidled by.

Jane looked up. Her spoon was halfway to her mouth, held where she'd been blowing on it to cool off the contents. A bowl of the chili con carne sat by her elbow on the chair's wide armrest.

Vegan? Jane's eyes flicked to Amy, who gave a subtle nod.

Jane shrugged. "I got tired of it."

"What a surprise," Allison said, rolling her eyes. She paused over the food again, then darted down and plucked a single square of cornbread from a basket, like a cat pouncing on a laser dot. With nothing else on her plate, she rounded the table and sat as far from Jane as she could.

Jane put her spoon down. She watched Allison, who was now thoroughly ignoring Jane as she tore tiny corners off of her cornbread and popped them into her mouth one at a time. A fine trail of yellow crumbs grazed her lips and dotted her fingers.

A sister. Jane still didn't even know what that meant, not *really*. Siblings at all were a foreign country to her, but sisters in particular provided an even greater puzzle. Clair had four brothers, but they were all so much younger than her. She and Jane used to babysit them, earning pocket money and changing diapers. Hardly a help.

So what did it mean, then? Jane wondered. What kind of childhood games had Allison and this world's Jane played, what kind of secrets had they kept? She thought about the complaints that Marie had about her sisters—stolen makeup and clothes, fights about who got the middle seat of the couch. One of Marie's sisters was into marathons, and kept trying to convince Marie to join her.

Try as she might, Jane couldn't quite put any of these things together with the woman sitting across from her, nibbling on her cornbread. Nobody had warned Jane about Allison, and why would they have? It made sense to assume that she'd have been in Jane's real life, too. Jane tried to picture it. She brought up a selection of her childhood memories, adding in a fuzzy image of a girl that looked a lot like Jane. Jane knew enough of her family history to understand that her parents had experienced difficulty conceiving—there had even been a miscarriage, about two years before Jane had finally been born.

Jane froze.

A miscarriage. She stole another look at Allison, trying to judge the woman's age, though it was impossible to tell. Certainly she was *near* to Jane's.

As if sensing the attention, Allison snapped her head up. Her gaze was already narrowed. "*What?*"

"Nothing," Jane said hurriedly. She drew the bowl of chili con carne closer, and tucked her legs up in the chair beside her so that she could curl around the warmth of her dinner without it seeming too weird.

Mrs. Maxwell cleared her throat. She sat to Jane's left, a plate balanced across her knees. Tiny portions of everything were evenly divided across the plate, pushed around so that it appeared as if she'd been eating. "So, Jane: tell us some of what you've been up to lately? It's . . . it's been a while."

Jane bit her lip. Right—the fight. Mrs. Maxwell had been so warm and welcoming that Jane had almost forgotten that in this version of reality, the two of them had been estranged for more than a year.

"Oh," Jane said, shrugging as she dug her spoon through her dinner. "Not much. Just . . . you know, the usual."

She took a large bite, the better to avoid answering follow-up questions, but the meal was still too hot. Jane lurched forward, only just stopping herself from spitting the chunk of searing meat back into her bowl. She snatched the glass of water from Amy's chair instead, downing it in huge gulps that nearly choked her.

Allison snorted. "Smooth."

Jane shot her a look as she wiped her mouth with the back of her hand.

Mrs. Maxwell raised an eyebrow. "I see. Well"—she shrugged —"if you don't want to talk about it—"

"Jane's just being modest," Cal said.

"There's a first," Allison said.

Jane looked up. Amy was shooting her an uncomfortable look, as Cal thumped Jane twice on the back.

"We're all very proud of our little star here," he said.

Jane forced a smile. Mrs. Maxwell was positively beaming at her.

"I can't tell you how happy it made me to read that you'd gotten back to painting," Mrs. Maxwell said. "Though I thought the piece in the *Times* could have been a bit more positive about it."

"Why?" Allison asked. "Her work is shit."

"Allison!"

"What? I'm just being honest. You'd think that being an art dealer would teach her how to recognize good art, but apparently not."

"That's *enough*," Mrs. Maxwell said. "Jane, I loved your pieces. They're very, um . . . expressive."

"They're depressing," Allison said.

Jane looked Allison square in the face. "Maybe they're supposed to be."

"Maybe," Allison said. She tore another corner off of her cornbread. "But who wants to go to a gallery just to see a dead bird? I mean, what's *that* about?"

A loud *whoosh* swept over Jane, making her head spin. She felt disconnected from herself, like she was only half there. She saw the scene: the gathering on the patio, the posh details of perfectly trimmed grass and expensive furniture; a collection of people that might as well have stepped off a movie set. A mirror of her own face, or close enough, staring back at her across the glow of the fire pit. Allison's expression had gone slack, like maybe she'd realized that finally, for reasons that she couldn't understand, she'd stepped too far.

Jane's heart was thundering in her ears. All that she could think about was the opening of the Spectral Wars, the dozen sketches that she'd drawn while crouched on a freezing stoop, in the middle of grief so deep that she couldn't even see the surface above her head. She did not hear the words that Cal said next, though it sounded like he was rising to her defense.

An awkward silence followed. Just when Jane didn't think that she could take it anymore, the door to the house opened, and a Hispanic woman stepped out onto the patio, her arms loaded down with two more trays. She wore crisp tan pants, a sharp white blouse. Her hair was woven into a braid that ringed her head like a crown.

Cal turned, instantly beaming. "Juanita! Your salsa is as amazing as ever."

The woman smiled patiently. *"Gracias, señor."*

"De nada!" Cal said proudly, stressing the emphasis of each word longer than was reasonable, as if he was trying to make a point.

Devin rolled his eyes.

"See?" Cal said, once the woman had deposited the food and disappeared again.

"You're such an idiot."

"I think I missed something," Allison said.

"No," Devin said. "Just the usual."

Jane shook her head. Her glasses had slipped, and she balanced her bowl in her other hand as she nudged them back up the bridge of her nose with her knuckle.

"Hey, Allie," Cal said as he leaned over to scoop up another large spoonful of the famous salsa, "you never did say where Mr. Awesome is this evening."

Allison made a face. Jane paused, midchew, trying to remember if there was a character somewhere in the universe of her heroes that she'd given such a horrible superhero alias. She didn't think so, but . . .

Allison deposited her plate on the table. The cornbread, at best half-finished, looked as if it had been gnawed on by mice. She picked a large glass of wine up from where it had been resting on the patio stones by her feet. "Alex and I thought it would be better for the kids if they stayed home for now. At least until . . ." She paused, took a drink.

Mrs. Maxwell leaned over, stretching far around the side of the table to pat her daughter's leg. "It's all right, honey."

"It's *not* all right," Allison said. "My father is *dying*, and we're trusting in a bunch of trick-or-treaters to sweep in and—"

Amy whipped her head up. "Wait!"

Jane was surprised when Allison drew herself short, although perhaps it was just a good excuse to bury her nose in her wine-glass again. Allison scowled as she knocked back the last of what had been a good helping of wine a moment ago.

Amy turned, peering into the bushes near the corner of the house.

"Amy?" Mrs. Maxwell asked, but Amy only held up her hand. She'd chosen a pale pink for her fingerless gloves, and they blended in with the soft light of the patio.

There was no warning. One moment Amy was sitting there, pensive, paused, and the next she was on her feet. She'd somehow dropped her plate off in her seat as she rose, one seamless motion, and Jane watched in fascination and dread as Amy dashed across the expanse of patio, Devin and Cal springing up to follow fast on her heels.

"What the—?" Allison asked, but her question was answered a second later.

A yelp and a flurry of motion burst out of the bushes as a figure—a camera swinging wildly around his neck—was flushed from his hiding spot. He wore all dark, blending in even now, as he sprinted across the lawn. Jane's friends were giving chase, shouts of "You asshole!" and "Get back here!" breaking free into the night.

The Maxwells turned, looking at each other. They were the only ones left on the patio. Too late, Jane realized that Mrs. Maxwell was studying her curiously, and it was only in that moment when Jane realized that her double probably would have gone running after the man as well. Captain Lumen: always the hero.

A flush crept up on Jane as she looked away.

"Fuck," Allison muttered. She got to her feet, grabbing a wine bottle off of the table. "That's just *perfect*. That's *exactly* what I need right now."

"Sweetie—"

"No." Allison pointed at her mother, the bottle hanging from the curl of her fist. "This is your fault. You told me that security would take care of them."

"They *are*."

Allison snorted. "Yeah, great job they're doing at it, too." She stepped around the chairs, the scattered remains of the plates and glasses, as she fished a phone from her back pocket. "I need to call Kylie. We need to get out in front of this thing before it blows up in our faces."

Mrs. Maxwell shook her head, but she made no effort to stop Allison. Allison was already holding the phone to her ear as she stepped through the glass doors. Jane watched her go, her head swirling with even more questions than she'd had when they first sat down.

And then they were alone.

CRICKETS CHIRPED. THE FIRE PIT CRACKLED. WAVES MADE seashell noises against the beach. The whine of a mosquito came and went, and Jane marveled at whatever (no doubt expensive) method was being employed to keep them at bay, because that was the first one that she'd noticed all evening.

"I'm glad that you felt that you could come back here," Mrs. Maxwell said, breaking the silence.

Jane stared at the bowl in her lap. What had Amy said, about maintaining the pretense of this Jane? Haughty disinterest?

Jane shrugged. "Yeah, well, it's not like we had much choice."

"I understand . . . Cal's text said that—that your other facility had been compromised? Is that true?"

"That's overstating it somewhat." Jane felt herself icing up, the protective walls of obfuscation and deflection rising fast between them. *Yes*, she thought to herself. This felt right—this felt like the aftermath of an argument with her mother.

She remembered how awkward it was, when her mother first reached out to Jane after the Thanksgiving debacle. Jane had kept her at arm's length for months.

"It didn't sound like an overstatement. I mean," Mrs. Maxwell lowered her voice, "UltraViolet, in the command room? How is that even *possible*? I thought the computers—"

"If you already know about it, why are we even talking?" Jane asked. She shot her mother a level gaze.

No, she reminded herself. Not her mother.

It looked like her mother, though. In the dimming light of the patio, the effects of the plastic surgeries seemed less pronounced. Mrs. Maxwell's eyes searched Jane, hurt and loss and hope mixing equally in the palette of her face.

Maybe she deserved to know. That Jane wasn't really her daughter, that they weren't really fighting.

But it didn't seem to be Jane's place to make that decision, and anyway, now Mrs. Maxwell was pulling herself together. She brushed it off, as easily as brushing away the stray fleck of tortilla that had fallen onto the seat cushion. "I understand. Cal said that you were taking this all rather hard."

"You talk to him a lot, do you?" Jane asked. She had no idea where the question had sprung up from.

Mrs. Maxwell looked startled. Her hand flew to the base of her throat. "What? No, I—Someone had to tell me you'd be coming. That you would all be coming. I assumed that you told him to."

"No," Jane said. "I didn't."

"Oh." Mrs. Maxwell tucked her perfectly done hair behind her ear, then immediately untucked it, patting it smooth.

The rustle of grass announced the return of the others. Jane turned to see sour faces, and a small cut near Devin's eyebrow.

"He got away?" Jane asked.

Devin shrugged. "Well, we couldn't exactly give it all that we've got. Not unless you want a front-page headline instead of just some random celebrity gossip."

Mrs. Maxwell winced. "You think that he got a photo?"

"It could have been worse," Amy said; not really an answer. "It was just a dinner party."

"While my husband is being held hostage at City Hall," Mrs. Maxwell said. Her face was drawn tightly together, a similar expression to what Allison had worn as she'd gone into the house. "Shit. This is going to kill his chances at a senate run."

Cal stepped over, and rested his hand heavily on Mrs. Maxwell's shoulder. He gave it a quick squeeze. "Hey. Olivia: It's going to be okay. We'll make it okay."

Jane raised an eyebrow. She studied her mother in fragments, like smaller pieces of a larger panel: the slightest flinch, tactfully suppressed; the dart of Mrs. Maxwell's eyes as she glanced at Jane and then away again just as quickly; her hand, resting on Cal's as she gave him a pat of thanks, which also served as an excuse to pluck his grip from her shoulder.

"I appreciate that, Cal, thank you," Mrs. Maxwell said. Her words were warm, but her tone was formal and dismissive, as if she was speaking to an aide who'd brought her ill news. Jane watched the space open up between them like an ellipsis as Mrs. Maxwell stepped away.

THEY SPENT THE NEXT DAY TRAINING. JANE BARELY SAW her family—here and there, usually as she was coming up to the kitchen for glass after glass of cool water, or ice packs as Jane nursed first one injury and then another. Allison watched as Jane passed her in the hall; Jane reeked of sweat, dripping as she sidled past Allison, a bottled water gripped against Jane's neck as if it was an old land-line telephone receiver.

"God, Jane," Allison sneered. "Is this really the time to be worrying about a *marathon*?"

"It's for charity," Jane said. She plucked the water bottle free and twisted off the cap, downing nearly half of it in one gulp. Not because she was particularly thirsty, but more in the hope that it would provide a long enough gap that she could leave Allison behind.

As cover stories go, it wasn't *bad*: that Jane and a few of her friends were scheduled to participate in the Grand City Marathon as a group, raising money to help fund research for a rare form of children's cancer. Training in the city under these circumstances would be impossible, what with the press hunting Jane down to see how she was handling the kidnapping of her father, so they'd retreated here, for some peace and privacy. The story settled well enough with the press, but it was clearly not doing its job for Allison. Jane was grateful that she had her glasses off to train, so that she couldn't study the glower of Allison's face in detail.

"Don't worry about Allie," Cal said to her a few minutes later. Back in the secret subbasement, Jane had tried expressing her concern. Cal raised his arms into a block posture. "Again."

"It's just—" Jane started, but then she yelped as a burst of wind and color blasted past her. Despite the fact that Devin was hitting her with "merely" the softest Nerf bat sold, physics still left Jane with some nasty bruises from his flyby swipes. "Hey! I wasn't ready yet!"

"Did I *say* that we would always wait until you were ready?" Cal asked. "UltraViolet won't."

"That's *different*," Jane said.

Cal snorted. "How?"

But Jane had no particular answer to this, so she kept her mouth shut.

As much as she hated to admit it, Cal's teaching methods did seem to be working. No, it wouldn't turn her into Captain Lumen overnight, but nothing would achieve that. Their goals were nowhere near so lofty as *that*. The plan, as the rest of the Heroes explained it, was merely for Jane to display enough of Captain Lumen's abilities to not be detected immediately as a fraud. On the side, it would be nice if she knew enough self-defense techniques not to be completely helpless in a fight, though the Heroes assured her that they would be doing the primary work of keeping her safe.

"And if you can't?" Jane asked, the morning after they'd arrived. They had only been working for an hour, and already Jane was covered in sweat, every muscle in her body aching.

Amy shrugged. "You'll be okay," she said. "I promise."

Somehow, despite everything, that did actually help.

Training had continued. Jane tried to take solace in Amy's encouragement, but as time wore on, the power of her words had grown thin. By the time night rolled around, and they entered the final countdown to the morning, Jane's confidence had been pummeled out of her.

They knocked off early that evening, to let Jane's body recuperate, and because there was very little to be done by that point. If she hadn't learned enough yet . . .

Jane tried not to think about that.

She tried not to think about anything.

Not her powers. Not this other life she might have had, if circumstances were different. Not her mother, or her father, or the alternate version of her father. Not her would-be sister, whose narrowed glares and sullen silences bored holes straight through Jane every time their paths crossed. Not Clair, or Amy. Not the rest of the Heroes.

It was a lot to avoid thinking, and the effort of it was almost more challenging than the training had been. Jane ate a huge dinner, took a long shower. Laid down in bed early, staring at the unfamiliar ceiling, and tried to quiet her mind.

It wasn't working. What if none of it was working? What if Jane's powers failed her at the critical time, or the Heroes looked away at the wrong moment? What if, for all their efforts, the plan wasn't going to work *anyway*, even if everything went *perfectly*— what if, after everything, UltraViolet was just too smart, too powerful, too evil to be stopped? Jane knew nothing about her, after all, none of them did. Doctor Demolition had given up only the woman's assumed name, and the Heroes were convinced this was all he knew.

Oh, if only Jane had written more about this woman. But even that was a silly regret, because it's not like Jane's stories *controlled* this universe. They just . . . happened to be right, more often than not.

Kind of a disturbing amount, really. If Jane stopped to think about it.

Which she *totally* wasn't. Because she wasn't thinking about any of this.

Nope.

Not at all.

Jane sighed. She sat up, squinting at her phone. It was nearly two o'clock, long after she was supposed to be asleep, but fuck it. Jane pulled on an extra sweatshirt from her closet—a crisp Sutton University logo emblazoned over her chest—slipped on her glasses, and toed down the main staircase.

Low light flickered from one of the living rooms, the telltale sign of a TV. That would do. Jane hadn't even realized until presented with the possibility of some company, just how badly she didn't want to be alone.

She entered the room, but hesitated on the threshold when she spotted Allison's hair peeking over the top of the couch.

Maybe this really wasn't the best person to be spending time with, only . . . dammit, Jane was tired of avoiding her.

"You're still up," Jane said.

Allison turned, raising herself up just enough to peer behind her. "So are you."

Jane inched farther into the room. How did you do this sort of thing, with a sister? All that Jane had to go on were movies and books, comics and television: two people up late, sharing a hot chocolate or something while they bared their secret confessions.

Somehow, that didn't seem likely to happen here.

Allison was curled sideways on the couch, feet tucked under a heap of blanket, head propped up on her hand. Her other hand held her phone loosely in her grip, thumb scrolling down what looked like Facebook. She watched the screen as if she didn't really see it, as if it didn't matter. Across the way, a TV was on mute, some news anchor talking soundlessly out of the frame. Jane glanced at a clock in the corner of the TV, a countdown to UltraViolet's deadline superimposed over the corner of the news anchor's desk. 15:22:31, 30, 29 . . .

Jane's stomach twisted.

Allison looked up. "He's trending," she said, flashing her phone at Jane. "Our father's life has become a hashtag."

"Captain Lumen will save him," Jane said. She tried to sound more confident than she felt, tried to remember the surety that their mother had spoken with the day before.

Allison snorted. "Yeah, okay." She went back to looking at her phone, her back to Jane. After a moment, though, she threw it down onto the area rug. "God, how can you just *believe* that?" she asked as she sat up. The blanket tumbled down to the floor with her feet, and Allison kicked it off with irritation.

Jane started as she realized that Allison wasn't just asking rhetorically. Allison had turned, and was glaring over the back of the couch at Jane, as if she was personally responsible for what was happening to her father.

Which she kind of *was*, Jane supposed—not that Allison knew that.

Jane shrugged. "I don't know. It's better than giving up, though, isn't it?"

"It's called being *realistic*, Jane. The Heroes' track record hasn't exactly been stellar lately. What makes you think that our father is even going to *make* it to UltraViolet's deadline? And why push it so close, anyway? I mean, if the Heroes were planning to do something, why don't they just *do* it?"

"I don't know," Jane said again. She edged around the couch, perching on the armrest.

Allison wasn't looking at her anymore. She stared at her own knees, her lips drawn in as if she was trying to hold herself together, and suddenly Jane's heart was aching. Because one thing was clear: even if Jane had beefs with her father, and even if this world's Jane followed suit . . . Allison clearly didn't. In the dark, half-lit by the TV, she looked like nothing so much as a little girl missing her daddy.

Jane reached out, gripping Allison's hand. "Maybe you're right," Jane said, "maybe . . . maybe there's nothing they can do. But I can promise you, Allison, and I know this for sure: they're going to try their absolute hardest. And if it is at all within their capability . . . they'll bring your father back to you. I *promise*."

Allison gave a messy snort. "You can't *promise* something like that," she said as she looked up. Her eyes settled on Jane, the faintest trace of hope dancing somewhere around the edges. "But . . . thanks anyway."

9

A NEW DAY DAWNS.

They left early, packing into Cal's SUV and trekking back to the city before the rest of the household was awake. Even Juanita still hadn't come in yet, and so breakfast consisted of cold cereal and weak coffee, because no one could figure out how to properly work the top-end coffee machine.

Jane just kept breathing: in through the nose, out through the mouth. She watched the morning pass with an artist's eye, laying it out as if this was just another issue of *Hopefuls*. Bleary eyes and hands wrapped tightly around travel mugs, jangled keys, the vistas from their trip here, now in reverse: the ferry, the main island, cow country, highways. The city, looming in the distance, a gray haze shrouding the taller skyscrapers from view.

They returned to the primary headquarters, long enough to suit up and move out. That was the plan, anyway, though Jane was finding the reality of it, like so much else, much more complicated than she'd ever expected it to be. Several hours after waking up, she stood in the middle of Captain Lumen's room, bits and pieces of clothes scattered to the high winds around her. Jane had her glasses off as she dressed, which helped; she was trying not to look at the room too much, because it was both familiar and not, because the version that she'd always drawn had been for Cal, and this one was distinctly . . . hers, in a way that was hard to put her finger on, but impossible to ignore.

A knock sounded at her door.

"Jane? Are you okay in there?"

Jane let out a yelp of frustration. The suit was halfway on, more or less, although a loop was snagged somehow around Jane's elbow. It pinned her arm against her, as if she was wearing a sling.

This looked so much easier in the drawings. Jane had sketched this suit a million times, both on her own body and then modified to fit Cal in the QZero versions, yet somehow she was stymied when faced with the actual thing. What, Jane asked herself, had compelled her double to design it with so many *parts*? A base layer to whisk away sweat, which wrapped around her stomach but still showed off her boobs (Why? Jane could not say); an armored piece that she was currently struggling with, so tight that her arms were getting tangled up; a short jacket, just over her chest, that zipped diagonally. To say nothing of the skintight pants, which Jane wasn't even sure her ass was going to fit into. All this, and Jane hadn't even *started* trying to work up the nerve to put in contacts—her fear of touching her own eyes made that a whole other hurdle to overcome.

"Jane?"

She went over to the door, hiding behind it as she peeked through the gap. Amy, slightly blurry in the hallway, was already dressed: trench coat, mask, fedora, blood-red lipstick. Fingerless gloves, although that was normal for this Clair-not-Clair. Jane reached out, yanking Amy inside.

"Don't laugh," Jane said, as she shut the door behind them. Then she stood back, motioning at her half-completed ensemble. Well, thirds-completed. A quarter, at any rate.

Dammit, she was useless at this.

Amy bit down on a giggle at the last second. Her shoulders

had already lurched, her lips starting to curl. Her white teeth were shocking against the red of her lipstick. "Okay," Amy said. "Okay, let's get this sorted out properly, shall we?"

Jane twisted so that Amy could unhook a strap from her elbow. "Don't tell the others."

Amy made a zipping motion in front of her face. "Mum's the word. Right, I need you to lift your arm a bit—there we go."

"What was I thinking when I made this?" Jane asked with a groan.

Amy shrugged. "You said it was badass."

"Yeah, well, it's not exactly going to be 'badass' when I don't even show up in time because I'm stuck in my costume."

"Uniform," Amy said. She glanced at Jane, then smiled. "Nobody on the team liked the word 'costume.' They said it made it sound like they were playing at being heroes."

"Huh. I didn't know that."

"Turn," Amy said, and Jane did as she was instructed. Amy tugged at a portion of Jane's uniform, trying to straighten it out. "I guess there are bound to be some things about our lives that didn't make it into your comic."

"I guess . . ."

Jane supposed that this should be embarrassing—having Amy dress her, standing half-naked in the same room as the doppelgänger of her dead wife—but it wasn't. She couldn't decide if it was because Amy wasn't enough like Clair for it to matter, or if she was *so much* like Clair that asking for her help was instinctive. She couldn't decide if she needed to decide.

Amy sighed. "Okay, you know what, I can't fix this. Arms up. We're starting over."

"Yes, ma'am." Jane raised her arms. Amy yanked the armor up, and Jane slithered down. She popped out the bottom, already breathing a sigh of relief—the thing was so tight that Jane couldn't even imagine how it was going to feel to try to *fight* in it. She stood back up, pushing away several stray bits of hair that had come loose from her ponytail.

"It helps if you loosen this part first," Amy was saying. Her attention was on the armor, where Jane spotted a row of lacing, like you'd find on a corset, running up the sides.

"Ah," Jane said. "See, I never drew it like *that*."

Amy nodded. She hooked the lacing piece by piece with her finger, pulling it open. "It's amazing that you got as many details right as you did." Amy glanced toward Jane. "I wouldn't have thought—" she started, but a double-take cut her off.

Jane looked down, following Amy's line of sight. At first she flushed, and went to cross her arms over the neon-yellow bra that now felt less "whimsical" and more "tacky" than it had when she'd bought it—but Amy wasn't staring at her chest, or the garish piece of underwear covering it. Instead, Amy reached out, stopping herself only inches from the chain hanging around Jane's neck.

"What's this?" Amy asked, though her voice was so small that she had to know the answer already.

Jane's fingers found Clair's ring without being told. They wrapped protectively around the metal, and only then did Amy look away, abashed.

The ring was identical to Jane's. Clair had wanted her body donated to scientific research; there was nothing for Jane to bury. They'd given her the ring in a plastic bag with the rest of Clair's possessions. Jane had gone immediately to a department store to buy a chain, and now she wore it next to her heart. It wasn't hard to guess that it used to belong to Clair, and it was only just now occurring to Jane that Amy probably hadn't known that Clair was dead.

"I'm sorry," Amy said. She was turned away from Jane, still holding the pieces of Jane's uniform in her hands.

"I know."

"How did she—? No, never mind. I shouldn't ask."

"You can ask," Jane said, "though it's not a complicated story. It was a car accident."

Amy turned back. Though her face was partially obscured by the mask and the hat, it wasn't difficult to read the grief and pity splashed across her features. Jane had seen the look so many times, over the last year and a half, that she would recognize it anywhere, even if it wasn't on the face that she knew best in all the world. "I'm so sorry," Amy said again.

"Yeah." Jane shrugged. "This is where I'm supposed to say

that it's okay. Then you offer up some platitude, and I act like I agree with it." She stepped aside, and sat on the edge of the bed. She held Clair's ring, still tight in her fist, against her heart. "Do you want to know the truth?" Jane asked, looking up at Amy. "It's not okay. I don't think that it's ever going to be okay, and I wish, just *once*, that someone could accept that, instead of telling me that time will make it better. How can time make it better, when the only thing that could make it better would be if something could *give me my Clair back*?"

Jane's voice cracked as grief struck thick and fast. A knife to the chest. Jane ducked her head, embarrassed, as tears cut hot tracks down her cheeks.

She hadn't meant to say that. She knew her role as a widow. Oh, sure, everybody has sympathy—for about six months. For six months, you can get away with crying at random, with your face twisting up in agony when a song comes on, with needing a moment to step away and collect yourself. But after that, well . . . people start sighing. *This again?* their faces say, even if their words are: "No, of course, of course, I understand completely." People start shuffling away uncomfortably. They start saying phrases like "meet new people," and "don't you think you should get out of the house a little?" A weeping widow at six *weeks* is an object of sympathy, their grief allowing you to feel better about your own life. At six *months*, she's an uncomfortable reminder of the frailty of life, the wreckage that death can leave behind in its wake. At a year and a half? She becomes, at best, a burden.

So Jane swiped hurriedly at her face. But the harder she tried to suppress it, the worse it bubbled up. True grief never really gets *better*—this is the uncomfortable truth that weeping widows bring to light. The best you can hope for is that it doesn't hit you as often, or that when it does, you'll be able to ride it out without breaking down.

Without a word, Amy sat down next to Jane. She did not tell Jane that everything was going to be okay. She did not say, again, that she was sorry. She did not offer up any platitudes.

Instead, she put her arm around Jane's shoulders. Leaned her head against Jane. It was the same move that Clair would do, when she was trying to comfort Jane after a particularly bad day, and feeling it again in the midst of this grief should have been even more heartbreaking—but it wasn't. It was the one thing that she'd wanted, for a year and a half, every time that she'd been crying. Jane tucked herself into the sideways embrace, folding underneath Amy's arm. Amy kissed the top of Jane's head, smoothed out Jane's hair.

It didn't solve anything. Nothing would ever solve this. But for the first time in a year and a half, a tiny fraction of Jane's heart felt soothed. They just sat like that, for several long minutes, as Jane listened to the beating of Amy's heart. Steady and working.

Finally, Amy brushed back Jane's hair. "Come on," she said, gently unfolding Jane from the crook of her arm. She gave Jane's shoulder an encouraging squeeze. "It's time to be a hero."

THE FIRST PROBLEM WITH THEIR GRAND PLAN IS THAT JANE COULDN'T RIDE A MOTORCYCLE.

"You didn't think to mention this *earlier*?" Marie snapped, as the group stood around in the underground parking garage of their headquarters. Low-slung cars and bikes in sexy shades of black and red and yellow filled the spaces underneath the buzz of movie-filter green light. Jane had always taken special care in drawing this place: she followed the blogs of car enthusiasts to learn how to capture the beauty and grace of the cars' angles, the hungry curves and vicious slashes that made up their design. She'd developed an appreciation for them over the years, though she'd significantly toned down her drawings of high speed chases since Clair's accident.

"It . . . didn't occur to me," Jane answered truthfully. In the early years, when the Heroes of Hope were still just a pet project and Jane didn't have to make them appeal to key demographics, vehicles had featured very little in the drawings that lined her portfolios. She'd only given them special thought once she'd gotten serious about pitching it to QZero, and by the time she started figuring out exactly who would be driving what, Captain Lumen was already a man. It was *his* signature arrival, to come streaking in on a yellow bike, the squeal of brakes a terrible omen to the bad guys. Jane would draw him kicking the bike sideways, tearing off it and letting it slide into position without him.

Several of the Heroes exchanged a meaningful glance, but Amy stepped right into the middle of them. "Hey now—it's not like Jane could have learned how to do the captain's moves in such a short time even if she *did* say something, all right? So let's just deal. She can hitch a ride with me if she wants to."

For a brief moment, a queasy flutter stirred in Jane's stomach. She pictured it: Amy's bike, vintage like everything else about her aesthetic, rumbling underneath them; Amy's hair flapping in Jane's face; Jane's body tucked up behind Amy, thighs clutched tightly around hips to hold steady. Jane blushed and looked away, to where Cal's car stood open and waiting.

Cal nodded. "Amy's right. We don't have time to worry about this. Jane, come with me—we're supposed to be the first to arrive anyway. Tony, Marie: keep a wide perimeter, in case UltraViolet has any surprises planned. Dev, Keish, you'll approach from the roof. Scout out the building. Meet up *only* once you get the signal—we don't want UltraViolet figuring out what we're up to. Amy—"

"I know," Amy said. Was it Jane's imagination, or was there a touch of petulance in her voice? "Hang back. Don't worry, I know the drill." She was already stuffing her helmet on, her hat tucked away in a bag on her bike. Jane's heart warmed at the safety gear, though she'd never drawn it in the comics for aesthetic reasons.

"Okay," Cal said. He clapped his hands together, and for a moment Jane almost forgot that he *wasn't* Captain Lumen, that it was supposed to be *her* giving out the assignments and rallying the troops.

Cal nodded again, to indicate they were ready. "Let's go."

AN AERIAL VIEW OF THE CITY. STREAKS OF COLOR ZOOM through an otherwise muted collection of cars jammed so close together that they may as well have been standing still. Close-up shots of tires, of Amy's vintage boots kicking the gear shift on her bike, of eyes narrowed in concentration. One panel, by itself, low and wide like the car it captures.

It was easier to focus on the imagery. It helped to ground Jane as Cal's car swerved and accelerated, each turn and pitch tightening the already queasy knot in her stomach. The reality of what they were about to do was threatening to overpower Jane. She gripped the door and the seat, her knuckles aching, as more and more panels filled the pages of her mind. Two full spreads at least, though she would never have devoted that much space to them in the real issues.

City Hall appeared in the distance as they rounded a corner, and then in the span of a blink they had shot up right beside it. The building was a piece of modern art, all mirrored windows and angled lines. A circle of police cars surrounded it like cats who'd heard a can opener. Officers held a ring of reporters and gawkers at bay. Every move was captured in flashes as Jane and Cal leapt from the car. *Good thing we're not going for stealth*, Jane thought as Cal struck an unnecessary pose of bravery and heroism.

No, Jane remembered. Not *Cal*, not while they were in uniform. It was a piece of advice that Keisha had given her, just before they'd headed out—on the job, she'd said, it's best to think of everyone as their superhero personas. Helps keep you from getting too emotional, she'd said. Jane tried it out, then, watching *Deltaman* as he accepted his accolades and applause. Deltaman . . . not having the history of the comics to draw from, that one was going to be the hardest to get used to.

Jane ducked her head and cut a straight line for the door. Her heart was pounding as heavily as the percussion of questions being lobbed at her back. There was something vaguely *wrong* about the whole situation, though Jane couldn't be sure that she wasn't just imagining it out of sheer nerves. She tried to tell herself to focus, to remember her training. As if in response, a tickle built in her fingertips as she pulled open the doors.

The sound no doubt reached her first, but it was the weight of Deltaman's body slamming against hers that Jane registered before anything else. "Captain!"

They hit the floor as a spray of bullets peppered the front doors and windows. The sound of glass shattering and the sparkle as a wave of window fragments pinged off of the marble floor tiles. Jane's chin hit the ground and a flare of pain sent her head spinning. She stared, transfixed, at the glittering floor, at the bullet shells littered by the feet of a turret mounted in the lobby.

A rookie mistake. Even Jane recognized that. She'd have never scripted Captain Lumen to do something so stupid as to waltz right in through the front doors, as if UltraViolet wouldn't have some kind of trap waiting for them. It didn't matter if this was what UltraViolet had asked her to do—she was a supervillain, so there would always be a trap.

Deltaman rolled off of her. He drew himself into a low squat, gun at the ready. His cape spread over Jane's back like a blanket, and for the briefest moment, Jane was tempted to curl up with it and squeeze her eyes shut. As if that would help.

The turret, sensing movement, began to swivel back toward them, but Deltaman had already tossed a grenade or something in the turret's direction. He ducked down as the *shunk* of the device magnetizing to the turret sounded through the lobby, and before Jane could process what was happening, the device exploded. She shrieked in an entirely un-superhero-like way as the turret was knocked off its tripod legs, clattering to the floor. It fritzed and sparked, its gun mount swiveling like a head trying to clear fog, and then gave up with a pitiful wind-down whir.

Gently, cautiously, Deltaman raised himself to his feet. When nothing else immediately began to shoot at them, he turned and held his hand out to Jane, still sprawled across the marble tiling.

It took every ounce of self-motivation for Jane to drag herself up. Her knees wobbled underneath her for a moment or two, and she had to grab hold of Deltaman's arm to stabilize herself.

A projection snapped to life in front of them. It seemed to spring up out of nowhere, hovering translucent in the middle of the lobby. A square image, like a screen, like a comic panel, filled their vision.

UltraViolet's masked face, shimmering in and out of focus. Her wicked smile was the only clear point in a sea of purples that looked as if they'd been smudged for artistic effect.

"Captain Lumen. How good of you to come."

In comics, this would be a moment for a brave or witty

comeback. *You didn't leave me much choice*, perhaps, or *We have to stop meeting like this*, or *It's over, UltraViolet*. Speech bubbles floated around Jane, begging her to strike a pose, to pluck them from the air and slap them over her head. She knew what she would have Captain Lumen do, if she was writing this. The real Captain Lumen, as far as Jane was concerned, the one that lived in her art—Cal's Captain Lumen, who knew what to do when facing down a maniacal supervillain.

But that person didn't exist, even here. All that they had was Jane, and Jane's throat was dry, her knees locked in fear.

As if on cue, Deltaman stepped forward. Positioned himself just in front of Jane, blocking a portion of her body from UltraViolet's view. Jane peered around his shoulder, where the shimmering projection continued to taunt them from above the broken turret.

"If you have something important to say, UltraViolet, just say it," Deltaman said, and Jane cursed herself for not thinking of that line on her own. "Otherwise, let's get this over with. I believe we have a deal to complete."

UltraViolet's smile snapped off. "Very well. First, though, I want proof that you've brought me the rest of my demands."

Deltaman tapped his earpiece. "Bring it in."

Jane turned. Beyond the glass doors of City Hall, a SWAT van had pulled up at the base of the stairs. Its back doors flew open, and a half-dozen policemen—unarmed, unprotected—started hauling out black crates stamped with government seals. Deltaman directed them inside, pointing for them to line everything up in front of the projection. Jane watched the stacks grow taller, the row wider, her heart thundering loudly in her ears. She knew that the acid UltraViolet had asked for had been replaced with a dud version, that the AF-72 assault rifles were missing a key component, rendering them harmless. That the hundred-dollar bills in the duffel bag that they brought in next were marked, and even if UltraViolet tried to spend them, the police and the Heroes would come down on her in an instant.

None of this settled her stomach, as the sound of a helicopter approaching began to beat overhead to match the pounding of Jane's heart.

The police retreated. The crates formed a protective wall between Jane and the projection of UltraViolet, who'd been studiously watching the whole process.

"Very good," UltraViolet said, as Deltaman stepped forward to open first one crate and then another. Guns and chemical canisters filled the padded lining, each one deadly in its own right.

UltraViolet gave them a slow-clap, her purple gloved hands looking only marginally more solid than her face.

"I'm impressed. I honestly thought you might let your mayor die, rather than give in to my demands. I hope he appreciates your loyalty—assuming that you get to him in time. Which reminds me . . ."

In the projection, Jane could see UltraViolet reach out for something, a nearby button or a switch. The elevator light snapped on, a cheerful *ding!* breaking through the hush of the lobby.

"It's time to come and get him, Captain Lumen."

Jane's depth of field collapsed. All of the lobby fell away, leaving only the gaping maw of the open elevator doors. The inside gleamed of orange and brass and red trim, glowing like the pits of hell. Jane would have drawn it with gently luminescent tendrils stretching out, twisting through the air as if trying to ensnare her in their grip.

The plan felt feeble, suddenly. Something to be played out with paper dolls, not real and breakable people. Staring at the elevator, Jane felt her body in a way that she never had before. All the interconnected parts, each frail joint, each snappable bone, the delicate network of veins and nerves stringing it all together. UltraViolet could kill her in a thousand different ways.

Deltaman's hand on her shoulder made her jump.

"Easy, Jane," Deltaman muttered, low enough not to be overheard. "It's just an elevator."

UltraViolet laughed. "Tick-tock, Captain. Your mayor doesn't have long now."

Jane swallowed down a heavy lump in her throat. Somehow, mechanically, one of her legs moved forward, and then the other. Deltaman's hand stayed heavy and supportive on her shoulder.

"Ah-ah-ah," UltraViolet tutted. "I asked for one Hero, not two, remember? And while I'd love to believe that you're just surrendering yourself as an added bonus, Deltaman, I'm not stupid. Stand down, or the deal is off."

Jane stole a desperate look, not at Deltaman, but at Cal hidden behind the persona. With her eyes hidden behind her mask, she tried to pour the terror into the rest of her face. Okay, Cal may not be her favorite friend, sure—but he was a steady, stable presence by her side, and, as Deltaman, he was an *armed* one at that. *Don't leave me*, she tried to tell him, signaling with all that she had, *don't leave me, don't leave me, don't leave—*

"I'll be right behind you," he muttered as he stepped away. Leaving her.

A tiny flare of light filled the space between them, a literal flash of panic before Jane could stamp down on the impulse. She just stood there a moment, twisted to look back over her shoulder at Deltaman. On some level, Jane knew that she was supposed to be leaving, that she should continue into the elevator, follow the plan. That if she stood there much longer, the whole thing was going to fall apart. UltraViolet would see her hesitation as weakness, and it wouldn't take much for her to work out that Jane wasn't the real Captain Lumen. Everything hinged on Jane, right here, right now, and she had to get moving, she had to play her part, but she was alone, and her chest constricted, and she couldn't think, she couldn't do it, she was a failure, they were all going to die, it was all her fault, and—

Clair's voice filled her mind: *It's going to be okay, Jane.*

Jane closed her eyes, just for a moment. A deep breath, held to the count of ten.

You can do this, Clair continued. *You need to do this.*

A memory sprang up, seizing Jane whole. Jane and Clair at seventeen, their future nothing but blank pages in front of them. Jane's parents were in the kitchen, and Jane and Clair stood on the back steps just outside, night falling all around, being eaten alive by mosquitoes. The sounds of cooking and petty bickering drifted through the screen door. All Jane had to do was pull the handle. But she couldn't, because inside was a conversation that she didn't want to have, that she'd put off having for two years, and it couldn't wait any longer, except for these few minutes that she could stand there, putting it off, getting bitten.

Clair stood, patient, beside her. They'd done her parents first, earlier that day—turns out that Mrs. Sinclair had worked it out ages ago, had just been waiting for them to admit it to her. More than anything, she was hurt that it had taken so long.

"*Come on, Jane,*" Clair had said, finally, the whine of mosquitoes getting louder all the time. "*It won't be so bad, you'll see.*"

Come on, Jane, Clair said again, now, the memory of her voice whispering in Jane's ear.

Like everything else, life had been more complicated than Clair's cheerful assurances had said it would be, all of those years ago, and no doubt it would be more complicated here as well. But it had always worked before, whenever Jane lost her nerve, and it worked here, too. Jane drew herself straight, shoulders back, and she stepped through the elevator doors.

For Clair, she could always be brave.

The doors were just closing as she turned back around, and the last thing that she saw of the lobby was Deltaman giving her a steady nod.

"Good job, Jane," said the voice in her ear, and with a jolt, Jane realized that it had never been Clair, after all. Merely Amy, or rather Mindsight, through the interconnected earpieces.

"Thanks," Jane mumbled, embarrassed. The elevator flipped Jane's stomach as it set off. She watched her reflection, hazy in the polished brass of the doors. In the panel of her mind, she saw herself sketched as a child: in costume, tiny hands on her hips, standing in the vague shadow of something much larger and greater.

She counted floors. The mayor's office was on the sixth floor, all the way at the top, but the elevator stopped immediately, just one floor from ground level. Jane gulped down her panic as the doors slid open. Because there, waiting for her, were two Shadow Raptors. Jane's eyes widened, a close-up of her terrified face.

This is where the issue would end.

10

PANIC.

Her training must have done *some* good, at least, because Jane was able to analyze the situation in an instant: the only exit, blocked by the Shadow Raptors; no place to hide inside of the elevator, not even a bench or a potted plant; trying to close the door again would take too long. This knowledge did not, however, provide her with any useful idea of what *to* do instead— fighting did not even enter her mind, perhaps because she was too much of a chicken, or perhaps because she knew her odds were nil—and so she leaped first to one side, then to the other, then accidentally flashed a burst of light at the Shadow Raptors, which did absolutely nothing.

Humiliation burned through her. God, she was a terrible superhero. Even she wouldn't read a comic about herself. She ducked down, throwing her hands over her head, all sense of dignity now lost.

It was only once the Shadow Raptors did *not* launch themselves in an attack against her that she realized something else was going on. Jane peeped up through a protective tangle of fingers. The Shadow Raptors were regarding her with blank, reptilian expressions. They blinked, their sideways eyelids snapping like camera shutters.

Jane quickly got to her feet.

They just stood there. Their signature obsidian daggers hung from silk ties around their waists. One of them, slightly taller, stepped to the side. It gestured for her to pass.

Then understanding kicked her in the stomach. Dear lord, of course. UltraViolet had been expecting her to come here. And yes, okay, perhaps her plan was to kill Jane—kill Captain Lumen, Jane forcibly reminded herself—but apparently that wasn't going to happen *yet*. Not right here, right now, like this: trapped in a corridor still four stories down from her father (not her father), facing a pair of Shadow Raptors that she stood no chance against.

Jane almost laughed, the relief was so palpable. Except that it really wasn't funny, and none of the danger had actually changed, and that realization soured her good humor in an instant.

"Smooth," Tony, as Rip-Shift, said through the earpieces. Jane tried not to think about how much of her spectacle the team might have overheard, as she edged past the slithery chests of the Shadow Raptors. Their breath was terrible up close, rank with rotten meat and vinegar.

"Where are we going?" Jane asked. She didn't know if the Shadow Raptors would answer her, or even if they could answer her—she'd never written them to have dialog bubbles—but asking was better than not asking.

The only answer that she got was a weary sigh. Jane stole a fast glance over her shoulder, but she couldn't tell which of them had done it. They gave her a shove, and Jane quickened her pace.

This was all wrong. They were supposed to go straight up to the mayor's office. The *whole point* of Jane pretending to give herself up was to get someone inside—she was wearing a special kind of tracker, designed by Marie, which would (in theory) create a point for Rip-Shift to latch on to without having to maintain a direct line of sight. It had worked once already, in an issue that came out about a year back, though it tended to strain Rip-Shift's powers to the limit and wasn't something they liked to rely on. The fact that they were willing to use it now spoke volumes about how important this mission was to them.

Lights flickered. Once, twice—off. Jane shut her eyes, trembling in the darkness.

A man's voice filled the hall, digitized to be low and ominous. "Did you really think that we would let you take her that easily?"

It wasn't the plan, but fuck it. Relief flooded Jane anyway, as a shadowy figure swept first one direction across the hall in front of them and then, a moment later, swept the other direction behind.

The Shadow Raptors hissed. They clicked their tongues between them, as if having an argument, and then abruptly cut themselves off.

One of them grabbed Jane's upper arm. She shrieked, damn near pissing herself, a burst of light slipping free before she could stop it. An obsidian dagger flashed in front of her, heading for her throat, and okay, now *this* was surely it, right here, right now, and the Heroes had failed her, and she couldn't protect herself—

But a yelp from his companion distracted the Shadow Raptor threatening Jane. It whirled instead, its weapon thrusting into the darkness around them. The crunch of glass beneath its talons filled the hall as they sidestepped out of the way.

The Shadow Raptor threw its head back. Their signature whistle sounded, louder and shriller than anything that Jane had ever heard or imagined. She clamped her hands over her ears.

A heavy dart, so thick that it was almost an arrow, landed in the Shadow Raptor's neck with a hideous, wet *thunk*. The whistle died.

The Shadow Raptor fell to its side. It clutched at its neck, writhing, its tail whipping through the air. Jane leaped back, narrowly avoiding being knocked over. The Shadow Raptor made no noise, though, not a scream, not a whimper, and somehow that made the sight of it so much worse. Jane's stomach heaved, as she fiercely remembered one afternoon when a boy in her class had smashed a toad on the playground with a rock, a horrible mess of red and tan and asphalt.

When Deltaman appeared beside her a moment later, she almost screamed again just from the shock. Every muscle in her body was taut and a headache ran hot, temple to temple. This mission could not have been stressing her out more if it had *tried*.

Deltaman's hand settled on Jane's shoulder. "Hey. You doing all right?"

"No!" Jane didn't mean to shout. It came out anyway, a single shrill word piercing the hallway.

And Deltaman just chuckled. *Chuckled!* Like Jane was being *cute* or something: oh look, precious little neophyte superhero, baby fresh in her ass-kicking boots.

She turned away from him. Stalked down the hall, footsteps pounding on the tile floor. She didn't know where she was going—certainly nowhere that would help. It didn't matter. If this is what it meant to be a superhero then . . . then maybe she just wasn't cut out for it.

A Shadow Raptor leaped out of the darkness.

Correction: a whole *swarm* of Shadow Raptors leaped out of the darkness. Jane froze, or rather the world froze around her. A part of Jane's mind processed what she was seeing, because of course, yes, there they were, right in front of her. A second part of her denied it, simply because the idea was too much, too much, too much, too much.

It was the third part of her that saved her life.

They say that fear is a survival mechanism. In one fluid movement, Jane's fear took control and made her do three things: duck, because that was always a good idea when something sharp and shiny and terrible is *leaping* at you; flash a widespread burst of light in a balloon around her, momentarily obscuring her exact location from the Shadow Raptors' sights; and press the button on the tracking device Granite Girl had slipped around her neck.

Within the span of a single pounding heartbeat, a rip appeared in the fabric of Jane's reality. Never before had one of Rip-Shift's rips appeared so glorious. A glimmering blue line, heavenly light pouring through, and then, appearing like vengeful angels: Keisha as Pixie Beats, Marie as Granite Girl, Devin as Windforce . . . and Mindsight. They flooded the hall, weapons firing, wind kicking into a frenzy, arms and legs whirling in the elaborate dance of combat. Rip-Shift sauntered through last, straightening his long leather jacket and then reaching behind him with a zipping motion.

He glanced down at Jane. An eye of cool in a storm of chaos. "That's how it's done," he said, as he sliced reality to both his left and right, sending a charging Shadow Raptor straight through a plate glass window in the next room.

A flicker of hope and confidence stirred in Jane. Her reflection in Rip-Shift's mirrored sunglasses was biting down on a guilty smile. Rip-Shift twisted, jumping with excitement into the fight now churning up the hall.

Jane sprang to her feet. Mindsight spun toward her, throwing her arm wide to sweep Jane out of the way of an oncoming Shadow Raptor. They slammed into the wall together, their breaths escaping them, as Pixie Beats spun by in a series of deadly pirouettes; she shrank as small as a butterfly, dodging a blow, and expanded back to full size in time to deliver an uppercut from a duck-and-stand dance maneuver.

Everywhere she looked, the Heroes were doing what they did best. Mindsight downed two Shadow Raptors with her revolver, Pixie Beats continued her homebrew, dance-inspired martial arts routine, Granite Girl smashed and slammed and sent Shadow Raptors bursting through office walls. Windforce summoned gusts through the hall that lifted Shadow Raptors off of their feet, hurtling them through rips that Rip-Shift would create with a lazy flick of his finger. Deltaman . . . well, Jane didn't see Deltaman much, but there were so many things to keep track of that this wasn't surprising. Flashes of his cape appeared around the periphery of the fight now and then.

"Captain!" Pixie Beats shouted. An opening had sprung up in front of Jane, a straight shot between her and the window that Rip-Shift had broken earlier. Pixie Beats kicked a Shadow Raptor, stumbling it into the space in front of Jane, and without a second thought, Jane narrowed a beam of light from her fingers and directed it straight at the Shadow Raptor. The Shadow Raptor wailed, staggering backward as it clutched its chest—backward, far enough for Windforce to conjure a gust around its feet and send it toppling through the broken window.

The last one. Silence filled the hall.

Jane burst out laughing. Her head spun with relief, as first Mindsight and then the rest of the team all gathered around her to slap her shoulder or offer a triumphant hug. The unreality of what had just happened was still processing in Jane's mind, terror and bliss mixed up all in one as she realized that they were all okay. That she was okay. "That was . . . !" Jane started, but she had absolutely no idea how to express what that was. All that she knew was she was grinning like a fool, an expression she could see hiding in the faces of all of her companions.

Her teammates.

Her elation was cut short, however, as another projection sprang up out of the body of one of the Shadow Raptors like a terrible ghost. UltraViolet, her face just clear enough to see the glower that she was casting them.

"That wasn't the agreement," she said, as she reached behind her and, without even looking, shot one of the hostages in the chest.

JANE DIDN'T HEAR THE SCREAMS OF THE HOSTAGES, OR the gasps and outrage of the Heroes. Her world reduced: the pounding of blood in her ears, heavy as funeral drums; the sight of the man that UltraViolet had shot. The image stayed with her, long after the projection itself had snapped off. His final moments played on a loop in Jane's head. His eyes, first widening with shock and fear, then squeezed so, so tight, like maybe if he just held himself together, just a *little*, maybe, maybe . . .

None of the other hostages had made a move to help him.

By the time Jane regained a sense of time and place, the Heroes were already on the move. Jane blinked, and found herself climbing a stairwell, the rest of the team spread in a careful formation above and below her. Rip-Shift was nowhere to be seen, probably scouting a path ahead. Jane held on to that knowledge, the fact that she could put something like that together for herself. It helped keep her from sliding back into her personal hell—the man, the gunshot, the way that he'd clutched his chest as he toppled over.

She wondered who his family was. Not *if* he had family—it was Jane's experience that *everyone* had family, in some form or another, no matter how distant, no matter how small. Who was going to tell them that he was dead? Whose job was it, to find out the list of names to call?

The call. Jane fought against the urge to dry heave, remembering the call.

A gentle hand rested against Jane's back. For an instant, she just assumed that it was Amy, but when she turned, it was Keisha's reassuring smile that greeted her behind Pixie Beats's mask.

"Hey," Pixie Beats said, moving up a step to walk beside Jane. "You holding up okay?"

Jane found herself nodding. She hadn't planned on it, and wouldn't have thought that this would be the correct answer, but there it was.

Then a horrible thought struck her. "Oh shit," Jane said, "Keisha . . . Dominick's not . . . I mean, he wasn't—"

"Nah, he's all right. Wasn't at the meeting. Thanks for asking, though."

Jane nodded once, acknowledging this. In the comics, Keisha's husband had recently been appointed Assistant Mayor of Grand City. Of course, he was working for a third, entirely fictional mayor, someone Jane had based off of her ninth-grade geography teacher. And Jane had no way of knowing, before she'd asked, if this version of Dominick had even followed that path. Still . . . she should have been more sensitive.

"I'm sorry, I didn't even think of it before," Jane said. Then her eyes widened, realizing how horrible that sounded. "I mean—! It's just that, in my world, you know, he helps run a non-profit."

Even behind her elaborate, masquerade-ball mask, Pixie Beats's amusement and delight were obvious. "Really?"

"Oh, yeah," Jane said. "You both do."

Pixie Beats went quiet, considering this. The aesthetic of her superhero persona was designed to create an aura of don't-give-no-shits—asymmetrical, multi-layered ballet skirt down to her knees; thick tights; beat-up sneakers; jean jacket with band patches sewn up and down the sleeves; a lock of neon-green hair that she clipped in before each battle—but Jane knew that she was actually a huge softy. She and Dominick had five kids, two dogs, and a turtle named Martian, and Keisha somehow found time for each of them.

"Who do we help?" she asked finally.

Jane knew that she wasn't asking about the name of the organization. When Pixie Beats wanted to know who she helped, she meant who she *helped*.

"Inner-city school kids. You set up programs where poor children can bring their laundry in for free, so no one has to come to school in dirty, beat-up clothes."

Pixie Beats smiled. "Good."

A noise made them look up. Rip-Shift had returned, stepping through a rip and sealing it quickly behind him. Deltaman was on point, waiting, and the two of them spoke in a frenzied whisper for a moment.

"Hey, boys," Granite Girl called from behind Jane, "care to share with the rest of the class?"

A gust of wind blew past them, Windforce's arms spread as the air carried him up the empty space in the middle of the stairwell. He landed easily beside Deltaman and Rip-Shift.

"I *hate* it when they pull this shit," Granite Girl said. She shoved past Jane and Pixie Beats, her heavy footsteps clomping loudly on the cement stairs.

By the time Jane and Pixie Beats caught up with her, though, Granite Girl's expression had gone as stony as her actual face. Mindsight trailed behind, three steps down, and they all listened in silence as Rip-Shift gave his report.

The good news: there were no Shadow Raptors patrolling the halls, no weapon turrets surrounding the mayor's office. The sixth floor was, in fact, completely sealed off, both UltraViolet and the hostages secured inside.

The bad news: the sixth floor was, in fact, completely sealed off, and a new lock had been installed in the already reinforced door. One that required a specific series of light pulses and laser beams to disarm. Not *difficult*, no—Granite Girl could whip up a gadget to open it easily, sure, assuming that she had the time.

Nobody turned to look at Jane. That was the worst part.

Instead, Rip-Shift held out a piece of paper.

"This was taped to the door," he said, his voice weighted with apology.

Jane took it. A typed message, diagrams explaining exactly how to open the lock. It was so complicated, far more complicated than anything that Cal had put her through in her training. So it was a test, then. For her. Only a single line of text preceded the instructions, two words taunting Jane in their false simplicity.

Prove it.

"MAYBE I CAN HACK THE FLASHLIGHT FUNCTIONALITY," Granite Girl said, already pulling her phone out of her pocket. She turned away from the team for better concentration, but Deltaman laid a heavy hand on her shoulder.

"There's no time for that," he said. "It has to be Jane."

"She can't *do* it, though!" Granite Girl said.

"Yes, she *can*," Deltaman said. He turned to look straight at Jane. "I believe in her."

Which was harder to bear: Deltaman's confidence, meant to be inspiring? Or the way that Mindsight's eyes skittered away from Jane's whenever she tried to catch them?

They were so screwed.

And yet, what other choice did they have? Retreat, and allow not just the mayor, but all the hostages and possibly large swaths of the city, to die? Sure, Granite Girl might be able to hack something together—ignoring Deltaman, she already had the back of her phone open, and was pulling the circuits apart with the skill of a surgeon—but would it be enough? Would it be fast enough?

Jane pushed her way to the top of the stairs. She had to move quickly, to stay ahead of her terror. The rest of the Heroes followed close behind.

There it was, then. The door.

It was barred by a complicated, aftermarket locking mechanism. An input panel glowed red in the middle, bars jutting out in an X to stake the doorframe. Briefly, Jane wondered how UltraViolet had attached it if she was really locked inside, but this was frankly the least of her worries. She stepped up to the input panel, light gently pulsing into the hall.

Now all she had to do was *do* it. Sure, as if it was that easy.

Jane wriggled her fingers, shaking them out. It didn't help— she did it anyway. She glanced at the note in her hand, which was already turning damp with sweat. The instructions looked like gibberish, like the scribbles of a child's drawing. She shut her eyes.

Prove it. The words entered Jane's mind, laughing at her. This was never the plan. The whole team had assured her that her limited powers would be enough. They really just needed a small light show, to demonstrate that Jane even *had* the powers, that was what they'd said. That would do it.

Jane opened her eyes. The input panel still glowed just as angry as it had a moment ago.

This wasn't going to get any better.

She raised her hand.

A burst of uncontrolled light struck the input panel; it beeped with all of the disdain of Jane's nasty third-grade teacher. Jane winced, a reaction that rippled through the rest of the Heroes.

The next attempt was a little better. It was a beam, at least, although not quite focused enough for the input panel to accept. Then the focus was okay, but the color was off. Jane bit her lip. Her contacts felt strange in her eyes, and she was quite certain that her deodorant had stopped working somewhere around floor three.

By the time one of the lights on the panel turned green— there were nine of them, laid out in a grid—Jane felt as if she'd been standing in this hallway forever. This was worse than every final exam ever, worse than the driver's test that she'd had to take twice, worse than the oral presentations she'd been made to do in college, worse than her job interview at QZero.

The rest of the Heroes shifted restlessly behind her. Jane tried not to worry about how long this was taking. She was grateful that she wasn't wearing a watch.

Three lights later, just as Jane was beginning to truly give up hope, just as Granite Girl swore from where she was sitting cross-legged on the floor to work on her phone, a miracle happened: the rest of the panel lit up green, one and then the next and then the next. The speed of it unlocking sounded like a slot machine on a winning spin: *jackpot!*

Jane's mouth dropped open, a soft "oh!" of alarm escaping her. Nobody heard it, though—the instant that the door unlocked, they'd rushed up behind her, and the bars clanged to the floor. They shoved Jane back, creating a barricade between her and the dangers waiting just on the other side of the door. Jane let them, retreating on shaky legs.

They threw the door open. Sight unseen, Windforce sent a strong gust crashing into the hallway beyond.

It was a good thing that he did, because it turns out that the hall was *packed* with Shadow Raptors. The wind was a good start to hold them back, but it wouldn't last long, and so Granite Girl crashed headfirst into the fray, like a bowling ball through pins. Shadow Raptors toppled, scrambling to regain their footing. Pixie Beats and Deltaman closed ranks, fists flying as they held back the Shadow Raptors at the entrance.

Rip-Shift wasted no time, either. As soon as Granite Girl had barreled in, he began slicing rips beneath the feet of the Shadow Raptors. They tumbled through, falling out of a corresponding rip hovering in the middle of the stairwell. The wail of the Shadow Raptors echoed off the bare walls. Their tails and claws whipped out in an effort to find purchase on something. Jane flinched back, and Mindsight shielded her as the first of the Shadow Raptors from the hall managed to burst free of Delta-man and Pixie Beats's blockade.

This was all so much *more* than Jane had ever pictured it. The crack of Mindsight's gun and the shrieking of the Shadow Raptors and the shouts of the Heroes and the whistle of the wind and the smell of blood and gunpowder jamming up her nose so hard it made her gag. Jane felt the edge of the panels closing in around her, packed tight with explosive bursts of color.

And then everything cut away—the chaos and the noise, the smell, the terror—as a Shadow Raptor leaped up from the stairwell, landing on the railing in front of Jane. It must have caught itself as it fell from Rip-Shift's rip, vaulting with an impressive display of acrobatics. Its claws dug into the metal of the railing, scarring the paint.

For a moment, everything was still.

Jane felt the breath that filled her. The expanse of her lungs, the way it straightened her spine, drew back her shoulders. It whispered to her, *do it, do it, do it*, and Jane did not think, she just did.

She saw the beam of light that shot from her fingertips. Watched it strike the Shadow Raptor, watched the beast tip backward until it fell. A flood of euphoria swallowed Jane, and she let it propel her forward. She did not think. Another shot opened up, farther up the stairs, and she took it. Then another. Another. The Heroes parted around Jane, folding her into their midst as if she belonged.

"Go, go, go!" someone shouted a moment later, and they charged. Straight up the last step, through the open door. Granite Girl and Rip-Shift had managed to largely clear the hall, and it was all the opening that the Heroes needed. They poured in. Pixie Beats shrank and expanded, leaping from walls and crashing into Shadow Raptors. Windforce threw Shadow Raptors through Rip-Shift's newest rips, the exit still hovering deadly in the stairwell. Mindsight's revolver cracked behind them, taking care of any stragglers that managed to claw their way back up. Granite Girl charged ahead, crashing through windows and over conference tables in the meeting rooms that lined the hall. Deltaman swept through, a dark and ominous phantom.

And Jane . . .

Jane laughed. Her powers flowed like water, singing a joyful tune in her ears. The Shadow Raptors became target practice, and though her aim wasn't perfect, it wasn't *terrible*, either. Each time she struck a blow, it was like a little piece inside of her shone brighter—like a portion of her mind cleared, nothing but pure light in the space where her worries used to be. What did it matter, then, if they were in *danger*? What was danger, in the face of this? What was care, what was sorrow, what was grief? Jane felt their absence like a weight finally taken from her shoulders, like shackles finally removed from her ankles. She laughed and shot and spun like a school girl on the playground, arms outstretched. She was searching for her next attack. Because surely there had to be another, surely that wasn't it, surely she wasn't *done*, they couldn't be *done*, she may never be *done*—

Her attention landed on another figure, and Jane raised her hands, ready to go, but it wasn't a Shadow Raptor.

Mindsight was staring at her.

Jane jerked herself back. "I wasn't—" she started to say, but a crash drew their attention.

They had finally reached the mayor's office. Granite Girl lifted a Shadow Raptor, injured but alive, and threw it through the doors. They *cracked* apart, flying inward.

There was no time to lose. The Heroes charged in as a pack— and stumbled to a halt, bottlenecked in the open doorway.

"Not so brash now, are you?" UltraViolet asked them.

Jane swallowed, trying to clear the tangled lump knotting up her throat.

UltraViolet stood in front of the mayor's desk, and she was not alone. Somehow, despite his ill state, she had managed to prop the mayor up in front of her. She had the scruff of his shirt collar caught tight in her fist, and a gun to his sweaty, green-tinged temple. His eyes were half-open, rolling back in his head more often than not. But he was *trying* to look at them, and for a moment Jane could have sworn that he was trying to look at *her*.

Standing there, covered in sweat, shaking as he leaned against UltraViolet, he didn't look like Mayor Maxwell anymore—the man whose picture she'd seen plastered all over the news, the man who smiled out of frames in her mother's office, the legendary figure who had brought about a record low unemployment rate to Grand City.

Now Jane saw her *dad*.

And not even the one that she was angry with. That one was a tower of vigor and vitality: a gym-rat, obsessed with his image, who had taken up *parasailing* during his last trip to Maui. The person in front her now was nothing like that. This version, reduced, had rolled back time. This version was the one that had helped Jane learn to ride a bike, telling her stories about all the places he used to go on his own bike as a child, as he held fast to her seat and ran behind her. This version was the one that had gone with her to Girl Scout father-daughter dances, both of them drinking too much punch and proudly dancing the hokey-pokey to every song, because it's the only moves they knew. This version was the one that took her to a baseball game when she was nine, because she'd just watched a movie about Jackie Robinson in school and thought for about a summer that maybe she would become an athlete. This version was the one that used to make her mother laugh, that remembered Jane's birthdays, that carried her on his shoulders when she was too tired to walk.

Forget the others: this one was dying.

Jane pushed her way to the front of the pack.

"*Captain!*" Mindsight hissed, but Deltaman held her back. "No," Deltaman muttered. "Let her do this."

UltraViolet cocked her head. Waiting. In person, her shimmering haze was even more distracting than it was in the video. Jane's head hurt just to look at her, but that didn't matter. Jane made herself look, made herself plant her feet wide, square her shoulders.

Power stirred in her mind. Her fingers were tickling so much that she wanted to rip at the skin with her nails. *Do it, do it, do it, do it.*

"Let him go," Jane said.

UltraViolet laughed. "Or what?"

Do it, do it, do it, do it.

Jane licked her dry lips. She felt her fingers twitch, stallions ready to burst free of the gate.

Could she, though? That was the one test that she hadn't yet been put through. It was one thing to use her abilities against a lab-grown beast, mindless, one copy of many. How far was Jane willing to go against a *person*, though?

How far was she even capable of?

Do it, do it, do it, do it.

"Well, Captain?" UltraViolet said. Her voice pitched low, challenging. "Whatcha gonna do to stop me?"

Jane narrowed her eyes. Her arm thrust forward before she'd

made up her mind to do it. She saw the moment, frozen in time: drawn from behind, the side of her head and her shoulder framing the lower corner of the panel. The reader's line of sight follows the long stretch of Captain Lumen's arm, her iconic red uniform made brighter by the flash erupting from her fingertips.

The beam was both stronger and more highly focused than anything Jane had managed to conjure so far. It cut a straight path over UltraViolet's head, just barely missing her—yet UltraViolet did not duck, did not even flinch. She turned to study the wall, and the painting upon it, which had received the brunt of Jane's attack. A smoldering hole was burned through the canvas, bits of teal and yellow curling in the middle of the frame.

Jane gasped. She yanked her hand back, as if she'd been caught in a fire. Her stomach pitched as the smell of rage and smoke drifted through the office.

UltraViolet turned back to Jane. A single smirk emerged through the flicker of her distortion, gone as fast as it had appeared.

A chill swept over Jane, chasing the last of her powers back to wherever they'd come from. This whole thing felt *wrong*, suddenly, like she'd just woken up from sleepwalking to find herself in the middle of a dark woods. If she didn't know any better, she'd say that UltraViolet had *wanted* this—but surely that was ridiculous . . . wasn't it?

There was no time to consider it. UltraViolet straightened up, dragging the mayor even higher on his feet. "Very well!" she said, her voice carrying as if she was on the steps of City Hall making a statement to the press. "You want your mayor so much? Have him!"

She threw Jane's dad forward.

All of the Heroes advanced as one, but it was Jane that caught him, just before he tumbled to the floor. The haze of a purple smoke bomb stung at Jane's eyes, and she did not need anyone to tell her that UltraViolet had disappeared.

Never mind that—UltraViolet was a problem for another time. Mayor Maxwell was a dead weight in her arms, and Jane staggered as she laid him on the floor as gently as she could. His breathing was shallow, hitching in his chest with each inhale.

Jane brushed some of the sweat from his forehead, his skin oddly cold beneath her touch. Her promise to Allison rang through her head, but what good did it do? Look at him: he was clearly dying.

Jane looked up, desperately searching the Heroes' faces. "Somebody do something!"

"Paramedics are on their way," Granite Girl said.

"What good is that? We need the antidote!"

Granite Girl threw her hands up. "Yeah, well, we don't *have* it! *Maybe*, if UltraViolet hadn't escaped, we'd have some idea of where to look, but—"

Deltaman's hand landed on Granite Girl's shoulder. Granite Girl clamped her mouth shut, a perfect line carved in stone.

"Okay, but there's got to be something else," Deltaman said. He turned to the rest of the team. "There's always something else. *Think*, people! What else do we have to work with?"

"Nothing," Granite Girl said. "There's *nothing* to work with. All we have is an office full of hostages, and dead Shadow Raptors."

The taste of bile crept up the back of Jane's mouth. She got up and stepped away, unable to look at Mayor Maxwell any longer. Instinctively, Jane found herself searching out Mindsight.

They had been so busy arguing that nobody noticed Mindsight break off from the rest of the group. By the time Jane spotted her, she was in the hallway, almost out of view, crouched beside one of UltraViolet's Shadow Raptors.

One of her gloves was off.

"Mindsight?"

But Mindsight didn't look up. She stared at the creature, focused as if steeling herself for something.

Deltaman glanced over, drawn by Jane's distraction. The argument that he was making to the others died on his lips, as an understanding of the situation hit him before anyone else.

"Mindsight, stop!" he called, too late.

Mindsight cupped the Shadow Raptor's cheek.

IN THE WORLD OF JANE'S COMICS, IT'S CALLED A FLARE.

There's some nonsense science to explain it, something that Jane picked Devin's brain about when she was first writing up the proposal scripts for QZero. The science doesn't matter. In essence, a flare is a hyperstimulated version of the Heroes' powers. It can be caused by a lot of things: stress, sometimes, or overtaxing your powers, or pushing yourself too far, too fast, when learning a new facet of your abilities. It was one of the reasons why Cal's training sessions focused only about half on Jane's budding powers, and half on standard self-defense and combat. Once in a while, the dastardly villains of the comics would also use techno-gizmos to cause the Heroes to flare on purpose, harnessing their abilities, siphoning off their powers . . .

Or, in Mindsight's case, attempting to duplicate their personality by taking over her consciousness.

Jane had never understood why Clair insisted that this was the ultimate height of Mindsight's powers. It's not that she didn't get the idea of absorbing the essence of another person—but why, she'd asked time and time again, did it have to mean that Mindsight was subsumed, the new personality wholly taking root?

"It just does," Clair used to say, as if the matter was settled.

In fairness, the issue where this was revealed was a huge success. Mindsight was nearly overtaken by the essence of a villain named Dark Atom, already a fan favorite. The issue sold out, and the fandom exploded with arguments about how this weakness might play out in future storylines.

Of course, by itself, physical contact between Mindsight and another person doesn't necessarily cause a flare. Certainly little touches don't, and even a full grip is not enough to do it.

But this wasn't exactly a person. Grown in the lab, first to do the bidding of Doctor Demolition and then overtaken by UltraViolet, a Shadow Raptor was barely even a proper life form. Tapping into its mind would push Mindsight's powers beyond normal—and a flare, even without the threat of being subsumed by another personality, could easily turn deadly.

A scream ripped itself from Jane's throat as she ran forward. Not "stop!" or "no!" or even "Amy!", this was deeper and more primal than any coherent thought. She surged toward Mindsight, but a pair of strong hands grabbed her from behind.

"Don't!" Deltaman said. He pulled her close even as she fought against him, holding her against his wall of a chest. "Interrupting a deep empathic link can be fatal, remember?"

Jane did remember (she'd written it, after all—an issue where they'd seen a terrible future, the destruction of everything they'd worked for), but the memory only came to her now that he'd said it. The difference between knowing something from a book, and knowing it in your heart.

That knowledge, however, did not make it easier to stand there and watch it happen. From the outside, perhaps, it was nothing flashy: Mindsight's hand on the Shadow Raptor's scaled cheek, leaning over it as if ready to whisper all of her secrets. There were no fancy special effects, no swirling lights or wobbly shimmers like Jane might have drawn. And Amy's face, hidden by her Mindsight persona, did not appear to anyone else in the room to be displaying any particular level of distress.

Only a wife would see it.

Jane saw it. The subtle tightening of Amy's jaw, the grinding of her teeth. It was a look that Clair used to have sometimes after waking up from a nightmare, as she'd gotten out of bed for a cooling glass of water and to pop a few frozen grapes. She never liked to talk about her nightmares, so Jane had to learn how to read the unspoken emotions in the focus of her eyes and the smoothed-out wrinkles of her brow.

Hidden pain coursed through Mindsight's face as she searched the Shadow Raptor's mind. Then, with a gasp like she was coming up for air, it was done. She dropped her hold, falling to her side, and Jane ripped herself from Deltaman's grip to rush to her.

"Amy?" Jane whispered as she tucked the short strands of Mindsight's hair behind her ear, surreptitiously checking her temperature as she did so. "Are you all right?"

Mindsight nodded. "I'm okay. I'll—I'll be okay." She looked up. "There's a vial of antidote in the mayor's desk—top drawer, left. The rest of it is in the basement. Records room. Two Shadow Raptors on guard."

Nobody needed to tell the team to spring into action. Before Mindsight had even finished talking, Pixie Beats was at the mayor's desk; she rummaged for only a moment before shouting, "Got it!" and tossing a vial to Deltaman, who caught it with ease. Rip-Shift had swatted Windforce's shoulder, and the two of them were off, heading no doubt for the records room, as Deltaman rolled up Mayor Maxwell's sleeve to administer the antidote. The whole thing was clockwork, a collaborative dance born of years of choreography.

Jane had no place in it, not yet, not anymore, and so she did the only thing that she could. "Stay here," she said to Mindsight. She rushed down the hall, searching out a water cooler that she'd thought she spotted earlier in the chaos.

"Here," she said a few minutes later, handing Mindsight an impersonal paper cup. Jane made sure to avoid touching it too much, not wanting to make it her own and thus imprint an emotional stamp upon it. She kept her fingers out of Mindsight's way as Mindsight accepted it. The aftereffects of a flare varied from person to person, but right now any use of Mindsight's powers would probably be too much for her.

Mindsight downed the water with enough vigor to best the efforts of someone dying of thirst. She'd scooted back since Jane left, enough to sit up against the wall, and now she leaned her head back, trying to recover herself.

Jane sat down across from her, cross-legged on the floor. "You shouldn't have done that."

"I had to," Mindsight said. She wasn't looking at Jane, but she put on a brave smile anyway. "It's what superheroes do, isn't it?"

"Amy—"

"Don't," Mindsight said. *Now* she looked over. She locked eyes with Jane, and their respective masks seemed to fall away. Amy's eyes, Clair's eyes. Wife to wife. It was almost too much to bear. "I can't fix your other loss, Jane. But I'll be damned if I'm going to let you suffer another."

EVEN IF THERE WASN'T A LAYER OF HAZE FROM DOCTOR Demolition's superweapon shrouding the heart of Grand City, the view in front of Jane now wouldn't have been ideal.

Technically, she was looking at a district called South Grands. Locally, though, it was referred to as South Shits. Buildings packed too closely together, too many of them falling into disrepair. Jane took in the view of rusted-out fire escapes, of peeling advertisements long since graffitied over, of street corners overflowing with piles of trash. Broken windows and broken bricks made up most of the walls, the houses and shops flashing gap-toothed grins at her.

She hadn't questioned Cal as he drove her here, as they met up with the rest of the Heroes on the rooftop of an old brewery, long since out of business. She had still been too worked up from her experience at City Hall. Every time she shut her eyes, it came back to her in panels: the hall, flooded with Shadow Raptors; her own face, overeager as she launched herself into the fight; the smoldering painting, a hole burned straight through an abstract field of yellow and teal waves, like the ocean on fire. And Amy . . .

It was better not to think about Amy at all. What she'd risked, why she'd acted—the look that she'd given Jane, in the moment when things had gone too far.

Because Jane *had* gone too far. She knew this, a cold certainty settling in the pit of her stomach as she'd watched the rest of the Heroes hand matters over to the police. Keisha's husband had arrived by then, taking charge, like he'd been taking charge of the city over the past few days. Jane didn't know how to process what had just happened, and so she'd found herself shutting down, piece by piece. It was like Clair's funeral all over again. Jane had followed Cal from the scene with a numb acceptance that her fate was no longer her own, and he had taken her to this rooftop.

Why? She did not ask. She did not care.

A sudden *pop!* from behind her sparked a panic somewhere deep in Jane's fog. Jane whirled, her fingertips already flashing as she brought them up in a block. Images of guns filled her senses so strongly that she could already smell the powder, could already feel the heat of a bullet whirring near her skin.

So the laughter that she found instead, the jolly scene of camaraderie and friendship playing out on the roof, did not seem entirely real to her at first. Cal stood in the middle of the group, his hood thrown back, his arm raised triumphantly to hold a cheap champagne bottle aloft.

A sea of empty glasses was already raised in his direction, waiting to be blessed.

Jane dropped her hands, embarrassed by the overreaction to what she now realized was only the sound of the cork popping. Waves of anxiety crashed over her, but she bit her lips tight and tried to take deep breaths through her nose. Her mother had managed to drag Jane—once—to a yoga and meditation class, and Jane desperately tried to remember the lesson now, as tears and the soot of South Shits both stung at her eyes.

"—and of course, we can't forget the real hero of the day!" Cal said, and only then did Jane realize that he'd been speaking at all. He held a glass out to her—no, Jane realized, a paper cup, like you might use for coffee at a cheap cafeteria. The whole affair had a decidedly cobbled-together air about it, like they'd run into a gas station with only the change they could find in the seats of their car.

He passed her the cup, wrapping both her hands around it for her.

"To Jane," he said, deep and steady as he looked into her eyes.

Jane swallowed, as an overlapping chorus of *Jane!* filled the air.

"And a damn fine job she did, too," Devin said.

Jane flushed. "No," she tried to mumble, but everyone else was piling on, heaping Jane with praise for what now felt like a meager performance. Only Amy remained quiet, smiling a practiced smile but spending more time looking into her paper cup than at any of them.

"No, really," Jane said, louder. "I didn't do anything."

"Bullshit," Devin said. "You held your own for a while there."

"And you unlocked the door," Tony said.

Jane shook her head. "I'm . . . I'm not sure I did."

"*Plus*," Cal added, ignoring this, "you scared off UltraViolet, and that was no easy feat."

"Yeah," Keisha said. "Give yourself some credit, Jane."

"Hear, hear."

"Absolutely."

"No, but," Jane started, waving her hand to cut down their arguments, "don't you see? It *wasn't* difficult. That's the whole point. The door unlocked itself. UltraViolet ran at basically the first sign of my powers. Doesn't that *bother* anyone else?"

Marie jerked her head in Jane's direction, her hair loose now and fluttering in the breeze. "*Someone* doesn't know how to take a victory."

"But why would she just give up that easily? And why did she just so *happen* to have exactly the right amount of antidote that we needed? Why was a vial of it *right there* in the office, right where we needed it? You can't mean to tell me this was normal."

"Sometimes you get lucky," Tony said.

"But—!" Jane started, but Cal placed a heavy hand on her shoulder.

"Main Jane." His brow was arched at her like she was a puppy who just didn't understand how the sliding glass door to the patio worked. "I understand that this is all new to you, but you should at least *try* to embrace your successes when you get them. Believe me, it doesn't always go your way out there."

At this sobering thought, the rest of the team turned and looked into their drinks. Behind them, Jane could just make out the gap in the cityscape where Woolfolk Tower should have been.

Jane sighed. He was infuriating, and it didn't exactly answer any of her questions, but . . . oh, hell. Maybe Cal was right, maybe not. Either way, it wasn't going to be Jane's problem for much longer. She'd done what she agreed to do, and now it was almost time for her to go home. Jane took a sip of the cheap champagne, then spit it out almost immediately. The rest of the Heroes leaped back to avoid the spray of flat, warm piss water that was trying to pass for something fancy.

"Ugh," Jane said, staring incredulously into her cup. "Where did you even *get* this? It tastes like the underside of someone's tongue after they've barfed."

"And you'd know what that tastes like because . . . ?" Tony asked.

Devin smirked. "Hey, don't knock it. This is kind of a tradition for us, see. Started way back when we beat our first baddie."

"Hell of a night," Tony said.

Cal grinned. "The look on his face!"

"Never mind *his* face," Keisha said, "what about *yours*, after your uniform—"

"Okay, okay, Jane doesn't need to hear about that!" Cal said, shouting to be heard over a cackle of laughter that erupted from the rest of the group. All save for Amy, still hovering on the edges.

"The point is, we've been coming here ever since," Devin continued.

"You'd think we could have started buying better booze, though," Marie said.

Devin raised a finger. "Don't mess with what works."

Marie rolled her eyes.

"Wow," Jane said. "I didn't write *anything* like this into my comics."

Keisha shrugged as she pulled a phone out of her jean jacket. "Some things should be a surprise, though," she said as she tapped the screen awake. "Otherwise, what's the point?"

Jane didn't feel like there *was* a "point" to any of this backward version of reality, though she held her tongue. She'd been in enough battles today, and besides, Keisha wasn't even paying attention anymore, her gaze fixed on the screen in front of her.

Not for long. Keisha took in the text on her phone in an instant, and immediately her eyes flicked back up, straight to Jane's face. Pinning her in time and place, like the look itself had trapped Jane there. Jane knew, even before Keisha spoke, that she wasn't going to like what she heard.

"The mayor's awake."

THE LAST TIME THAT JANE HAD SEEN HER FATHER, IT WAS BY ACCIDENT.

You'd think, in a place as large as Grand City, it would be easy enough to avoid someone, and for the most part you'd be right. Jane and Clair fastidiously kept their distance from any social circles that might brush up against those of hotshot law firms—and while occasionally one of the older partners would take an interest in donating some money to the museum in an effort to appear philanthropic, there really wasn't much cause for their paths to ever cross.

Jane had lived there for years without an issue.

Until one day.

"Tell me again why we're attending this thing?" Jane asked. She and Clair were trudging up the sidewalk underneath the towering brownstone face of one of Sutton University's buildings, their hands buried deep in the pockets of their winter coats. Wet snow spat at them from ominous gray clouds, landing on damp wool and clinging to the outer wisps of Clair's hair like fairy dust. All Jane wanted was to get inside—they'd been walking for what felt like half of the city by now, and her toes were frozen inside of her Converse.

"Because it'll be interesting," Clair said.

Jane huffed, her breath misting in front of her like cigarette smoke. "Interesting, sure. During the summer months, maybe. I don't see why they had to stage it *now*. I thought the whole idea of Shakespeare-in-the-park was to be, you know, in the *park*?"

"I said it was *like* Shakespeare-in-the-park," Clair said. "It's . . . a little different."

"How different, exactly?"

Clair grinned. She reached over, patting Jane's arm. "Patience, love."

But Jane didn't need much patience, because they'd already arrived.

It was held in the Jewish community center of Sutton's arts and culture department. Jane and Clair climbed the stairs with a small trickling of other attendees. They nodded hellos to the two greeters by the door, who were passing out programs. Traces of melting snow fell from Jane's hair as she accepted hers, softening the bright red paper in her hands. Her vision was spotty from the drops on her glasses.

They moved to the side. They were in a narrow room with a high ceiling, marble floor underfoot, wood-paneled walls. A foyer of sorts, with a bulletin board and a table full of informational sheets about upcoming programs and events. Jane handed her program to Clair as she took her glasses off, trying to shake the water droplets from the lenses.

She didn't see him approach.

"Jane?"

More than a decade since they'd last spoken, but his voice was as recognizable as ever. Jane froze, rooted in place, her glasses loose in her hand. Instantly, she was ten years old again, in the kitchen of their house before her mother had remodeled. Jane used to do her homework at the table while her mother made dinner, and her father's voice when he came home would boom into the kitchen from the door to the garage. *There's my girl!*

His voice drew nearer. "I thought that was you."

Clair's hand rested steadily on Jane's shoulder as she answered for them. "Mr. Maxwell. This is unexpected."

"Well, I . . . that is, we—Leena and me—we've been coming here for a while now. She's Jewish," he added. "And quite the budding actress, if I do say so myself."

There was a cheerful lilt in his voice, and a trace of forced laughter. Jane put her glasses back on and turned around.

"How nice for you."

She wanted to see a monster.

This was what he had become in her head, after all. Jane had never drawn it, not explicitly, but now that she turned and she saw him—framed by the walls and the arch of the ceiling, a milling crowd blotting up the background, light catching his wire-rimmed glasses—she realized that she'd been pouring the *idea* of her Evil Father into so many villains, over the years. The cool poise, the steady dismissal. Perfectly trimmed hair, cut close to the scalp, and the stern line of a jaw that had never supported a smile in its life. Pressed suits, the lines sharp enough to cut anyone that dared to approach. Calculating eyes, slicing up whoever he was looking at. An expensive drink, held loosely in the fingers.

That was not what she saw now, and the *lack* of seeing it made Jane's head spin. It was only upon the absence of this very real and clear image that she realized she'd been harboring it at all.

What she saw was her father. Nothing more, nothing less. His hair—short yes, but not as short as her imagination had cut it—frizzed a little in the damp, bits standing up where they should have lain flat, accenting the traces of gray now encroaching from the temples. Instead of the suit, he wore loose slacks and loafers, a collared shirt and v-neck sweater visible beneath an open pea coat. Jane took in the crow's feet beside his eyes, left untouched by Botox. A salt-and-pepper beard (that was new) rose up on either side of his mouth as he offered a tentative smile.

"You look good, Jane," Mr. Maxwell said, as if they were former neighbors that had run into each other at the grocery store. He glanced at Clair, extending his hand. "Clair. Nice to see you again."

Clair accepted the gesture with the practiced ease you'd expect from an assistant curator at the Grand City Museum of Fine Arts. Her professional smile—just enough to be polite, just enough to put you at ease—was firmly in place. "It's been a while."

"Yes, it has." He didn't even flinch at the admission.

Then his attention was back on Jane, heavy with expectancy. He was both softer and older than Jane remembered, his whole countenance infused with the wizened air of a guru. He looked like he should be on some talk show promoting his newest self-help book, or giving TED talks about managing stress in one's life. He put his hands into the pockets of his coat, nonchalant, as he waited for Jane to say something.

But when it was clear that she wasn't, he cleared his throat. Tried again.

"I read your comic."

"Did you."

Clair's hand rested softly on Jane's shoulder, the unspoken command of *Be nice* running instantly between them. Jane shrugged it off.

"I did," Mr. Maxwell said. "It was very . . . imaginative."

"So, you hated it, then."

Mr. Maxwell smiled, gave a soft shake of his head. "I didn't say that, no. It wasn't entirely my cup of tea, I'll admit that, but hate?" The slightest pause. "I could never hate it, Jane. And I hear it's been quite a success. There's talk of a movie, isn't there?"

"Talk," Jane said. "It'll never go anywhere."

"Oh, now, don't say that! You need to believe in your dreams, honey."

"They're not my dreams." Jane glanced at her watch. "We're going to miss the performance."

She hooked Clair's elbow. The two of them brushed past Mr. Maxwell, and though Jane was tempted to "accidentally" knock against his shoulder on the way by, she stamped down on that impulse. They entered the main room just as the overhead lights were dimming.

* * *

JANE WAS THE LAST OF THE FAMILY TO ARRIVE.

If you could even call her that. She hadn't wanted to come in the first place—if she didn't have any interest in seeing her *real* father, then what possible motivation could she have for visiting this version? Besides, her duty was done, she was going home— or so she'd thought.

"What do you *mean*, 'It's not going to be ready until tomorrow'?" Jane asked on the rooftop, about five minutes after Keisha broke the news of the mayor's recovery.

Marie rolled her eyes. "Gee, I don't know how I can make it any clearer. Let's see: maybe I mean that it won't be ready until tomorrow?"

"But you said—"

"I gave you an *estimate*," Marie snapped. "Okay? It was just a fucking *estimate*, and we're dealing with a piece of tech that we didn't invent and still don't fully understand, but that literally rips a hole between two universes, so forgive me if I can't predict its recharge rate down to the last second."

"But—!"

"Look, it's not a bus. You're not going to miss your ride if you're not there on time." Marie crushed her champagne cup in her fist, her fingers turning to granite as they compressed around the paper with a sickening *crunch*.

In the end, there was no arguing with her. If it wasn't going to be ready until tomorrow, then it wasn't going to be ready until tomorrow.

Which still didn't mean that Jane had any obligation to go and see Mayor Maxwell in the hospital, although Amy didn't see it that way. She argued that, once they got *their* Jane back, the last thing that she should have to deal with is the repercussions of snubbing her gravely ill father—and though the point didn't exactly thrill Jane, a twinge of sympathy tugged at her gut. Jane still wasn't sure that there *would* come a point when they found their Jane, but she wasn't about to tell Amy that. The look on Amy's face as she spoke . . .

Besides, Jane had never been able to say "no" to Clair. Amy. Whatever.

So here she was: standing in front of the door to her father's hospital room, trying to settle her shaky hands. At least she'd taken out her contacts by now, though the dry air of the hospital meant that her eyes were still itching, making it hard to fully calm down. Jane glanced to the side. Two bodyguards stood sentry by the door to Mayor Maxwell's room, their ears wired up. They'd already cleared her to enter, though Cal (who'd insisted on coming along for moral support) had to stay outside. He'd wandered down the hall in search of a vending machine a few minutes ago, when the guards had explained the security rules. Jane watched him go, wishing he didn't have to. As if sensing her attention, he'd held up a fightin' fist in solidarity, like a protester on the march.

There was nothing left to do but to face it.

Mayor Maxwell's head snapped toward the door, but his face fell into a scowl of disappointment as Jane stepped in.

"Oh. Jane."

Jane gave a curt nod. What did her double call him, in her world? "Dad"? "Daddy"? "Father"? What level of love, if any, existed between them? It was easier to stay silent.

Mrs. Maxwell stood up. She edged around the table with the remains of Mayor Maxwell's dinner on it, and came over to wrap her arms around Jane's shoulders. "It's good of you to come, sweetie. I'm sure that your father actually does appreciate seeing you. Don't you, Paul?"

Mayor Maxwell gave a grunt that was neither agreement nor dissent. Allison was already seated on a chair that she'd pulled right up next to the bed, and she patted her father's hand as if to say, *It's okay, at least one of your daughters cares.*

Jane pinched the bridge of her nose. Or maybe she was completely wrong, maybe she didn't know how to read this jumbled-up version of her own family, these people that both were and weren't the faces that she'd seen over the dinner table, the parents that she both had and hadn't bought Christmas presents for, drew pictures of, came crying into their bedroom in the middle of the night.

"Listen, Jane, I'm . . . sorry," Mayor Maxwell said, and Jane looked up in wonder.

In all of her years, had her real father ever uttered those

words? Okay, so these were said with a snarl of resentment, like he'd only bitten them out from some twisted sense of obligation, but it was still *something*.

Mrs. Maxwell smiled. She left Jane, then, and sat back down and crossed her toned legs, duty done.

"I really do appreciate you coming out," Mayor Maxwell continued. "Your mother is right. It's just that I've sent Craig with a message for the Heroes, but they haven't responded yet, and . . . when the door opened, I was hoping it was one of them."

Jane tossed a glance at Mrs. Maxwell, who arched one eyebrow at her.

"Oh," Jane said. She hadn't heard anything about a message, or the mayor wanting to speak to them, but then . . . she supposed it didn't really concern her anymore. She'd done her job.

Still.

"Um . . . is it something terribly important, then?"

Mayor Maxwell scowled. "No, I just want to swap recipes. *Yes*, it's important."

"Paul," Mrs. Maxwell said, his name drawn out in her warning tone.

"Oh, for fuck's sake, Olivia, give it a rest. I'm done playing the happy family game today, all right? My daughter asks a stupid question, she's going to get a stupid answer."

"All I was *saying*—"

"Do I look like I give a shit what you were *saying*? This isn't the time for family therapy."

"Hey!" Jane said. "Don't talk to her like that."

Mayor Maxwell pointed at Jane. "You stay out of this. You're in enough trouble already."

"Me?"

Allison rolled her eyes. "Don't pretend like you don't know. How many times, Jane? When we text you, it's because it's *important*."

"I was *busy*."

"Yeah, sure." Allison snorted. "Doing *what*?"

Jane's jaw bobbed open and shut, open and shut. "I—"

"That's really not what matters right now," Mrs. Maxwell cut in, saving her.

Allison rolled her eyes. "Oh, no, of course not. My issues are never important when compared to protecting the almighty *Jane*."

"Allison!"

"Enough!" Mayor Maxwell snapped. "God, you three are going to drive me to an early grave. Is it any wonder I work late?"

Mrs. Maxwell's mouth tightened.

And then Jane knew: this world really wasn't *so* different, after all.

"Sure," Jane said, before she could stop herself. "'Working,' let's call it that. I'm sure that makes it all sound so much better in your head."

The room was cut with a heavy silence. Jane saw each of her family's reactions, as if their faces were framed in three narrow panels right in a row. Mrs. Maxwell, somehow mortified and smug all at once. Allison, confusion drawing her brow together, with just the slightest hint of understanding beginning to creep into her doubtful eyes. Mayor Maxwell, jaw set, battle ready. He glared evenly at Jane.

"Is there something you'd like to say to me?"

Jane snorted. Oh, where would she even begin?

"Sure," Jane said. "Why not? God knows I've wanted to tell you this for a long fucking time, so sure. You're a complete piece of shit."

"Jane!" Mrs. Maxwell gasped.

Jane ignored her. "You're such a hypocrite. No one else has ever been able to set a foot out of line, but you can apparently just do whatever the fuck you want, and it doesn't matter who gets hurt. You know what? It would have been better if this had all just come out *years* ago. I don't know how you've managed to keep Mom quiet, but I *know*. And if you think I'm just going to stand here and pretend like you don't cheat on Mom every chance you get—"

"That's *enough*!"

Jane's rant stumbled to a halt. She'd been expecting to be cut off, the truth shut down before she had a chance to tell it all— but she hadn't been expecting the admonishment to come from *her mother*.

Or, well, Mrs. Maxwell, anyway. Close enough.

"Seriously?" Jane asked. "You're going to defend him?"

"This isn't the place," Mrs. Maxwell said. She moved over to stand beside the hospital bed, where she actually laid her hand on Mayor Maxwell's shoulder. "And your father has done so much for our family, that . . . we owe him our loyalty. I'm sorry that you can't understand that."

For a moment Jane just stared, agog. Mayor Maxwell sat up in his bed, looking smug, as Allison clung to one hand, Mrs. Maxwell to the other. Like some kind of saint, revered by all. The overhead lights even caught the pale color of his hospital gown, lending an angelic glow to the scene.

"Oh, fuck *that*," Jane said. "That's the most apologist bullshit that I've ever heard!"

Mrs. Maxwell scowled. "Jane, you will apologize right now."

Jane rolled her eyes. "Yeah, not happening."

"Young lady, I didn't ask you."

"I don't care," Jane said. "You want to stay here and suck his every lie, fine. I'm done. I shouldn't have come here in the first place."

She was already at the door as Mrs. Maxwell started calling after her. The guards didn't even flinch as Jane stormed into the hallway. She barreled past them, barreled straight into Cal as he rounded the corner.

"Whoa!" Cal said, catching her by the shoulders. "What's the rush?"

"We're leaving," Jane said.

Cal studied her face for just a second before nodding. "Okay."

They were just turning away when Mrs. Maxwell's voice caught up with them.

"Listen, I don't know what's gotten into you lately, but—oh," Mrs. Maxwell cut herself off as she rounded the corner and spotted Cal. Instantly, her whole demeanor cooled. She straightened her shoulders, smoothed her expression. "Cal."

Cal smiled at her. "Olivia."

Jane frowned. Her mother had always been somewhat image-conscious, and certainly this version of Mrs. Maxwell—being a public figure, or at least the wife of one, under constant scrutiny from the media—had plenty of reason to worry about airing their family's dirty laundry in a hospital corridor, in front of guards and orderlies and nurses and people pushing dinner trolleys back and forth. And yet, as Mrs. Maxwell stepped toward Jane, lowering her voice, something else seemed to be going on. Call it daughter's intuition. Her mother was flustered, by more than just the fight.

"Janie, you know why we can't make a fuss about this. Please, can you just come back inside? For me?"

"No. I shouldn't have even come," she repeated. "I'm sorry, Mom. Really, the last thing that I want is to make things complicated for you. But I won't apologize to him."

Mrs. Maxwell's mouth compressed into a tight line. "I thought that you'd changed. After all that you've been through . . ." She shook her head. "Fine. Run away from your messes again. Don't listen to me. *Again.* See what good it does you."

Cal cleared his throat. "Jane?"

Jane didn't answer. She couldn't speak to either of them right now, and so she did the only thing that was left for her to do. She turned on her heel and stormed out of there.

"JANE!"

Jane ignored Cal. She tore out onto the street, her footsteps making satisfying thumps against the pavement as she wended toward the subway. Her world narrowed down, divided into tidy chunks: a couple, scrambling to get out of her way as she barreled past them, frowning at her in annoyance; a flock of pigeons taking flight from the sidewalk, the colors of their plumage catching neon in the lights of the city; a guy leaning against a lamppost, head down, hoodie up, tapping his legs to the music in his earbuds. A subway sign glowing bright, the shadow of Jane's profile against it as she headed down, down, down.

A train was just arriving. Jane hurried into the flock pouring inside.

"Main Jane!"

Cal's tone was light, friendly even. The perfect way to blend in, as if there was nothing more to their interaction than Jane had forgotten her wallet and he was rushing to return it for her.

Jane found an empty seat. Slumped low, crossed her arms, shut her eyes. She tried to pretend that she was just another passenger, just another citizen of Grand City, that this was just another evening. That she hadn't just defeated a super-villain, almost lost the woman that wasn't exactly her dead wife but close enough, drank champagne on a rooftop, met the double of her estranged father, gotten into a fight with her mother-not-her-mother.

She wasn't in the mood. Not for Cal, not now. Not for anyone. She longed for her bed—her real bed—with an intensity not felt since her very first time waking up in this place. Her apartment may be empty, lonely, an aching wound that would never heal; it was still *home*.

Cal's weight dropped in beside her.

To Jane's surprise, he allowed several minutes of silence to pass between them. The subway car lurched forward, swaying gently underfoot. Somewhere nearby, the faintest hint of bass from another passenger's headphones provided a counterpoint to the rhythm of the rails. Cal's fingers tapped against his elbow, his arms crossed, syncing up without conscious thought.

"So . . . do you want to talk about—"

"No," Jane said.

"Are you sure?"

"Yes."

Cal sighed. "Cut her some slack, Jane. Your mom's just trying to—"

"Yeah, forget about me and my mom for a minute," Jane said. "What's up with *you* and my mom?"

She didn't realize it until she asked. *That's* what had caused Mrs. Maxwell's discomfort: Cal. Every time, every interaction, ran taut with invisible tension.

The smallest flush colored Cal's cheek as he turned toward the window; then he seemed to realize his mistake, and made himself look straight back into Jane's eyes. The whole thing took only an instant, but it was enough.

"I don't know what you're talking about," he said.

Jane raised an eyebrow. "Cut the crap, Cal. I'm not stupid."

A blink of surprise. Then Cal turned downcast, his shoulders drooping in defeat. "No," he said, "I know you're not."

"So . . . ?"

"Is this really where you want to talk about it?" Cal was squirming where he sat, like a little boy caught stealing candy.

Jane looked around the train. There was a certain privacy in the kind of crowds that cities provided, a total lack of fucks given for those around you. Across from them, a pregnant Hispanic woman sat leaning her head back against the window, thick headphones blocking out the world; beside her was an older black gentleman, clean-cut and academic, reading a well-thumbed paperback; two pale and scrawny teenagers stood making out not far from them, one with her hair dyed purple, the other's streaked white-and-black like a zebra.

"Just tell me."

Cal ran his hand across his jaw. The rough scrape of early stubble grated like sandpaper.

He wasn't looking at her as he spoke, not directly. The reflection of the window right beside them would do just fine. It framed them like a comic panel, two people heading home after a long day.

"I . . . *may* have . . . ," his voice lowered to a mutter, spitting it out fast, "slept with her."

"You *may* have?!"

The question exploded out of Jane, louder and more of a shriek than she intended.

"Shh!" Cal turned back, scowling hard at Jane. "Quiet, will you?"

"Well, *did* you," Jane asked, lowering her voice to a tense hiss, "or *didn't* you? And don't you dare try to tell me that you don't remember."

Cal's scowl deepened. The lines of his face were hard as marble, thrown into stark relief underneath the stale-piss lights of the subway car. "Fine," he said, biting the words out. "Yes—I *did*, all right? But it was *one time*. It meant nothing."

"That's supposed to make me feel better?"

"You asked."

"You're right," Jane said. "I did."

And really, it's not like it was surprising. Isn't this what Jane had always suspected, deep down, as soon as she'd seen the way they were acting around each other? Isn't it what she'd known that she'd hear?

Still, she couldn't bring herself to just sit there and look at Cal right now. Jane turned away, studying the grooved runner that cut down the aisle of the subway car.

"Jane . . . I'm sorry."

"You slept with my *mom*," Jane said. Her mouth twisted up as she spoke, an urge to vomit twitching in her stomach.

"Well . . . technically, she's not really *your* mom."

Jane looked back up. Now it was her turn to scowl. "Not helping your case, man."

"No, I don't suppose it does." Cal sighed, regripping his hold on the seat's support pole. "Listen, not to make things worse, but . . . I think that might be what the big fight was about. With your mom. The fight was—was not long after it happened. When Jane got back, she was . . . different."

Jane shut her eyes for a moment, gathering herself. "Don't you think you should have told me this sooner?"

Cal winced. "Yeah," he said, his voice small. "But it's not like I can prove anything. I mean, Jane never talked to me about the fight. It could have been about something else."

"Uh-huh."

"Look, I'm *sorry*, all right? I wish I didn't do it, but I *did*, and nothing's going to change that."

"You slept with my *mom*," Jane repeated, as if saying it again might make things more palatable. The words didn't taste any better this time than they had the last.

Cal's phone chimed. He pulled it out of his pocket, and frowned as he read the message on the screen.

"Your dad wants a meeting."

"I'm not going back there."

Cal sighed as he ran his hands through his hair. "You understand that he doesn't know who we are, right? He's not going to fight with you, if you show up as . . . well, you know."

"Don't care," Jane said as she adjusted her glasses. "I'm done with that man. If you want to meet with him, fine. But don't expect anything that he says to be of use. He's always been more talk than substance."

"That's . . . not exactly been our experience with him."

"Then you just haven't met him properly yet."

Cal sighed. "People do change, Jane."

"Some people." Jane shook her head. "Not him. Not even a new universe can fix him."

THEY WATCHED THE MEETING FROM THE COMMAND ROOM.
It was easier for Jane to see her father this way: his image plastered on a large screen, like he was nothing more than a television character, and they were binge-watching some new superhero show on Netflix. Jane sat in one of the chairs, swiveling back and forth, her feet propped on the edge of the curved conference table. She didn't know why she was here, because it's not like she cared what Mayor Maxwell had to say. Everyone else stood around on-edge, arms crossed, faces grim. The light was turned down low, the screen dark as Cal's video feed showed him, as Deltaman, scaling the side of the hospital.

He snuck in through the window. Mayor Maxwell was asleep, his room still and empty. The Heroes had purposefully waited until after visiting hours, to ensure they'd be alone. Monitors displaying Mayor Maxwell's vitals lit just enough of the room to catch his profile, slack and unaware. His mouth hung open, his hair lightly askew. Jane flinched, watching him. He looked *old*, older than she was comfortable with.

It wasn't clear what Deltaman did to wake him. One moment a faint snore filled the room—the next, Mayor Maxwell jerked awake, blinking rapidly as he seemed to take in his surroundings. His attention settled on Deltaman.

"You're here," Mayor Maxwell said.

"Your message said it was urgent," Deltaman said. His voice came through distorted, digitized by the same type of device UltraViolet used. It was a necessary precaution, in their line of work, and one that Jane had never had qualms writing into the comics—but there was something unsettling about hearing it from someone that she knew. A voice that should have been familiar, but wasn't.

People change, she heard Cal say, but Jane shook her head.

"It is urgent," Mayor Maxwell said. He shifted, sitting up higher in his hospital bed, as if the full brunt of what he had to say had finally come back to him again. He paused just long enough to retrieve his glasses from where they were resting on the bedside table, right next to a paper cup of water.

Jane shut her eyes, trying not to think about the bedside table that she'd always had to sneak past when entering her parents' room as a child, in the middle of the night after she'd had a bad dream or wet the bed. The glasses, the water, the book with its pages folded in to mark their place.

"The city is in terrible danger," Mayor Maxwell continued, drawing Jane back to the situation at hand.

Deltaman raised his hand. "It's okay—the antidote is already being distributed."

"No, not that. Listen to me: I heard things, while I was being held captive. They thought that I was so far gone because of the sickness, but I had my moments of clarity. This whole thing . . . it was just a distraction. UltraViolet never had any intention of killing everyone, not this time anyway."

Back at headquarters, the room took a collective breath. Amy snuck a fast glance at Jane, but Jane was staring at the screen, glued to what was playing out.

"I'm listening," Deltaman said.

"The weapon that destroyed Woolfolk Tower was a test. Ultra-Violet is building another, large enough to wipe out the entire city. While you were busy saving us, a robbery was taking place. Wilson Labs."

"On it," Marie said. The message was transmitted to a discreet earpiece, and Deltaman waited for more information before replying to Mayor Maxwell.

Marie sat down and typed quickly on a laptop, accessing the Heroes' central database. She grimaced as the information she'd been looking for popped up.

"Confirmed," Marie said. "Though it seems that Wilson Labs isn't exactly keen for anyone to know. The police weren't notified of the crime, and the only record of it was logged as a false-alarm glitch of the lab's security system."

"Do you know what they took?" Deltaman asked. The question was both for Mayor Maxwell, and for Marie, through the earpiece.

Mayor Maxwell shook his head. "They didn't say."

"Oh, well, that's helpful," Marie muttered, as the sound of her typing revved up once more. She tapped her own earpiece. "Cal? The alarm was triggered in their Research and Development department, at the Experimental Sciences vault." A nervous laugh tinged her voice as she added, "So that's not disturbing at all."

"We'll handle it," Deltaman told the mayor and the team both. His voice was deeper than normal, full of confidence in the Heroes' ability. Jane didn't know if it would necessarily convince the mayor—her own father was notoriously difficult to impress—but Jane could *feel* the tension level of the group around her lower just a fraction as determination replaced fear.

She couldn't help but feel that, between the two of them, he really was the better leader of the group—collected, organized, unflappable. Granted, Jane didn't know what this world's Jane was like, but by contrast Jane herself was a trembling leaf, just barely hanging on. She looked around the room, at the faces of their team, grateful that there was someone capable to step up and fill the void that her double had left behind.

It was a good thing that she was leaving tomorrow. Because

one thing was clear to her, now more than ever: she would never be a proper replacement for Captain Lumen.

"HAVE TIME FOR A COFFEE BEFORE YOU GO?"

Jane paused. She was halfway through twisting her damp hair into a ponytail. Amy had found her as soon as Jane had stepped out of her suite, the morning sunlight pooling into the hall. The timing was too perfect to be coincidental.

"Is this where you take me somewhere, seemingly innocuous, but in fact you've got this big speech ready to pull at my heart strings so I'll agree to stay?"

A blush tinted the tops of Amy's cheeks. "Would it make a difference?"

"No," Jane said, as she finished her hair and dropped her hands. "I'm sorry, but . . . really, no."

This had started the night before. Just after the meeting between Deltaman and Mayor Maxwell. The screen had gone dark as Cal returned to base, and one by one, the sets of eyes had turned to settle on Jane.

Immediately, she'd put her hands up. "Oh, no. I've done my part."

It didn't take a genius to work it out: the last time Doctor Demolition's weapon had threatened Grand City, Captain Lumen was the key to defeating it. Just because they hadn't arrived in time didn't mean that the plan wasn't sound. Now, with no Captain Lumen . . . it only made sense for them to turn to, in their words, "the next best thing."

It should have been flattering.

It wasn't.

So now they were resorting to emotional blackmail. Jane couldn't *fault* them for this, but that didn't mean that she had to go along with it like a pig to the slaughter.

She brushed her way past Amy—not unkindly—and headed for the kitchen. She'd written this place to have a wicked kitchen, with a piece of tech that they'd stolen from the future that could whip up just about anything you were craving in twenty seconds flat, and she was eager to see if it existed in real life.

Real life. Jane frowned, shaking her head as she walked. Since when did she start thinking of this place as real?

Amy followed. As Jane knew she would. Her footsteps were light in Jane's wake, a careful tread that said more than words ever could.

"I'm not going to change my mind," Jane called over her shoulder.

"Oh, I know," Amy said. "I just haven't eaten yet, either."

It was a lovely lie, though easily spotted. Which meant that Amy wasn't even *trying* to convince Jane, which meant that she had some other plan up her sleeve, which meant . . .

The rest of the Heroes were waiting for Jane in the kitchen.

"Seriously?"

Cal was fast to his feet. "We're not trying to make you do anything you don't want to do—"

"Oh, bullshit," Jane said. "God*dammit.*"

"We have a proposal," Keisha said.

"One that's very reasonable," Devin said.

"Even for you," Marie said.

Jane threw her hands up. Cal blocked her path, his broad chest creating a barrier.

"Cal."

"Jane."

Jane pinched her nose. "Can you at least let me get to the fucking cereal cabinet before you ambush me?" She didn't even care about elaborate meals anymore, not if *this* was going to be her morning.

Slowly, so slowly, Cal moved aside. Jane didn't know what he was so worried about—Amy was already blocking the closest exit. Jane muttered to herself as she crossed the kitchen. She found a bowl, a spoon. Some milk. She had finally figured out what the point of milk was, several months ago. Their cereal selection was shit, mostly sugar-bombed frosted fruit puffs with chocolate and marshmallows, but hidden in the back was a box of the blandest bran flakes.

She poured herself a bowl. Jane grounded herself in the images of her routine: her hands, framed from counter height, as she rips a banana from its cluster; her back as she rummages in the fridge, light stealing out around her and turning her into a silhouette. One shot of her face, eyes and mouth both level and tugged just to the side, where the readers can see the blocky colors that outline where her so-called "friends" are gathered behind her.

There was no way that she was going to say "yes."

She was totally going to say "yes," wasn't she?

"No," she said, as she turned around. Milk sloshed, threatening to topple a slice of banana and several bran flakes from her overfilled bowl. She hooked a chair with her ankle, and sat without ceremony. "I'm just telling you that now, so that we know where we stand. I'll listen. But I'm saying 'no.'"

She didn't wait for them to answer before she shoved a giant spoonful into her mouth. Milk dribbled down her chin, and Jane wiped it away with the back of her sleeve.

"We're not asking you to risk your life," Cal said. As usual, the leader of the group. He sat across from her, the whole kitchen gleaming white and spotless around them. Even the table, round and sixties-retro, was white, with stupid little egg chairs that required far more balance than they had any right to.

Jane crunched. She didn't look at Cal. She didn't look at any of them. Her bowl; the cereal. Banana slices, slimy in the overhead light.

"What we're asking you to do is just to *stick around*. For a little while. Until we can figure out a better option."

"You mean until you can guilt me into doing your bidding."

Dammit, she wasn't going to say anything. She frowned. Why had she said something? She tried to reduce her world: she was the only thing in her panel, just her and her cereal bowl.

Crunch.

Not my problem, a square, thought-bubble box said beside her head.

"Marie is going to try to replicate Captain Lumen's power artificially," Cal continued. He was clearly working from a script, and Jane wondered how long he'd spent rehearsing his lines in the bathroom. That was what he'd have done if he really *was* Captain Lumen, anyway—Jane tried to write some vulnerability into him, whenever she could.

Crunch.

Nope.

"And we're going to redouble our efforts at finding *our* Jane. There's really every reason to believe that one of these options will pan out, long before you would—long before anything would actually happen."

Crunch.

Jane's head tipped down, and her eyes moved up. She looked at Cal heavily over the tops of her glasses. "You should have practiced longer," she said. She pointed at him with her spoon, then quickly pulled it back to lick a flake off the gentle curve.

Cal's jaw tightened. "Look, Jane—"

"Why don't you just pop to another universe?" Jane asked. She dug her spoon through her cereal. "I mean, you have the tech, right? So find another Jane, someone that already *has* the right powers—bam, there you go. Problem solved."

She knew that it couldn't be this simple—that if *was*, they'd have already put the plan in motion. Still, if they were going to ask this of her, she was going to be damned sure that there wasn't another way. *Any* other way.

Not that she would agree, even so. But.

All the same.

In the end, it was Marie that answered first. She sighed. "We . . . don't know how."

Jane snorted. "Of *course* not."

"Look, it's complicated, all right? I didn't *invent* these things."

"No, you just use them to kidnap people and force them to help you."

"Jane," Cal said. "It's not like that."

"It's *exactly* like that!" Jane threw her spoon down. Milk leapt from her bowl, splashing on the table. "Look at it from my perspective! I've gone along with your stupid schemes, I played the part, and it's still not enough. You're supposed to be *superheroes*. Can't you just find some other way? Hack a computer and track down who's been buying purple lipstick, or something?"

"Jane—"

"Forget it," Jane said, because she knew that her arguments wouldn't do any good. She picked her spoon back up, shoved more cereal into her mouth so that she didn't have to talk anymore. Tears stung at the corner of her eyes. Dammit, didn't any of them *understand*? They'd all chosen this life. They'd all felt some stirring, deep in their soul—a calling to do good, to rise up, to be more. You couldn't just throw that at a person, and expect them to be grateful for it.

That's not how heroes were made.

"What if we give you the device?" Amy said finally. "And that way, you can leave any time you want to."

The kitchen fell silent. Even Jane's crunching had stopped.

Jane watched the room. Most of the Heroes were within her line of sight, and she took inventory of their reactions. So they really *had* been planning to keep her here, then. Regardless of what she said, regardless of whether or not she liked it. That was good to know.

The scrape of a kitchen chair. Jane turned, addressing the only person that mattered anymore.

Amy was framed by the closed door behind her. Perfectly centered, perfectly poised. To either side was nothing but clear counters, the surfaces aligned with the hands folded in front of her. She was the only point of color Jane could see, but oh, there was *so much* color. Peaches and browns and the flecks of green of her eyes. Blue fingerless gloves with swirls of green and purple, like a night frozen in a northern hell. Yellow pants of spring, her green shirt blooming above them. A necklace . . .

Jane swallowed. She'd bought that necklace for Clair. Shortly before they were married, they'd found it in an antique store. Folded glass in an abstract origami, expertly crafted.

If UltraViolet was allowed to continue, that necklace might be shattered. Amy could easily get caught up in the explosion, snuffed out as swiftly as Clair.

Now here she was, asking for help.

What else could Jane do?

"You know that I can't stop it, right?" Jane asked. "I mean . . . I've barely scraped the surface of Captain Lumen's powers. I'm still playing with visible light. Widening the range into infrared would be hard enough, but wireless signals?" She shook her head. "There's just no way."

There. It wasn't a "yes."

It could never be a "yes."

But as Amy smiled, warm and reassuring, filling Jane's heart to bursting, there fell between them the simple truth: it also wasn't a "no."

For now, at least, that was really all the Heroes needed.

JANE DREW A MONTAGE.

Marie holed up in her lab: a portrait of her face, her lip scrunched up and caught between her teeth, her eyes narrowed in concentration; the straps of her safety goggles muss with her hair, and she's soldering something on a teeny-tiny circuit board that she holds in front of her. Behind her, you can see whiteboards filled with equations, gadgets half-completed, a spaceman helmet with golden wings and several wires sticking out of its neck as if it is still being worn by an android head, now severed from its body. A basil plant sits under a sunlamp near her elbow. In one panel she works, in the next she is downing an entire bottle of water, the next she works. Over and over and over.

Tony, in a police uniform at his GCPD precinct: in one panel, first, he chats amiably with Captain Daniels, then in the next something on the captain's desk catches his eye. In the next he's at his desk, watching in the reflection of his computer monitor as Captain Daniels puts on his coat, preparing to leave the office. Tony reaches underneath his desk, slices open a breach in reality, slices another through the open door of Captain Daniels's office. He reaches through the rip and takes the file, then slides it into the laptop bag by his feet.

Keisha as Pixie Beats, out on patrol: she is small as a mouse in a city packed with feet and coffee cups. She sneaks through the world, listening to conversations in bars and bathroom stalls and boardrooms. Some panels show her running through passages of duct work or along a railing of the subway; others are almost a game of *Where's Waldo?*, her uniform the tiniest splash of color in a sea of chaos, like a flower lost on the street.

Cal in a leather jacket and dark jeans: he's gone to a dive bar, someplace where they have contacts with the criminal underworld. In a corner, in the shadows, he slips money to a man with wide eyes and too many teeth. Literally too many teeth—he's not from this world, and his narrow, spiked incisors are laced with poison. He flashes them in a grin at Cal; Jane imagines that this creature has fancied Cal from a distance for years, that it's this reason that causes him to cooperate with the Heroes.

Windforce, soaring over Grand City: carried by currents, his blue-and-white wingsuit blends into patches of cloud and clear sky. His full-face spandex mask is broken up only by the reflective lens of his goggles, cutting a wide swath across his face. The goggles reflect the city below, the gleaming buildings, the paths jammed with traffic. Later, the stretch of suburbs, the industrial grime, the open span of fields and trees. He loops out beyond the edges of Grand City, circles back, loops out again.

Mindsight.

There is only one panel of Mindsight. Crouched in an empty parking lot that is surrounded by buildings on all sides. Fences block most of it off, but one is twisted, a broken gap allowing access. Cigarette butts and joint stubs litter broken pavement and puddles and oil patches. Mindsight traces her fingers along the ground, her eyes closed, her face frozen in concentration. Graffiti looms large on a wall behind her, overlapping messages of anger and joy and rebellion.

The pages surrounded Jane. In a tiny corner of the Heroes' headquarters, she made a space her own. Not Captain Lumen's room, not anybody's room. It was a junction between corridors, and so nobody could object as Jane dragged in a table and set herself up. She bought paper, pencils, paints. Most of her work at QZero was done on the computer, by necessity, but Jane had always preferred working with the old methods. There was something soothing about the scritch of a pencil, the resistance of the paper when she erased something. The smell of paint. The smudge of ink. Swirls became shapes became people. Jane finished each piece and taped it to the wall above her workspace, then moved on to the next one.

Now a blank sheet lay in front of her. She stretched out her fingers, working cramps from her knuckles in turn. It was long past time for a break, but stretching was all that Jane had allowed herself. Her shoulders screamed at her, and she ignored them. Her arms were heavy with effort, and she willed them forward.

Most of her pages were planned well in advance. Certainly for the real issues. Binders full of notes and loose scribbles would give her a framework to build on, as she tried out one pose, one arrangement, then another, then another. By the time she sat down at her tablet at her desk to compose the final page, she could close her eyes and see exactly what she was going for.

This time, there was nothing. Jane leaned back and took a moment to clean her glasses, clear her thoughts. The paper stared back at her—empty, waiting. There was a certain expectancy to a blank page that Jane was never quite comfortable with.

Jane bit her lip, let her pencil make a line. A vague image strung her along, and she did not interfere. The outlines of a room gave structure to her drawing. Jane hummed under her breath. She made a figure, and then another. Swirls, and then shapes. By the time she realized that she was drawing Captain Lumen, the details had already started to creep in. Jane sat back, breathing deeply as if waking from a trance. She looked down at the drawing, still vague on the page, but there was enough detail to see what she was going for. Herself, in uniform, standing in the Vault below the headquarters. A prison cell stood before her, as Captain Lumen looked in on the man being held. He rested on a bench, his leg up beside him, hand laying casually over his knee. Doctor Demolition's black uniform was already partially filled in with thick layers of graphite, but his face . . .

There was nothing in the blank circle of his face. Jane had never drawn him without his mask before.

Her chair screeked underneath her as she stood up. She was still holding her pencil, tapping it thoughtfully against her lip as she walked. The drawings didn't truly *matter*, she supposed— certainly they served no purpose, other than a kind of meditation for Jane—and it's not as if they were entirely accurate, though she was basing them on conversations overheard. Still . . . how often do you get to see your own creations come to life?

She wanted to draw him as he actually looked. For real.

Jane was certain that she wasn't supposed to have access to the Vault. Though the Heroes wanted her help, needed her help, there remained a very clear distinction between them and Jane. She was like a freelancer, a temp, not truly part of the office. Not invited to the parties. Not trusted with the supplies.

To hell with what they wanted. Jane rode the elevator down, down, down, watching the gently pulsing panels of white that slid up the walls as she passed each floor. Jane was risking her life for their cause. She was owed one or two.

Besides, she was Captain Lumen, right? The computer recognized her, even if the Heroes would not.

The access panel outside of the Vault turned green. The doors slid open. Jane tucked her pencil into her ponytail, and stepped through.

And there, inside the cell, there he was. Doctor Demolition. The one and the only. The man who had been wrecking havoc on Grand City for more than a year now, who'd been defeated time and time again, only to rise with an even more dastardly plan a few weeks later. Or, as Jane knew him:

"Eddie?"

Eddie, the man that had fired her. Eddie, with his bobblehead collection and his habit of accidentally spitting as he talked. Eddie, who took credit for Jane's ideas at every opportunity, who never appreciated what she'd given to QZero, who seemed somehow angrier with each new level of success that the *Hopefuls* franchise achieved.

Eddie whipped his head up, his eyes wide and frantic, as Jane burst out laughing.

"Who the hell are you?" he demanded. His voice was overly strong the way that it got when he was trying to hide something. "How did you get that name?"

Jane's laugh condensed to a smug grin. "Oh, this is rich."

"Listen, whoever you think I am, I'm not," Eddie said.

Jane raised an eyebrow. She crossed her arms. "Really? So you're not Edwin Easton, formerly of Clear City, husband to Maxine, father of Lucy and Thomas? And I suppose that you don't really like Tycho's Tacos with an unholy passion, especially if they give you extra packets of hot sauce?"

The absolute stillness that radiated off of him told Jane all that she needed to know.

Jane smirked. Oh, she was going to enjoy this.

"What do you want?" Eddie managed to say. Though it took him three attempts, and even then, his voice was stiff with tension.

"UltraViolet." The answer came automatically, as if this was always the reason that she'd come down here. She leaned in, until she was just on the other side of the glass barrier that separated them. "Who is she?"

Eddie shook his head. "I don't know. Truly! I've told your Heroes that, and I mean it. She came to me about a year ago. Wanted me to cause chaos in Grand City. But she's never divulged her secrets to me. I've never even seen her face!"

"You expect me to believe that?" Jane asked, though in fact she did. Eddie was so many things, but not a skilled liar. Especially when he was stressed or intimidated. Jane remembered one time, running into him talking to a corporate bigwig in the hallway, how Eddie had folded so easily under pressure, like a wet comic book.

"It's the truth!" Eddie said. A layer of sweat had sprung up on his brow. Next would come his habit of gnawing on his lip.

As if on script, Eddie's teeth appeared, drawing his lip in. He chewed, chewed, his wide eyes never once leaving Jane's face.

Jane sighed. She dropped her arms. "Okay, fine. But listen, you have to be able to tell me *something*. Why does she want to destroy the city? What's her endgame?"

Eddie stopped chewing. His eyebrows raised up—first one, then the other. His mouth was red and irritated as he said, "You mean you really don't know?"

"Apparently not," Jane said. "So why don't you just tell me?"

"She wants to destroy you."

Jane frowned. "You mean the city? Or the Heroes?"

"Both," Eddie said. He stood up, his face turned serious, like someone had flipped a switch. When he took a step forward, closer to the glass barrier, Jane suddenly felt an urge to step back. "But mostly, she wants to destroy *you*." Eddie jabbed his finger at the glass, straight at Jane, making her jump. His grin cut the room like a knife across her skin. "Jane Maxwell. Did you really think that we wouldn't know who you are?"

Jane's blood went cold. She reached behind her, fumbling for the door controls, as Eddie—as *Doctor Demolition*—reached into his uniform and removed the smallest piece of tech. He crunched it between his fingers, and a pulse shot out around him.

Later, Jane wouldn't remember hitting the floor. The explosion would exist in fragments: the sound of glass splintering, the burst of heat hitting her square in the chest, the ringing in her ears. Her world blinked in and out, as heavy black boots stepped over the rubble, coming toward her. Lights flashed red, alarms sounded from so far away. Sparks made her wince. Her breath squeezed tight as Doctor Demolition's face, now masked, came into focus above her. He pinched her chin, turning her head toward him. His voice seemed to come from everywhere.

"The Spectral Wars are coming, Captain. And there is nothing you can do to stop it."

Fear turned Jane's world black. Like a curtain falling, she slept.

WITHIN DAYS, JANE'S FAMILY HAD RETURNED TO THEIR normal lives. Allison drove down to D.C. (though she promised to visit again soon, to see how her father was doing). Mayor Maxwell went back to work. Mrs. Maxwell retreated to Charlotte's Landing.

"I suppose I shouldn't be surprised," Mrs. Maxwell said, opening the door for Jane and Cal. She stepped aside, motioning to the foyer. "Well, help yourselves. You know where the basement is."

"Thanks, Olivia," Cal said, as he breezed past her like he owned the place.

Jane hung back. Even though it wasn't really *her* mother, the words that they'd shared last time sat prickly between them. She wanted to talk about them. She didn't want to talk about them.

"Oh, don't worry," Mrs. Maxwell said. "I have a busy schedule—you'll barely even notice that I'm here. As I'm sure you're counting on."

"I'm not—" Jane started, but Mrs. Maxwell was already shaking her head. She turned away, leaving Jane to enter the house and close the door on her own.

Jane picked her way inside.

Honestly, she'd have been just as happy to never see this place again. But something had changed, since talking to Doctor Demolition. The threat of UltraViolet's weapon hung over everything now, coloring Jane's world. She couldn't just ignore it anymore, as much as she might want to. She had to be honest: the rest of the Heroes' efforts may not be enough. And neither, realistically, might Jane's—but she had to at least *try*.

She'd never be able to look at herself in the mirror again if she didn't.

So here they were. Training again, isolated from both the city and the rest of the Heroes. Part of Jane felt like a little kid, shuffled off to summer camp to get out from the adults' hair, but she couldn't really argue. While they didn't exactly *blame* her for Doctor Demolition's escape, neither was Jane the most popular person among the group right now. And not having to look at them every day, see the mix of judgment and uncertainty in their eyes . . . it might help.

Days passed. Not many, but so full that Jane lost track of them easily. During the day, Jane ran and fought and ducked and scrambled. Lights flared—over and over and over again, so much that Cal had taken to wearing his sunglasses even indoors. Jane's head throbbed. At night, she counted her bruises, took stock of each sore muscle. Once, in a fit of frustration, Jane yelled at Cal that he was putting her through basic training, only to have him answer that that's exactly what he was doing. This version of him used to be in the military, after all. He knew how it was done.

Jane didn't know what to say to that. Cal shrugged—then barked out another order for her, and she sprang into action as if she was a puppet on strings.

She slept deeply. Chugged gallons of water. Juanita, or whatever her name really was (she never said, even when Jane tried to ask), made Jane dinners fit for a king. Heaps of protein, full green salads, rolls slathered in fresh butter. Jane would eat by herself, by choice, alone in the formal dining room. She carried her plates back and forth, loading up course after course.

". . . thought we were pals!" Cal was saying one evening, as Jane came back into the kitchen. "Amigos! Compadres!"

Juanita blinked up at him. She held up a plate of fresh cheesecake, right under his nose as if to distract him. Jane sidled up, just long enough to steal a slice of cheesecake for herself, and left them to sort it out.

Every day, there were more stupid exercises. Another routine designed to jar her powers, another test for Jane to pass. Jane had been afraid, at first, that her powers might prove overwhelming, that the voice that had egged her on at City Hall would return, but so far it was all routine. She certainly *felt* in control—even the day that she'd finally managed to break through into infrared, the whole of the darkened basement now visible to her, she'd been in control.

So . . . maybe the voice had been nothing, after all. A freak occurrence, like a snow squall in July.

Now she stood on the docks, alone, trying to focus her breathing. Her powers hummed through her, but Jane kept a comfortable leash on them. Even the tickle in her fingers was becoming familiar.

Jane stared out at the water. There were several targets bobbing in the distance, buoys that Cal had positioned earlier that day. Jane didn't understand the *point* of this one, but when did that ever matter? The buoys flashed wide stripes of red and white, red and white, as the currents tugged them over and over. The sun beat against Jane's back, the exposed length of her neck. Six new bruises yesterday, and by now every muscle ached down to the bone. She was sweaty, cranky, crusty with salt from a two-mile swim.

She was just about to target them when the sound of a door slamming shut broke the stillness.

"Cal, I swear to God, if you've come to tell me *one more*—"

But when Jane turned, it wasn't Cal cutting down through the slope of grass.

It was Amy.

Jane felt as if she'd fallen into a dream. Amy smiled. Waved.

She had on an a-line skirt, and a sleeveless blouse with a Peter Pan collar. Bare legs led way to flat sandals tied in place around her ankles. A red belt cinched in at the waist, drawing together the yellow and blue and white of the rest of her outfit. With her bobbed hair, she could have been a model for an upscale thrift store, vintage clothes curated for the highest quality. The mere sight of her lifted some of the weight from Jane's chest. The view cut a perfect picture: Amy backed by a sprawling green lawn, a white beach house and the blue sky framing her. Every color popped, the image screaming of summer, of lazy days, of long nights at the beach, of sparklers, of steaks cooked over a charcoal grill.

"How's the training going?" Amy called as she approached.

Reality crashed back into Jane, and she made a face. "Don't tell me you came all this way just to ask me *that*."

"Why not?" A trace of laughter clung to the edge of Amy's voice like perfume. "Aren't I entitled to fuss over you?"

Jane flushed. Her eyes found the wood of the dock, the wet splotches from her bare feet.

Amy had reached the dock by now. She picked her way along the planks, walking along them as if they were stepping stones. Up close, Jane could see that she'd chosen white lace fingerless gloves for the day, like she was expected for tea with the Queen.

"How do you *do* it?" Jane asked. Amy glanced up, puzzled, so Jane added, "Handle being a superhero. I've been here for less than two weeks and already it's exhausting. And you . . . I mean, you can't even touch things without absorbing their emotional energy. Doesn't it drive you *crazy*?"

Amy shrugged. Her hair fluttered in the breeze, dragging loose strands across her cheek. "You get used to it," she said as she brushed them aside. She laughed. "I'm sorry, that's probably not very helpful to you right now."

"Not really, no," Jane conceded. She looked down at her hands, reflecting brightly in the sun.

You get used to it. Jane snorted. She doubted that she'd ever get used to any of this—not just the superpowers, but the whole package deal of her double's life. The house, the money; the parents, their fractured marriage locked up inside; a sister, so new to Jane and already not speaking to her; training sessions that left Jane feeling like she'd been pulverized with a baseball bat.

Without a word, Amy ran a reassuring hand up and down Jane's shoulder blade. Jane closed her eyes. Amy . . . That much, at least, Jane felt like she might be able to get used to. Not Clair, no—nothing would ever be the same as Clair. But there was just enough of Clair in Amy that it was easy to forget sometimes, easy to allow the familiar gestures of comfort and support. Tiny bits of Clair in an otherwise empty and cruel world.

In the grand scheme of things, it was barely anything—table scraps at a pauper's supper—but it was more than Jane would ever get back in her own world, in her own life.

"You know what I think you need?" Amy asked. She wore Clair's bright tone in her voice, the I'm-going-to-fix-everything tone that Jane thought had been lost forever.

"No," Jane said. "What do I need?"

"A break." Amy smiled. She threaded her hand down until she'd taken Jane's, careful to avoid contact between their bare fingers. She gave Jane a gentle squeeze. "Come on. I know just the thing."

"WHERE EXACTLY ARE WE GOING?" JANE ASKED FOR THE HUNDREDTH TIME.

"*Patience*," Amy said. "Honestly, Jane. You were never good at waiting for anything, were you?"

"No," Jane said, so directly that Amy laughed. It used to make Clair laugh, too; she had endless patience for Jane's impatience. In fact, Clair used to revel in concocting elaborate scenarios to torment Jane—every birthday, anniversary, Christmas. She dragged out Jane's presents all day, hiding them behind the furniture like Easter eggs.

"*One more*," Clair would say, whenever Jane stumbled across another one. She'd grin, a wicked, evil, grin, because there was never any way of telling if there truly was only one, or still another half-dozen scattered among the apartment.

"*God*," Jane would whine, "*you're killing me here*," though that was a lie. As much as it drove Jane crazy, she loved the thrill that it gave Clair, and would dutifully scour each room top to bottom, knowing that Clair was sneaking off to rearrange the hiding places while Jane's back was turned.

"Okay, we're almost here," Amy said, snapping Jane back to the moment. The summer day returned in force: the heat off of the interlocking brick sidewalk, the drawling chatter of the Landing accent, the smell of ice cream twisting along the breeze.

Amy stopped. Jane stood beside her and looked around, but, not being familiar with the island, she wasn't sure why Amy had brought her to this particular street corner. It looked the same as every other one that they'd passed: a coffee shop (independently owned, none of the corporate sellouts for *this* tourist town, oh no), a bank, a preservation society. An old couple walking side by side down the sidewalk, a middle-aged woman with hair frizzed to high heaven, a young mother out pushing a jogging stroller, a cradled poodle with a wig.

"I don't get it," Jane said.

Amy smiled. "You're not supposed to—yet. Here"—she reached into her purse, drawing out a cheerful, cherry-patterned silk scarf—"tie this over your eyes."

"You're joking."

"Nope." She shook the scarf, as if it might entice Jane into taking it.

Jane crossed her arms over her chest. "I am not blindfolding myself in public."

"Oh, I think you will."

"Do I even want to know why you have that in your purse?"

"Now that *would* be telling," Amy said, flashing a knee-weakening grin in Jane's direction.

Jane looked down, hoping that her hair would cover the flush creeping up her cheeks. She supposed that it was her own fault—she'd kind of started it.

She snatched the scarf out of Amy's grip. Took off her glasses, tucking them into her shirt pocket. Tried to ignore the curious looks that she was drawing as she lifted the scarf in front of her own face and closed her eyes. The scarf smelled like jasmine and turpentine—like Clair—and the silk caressed her skin with the softest kisses. Jane fumbled to tie a knot. Warm fingers fluttered against hers, shooing them away, as Amy took over the process. A few short tugs later, and the blindfold was secure.

"This way," Amy's cheerful voice said. Her touch ran down Jane's arm until their hands were folded against each other, and then Amy lifted both of Jane's in hers. Soon Jane found herself holding the tops of Amy's shoulders, the light fabric of Amy's blouse cool underneath Jane's fiery palms.

Jane swallowed hard. The slope of Clair's shoulders, the rich pull of muscle against bone as they flexed strong and full of life. With what Jane considered to be her primary sense shut off, the rest of them jumped to attention, eager to prove themselves. The way that Amy had positioned Jane's hands, Jane's index fingers just brushed Amy's neck; the skin was baby smooth, Amy's pulse beating beneath the surface. They toddled down the sidewalk together, taking slow steps so that Jane didn't stumble. Jane's finger traced familiar lines against Amy's neck until Amy reached up and gripped her hand so hard that Jane jumped.

"Sorry," Jane muttered, though it was impossible to know if Amy had heard her, because a moment later they'd stopped, and the heavy *shunk* of a door opening broke the air.

Jane expected a bell to tinkle, announcing their arrival, but it didn't. A soft breeze wafted out, tinged with the smell of a dozen different perfumes. Jane heard the soft intake of breath that should have preceded a question, and felt from the shift of Amy's muscles that she held her finger to her lips. Their footsteps changed pitch underneath them as sidewalk was replaced by wood flooring.

"Can I take this off now?" Jane asked.

There was a grin in Amy's voice as she said, "Almost."

Jane sighed. "Amy—"

"*Al-most*," Amy said, drawing the word into two distinct syllables. "Trust me, it's worth it."

"Fine," Jane said, with far more ill humor than she actually felt. In truth, her heart was racing, though how much of that was due to the surprise, and how much was the simple chemical reaction of her hands on Clair's (not Clair's) shoulders, it was impossible to say.

"All right," Amy said. She came to a stop, Jane came to a stop. Jane tried not to feel a flush of disappointment as Amy stepped out from underneath her grip. "Ready?"

Jane nodded. She felt Amy move behind her, the gentle tug as she undid Jane's blindfold. She was warm at Jane's back, her hand rubbing Jane's arm as she drew away the scarf. Her voice came softly in Jane's ear: "Ta-daaaah."

The silk fell away. Jane opened her eyes. A panel of black, and then a blurred, almond-shaped view of the world around her, and then the room.

The room took Jane's breath away. She hurriedly put her glasses back on, taking in the details.

They were in the middle of an art gallery. A large space with a domed ceiling high overhead, pale wood underfoot. The walls, solid white, had tastefully spaced paintings of a variety of sizes and styles. Interior walls divided the room like a maze of cubicles, the better to utilize the otherwise empty floor space.

Jane grinned. "You didn't."

"Oh, I did." Amy grabbed a tiny plate off of the tray of a passing waiter: three grapes, two canapés, several waferlike disks of pale pink and green. Amy popped a grape for herself, then passed the plate to Jane. "Canapé?"

It was all that Jane could do to keep from laughing. She and Clair had a ritual: whenever Jane had gotten into a funk from overworking herself, Clair would drive her out to the most self-important art show she could find. Clair's work as Assistant Curator at the museum gave her an inside edge into the gallery world, and she always knew exactly which ones to bring Jane to. Sometimes they were actually good: pieces that shocked Jane, pieces that used color and texture in ways that she didn't expect, or amateur artists where you took *one look* and knew they were destined for greatness. But more often than not, Clair tried to find the shows that would amuse the hell out of Jane. Poor copies of the world's greatest artists, or abstract art that took the concept of an installation piece just a little too far, or still Jane's personal favorite: the one show they went to, shortly after their wedding, that was nothing but paintings of the same porcelain doll from fifteen different angles. The doll itself was one of those creepy

Victorian-style girls that you could find on the Home Shopping Network, and the artist hadn't changed the background or the lighting or *any* piece of the setup from painting to painting. Its eyes stared out like satanic pools, its mouth slightly parted as it smiled at you.

"*See, it's about the futility of modern commerce,*" Clair had said, as the two of them stood in front of the fourth painting and tried to look as if they were taking it Very Seriously.

"*It's about the desperation of being alone at two in the morning,*" Jane said.

"*The tragedy of a maxed-out credit card: only being able to afford one doll.*"

"*Do you choose the doll, though, or the genuine carbon steel knife set?*"

"*Oh, the doll, always,*" Clair said. "*It's far more lethal.*"

This was the point when Jane had dissolved into unstoppable giggles, the two of them rushing for the bathroom so that they could calm down away from the scrutiny of the beady-eyed old ladies running the show.

The memory of it brought a sad smile to Jane's face.

As if sensing the melancholy turn, Amy took one of the pastel wafers from her plate and held it up to Jane's mouth. Amy did her best to keep her fingers from touching Jane's lips, but as the minty confection hit Jane's tongue, the softest brush of skin passed between them. Something deep in Jane's core stirred, a slumbering thing half-roused from its hibernation.

"Ready?" Amy asked, smiling at Jane as if this was all the most natural thing in the world.

A sense of calm settled over Jane. *Ready.* For the first time in a long time, she felt like she actually was.

"BUT WHAT'S IT *REALLY* LIKE?" JANE ASKED.

It was several hours later. Amy had led Jane through the gallery, which was a seemingly random mishmash of local artists and featured pieces that were both profoundly beautiful and incredibly twee. They'd exited in high spirits just as the sun was beginning to set, and after poking around some local shops, they'd found themselves standing in front of the most incongruous restaurant imaginable: a steakhouse, surrounded by the sea.

It took only a single shared grin for them to decide to step inside. They entered and were promptly seated at a table in the corner. A light crowd filled the place, mostly locals from the looks of it, while a single musician sat on a bar stool in the corner under the bright lights, crooning and strumming his acoustic guitar. Now they had ordered, and were waiting for their appetizers, glasses of iced tea sweating between them.

Jane tore a straw out of its wrapper as she waited for Amy to reply. She'd drawn an artist's interpretation of Amy's powers a hundred times over, but had never been happy with the result. It had always felt too pat, too cliché. Amy's eyes closing, then a swirling, fade-to-dream effect across the bulk of the page, a faint image emerging in one long panel along the bottom. These drawings had never made it into the comic. Jane had scrapped them every time, choosing instead to let Mindsight relay what she had learned. Some critics lambasted Jane for her choice; while, conversely, there was a popular fan theory that Mindsight's powers were something entirely different, and the whole "empath" story was a clever ruse to fool either the reader or the rest of the team.

Amy smiled softly as she considered Jane's question. She looked at her hands, forever ensconced in the fingerless gloves. Her nails were freshly manicured, trimmed short and painted bleach white. The tips of her fingers were still enough to pick up senses from the world around her, but it was large amounts of contact that got her into trouble: gripping something tightly in the palm of her hand, a full-bodied hug if she wasn't wearing enough layers, falling asleep on someone else's pillow.

"It's hard to describe," Amy said finally. She picked up her fork. Pinched it between her bare fingers, held it out toward Jane. "You've heard of synesthesia, though, right? How some people see letters as different colors, or associate different tastes with sounds?"

Jane nodded. "Yeah . . . Doesn't Devin have that?"

"Exactly. Right, so, this fork? It doesn't really belong to any one person, but it kind of belongs, temporarily, to everyone that uses it. *You* see it, and it's just a fork. You can see the scuffs along the edges, the shine of the metal . . . when you touch it, it's either hot or cold, the handle is smooth and heavy. These signals are relayed through a series of nerves to your brain, and your brain understands them and processes them into words that you can express."

"Okay."

Amy turned her attention to the fork. Her eyes shifted slightly, as if she wasn't really looking *at* the fork so much as *into* it. She rubbed it idly between her fingers. "The last person that ate with this fork didn't know how to come out to his family as trans. The waitress that brought it to us is worried that her daughter might be dealing." She shuddered, setting the utensil down hastily on the table. A shrug later, and she'd brushed off whatever sensation the fork had given her. She smiled at Jane—patient, polite. "It's just *there*, the way that texture or color or smell is. And like how a smell can vary in intensity, the impressions left behind vary depending on how much time a person spent with an object, how important it was to them . . . things like that."

"And you know it all," Jane said. It wasn't a question, though a hint of awe did leave her statement open to either confirmation or rebuttal.

Amy made a noncommittal head tilt. "I know enough."

"You don't always have to be modest, you know."

"What, you mean that Clair wasn't modest?" Amy said.

Jane looked away.

No, Clair was modest all right. She never wanted coauthor credit on any of Jane's comics, no matter how many of the ideas had come from her, no matter how many times Jane had sat up late picking Clair's brain as she tried to untangle a plot twist. She took compliments simply, politely, smiling and saying a genuine "thank you," but never lingering, never wanting to then tell you how she'd done something, where she'd bought it, what had inspired her choices. She tried to give more than she took.

"I'm sorry," Amy said a moment later. "I didn't mean to—"

"It's okay," Jane said. She made herself look up, made herself look into Clair's face. Not Clair's face. She didn't have to make herself smile, though—that happened naturally, her chest loosening as she took in Amy's familiar features. "I'm glad that you're here."

A tinge of pink tinted Amy's cheeks. "I'm glad that getting away for a while is helping."

Jane shook her head. "That's not what I meant. I mean . . . just, *here*. In this world. With me. I'm glad that . . . somewhere, in some way, that there's still an Amy Sinclair. Even if she's not mine."

"Ah." Amy bit her lip. She gave Jane a tight smile, and raised her iced tea as if for a toast. "Glad to be of service."

The *clink* of their glasses coincided with the arrival of the appetizers.

"You ladies out celebrating something tonight?" their waitress asked as she set down first one and then the other enormous plate, so large that the word "plate" felt inadequate—these were more like platters, laden down with enough food for an entire family. And this, just the first course.

Jane opened her mouth to say something, but then she glanced at the waitress and remembered what Amy had said about her, how she was worried that her daughter might be dealing. The restaurant felt crowded, suddenly, this woman too close, the information too personal. She didn't *look* like she was worried about anything, except perhaps how many tips she was going to make that night, if she was going to spill any of the plates she had to juggle.

How did Amy *do* it? Live with all this insider knowledge? Look at people, and smile like she didn't know anything?

"Nah," Amy said, giving the waitress an easy smile as she shook her head. "No celebrations. Just good friends who haven't seen each other in a while."

The waitress grinned. "Then I'd say that's a celebration, after all. Let me get you something stronger," she said, nodding at their iced teas. "On the house."

Jane and Amy exchanged a look, then a shrug.

"Why not?" Amy said. "We're taking the ferry back, anyway."

The waitress laughed. "That's the spirit, darlin's. You only live once, right?"

"More or less," Jane said. She ignored the funny look the waitress gave her, her whole attention fixed on Amy. Clair's smile, Clair's blush. Amy, but not Amy. Clair, but not Clair.

You only live once, true.

Unless you live in comics.

THEY MISSED THE LAST FERRY.

It was obvious even as they were racing down the darkened streets: the ticket booth was shut down, the shutters drawn against the rain that had sprung up toward the end of dinner. A chain ran across the dock, but that didn't stop Jane and Amy from running up and pounding on the window as if somehow a magical ferry elf might pop up and summon the boat for them.

"Shit," Amy said. She banged on the window frame again for good measure, her palm slapping against the rain-soaked wood.

Jane shivered. Water was pouring down her back. Her clothes and hair were plastered against her. She could barely see through her glasses, though at this point what was the sense in taking them off? "I don't suppose there's an emergency number . . . ?"

Amy snorted. "No. They'll only operate off-schedule if the police show up, and even then they charge two hundred dollars."

"They *charge* the police?"

"Welcome to Charlotte's Landing," Amy said. She hugged herself for warmth, turning back toward the town. "I suppose that we'll just have to find someplace to stay. You can't exactly fault this place for a lack of B&Bs."

"Do you have any more cash on you?"

"Some," Amy said. "And a credit card that's almost maxed. You?"

"I guess we'll find out."

The closest was two blocks down, a three-story Victorian called the Horse and Tack. The proprietor, a middle-aged man with a port wine stain on his cheek, was none too happy about being roused just after midnight, and had little sympathy for their story about missing the last ferry.

"You say you're from around here?" he asked, as he nonetheless took the last scraps of their money. Before they could answer, he added, "Then you should know better than to stay out this late."

Jane shot him a nasty look, though Amy had the sense to look abashed. They were dripping on the man's carpet, after all.

"Don't wake my other guests," he said, his voice shooting daggers, as he handed over their key. "Top of the stairs; to the left."

It was the cheapest room in the house: an old attic-style bedroom with a slanted ceiling painted white, and a single brass bed. A bouquet of fresh daisies rested on a white end table. A stiff and overstuffed loveseat sat opposite the bed. The bathroom had a claw-foot tub with a rubber stopper, and crystal handles on the pedestal sink.

They took turns showering—Amy first, then Jane. The pounding of the rain echoed the drumming of the water against the base of the tub as Jane washed the day from her skin. She ran the shower as hot as she could stand it, the better to fight off the chill from the storm. The metal chain that held Clair's ring sparkled underneath the water and suds, brighter than brand new. Jane was flushed by the time she was done, pink contrasting sharply against the white fluff of the robe that she found on the back of the bathroom door.

Amy was sitting up in the bed when Jane emerged. Cross-legged, her own robe modestly arranged over her lap. She tossed Jane a smile as she looked up. Their clothes were already spread across the bars of the old-fashioned radiator, their shoes lined up neatly beside it.

Amy held her phone toward Jane, screen out. "What do you think?"

Without Jane's glasses, the screen was a little blurry at this distance, but Jane could still tell that it was paused on the opening shot of their go-to movie choice during all the giggly slumber parties they'd had together as teenagers.

"I was *going* to pop out and buy some ice cream and pizza rolls," Amy continued, "but aside from the fact that my clothes are out of commission, I'm still way too full from dinner."

Jane bit down on a giggle. She came around and flopped on her side of the bed. Amy had spread a fresh towel across the two pillows, to protect them from their wet hair.

"How many times do you think we watched that?" Jane asked, as Amy slid down until she was lying side by side with Jane. They tipped their heads together, the better to see the screen.

Amy made a hmming sound. "Nineteen thousand and five. Give or take."

Jane swatted Amy's leg. "Seriously."

"I *am* serious," Amy said, though the laugh in her voice betrayed her. She shrugged. "I don't know. A lot."

"We still watched it sometimes, you know," Jane said. "Me and Clair. Not often, but . . . whenever we felt nostalgic."

In fact, they'd watched it shortly before Clair's accident. A weekend earlier, maybe two. It had been ages since they'd seen it. They'd curled up on the couch, Jane on her side and Clair squeezed like a spoon behind her. A pillow propped Clair's head up just enough to see over the top of Jane.

Amy lowered the phone. "You two must have loved each other very much."

"We did," Jane said simply. "So much. You have no idea."

"When did . . . ?" Amy started, but then she trailed off. She shut her lips tight.

"What?"

Amy shook her head. "Never mind." She held the phone back up, her finger poised over the big *Play* button in the middle. "Ready?"

"I have a better idea." Jane took the phone from Amy, closing the movie. She tapped around until she found Amy's playlists, and sure enough, there was one that was exactly what Jane was looking for. Late-nineties alternative rock and grunge bands, lots of Goo Goo Dolls and Green Day and the Wallflowers mournfully crooning out their angst to melancholy guitar solos. Jane grinned as she started it up on shuffle. The sounds of their childhood broke free, and Amy was already laughing.

"Now you make me wish I *had* gone out for ice cream," Amy said.

"We didn't *always* have ice cream."

"No," Amy agreed. "But often enough."

That much was true. Like anything, the girls' sleepovers were steeped in ritual. Friday nights once a month (the most their parents would allow), almost always at Jane's house. Initially, it had been the whole pack of them: Jane and Clair and Marie and Keisha. A pile of girls tumbling into a nest of sleeping bags, giggling and shrieking to all hours of the night. Eventually, though, the others stopped coming. They feigned family obligations and stomachaches until it became obvious that it was something more. Jane and Clair never pushed them on it—in truth, everyone was happier with this new arrangement. Even within the group, it had always been Jane and Clair.

Now, Amy let out a contented sigh as she settled deeper against her pillow. "This song was always my favorite."

Jane smiled. "I know." She stared at the slanted ceiling, refurbished beams crossing overhead. "It's the song that you were thinking about as you worked up the nerve to tell me that you liked me."

"Really?" Amy said. She rolled onto her side, eyes wide and sparkling with curiosity.

"That's what you told me later. I don't know if it was playing or not—we listened to so much music during those sleepovers, remember?"

"It happened at a sleepover?"

"Just like any other," Jane said, still smiling. "Until it wasn't."

"I'd like to hear about it," Amy said. "That is . . . if you don't mind telling me. I'd understand if it upsets you."

"It doesn't upset me," Jane said, and was surprised to find that it didn't. Her memories of that night were already saturating the room like thick perfume. Every other time before when someone had tried to get Jane to talk about Clair—her friends, her mother, the grief counselor that her mother paid for—it had been like someone was stabbing Jane with a knife. She didn't even like to think about it. This night, along with so many others, had been tucked away in the trunk of her mind for more than a year, and now Jane sifted through it, lifting out the memories as if they were old photo albums. Her and Clair. Their honeymoon, their first crappy apartment, their wedding, the summer that they'd lost their virginity. This night—the start of it all.

The memory of it ached inside of her, but in a good way, a muscle stretching out after too much time being babied. Jane moved the phone to the nightstand. Their damp hair mingled on the towel that Amy had spread across the pillows earlier. They lay on their sides, face-to-face, just the narrow gap of the embroidered bedspread between them, their hands tucked up underneath their pillows. Was it a subconscious mimicry of the way they'd been on that other night, that other sleepover, or was this perhaps just a natural expression of their habits? The music continued to wash around them, low enough to talk over. Jane remembered that she had turned it down, last time, reaching to her bedside clock radio and twisting the volume knob back.

Past and present blurred together, the haze of time falling away. Amy's face, Clair's face, watching Jane expectantly. It had been up to Jane to start the last time, too.

"Well . . . it doesn't start very romantically, but we'd been talking about school," Jane said, and Amy smiled, already charmed. Jane shrugged. "There was some stupid dance coming up, and all week our friends had been gossiping and daydreaming about who would ask them out. I was just going along with it, picking the names of popular guys that everyone else kept insisting were hot, but you always balked whenever people would ask you."

"Wait . . . I remember this. It was Homecoming! You were insisting that Josh Grobeck was going to ask you."

"Did I?"

"Don't you remember? It was . . ." Amy bit her lip. "No, you wouldn't, I guess. In our world, your parents had just announced the move. This was going to be your last dance here. You didn't even know if you'd still be enrolled by then."

Jane fell silent, trying to imagine it. A budding teenager, a fresh new school year, her world abruptly yanked out from under her feet. The weeks leading up to the move, the dance looming uncertainly on the horizon.

She shook the picture out of her head. That wasn't her life, she told herself firmly. She dipped back into her own thoughts.

"Okay, so do you remember the way that the other girls kept teasing you about it? Insisting that you *had* to pick someone?"

Amy made a face. "They kept saying that if I didn't pick, then it meant that I wanted to go out with John Faulkner," she said, referring to the boy that was universally considered the worst choice in the whole school. Overweight, riddled with acne—he smelled like old socks and was always grabbing at his crotch whenever girls he liked walked by him.

"Well, anyway," Jane said, "that weekend you slept over at my house. And I was trying to make you feel better, so I admitted that I didn't like their game any more than you did." Jane smiled. "You were so surprised. You looked at me as if you were going to fall off the bed, because I had been so vocal about my choices at school. But I told you I only did that so they'd leave me alone. I said that I hated whatever his name was—Josh, I guess?"

Amy nodded.

Jane laughed softly. "See, I don't even remember that." She took a deep breath. "What I *do* remember, is that you asked me what boy I *did* want to have ask me out."

A gentle hush fell over the room. One song ended, then another began. In the real world and in memory, both, Jane fell silent, just studying the face across from her. The birthmark underneath Amy's right eye, the slope of her cheek.

The fullness of Amy's lips, as she asked, "What did you say?"

"Honestly, I panicked," Jane said, drawing herself back to the story. "I started babbling about how there were no good boys in our school, how they were all gross and rude, how maybe they would get better once we were in college. Something like that. And I remember, you just . . . it's like you shrank. Everything about you went still and small, and then it felt as if there was so much more room on the bed between us than there really was."

Jane could tell this, even in the semidarkness. They'd shut the main lights off already, had changed into their pajamas, watched their movie. Now they were just lying there, the soft glow of Jane's retro lava lamp casting moving shadows on the walls of her childhood bedroom.

"So you said, 'Why does everyone keep insisting that we need to find a boy all the time, anyway?', and later you admitted you were trying to act all cool and independent, like who even needs to get into a relationship? But I didn't hear it that way. And I didn't hear what you said next, because all of a sudden my heart was just pounding so loudly in my ears that it's like someone was playing drums in my room."

Amy smiled.

"I tried to laugh it off," Jane said. "I was like, 'Yeah, and what about if a girl doesn't even like boys?' I was ready to act all grossed out if you were, like it was all some kind of joke? But you didn't, and I guess I didn't sound very convincing about it being funny. Because first you went all quiet, but then you asked me if I thought there was something wrong with girls like that."

For the briefest moment, adult Jane shut her eyes, and teenage Jane filled up her senses. This was a moment that had always felt to Jane like it was literally suspended in time. The bedside clock was behind her, but she could see it reflecting in the mirror of her bureau, and Jane was so practiced at reading it backwards that she sometimes couldn't even tell that it was flipped. 1:46 am. It was like Jane had stepped outside of herself, trapped them both inside of a drawing. Looking down on her and Clair, lying there with expectation hidden in their faces. Jane knew, even then, that this was a moment that would define everything. Botch it, and she closed the door forever, the one that led to all her secret wishes, all the fantasies that she didn't dare ever say aloud. But if she got it right . . .

She couldn't even imagine what getting it right would look like. Did not even dare to think it. Thinking gave it form, and a shape that could be mourned if lost forever.

Jane's eyes eased open. Barely a moment had passed, Amy still watching, still waiting. Listening. She didn't know how this story ended, not the details of it anyway. The rain had picked up again, pounding on the steepled roof over their heads. It perfectly mimicked the memory of the flutter of younger Jane's heart.

For some reason when she spoke again, her voice was softer. Like some things were more naturally said in whispers. Or maybe she was lost in the memory of it, because she had spoken in a whisper then, too. "I told you no, I didn't think there was anything wrong with girls like that. I said that people should like whoever they like."

Jane's hand slid forward underneath the pillow, her fingers instinctively seeking out and hooking with Amy's. The night in her memory was so strong that it threatened to drown her, and she didn't know for sure if she was relaying young Clair's next line or not. *"It's just," Clair had said, "I don't want you to think less of me, if I tell you that maybe I'm one of them."*

"I won't," Jane said. "Clair . . . I couldn't ever think less of you."

Clair licked her lips. Took a deep breath. "Even if . . . even if I say that the girl that I like . . ."

". . . is you?" Amy whispered. Out loud, in the present.

Jane jerked, as if waking up from a dream. Her fingers unhooked from Amy's, slithering back to her own safe space underneath the pillows.

"I'm sorry!" Amy was already saying. Jane had pushed herself up onto her elbow, and Amy followed suit. Still facing each other, still inches apart. "I'm sorry," Amy said again. "I didn't mean to . . . It's just, well, you know about my powers and so when you touched my hand, I just, I assumed that you were trying to—"

"It's okay," Jane said.

Amy bit her lip. She flopped back onto the bed, her cheeks burning with embarrassment. She looked at Jane with much the same expression that Clair had, all those years ago. *I don't want you to think less of me.* "I don't tap into people's memories without their permission, I swear it."

"I know you don't," Jane said.

"I'm so sorry."

"I know you are."

Amy winced. "Are you angry with me?"

"No," Jane said, and in that moment it became true. The burst of irritation that had sprung up disappeared, blown away as if by a strong breeze. Amy/Clair, Clair/Amy. Jane could never stay angry with either of them. She smiled, twisting her wedding ring around her finger. "Do you want to hear the rest of it?"

"Always," Amy said quickly. "That is . . . if you're willing to share."

"Well . . . you already saw the best part of *that* day. I was too embarrassed to say anything, and I think you kind of took it as a rejection."

Amy's eyes widened. "You mean you didn't even kiss me?"

Jane shook her head. "Nope. We decided that it was probably for the best if we just went to sleep at that point, so you scrambled out of bed and got into your sleeping bag on the floor, and I turned off the light. I tried to go to sleep, but I just kept kicking myself for being so stupid. It's not that I didn't already know that I liked you. It's not like I was under the illusion that I was straight or something. But you were just so . . ."

"Direct?"

Jane shrugged. "Maybe." Her fingers traced the edge of her robe until they found the chain that held Clair's wedding ring. The links were warm from being against her skin. "I just kept lying there, watching hour after hour go by, and I kept telling myself: Jane, get out of this bed; go over to that girl—wake her up if you have to—and tell her how you feel." Jane dropped the necklace. She looked down at Amy. "I wanted to kiss you so badly."

Amy gave her a sympathetic smile. "But you didn't?"

"No," Jane said. "I didn't . . . But the next day, I promised myself I would never let another opportunity like that pass me by again. That from now on, if there was ever something that I wanted that badly, that I would just go for it, and to hell with the consequences."

"So, *then* you kissed me?"

"Then I kissed you," Jane agreed with a smile. "More or less."

"What's *that* supposed to mean?"

Jane went quiet. She looked at Amy: the subtle waves drying into her dark hair, the familiar angles of her face, the studded silver earrings glinting like a row of stars. The air was buzzing with comfort and nostalgia, and Jane thought about her promise to herself. She'd always lived up to it, ever since that day.

Amy was still waiting for Jane to explain herself. She had the smallest of frowns, crinkling between her eyebrows. Jane watched the skin smooth out as those same eyebrows arched in surprise when Jane leaned over.

"Why don't you find out for yourself?" Jane whispered as the last of the space disappeared between them.

UP TO LIP. BREATH TO BREATH. HEARTBEAT TO HEART-BEAT.

Time folded in on itself. Jane and Clair. The raw memory of a thousand kisses, but it all started with one. The images tumbled through Jane, disjointed and perfect:

But when I said that I liked you—

—I know. I know, I'm sorry.

Rough bark underneath Jane's fingers, smooth hair brushing over her shoulder.

Clair? Can we talk about something?

Clair's crooked smile, her lower lip caught between her teeth as she tried not to look too hopeful.

Don't just tell me what you think I want to hear.

The sparkle of the river, the shade of the tree.

The twist of Jane's stomach.

Jane . . .

Clair . . .

Their first kiss, the spark of contact. Mouths, warm and wet and awkward, trying to find their rhythm. The fear of getting caught, the fear of letting go. They mashed themselves together, driven by pure need and teenage hormones. Clair pushed Jane against the tree, and Jane caught herself against the bark to steady herself. Soft, sweet skin, and the smell of Clair's body spray, peachy and bright like summer. Jane swam through the memories, pushing them into Clair, letting them guide the two of them along.

Their first kiss, again, more than fifteen years later. The same spark of contact. Mouths versed in what they were doing. The fear of stopping, the fear of what they'd started. Lips as familiar as the beat of Jane's own heart. Her heart, which was singing, *home, home, home!*, like the chirrup of a bird in the springtime. *Clair.* A well of heartbreak and elation burst up from Jane's chest, an unstoppable tide. *Clair, Clair, Clair.* The one thing that Jane had dreamed of for a year and a half, the one thing she'd known she could never have again. Jane kissed her as if she was a miracle. She kissed her as if she was the last breath of life that she would ever taste. Clair arched underneath her, a whimper escaping as Jane's lips trailed down to her neck, her shoulder, her collarbone. Fingers traced familiar pathways up Clair's legs, across her stomach.

"Jane . . ."

"Clair . . ."

Jane's hand roved, but Clair's grip found her wrist. The whole of Clair had stilled underneath her; even Clair's breath had caught and started up again slower. Jane sat back, blinking, as if coming out of a daze. Clair's lips were flushed, and Jane's ached at their absence.

Jane frowned. "What's wrong?"

"I'm not Clair."

Another blink. This time the daze actually *did* fall away, and Jane's vision cleared for perhaps the first time all evening. Amy's face, both familiar and not, was looking up at her: flushed cheeks and tossled hair, hurt and sad and longing. Jane let her gaze trail down, the slip of their robes falling open, Jane's hand tucked underneath the terrycloth. She yelped, jerking her touch back as if she'd awoken to find herself with her hand in the fire. She sat up, turning away, cinching her robe tight. Her whole body seared with embarrassment and lingering desire and anger at the part of herself that was wishing that Amy had never said anything. She buried her face in her hands.

The shift of the bed behind her as Amy sat up. Not Clair,

but—spousal instinct painted an exact picture of Amy's movements, as she reached out, clearly wanting to put a hand on Jane's
shoulder, and then pulled herself back. Amy's arms wrapped
around her own legs instead, her knees drawn to her chest.

"Jane . . . I'm sorry."

"Don't be. I'm . . . I should apologize to you, I—"

"I wish that I *was* Clair," Amy said, and Jane's breath caught
in her chest. Amy sighed. "I shouldn't have said that. Please try
to forget that I said that."

Jane's voice came out tiny. "I can't."

Time slipped past. Eventually, Jane realized that Amy's phone
was still playing music, all the hits from their early teenage years.
She snatched it off the nightstand and swiped at it until it shut
up, plunging them into impenetrable silence. Even the rain had
stopped. The bed-and-breakfast held its breath.

I wish that I was *Clair.* The words tumbled through Jane's head
on a terrible loop, Clair's voice, Amy's words, until Jane's mouth
soured, her lips twisting in distaste.

Well, you're not.

"We should get some sleep," Jane said.

"I'll take the couch," Amy said.

"No," Jane said. She was already on her feet by the time the
word was out. She tugged her robe tighter around her body. "I'll
take the couch."

She was expecting another argument. Clair, Jane was sure,
would have argued the point further. Instead, Jane watched the
reflection in the bureau as Amy nodded. Jane looked away, fresh
shame burning through her as she settled on the stiff cushions of
the loveseat. She faced away from the room, faded roses filling
her view and the cloying smell of Febreeze assaulting her nose.

Not Clair.

Never Clair.

16

IN THE MORNING, THEY DIDN'T SPEAK. THEIR CLOTHES
had dried, and they took turns getting dressed. Amy spent the
morning on her phone, typing and reading in a manner to indicate that she was texting someone back and forth. They checked
out at the front desk in silence, walked to the docks in silence,
took the ferry in silence.

Cal was already waiting for them. SUV idling in the parking
lot, windows rolled up tight. Cold air and heavy beats pounded
against Jane as she opened the door. Jane climbed in, clicking
her seatbelt firmly in place.

"Morning," Jane made herself mumble. After so much silence,
it was hard to speak at all. Jane's tongue felt awkward in her
mouth, like it was going to trip over itself if she attempted whole
sentences.

Cal grunted. His fingers stretched and then gripped the steering wheel harder. His eyes were hidden behind his sunglasses,

despite the cloud layer still hanging fat and threatening across the morning skyline. Jane turned away from him, feeling oddly chastised.

He drove them back to the Maxwells' house. Amy disappeared inside without a word. Jane tried not to watch her go, and failed. Amy's skirt was wrinkled from the rainstorm, and her hair had dried in wavy chunks. Light and hope seemed to disappear with her, the sky darkening even more as the door shut in her wake.

"Come on," Cal said gruffly. "We're behind schedule."

He spun his keys around his finger before tucking them into his pocket, like some cowboy showing off as he holstered a gun. He rounded the house, heading for a different entrance.

Jane had no choice but to follow. She jogged to catch up; Cal wasn't waiting for her. Around the back of the house, he followed a narrow set of cement steps hidden behind a hydrangea bush. A secure metal door stood at the bottom, with a keypad that Cal *punched* the sequence into—never before had Jane seen someone take so much aggression out on a number pad. She worried that he would fritz something out, but a moment later the light on the keypad turned green, and the door clicked open.

He tore through the hallway, past the bunkers, to the weapons testing room that they'd been using as a gym. He gathered a set of paddles and tossed Jane some hand wraps. A moment later he was poised and ready, and he gave her a curt nod. "Begin."

For a while, Jane tried to ignore his odd mood. They needed to focus, after all. The fate of their lives, and perhaps the whole city, hung in the balance—it was hardly the time or the place to be worried about personal issues. And okay, maybe guilt at having wasted the day before was gnawing at Jane, just a little.

So Jane focused on the familiar moves. The punches, the dodges, the bursts of light to distract Cal from landing his occasional counterattack. It felt good to use her muscles, to work up a sweat. To shut down her conscious thoughts for a while. Jane couldn't claim that she had *forgotten* about the shame and embarrassment of the night before, no, but it had, at least, retreated to a smaller corner of her mind.

"No, no, *no!*" Cal said, as Jane's fist connected with his paddle.

"You're still throwing yourself off-balance as you punch. How many times, Jane? You want to plant your feet, and use your whole *body*."

"Right," Jane said. "Sorry."

"'Sorry' isn't going to save your life," Cal snapped. "What if you're jumped in the streets, huh? What if you *need* to defend yourself, and you can't, because you're *not paying attention*?"

"Okay, okay! Jesus, Cal. It's not a big deal."

"Right," Cal said with a huff. "Like how disappearing yesterday wasn't a big deal."

"What are you talking about?"

"Do you have any idea how frantic I went, looking for you? You vanish without a note, without a text, without a *word*, and I'm—"

"I didn't *vanish*. I was with Amy."

"*I didn't know that!*"

"Oh, well." Jane crossed her arms. "Excuse me, *mother*, I didn't realize that I needed to inform you when I left the house."

"That's not the point," Cal said. "This is a dangerous situation, and I can't *protect* you if I don't know where you are!"

"Yes—okay, I get that. But, honestly, what do you really think is going to happen to me *here*? It's like the safest place in the country."

Cal sneered. "*Safe*. You think you're safe? You think that *Jane* didn't think she was safe?"

"I—" Jane started, but then she bit down on what she was going to say, and shook her head instead. "That's different."

"How? Because she had even *more* training than you do? Because her powers were even *stronger* than yours? She wasn't able to protect herself. *Think* about that, Jane!"

Jane jumped back. In Cal's frustration, he'd ripped off the paddles and thrown them across the gym floor. He wasn't looking at her. He just stood there, breathing hard, grabbing fistfuls of his short hair until it stood up all on its own.

Jane opened her mouth. Shut it again. The waves coming off Cal—Jane would almost be tempted to describe it as dread, if she didn't know him better.

She cleared her throat. Tried again. "Cal . . . I don't—"

"Do you have any idea how worried I was?" He looked up now, his gaze pinning her in place. There was something in the way that he was watching her, the turn at the corner of his eyes . . . naked fear splayed across his Hollywood features, more raw and real than anything Jane remembered seeing from him since they were kids.

Jane tucked a stray lock of hair behind her ear as she looked away. It was in this momentary distraction that Cal rushed forward. She did not see him, not until he was right there. Not until he was pushing her back, not until he was literally in her face. He shoved her against the wall, and kissed her hard.

The shock of it held her in place for a moment. A deep mammalian instinct, of fear, locking up her thoughts. She felt out-of-body. She saw the scene as if she was watching from the shadows: the empty gym stretching out around them, paddles discarded on the floor; Cal and Jane, off in the corner of the frame, pinned as if in a lovers' embrace.

Rage sprang forth from somewhere deep in Jane's core. Power ripped through her, harder than she was used to, as she blasted him away. Her hands were stinging as he staggered back—he tripped over the paddles, falling to his ass, his mouth open in an *O* of surprise.

"What the *hell*, Cal?"

Jane's hands glowed as she wiped her mouth off, perfectly illuminating every crease of disgust upon her face.

"What do you mean, 'What the hell'?" Cal asked. He sprang to his feet. "What's *wrong* with you?"

"Wrong with *me*?"

"Yes!" Cal said. "You're acting like we've never done that before."

"Because we *haven't*!"

Cal frowned. "Well . . . no, I suppose, *technically*—I mean, not you and *me*, but . . . but . . . I mean, your Cal—"

"Oh God," Jane said. Dizziness overwhelmed her, and she had to crouch down, tucking her head between her knees just to keep from passing out. An image of the birth control pills that she'd found in her bathroom flooded her mind. The idea of her double being straight was bad enough, but *Cal*?

Cal snorted. "Way to flatter a guy, Jane," he said, as if reading her mind.

Jane forced down the knot in her gut as she stood up. "Cal, listen to me: whatever you had going on with this Jane . . . I mean, it's none of my business, but—"

"Of course it's your business. You're her, she's you." Cal stepped closer, and Jane's blood pressure spiked. She raised her hands, still wrapped from her training session, but Cal ignored them. He stepped right between them, as he brushed back the stray lock of Jane's hair with the back of his fingers.

"Jane," he said, "don't you see? We're meant to be together."

"No. We're not."

Cal smirked. Undeterred. He lowered his voice as he leaned in, somewhere halfway between a purr and a growl. "How can you say that?"

"Because I'm a *fucking* lesbian, for one!" Jane said. She shoved him again, though this time he was prepared, planted in front of her. Her efforts did nothing.

Cal threw his head back. A bark of laughter bounced off of the gym ceiling. He was already grinning when he looked back at her. "No you're not."

"Yes," Jane said, "I *am*."

A single moment, frozen in time. A whole page, just Cal's blank face. He stared at her, his lips slightly parted, as if he wanted to speak but couldn't quite form coherent sentences. A speech bubble, empty save for an ellipsis.

Finally, he blinked. "Wait, are you serious?"

Jane nodded. She crossed her arms, hugging herself. A wave of sympathy passed through her at the thought that she'd just crushed his dreams—then a flare of irritation rode in on its wake, that she'd fallen prey to the societal idea that she needed to *apologize* for not having interest in a man.

Cal shook his head, like he couldn't quite process this. "That's . . . This is . . ."

"A fact?" Jane offered.

"—so *hot*," Cal finished. He caught her eye again, a grin splitting his face. "Hey, do you think that maybe once we find the real Jane, the two of you could . . . you know . . . ?"

"*Excuse* me?"

Cal shrugged. "Can't blame a guy for dreaming."

"Actually, I can." Jane stared at him in disgust. She needed a shower, just to get the pervy off her.

She started to turn away, but Cal caught her by the elbow. "Aw, come on. You can't mean to tell me you've *never* made out with a girl to impress a guy."

"Cal!"

"What?"

"I don't . . . I can't *believe* you right now! Do you even hear yourself when you talk?"

Cal scowled. "Don't be such a prude, Main Jane. I'm not asking much. Just, you know, a bit of a show. Maybe tops off? Nothing serious."

"Oh my *god*," Jane said. She turned away, starting to storm off. Cal was already on her heels, wrapping his fat man-fingers around her arm. "Get *off* of me!"

"No. After all I've done for you, you owe me. I'm not taking 'no' for an answer."

A surge billowed in Jane's chest. "*Fuck off!*" she shouted, her powers coursing through her so hard that it left a ringing in her ears.

Except, that's the thing: it wasn't just ringing in her ears. In the instant just before she spoke, a current of rage had exploded out of Jane, pulsing through the air. The speakers of the gym buzzed, her voice amplified and pounding out of them with a squeal like it was from a microphone. Their phones chimed in their pockets, the control panel on the wall for the security system beeped rapidly, and a laptop that Cal had sitting on a nearby bench flicked on, as every screen in the room, right down to Cal's smartwatch, displayed two repeating words: fuck off, fuck off, fuck off, fuck off, fuck—

"Holy shit," Jane breathed.

Cal laughed. He pulled his phone out, turning it around for Jane to see the words repeated there, too.

Jane stepped back, uncertain. "What . . . what just happened?"

"It worked," Cal said with a grin. He rolled his eyes. "What, did you think I really *meant* all that crap? You wound me, Main

Jane." He put his hand over his heart in mock-pain. "No, I just needed to get you good and pissed. I've been thinking about it, and that's how our Jane's powers kicked into higher gear. I figured it couldn't hurt to try."

"Wait, that was . . . ," Jane sputtered, as she pulled her own phone out, the same *fuck off* message filling her screen. "Holy shit."

Cal clapped Jane on the shoulder. "Welcome to the big league," he said, still grinning. "Now. How about we head back to Grand City and kick some UltraViolet ass?"

THEY RETURNED TO HEADQUARTERS, BACK IN GRAND CITY.

Amy took her own car, the one that she'd driven up to the islands, while Cal and Jane rode back in uncomfortable silence. Cal hummed along to the music, tapping his hands, offering Jane the occasional stop for a bathroom break or a cheap burger, all of which Jane declined.

She stared out the window nearly the whole time, but what she saw wasn't the passing landscape. Instead, she was lost in her own memory. She kept going over what had happened in the gym: the smack of her fists against the paddles, the kiss that had startled her into action, Cal's leering face as he'd said all those horrible, perverted things. Okay, so he claimed that he hadn't meant any of it, but . . . how much of "it" hadn't he meant? That he and Jane had been together? That he wanted her to make out for his own entertainment? Or just how pushy he was about it?

Grudgingly, though, she had to admit that his technique had been effective. Every time that Jane remembered it, she could feel another piece of her powers itching to come back to life. She still wasn't ready to try using it again—and didn't know how good of an idea that would be, anyway, in a moving vehicle on the highway, one that was modern and full of electronics—but she knew that, whatever had awoken, it wasn't a fluke.

Traffic was light, so the trip took less time than usual. Jane breathed a sigh of relief as they pulled into the underground parking garage. She scrambled out of the car before Cal even finished cutting the engine.

They were scheduled to meet in the command room. Amy's car was already there, though Amy herself was gone. Still, Jane hurried up the elevator, leaving Cal behind to catch the next one. It wasn't until Jane saw the empty car that she realized how badly she wanted to talk to Amy. Which probably didn't make any sense, given what had happened between them, but . . . old impulses die hard.

The elevator reached the top, and Jane pushed herself through the doors as they were still opening. Amy was a distant smudge at the end of the hall, shuffling along with her shoulders slumped.

"Amy! Wait up!"

There was probably no reason for Amy to listen, but she did anyway, slowing and then finally stopping as she waited for Jane's footsteps to catch up.

They picked up side by side. Silence ran taut between them.

"Listen," Jane said finally, "I'm sorry about—about what happened at the B&B. I didn't—"

"Don't. It was as much my fault as anything. It's . . . it's just hard sometimes. You have all these memories of the two of us, and . . ." She let out a nervous laugh. "I guess I'm jealous. Isn't that weird? *My* Jane never felt that way about me, but God, I did. I never told anyone that before. But I did."

Jane looked down. Her wedding ring was on the wrong hand, but still there, a touchstone that Jane could retreat to any time she needed it. Her memories, too—for so long, Jane felt the pain of them whenever she looked back, but now she realized how much better it was to have them. This other life, this other version of herself . . . Jane couldn't even imagine it. Loving Clair had been the foundation of Jane's entire existence. She couldn't remember a time when she didn't love Clair.

"You're sure that your Jane doesn't feel the same?" Jane asked.

Amy snorted. "Oh, I'm sure. Though, actually . . . ," she trailed off, shook her head.

"What?" Jane asked.

"Nothing—never mind."

"Amy."

"I *said*, 'Never mind.'"

Jane reached out and touched Amy's shoulder without

thought or planning. The gesture came as natural as breathing, and it stilled the two of them in their walk.

"You know that you can tell me anything," Jane said. "Don't you?"

A sad smile crossed Amy's face. She avoided looking at Jane as she said, "You really don't want to hear it."

"Then that'll be my problem. Now, tell me."

Amy looked down, staring at the lines of her fingers as they poked out from her fingerless gloves. She shrugged, like it didn't even matter.

"It's just that I've always assumed that I was in love with Jane, but in fact . . . I realized a few years ago that it was more the *idea* of Jane that I was in love with. Who she *could* be. I used to have these dreams about her that were just—oh, they were *perfect*. She was perfect. Then I would wake up, and she'd be different, and eventually I realized that the woman from my dreams wasn't really Jane, and I had to accept that. No matter what, I had to accept that."

Amy fell silent. She turned her hands over, her trapped palms making the gloves damp with sweat.

"The thing is . . . ," Amy continued, still not looking up. She hesitated, half a breath waiting on her lips. "Ever since you got here . . . the more I get to know you . . . It's not *my* Jane that I dreamed of."

The words hit Jane like the pummeling force of Windforce's gusts. She closed her eyes, turned away. She didn't want to, but—dammit, she couldn't help it. The last twenty-four hours had been filled with so many emotional wringers, so many different pulls of her heart, that she just didn't know if she could take it anymore. She wanted to curl up in bed, not go to this meeting. Wanted to pull the covers over her head, snuggle down, block out the world until there was nothing left but the safety of her dreams.

Her dreams . . .

"I'm sorry," Amy was already saying from behind her. Her words tumbled out fast, tripping over each other. "I know that this isn't anything that you want to hear, and I can only imagine how painful this must be for you, I just—I just can't keep it to myself any longer. And I'm not expecting you to reciprocate, I mean, I get it, I'm not *Clair*. So it's okay, you know, if you'd rather—"

"Dreams," Jane said, as she opened her eyes. She turned back, her heart racing. Why hadn't she seen it before?

A pert little frown was wrinkling Amy's brow. "What?"

"You said that you saw me in your dreams. *Me*-me, not your Jane. You saw my life?"

"Um . . . sort of. Well, really just you, but . . . Why?"

"Come with me," Jane said. She took Amy's hand, guiding her down the hallway.

"Jane? What's—I'm sorry, but what's going on? Where are we going?"

"We need to get the others," Jane said, still not stopping. "If we're very, very lucky . . . I may have just figured out how we're going to beat UltraViolet."

17

"I'M SORRY, YOU WANT TO DO WHAT?"

Jane looked around the table of the command room, all the skeptical faces staring back at her. She adjusted her glasses, steadying herself. "I want to go back to my world, in order to retrieve Clair's journal."

Keisha raised an eyebrow. Devin frowned. Marie scowled. Tony looked on, amused. Cal just watched. This meeting wasn't going exactly how Jane had pictured it.

"Wait, I'm confused," Keisha said. "Who's Clair, again?"

Amy raised a tentative hand. "That's me. In the other world. Apparently, I hated the name 'Amy.'"

"The you that's dead," Keisha said, clarifying.

"The you that's a lesbian," Tony added, a chuckle just off the side of his voice.

Amy flushed as she looked away.

It shouldn't have surprised Jane, that neither of them were "out" in this world. Still, it had been weirder than weird, to stand there at the beginning of the meeting and explain about Clair, about their marriage. Several of the Heroes hadn't quite been able to look Jane in the eye since.

"Look, none of that's the point," Jane said. "Clair and Amy . . . I think they dreamed about each other's lives. *That's* how I got everything right when I started to draw the comics. Clair told me so many details, and we hashed out almost all the plots together."

"Okay . . . ," Keisha started, "that's all well and good, but what does that have to do with anything? Clair can't exactly dream you a solution if she's . . . I'm sorry, but if she's dead."

"Unless she dreamed of your future," Jane said.

Keisha shook her head. "Right. Now you've lost me."

"Actually," Marie said, "that kind of makes sense. Interdimensional travel has a slight time distortion *anyway*."

"It does?"

Marie shrugged. "A couple of hours, usually. Maybe a day or so. But yeah."

"Sure, of course," Devin said, chiming in. He tugged at his hair and sat up a little straighter, enthusiasm lending him buoyancy. "And if Clair had a low-level empathic sense—"

"One that she likely wouldn't even be aware of, if it's that small—"

"—then it's not going to be refined. She could have been picking up pieces of Amy's life, rippling back in time from the future—Oh! Amy wasn't even *aware* of Clair until recently! Once she was, that would have strengthened the link!"

"Making the connection even greater, and more accurate! Which then would have gone *backward*, right along the line of causality—"

"—and given Clair a series of premonitions straight to her dreams! God, that's so cool!"

"Wicked cool," Marie agreed. She turned to Jane. "How far into our future did she see, do you think?"

Jane started, thrown by the shift in Marie and Devin's attention. "Um . . . well, she definitely saw Doctor Demolition's weapon test, so she got pretty close to now."

"But she didn't say anything about you coming here?" Devin asked. "Not a word about UltraViolet?"

"We knew UltraViolet was the real villain behind Doctor Demolition," Jane said. "But . . . no, nothing about any of *this*. But she didn't always tell me everything immediately. Which is why I want to get her journal. She wrote all of her dreams down, as soon as she woke up. Always has."

"But we already *have* a plan," Tony said. "Cal said that you'd managed to focus your powers enough to access lower frequencies."

Jane sighed. "I *did*, but . . . Tony, that's a long way from being able to stop UltraViolet. We don't even know when she's going to strike. We might not have time for me to improve. What we *need* is more information. Clair might be able to provide that."

"Yeah, but—"

"Hang on," Cal said. He'd raised his hand, interrupting, and now he looked heavily across the table at Jane. "Look, I'm not going to pretend to understand everything that's been said here, but . . . all other issues aside, let's focus on the most important question. You think there's a chance it'll work?"

Silence hung in the air. Jane pressed her hand flat on the table, grounding herself.

"I think that I have to try," Jane said. "Because I'm going to say what everyone else is afraid to: there's no guarantee that my powers are going to stop UltraViolet's weapon. If there's any chance that Clair's dreams can show us what's going to happen, then we need to take advantage of that."

The room went quiet again, as they considered this. Clearly, nobody wanted to hear what Jane had said, but—going by their ducked heads, the way that Devin picked at his fingernails, the way that Keisha frowned at her phone—neither were they willing to argue the point.

Finally, Cal nodded. "All right," he said, and Jane knew that the matter was settled. Despite the skepticism still visible on some of their faces, they would never argue with Cal once he'd made up his mind. "But I don't want you going in there alone. Someone needs to be there to watch your back."

"I'll do it," Amy said.

"Um, are you sure that's such a good idea?" Marie asked. "I mean, if you're supposed to be dead . . . ?"

"I'll go as Mindsight. I won't get caught, I promise."

The table shared a look, clearly uncertain.

Cal shrugged. "It's fine by me. Jane?"

Jane looked at Amy. An unspoken exchange took place between them; it wasn't just Cal that was asking if this was all right.

A part of Jane wanted to say "no," of course she did. What would it be like, to bring Amy back there? For that matter, what would it be like to go in the first place?

In the end, though, it didn't really matter what it would be like, how hard it might prove to be. Because Cal was right: she shouldn't go alone. And Amy was right: given the options . . . she really was the only choice.

Jane nodded.

"Then it's settled," Cal said. He slapped his palm on the table as he stood up, as if he was sealing the deal. "Good luck, you two. I hope you find what you're looking for."

JANE AND CLAIR'S APARTMENT, SEEN FROM ABOVE AS IF it was a model: the place is long and narrow ("Like a shoebox," Jane sometimes muttered; "Like a train," Clair countered), each room leading way to the next and then the next, so that by the time you reached the bedroom you'd already traversed the living room/dining room combo, the lithe strip of a kitchen, and the travel-sized bathroom. Space was not efficient. Walls jutted where they shouldn't, and built-in shelves cut off huge swaths of otherwise usable floor space. The building had once been a townhouse for wealthy aristocrats, only to have been sold off and carved into tiny pieces at the turn of the last century. Jane and Clair's landlord was the son of the man that bought the house from the last line of the oil tycoons and bankers and newspaper moguls that had been trading it back and forth for generations.

The rooms were dark when Jane eased open the door. Pale moonlight spilled in through the high, north-facing windows that ran along one whole side of the apartment—their top-floor slice of the building was against the outside wall of the house, and during the day it was flooded with gorgeous, artistic light that bounced off of the pale walls and original wood flooring.

"Watch your step," Jane whispered as she moved through the door and stood aside for Amy, as Mindsight, to follow. It was decided that it would be best for this extraction to take place clandestinely, rather than have to take the time to explain Jane's absence to anyone that she might encounter. She left the lights off, letting herself through the apartment on muscle memory. Plus, it was just as well that Jane couldn't see all the details of her old life—her real life, Jane corrected herself. The living room still had framed pictures of her and Clair on their wedding day, their graduations, the day that Jane started working at QZero. Jane shoved them out of her mind as she moved through to the kitchen.

Her landlord hadn't sold her possessions, then. Someone must have been in since she'd left, to pay the rent in her absence, to empty the fridge and clean the dishes in the sink. She could just picture her mother (her real mother, Jane thought with a pang of longing), rolling up her sleeves and making sure that, wherever her daughter was, her apartment would still be waiting for her when she got back. So at least Ms. Holloway hadn't given up hope of seeing Jane again. Or maybe she was just in deep denial. That was also possible.

The bedroom had received a similar treatment. Jane's dirty laundry had been gathered up from the heaps on the floor, washed and folded and returned not *quite* to their proper places in her dresser, but close enough. The bed was made, one of the few times since Clair's death. Jane ran her hand over the quilt, a gift that Clair's great-aunt had made for them. The smells of Jane's apartment, of her life with Clair, were thick in the air. Jane closed her eyes, breathing it in. Fabric softener and jasmine perfume, coconut shampoo and the faintest traces of turpentine. It filled Jane's chest to bursting.

Jane forced her eyes open. In the darkness of her bedroom, she moved around to Clair's side and opened the top drawer of the nightstand.

Nothing had been packed away since Clair died. Not a single sock thrown out, nor a single jacket donated to charity, nor a single keepsake tucked into a box of mementos. Clair's hand lotion still sat beside the lamp, the book that she was reading still bookmarked as if she'd be right back to it. This stubborn hold was the biggest point of contention between Jane and her mother, and the one thing that Jane would not budge about with her grief counselor. No matter how many times she was told it was unhealthy, obsessive, wallowing—it didn't matter. Jane left her apartment untouched, a shrine to a better life. Her existence in the eighteen months since then was carved out in tiny corners, taking up as little space as possible, as if disturbing anything would break the spell.

She hadn't even opened this drawer, until today.

Clair's journal was right on top. Clair had a thing for note-books, though she wasn't a casual hoarder. Each one that she added to her collection was carefully chosen. Novelty notebooks from Barnes & Noble or the stationery aisle at Walmart wouldn't do, oh no. Nor, either, would Clair accept Moleskines, or the latest trend for bullet journals or day planners. She never ordered them online. Each book was selected by hand, in back-corner shops or used bookstores or pilfered from estate sales. Clair needed to hold them, to breathe in the smell of them, to feel the texture of the paper. To see if they *spoke* to her. Jane had learned a long time ago not to buy them for her as gifts.

And yet, that's exactly what this one was, Clair's last journal. Jane's hands trembled as she lifted it out, remembering the day that she'd spotted it. She was on her way to meet up with Clair for lunch when the sky opened up and a downpour rushed the city, sending everyone scurrying for shelter. Jane had ducked into a novelty shop, the bell tinkling overhead to announce her arrival.

"Fierce out there, isn't it?" the shopkeeper had said. Jane had only nodded, not even turning around. She was staring out of the window, watching the streaks of rain, tempted to dig out her sketchbook and copy the patterns.

When Jane spotted the notebook a few minutes later—browsing through racks of scented candles and dream catchers and beaded necklaces, because it seemed rude not to at least pretend that she might buy something while she waited out the rain—she didn't even question it. There was something *familiar* about the book, and for a while Jane worried that maybe Clair had already bought herself a copy, maybe this exact book was sitting back in their apartment right now. Still, Jane paid for it, and by the time she was done the rain had stopped, the clouds pulling back as suddenly as they'd appeared. The street outside was sparkling in the fresh sunshine, as if diamonds hung from the leaves and rimmed the overhang of apartments and restaurants.

She gave it to Clair at lunch that very day. Sitting out on the sidewalk, at a table mopped dry by the proprietor. Clair smiled as she drew it out of the bag, but then she saw it and her face froze as if someone had pressed pause on her.

"I can return it if it's not right for you," Jane said, knowing how Clair felt about this sort of thing. "It's no big deal." She was already reaching across the table for it, when Clair drew back.

"No," Clair said. The force of her voice surprised Jane. Clair clutched the notebook to her chest. "Don't return it. I love it."

"You're sure?"

Clair nodded, her smile returning. "I'm sure. It's perfect."

Perfect. Jane opened the notebook now, in her darkened bedroom. A paper fluttered to the floor, which Jane retrieved and tucked absently into a pocket on her uniform. Even in the dim light, she could see the inscription that she'd added to the notebook that day in the café, after she'd made sure that Clair had liked it. Clair's great-aunt had instilled the idea that you should never give someone a book without making it personal, and so Jane had pulled out her favorite drawing pen from her bag and cracked open the spine. She doodled a quick pigeon on the inside cover, and then across from that: *To my perfect Clair, with love. May all your dreams come true.*

MINDSIGHT WAS SITTING ON THE COUCH WHEN JANE RETURNED TO THE LIVING ROOM.

"All right, let's get out of—" Jane started, but cut herself off as she spotted the look on Mindsight's face. "What's wrong?"

Mindsight just sat there, rooted in place. Her eyes, tucked

behind her mask, were wide as if trying to tell Jane a thousand things at once, none of which Jane understood.

"Oh, don't mind her," a voice said from behind Jane. Digitized, its tone obscured. Nonetheless, it was unmistakable. "She's been instructed that if either of you say a word, you'll both be killed."

Jane whirled. A shimmering haze stood behind her, woman-shaped and vaguely purple. UltraViolet's face, as usual, was obstructed, as if Jane's eyes couldn't quite bring themselves into focus. Still, Jane *tried*. There was something maddening about UltraViolet, something that gnawed on Jane's subconscious. If she only had more light—though of course Jane knew from experience that due to whatever tricks UltraViolet used, light didn't help the matter.

UltraViolet held out her hand. A purple glove resolved itself, the only clear part of her appearance.

"I'm not going to waste time," UltraViolet said. "Give me the book, and you can both walk out of here alive."

Jane's grip tightened as a fierceness in her chest stirred. "No."

"Ah-ah-ah." UltraViolet stuck up a finger and tipped it back and forth like a metronome. "What did I say about talking? Now, let's try this again: Give me the book."

Her palm turned back up, flattening out. Open and waiting.

Jane knew what the real Captain Lumen would do: strike first, while UltraViolet felt that she still had the upper hand. Of course, the real Captain Lumen would have also brought backup with her, in case this very thing happened. Because the real Captain Lumen would have thought ahead. The real Captain Lumen would have never cut herself off from help like this, literally worlds away from everything that kept them safe.

"What are you going to do with it?" Jane asked. She spoke in a rush, in case UltraViolet decided to actually follow through on her threat.

UltraViolet shrugged. "I'm in a reading slump, and this one has such stellar reviews."

Jane blinked. "Uh . . ."

"Wow, you really are bad at this, aren't you?" UltraViolet said. "Look, what part of this don't you understand? Last chance:

the book, or your lives. I'm taking one. Be glad I'm letting you choose which."

Mindsight's voice, strong behind Jane: "Don't do it, Captain."

"Shut up!" UltraViolet snapped, as she leaned over to see the couch. "Did I ask you?"

It was all the distraction Jane needed.

She threw the journal high into the air. The motion drew UltraViolet's attention back, giving Mindsight the opening that *she* needed to leap to her feet and whip her revolver out. Jane ducked, as Mindsight fired through where Jane's head had been only moments earlier.

Jane's heart pounded as loud as the gunshot, as UltraViolet staggered back and swore. The journal had hit the floor beside Jane, its pages falling open somewhere in the middle. Jane scrambled to retrieve it as Mindsight rushed to her side, firing off another round at UltraViolet.

It happened so fast. One moment they were in a standoff, the next Jane and Mindsight were barreling down the staircase at the heart of the old townhouse. Occasionally, a door would begin to crack open as someone peeped out to see what the hell was making all that racket, and Jane would throw a burst of light in their direction like a camera flash. Just enough.

They saw no sign of UltraViolet as they fled the house. "This way!" Mindsight shouted when they hit the streets. She dragged on Jane's arm, and Jane followed without question.

A crackle of purple lightning shot past them as they rounded the first corner. Jane yelped, but Mindsight was already on it: she dragged Jane down, ducking them behind a dumpster. Another crackle struck, the metal sparking at their backs.

"Shit, shit, shit!" Loose gravel bit into Jane's hand as she scrambled away from the dumpster. Her knuckles scraped the pavement, the journal still clutched tightly in her fist. "How did she know where to find us?"

"Never mind that!" Mindsight said. She whipped up, peering over the dumpster just long enough to fire off three quick rounds from her revolver before crouching back down beside Jane. Her chin jerked in the direction of Clair's journal. "Just what the hell is *in* that thing?"

It was a fair question. Jane looked down at the journal as another crackle of purple lightning shot overhead. Even streaked with dirt, the cover was so familiar, and so ordinary. It seemed hard to believe that anything dangerous could be tucked between its covers, but if UltraViolet wanted it . . .

Was it possible that she knew something Jane didn't?

It didn't matter. There was no time to ponder their circumstances. Mindsight grabbed Jane's hand, hauling her to her feet, and together they burst back out into the open. Lightning bit the air, so close that Jane felt it in her teeth, as they dodged around a car, and then a van, and then around the corner of a café. Jane heard screams from somewhere inside, and faces pressed quickly against the glass. The flash of a camera, several phones held in their direction. Jane was grateful for the anonymity of their uniforms—until she realized that this might get played up as a promotional stunt tomorrow, hyping the Spectral Wars storyline. Irritation clawed over Jane's skin. Of all the things to concern herself with, and yet . . .

They kept running. Kept dodging. Really, UltraViolet was a terrible shot. Unless she *wanted* them to escape, but that would be ridiculous—right?

No time for that, either. Jane's legs burned, her chest heaving as Mindsight led the way through the back alleys of Grand City. Jane did not question where they were going. They ran and ran, for what felt like forever. Once, it seemed as if they might have lost UltraViolet—but then she reappeared, directly in front of them, and they slid to an ungraceful halt and veered to the side.

They ran all the way to the bay.

At the park that ringed the water, Jane's feet slipped over damp grass. The paths were abandoned by this time of night, the benches empty. They ran, their backs exposed in the moonlight, straight to the water's edge.

There was nowhere else for them to go. Jane stood in front of the railing that edged the water, heaving, gulping in lungfuls of salt air. She leaned forward, resting her hands on her knees. Mindsight slid the journal out of her grasp, and Jane was too winded to care.

"Be ready," Mindsight whispered.

Ready for what? Jane wanted to ask, but all she could manage was a nod.

"Well!" a voice puffed out behind them. Jane whirled. She tried to summon a flash of light, but even her powers were spent. Her hands flickered only briefly, a lighter going out.

UltraViolet stood by a park bench, twenty-some-odd feet away.

"Not that I don't enjoy a good chase," she called out, "but really, Mindsight. What are you hoping to accomplish with this?"

Mindsight squared her shoulders. "You want the journal."

"That much, I believe we've already established."

"I know," Mindsight said. She clutched the journal to her chest. "But before we return to our own reality, I just wanted to make sure that you saw. So there would be no question in your mind, no reason to come after us."

A sick feeling settled fast in the pit of Jane's stomach. For a brief instant—just a flicker—it was like Jane had seen a frame of UltraViolet's face, her expression perfectly matching Jane's emotions, like they both realized what was happening all at once.

"Amy . . . ," Jane said, but too late.

Mindsight spun around, hurtling the journal out over the bay.

A narrow panel: the journal, midair, its pages fanned open. Glimpses of Clair's handwriting, the odd doodle here and there. Beside this panel is another slice, and then another, and then another, stacked up like frames of a movie as the last few months of Clair's life tumble through the night.

Beneath them, a wide shot of the bay. The journal lands, barely making a splash against the larger scope of the boats and the waves and the city lying beyond.

Time freezes, just for a moment. A panel of black as Jane shut down, unable to process what's happening around her.

Then the real world came roaring back to life, quite literally, as UltraViolet's scream of rage belted through the park. Jane just kept staring at the water, the way it lapped at the pages as the journal sank beneath the surface. It was Mindsight that threw her arm out, grabbing the wrist cuff on Jane as she activated her own. *I'm sorry.* The words floated, disconnected, and Jane didn't know if Mindsight had said them, or if she did, or if somehow they had come from Clair, like an echo on the wind. Jane's world shifted, lurching out from underneath her, as a crackle raised the hairs all over Jane's body.

She hit the ground, tumbling forward onto her hands and knees. Sunshine lit up the sidewalk, spitting back at her from the clutter of waves splashing madly in the bay. Jane raised her head. Across the water, she could see the hole Woolfolk Tower had left behind, a cigarette burn on a comic page.

A surge of anger pushed her back to her feet. "You shouldn't have done that!" She whirled toward Mindsight, ready to fight, but—

Mindsight was sprawled on the sidewalk. A scorch mark marred the back of her trench coat like a letter sealed with a lipstick kiss.

18

NOBODY QUESTIONED JANE ON HOW SHE KNEW THE
layout of the hospital so well. Instead they followed her, their
own personal ambassador through the lands of fear and grief.
Jane led the rest of the Heroes down the halls—a left, two rights,
another left. Around the edges of a crowded ER, to a tiny corner
with just enough chairs for them to wait. She did not stop to ask
for directions. She consulted no maps.

A year and a half later and an entire world away, and the
hospital hadn't changed at all. The smells: alternating between
a harsh disinfectant, cheap coffee, and the sweat of fear. The
sounds: the squeak of nurses' shoes, the conflicting beeps and
shrieks of the monitors, the whispered conversations. The ER was
still too warm, too dry, the floor of the lounge was still so polished
that Jane could almost see her reflection in the faux-marble white
tiles. There was still a smudge on the wall, a black mark at roughly
elbow level. A TV mounted in the corner blared the same talking
heads, the same worn-out problems of gun violence, bigoted

legislation, and hopeless elections, as if somehow these three things were not all heads of the same demonic creature. Jane sat in what she had come to think of as her chair. Its cushion felt the same underneath her ass, the wooden armrests had the same notches and grooves worn into it like veins. Time may as well have not progressed at all. Jane even spotted several of the doctors and nurses that she used to know, their tired faces passing over her without the slightest flicker of recognition.

This was the last place that Jane had wanted to come, but what other choice did she have? There wasn't time to bring Amy back to headquarters. The Heroes had begun talking in her ear almost immediately, having picked up the tracking signals of her and Mindsight's uniforms, and Jane could barely bring herself to answer them. "Help" was about the only word that had slipped out—over and over again, a frantic, frenzied prayer.

Now there was nothing to do but wait. Cal and Marie and Tony and Keisha and Devin were less versed in the art—they paced the visitors lounge like it was a cage, or gazed longingly out the windows, or stared at the clock with contempt, or blankly watched the talking heads on TV. Once, Cal and Devin got into a whispered argument in the corner. "Dude, I'm telling you, I talked to her! It's definitely Juanita!" Cal said, but Devin just shook his head. "What's it going to take, man? She *lied* to you."

"But—!"

"Look, sometimes people lie, okay? Even people we trust."

Cal's face twitched. He took a breath to argue, but Jane turned away with a sigh, trying to ignore them. She sat in her chair, so chosen because it faced nothing but a potted plant and a stretch of empty wall. Unlike the others, she did not try to distract herself to pass the time. She had learned through experience that it did not help. She did nothing. She said nothing. She thought nothing.

She did not, however, attempt to *feel* nothing. That, like pacing, like flipping through glossy magazines, like pointless arguments, would not work, not in Jane's experience anyway. In hospitals, dark moods clung to the shadows, growing until they blotted out the room around you. Jane sat in her chair, isolated from the rest of her group, and she cried in silence.

At five o'clock, her phone chirped. Jane pulled it out, swiped off the alarm with mechanical indifference. It wasn't until it had rung that she realized she'd set it on her way in, a habit from the last time she'd spent so much time in the hospital. It was something that her mother had drilled into her: food every five hours. Seven and noon and five and ten. Then bed, whether she wanted it or not. Up again at six, to repeat the cycle.

Jane got up. She wiped at her eyes beneath her glasses, turned to her companions. "I'm going to the vending machine."

She did not offer to get them anything, though she assumed they knew the offer was open. They said nothing. Cal grunted an acknowledgment, and Marie waved her fingers as she flipped a page in a magazine, and Tony looked at her, his expression blank. It had been more than three hours since they'd arrived, and they were starting to lose their earlier optimism.

Whatever. Jane turned away, shuffling down the hall to where she knew she would find a small alcove. Three vending machines—snacks, soft drinks, and coffee—sat next to a counter with a mini fridge and a trashcan tucked underneath, and a cheap microwave and tiny sink on top. Jane stared through the glass of the snack machine. The same labels, all unappealing: low-fat microwave popcorn, packets of cup-o-soup, potato sticks, honey roasted peanuts, Snickers bars, stale cinnamon buns. Jane's reflection hovered like a ghost as she listened to the ching-jangle of change going in, the click of buttons being punched. She did not even look at the keypad as she dialed in *1-3-4*, already knowing that a Snickers bar was going to be trundling forward on the spiral. It *clunked* to the base a moment later, though it took Jane another moment before she ducked to retrieve it.

Coffee next. Jane munched on her candy bar, chewing without tasting, as she waited for the coffee machine to *thunk* and *hiss* its way through pissing out coffee that would be both too weak and too hot at the same time. She rested her half-eaten Snickers on its wrapper as she poured in creamers and packets of sugar, thwacking them against her palm three times before tearing off the top. A coffee stirrer was clenched between her teeth. She was just pouring in the last of her creamers when a set of footsteps began *clacking* down the hall toward her, and a familiar voice cried out, "*There* you are!"

Jane jerked at the sound of her mother. Unfortunately, she had already curled her grip around the paper coffee cup, and now it went flying off the counter, landing on her shoes. "Shit!" Jane shouted, as searing hot coffee soaked through her toes and the hem of her pants.

She ignored her mother—who wasn't even really her mother anyway, and dammit Jane was tired of playing this game—as she grabbed a pile of napkins from the counter and crouched to try to mop up her mess. Mrs. Maxwell swept over, uttering apologies: didn't mean to startle her, blah blah, she came as soon as she heard, blah blah, wanted to be with you, blah blah. It was probably sweet, but it meant nothing to Jane. The comfort was as useless as the napkins, flimsy and falling apart as soon as they tried to be helpful.

"Oh, sweetie, here, let someone else take care of that," Mrs. Maxwell said. She placed her hands gently on Jane's shoulders, as if to guide her to her feet.

Jane jerked out from underneath her grip. "Leave me alone." She dabbed even more angrily at the spilled coffee, the sopping pile of napkins falling to pieces in her hands.

Mrs. Maxwell sighed. "Jane—"

"I don't want your help." Jane jabbed her glasses up her nose with the back of her knuckle. "I'm capable of cleaning this up on my own, *thank* you."

Unfortunately, Mrs. Maxwell—either version of her—was not one to be so easily dismissed. Jane kept her back turned, the level of her shoulders sharp and unwelcome. But a moment later Mrs. Maxwell was crouched right there beside Jane, a fresh pile of napkins pinched in her manicured fingers.

"Here," she said, holding them out to Jane.

Briefly, Jane did consider ignoring them—but that would just be petty, at this point. She took them without a word, sopping up the last of the coffee.

"You know," Mrs. Maxwell said, "I understand that this is hard for you, Janie. Really, I do. But you can't let your guilt make you drive *everyone* away. I let you push me away last time. I'm giving you fair warning: I won't be so easily dissuaded now. I'm your mother, and I love you, no matter what."

Jane frowned as she scooped up the mess of soggy napkins and stuffed them into the now-empty coffee cup. "Last time?" she asked as she stood up.

If she wasn't so consumed with worry and grief, Jane probably would have had the good sense to be a little more discreet with her question. The sharp line of Mrs. Maxwell's mouth was enough to let Jane know that she should have played things better, but as Jane threw her garbage away and stepped around Mrs. Maxwell to get to the tiny sink, she was suddenly overwhelmed with exhaustion. She simply did not *care* anymore, if she was playing this world's Jane correctly. She had far more important things to concern herself with.

Mrs. Maxwell straightened up. She smoothed out the pencil skirt of her neat little dove-gray suit. Randomly, it struck Jane that if this version of Mrs. Maxwell had been alive in the forties, she would have been the kind of woman whose stocking lines were *always* perfect.

Jane shook the idea out of her head. She washed her hands, using extra soap.

Mrs. Maxwell lowered her voice. "Look, I know you've been trying to pretend the whole thing never happened, and if that's how you need to deal with it, then . . . then fine. I'm done trying to change your mind on this, and I can only imagine how hard it must have been for you, watching her die."

Jane said nothing. She shook her hands off, patting them dry against her jeans.

"But listen," Mrs. Maxwell said—and here she actually took hold of Jane's elbow. "Listen: that *wasn't Amy*, all right? *Amy* is going to be fine."

A chill swept over Jane. She was still standing in front of the sink, still facing the little sign over the counter that instructed people how long you needed to wash your hands in order to properly kill all the germs. The cheerful blue-and-white letters seemed to swim in front of her, blurring as she lost herself in what Mrs. Maxwell had said. *That wasn't Amy . . . How hard it must have been for you, watching her die . . .*

Maybe it was nothing. Maybe . . . maybe this world's Jane had merely witnessed something horrific, and it had traumatized her with the possibility that it *could* have been Amy, if circumstances were different. She tried to ignore the creeping sensation working its way up her back, onto her shoulder, where it whispered in her ear like a little cartoon devil. *That wasn't Amy.*

Instinctively, Jane rubbed at the spot where her wedding ring was supposed to sit, as she turned toward Mrs. Maxwell. She didn't even realize that she was doing it, years of habit driving her thumb's actions, until she saw Mrs. Maxwell glance down.

Then they both went very, very still. Jane, out of fear that she'd done the wrong thing, that she'd finally been caught out in her lie—though how Mrs. Maxwell could have known, Jane couldn't even begin to imagine. But Mrs. Maxwell . . .

Mrs. Maxwell raised her eyes. Her gaze locked with Jane's, snaring Jane before she could react. Jane stood stock-still, terrified, barely breathing, as the piercing look of her mother seemed to pour down into Jane's soul, stripping back all her secrets. Her mother's voice filled her head, words repeated a thousand times during Jane's childhood: *I can always tell what you're thinking, Jane.* With the notable exception of the one truth she hadn't *wanted* to see, Jane's mother was always right. Mrs. Maxwell's eyes, gray like the first hints of weather on a summer day, narrowed as they studied Jane. They lacked the wrinkles that Jane's real mother sported, no doubt buffed and polished away by a careful plastic surgeon. In the hospital where Clair had died, Mrs. Maxwell's eyes looked more like the eyes that used to peer down at Jane when she was six, twelve, twenty.

Jane was never able to keep a secret from them, not forever. Not those eyes.

They widened. Abruptly, the grip on Jane's elbow released. "Oh my god," Mrs. Maxwell whispered, as she pressed one hand to her mouth, the other over her heart.

Mrs. Maxwell turned away. Jane watched, stepping out of the alcove, as Mrs. Maxwell marched straight down the hall, all the way to the end. A large window overlooked the parking lot, and Mrs. Maxwell stopped directly in front of it. Rose-gold sunbeams spilled across her head like a celestial spotlight.

She just . . . stood there. Jane could see Mrs. Maxwell's arms, wrapped around herself in a hug. The harsh plane of her shoulders, mimicking what Jane had tried to signal just a few minutes earlier: leave me alone.

Jane left her alone. She turned away, collecting the remains of her Snickers bar as she made her way back to the visitors lounge. Her heart thundered in her ears, louder than her footsteps, as she tried to make sense of what had just happened.

That wasn't Amy.

A FRAGMENT OF A MEMORY. IT MIGHT HAVE BEEN A DREAM.

So much of Jane's time at the hospital with Clair was blurred around the edges, shifting from one day to the next, shifting from awake to asleep to awake. Jane had forgotten about it, or she'd tried to, but it still clung to the edge of her memories like a dead leaf.

Sitting in the hospital chair, leaning forward so that her head rested on Clair's bed. Clair's unresponsive legs beneath her like a bony pillow. The bumpy pattern of the hospital blanket pressing into her cheek. Jane looked up, her attention drawn by the squeak of a shoe—was it a doctor, come to deliver news?, a nurse, checking Clair's vitals?, her mother, stopping by after work? No, the person in the doorway was already turning away, probably wasn't even supposed to be there in the first place, probably had the wrong room. She was wearing a short black jacket, a black baseball cap. Her eyes were obscured by black sunglasses, but there was something about her, when she started to turn back before catching herself. It felt like Jane was studying her own profile, like she'd somehow stepped outside of herself in her grief. Jane started to open her mouth, to call out, but a flare of light made Jane flinch, and by the time she looked back, the person was gone.

MRS. MAXWELL APPROACHED JANE ABOUT TWENTY MINUTES LATER.

"Can we talk?" she asked. She was standing just behind Jane's chair, out of sight. Jane motioned at the empty chair beside her, but Mrs. Maxwell hesitated. "Alone?"

Jane stood up. By the time she was fully to her feet, Mrs. Maxwell had already turned and was heading out of the visitors lounge. Jane followed at a distance. She didn't know why. It was perfectly safe to walk beside this woman that both was and wasn't her mother, but she couldn't bring herself to do it. She stalked her through the familiar routes of the hospital, and even when she was forced to get into the elevator with her, Jane kept her distance, always behind and to the right.

If Mrs. Maxwell was offended, she did not show it. But then, she wouldn't.

They reached the parking garage. The clack of Mrs. Maxwell's heels was especially pronounced against the cement, echoing from floor to wall to ceiling and back again. They had barely started to approach a sleek black town car when a driver stepped out, ready to open her door. Mrs. Maxwell held up her hand.

"It's all right, Tom. Why don't you go have a smoke break? Or here"—she reached into her purse, drawing out a twenty—"get yourself some coffee. My treat."

Tom was either used to this, or too well-trained to bat an eye at this request. He accepted the tip with a practiced bow. "Ma'am," he said, nodding at both Mrs. Maxwell and Jane as he set off.

Mrs. Maxwell opened the back door of the car. She motioned inside. "Have a seat."

A moment later, they were both settled on the leather seats. Side by side, but as far from each other as they could get without it being obvious that this is what they were trying to do.

Neither of them said anything. Jane stared sideways at the face of what her mother could have been, if fates were different. Mrs. Maxwell crossed her legs. She uncrossed them. She crossed them again. She smoothed out her skirt, picked at a piece of imaginary lint, brushed her fingers off on each other.

Finally, she cleared her throat. "First, I just want to know if *my* Jane is okay."

"I don't know," Jane said. There was no point in lying. "She's missing. We're looking for her."

Mrs. Maxwell nodded, accepting this. She folded her hands on her lap. She was studying a ring on her finger, a fat onyx oval set in silver and pearl.

Jane sensed the emotional hit before Mrs. Maxwell said a word. She closed her eyes, retreating inside of herself. Forget the car. Forget the parking garage. Forget this woman who wasn't Jane's mother. Forget the hospital, her friends waiting anxiously several floors above, the same stale faces of doctors and nurses bustling from one room to the next to the next. Forget, if she could, about Amy, somewhere up there in surgery. Jane floundered, searching the depths of her mind for a place where she could handle this, a place where she could weather the storm.

"I have to tell you a story, Jane."

Jane nodded, suddenly ready. She could do stories.

I HAVE TO TELL YOU A STORY, JANE.

About . . . a year and a half ago, my daughter came to my door. Bloodied, streaked with dirt. Now, I've seen her battle worn before, but this was something else. It wasn't just that she was in civilian clothes. There was something—something haunted about her eyes.

A battered finger pressing the doorbell. Dark strokes, the lines loose and careless. Muted colors indicating road rash, scratches, bruising. A streak of drying blood worn into the grooves of her knuckle. The background is bright and cheerful, soft pastels indicating a perfect day, a perfect porch.

The door opens. Just a slice of Mrs. Maxwell's face, not even fully in view before the lines of worry begin to wrinkle her brow and draw her lips together. A small, tentative speech bubble: "Jane?"

A wide shot. Jane, her designer clothes torn and stained with gray. Blood cuts a harsh angle down her legs, another across her shoulder. Again, the world behind her is bright and carefree, while her face tells another story. Slack jaw, hollow cheeks. A spark is missing from her eyes as she regards her mother with detachment.

I brought her in. Tried to get her to take a shower, change out of her awful clothes, but she just collapsed on her bed and began sobbing. No explanation. Nothing I did could pull it out of her. I thought about calling for a doctor, or Cal, but it seemed . . . I don't know, wrong somehow. Her grief was so pure . . . almost sacred.

I left her there. Let her work it out. I went down to the kitchen, and I was so restless, so worried, I just started making banana bread. I don't know, it was something to do. I used to make it for Jane when she was little, before the move, before her father started running for office, and it always used to cheer her up.

It was just coming out of the oven when Jane reappeared. I guess she had taken a shower after all, because she was in fresh pajamas now, and her hair was damp. She didn't say anything at first, just came into the kitchen and sat down at the island by the stove. I . . . I tried to offer her a slice. But she wouldn't eat it.

Speech bubbles overlapping each other:

"Are you sure?"

"Yes."

"I made it just for you. Do you remember, how I used to—?"

"Yes. But no. No."

Smaller text: "All right."

Mrs. Maxwell's face, chastised and downcast. The banana bread, steaming, untouched, on the counter. Folded hands, flawlessly manicured, rest next to it as Mrs. Maxwell waits to see what Jane is going to do next.

She told me that Amy was dead.

At first, I couldn't believe it. I actually had to sit down. The two of them were so close as children—inseparable—and even though they'd lost touch after we moved, I was so thrilled when they found each other again in Grand City. I mean, I knew things were different between them now. They had their whole group of friends back, and what with the Heroes, their work . . . I knew they weren't as close as they once were. But it was so good to see them working together. It was almost like having a lost daughter back. I don't think that I'd realized, until Jane said that Amy was dead, exactly how much the girl had meant to me.

This might sound arrogant, but I think that it was my own grief that finally snapped a little bit of life back into Jane. She narrowed her eyes, and it's like a part of her came back to herself, realized what she'd said. "No, not our *Amy," she told me, but of course I didn't understand what that meant.*

So Jane explained it. How she'd found a way to travel into a kind of alternate reality. Another Earth, another Grand City. I didn't understand it at first, but Jane said that we were all there. Her and Amy,

Cal and the rest of the team. Me. Her father. All the same, but different in a number of little ways. Like a kind of what-if story, or one of those Choose-Your-Own-Adventure books that Jane's uncle used to send her on her birthdays.

She didn't say it, but I think that Jane had become kind of . . . obsessed. There was something manic in her voice as she described it.

The spark of life was back in Jane's eyes. Sitting up straighter on the bar stool by the kitchen island. Jane's shoulders pulled back, her hands spread as if in the middle of gesturing widely. "We're all there! But it's not really us, it's like . . . we're different, like we'd made other choices. Gone down other paths."

Mrs. Maxwell, getting herself a cup of coffee. Glancing sideways at her daughter, her lips pinched tightly as she listens. The curtain of her hair provides contrast to the angled line of her face as she turns back.

"Other paths?" Mrs. Maxwell's speech bubble says next. Turned back now, coffee in hand. She's brought her shoulders in, her whole body tense. Poised.

She said that this other Jane was married—to Amy. That Jane was some kind of artist. Jane had been visiting them for months now, I don't know, maybe longer. Watching from street corners. Logging into this other Jane's social media accounts with the passwords that she would have picked for herself.

The scene cuts. The familiar streets of Grand City, stacked on top of each other. The corner bookstore, the one that used to be a bank back in the thirties, where Jane and Clair liked to meet after Clair got out of work. The two of them, browsing the stacks. The front doors of QZero, Jane pushing open the glass, a large drawing portfolio tucked under her arm. Clair giving a lecture at the museum, a darkened hall dotted with spectators. Their apartment, seen from outside: Jane and Clair singing as they cooked dinner, a spoon extended from Jane's hand for Clair to use as a fake microphone.

Always, in the foreground, a dark figure looming. Black baseball cap. Short black jacket. Black sunglasses.

I tried to ask her if she knew what she was doing—it all sounded a little . . . concerning, to me—but Jane wouldn't let me get a word in. She was talking so fast, it was hard to keep up with what she was saying. There was something she wanted to discuss with Amy. She said something about going to meet her, and then . . . then Jane went quiet.

Back in the kitchen, a moment without speech bubbles. The room from the doorway, wide angled. Jane and her mother look so small, standing in the middle of all that open space. The yellow of the walls is too cheerful for the evening. The sun has fallen outside, blackness pressing thickly against the windowpanes.

She didn't get the chance to talk with Amy. Before she could meet with her, Amy had already gotten into her car. Jane followed her. Amy went into the tunnel . . . but . . . the car—

"STOP!" JANE SAID. SHE WRENCHED HER EYES OPEN, trying to ground herself in the present. Her heart was pounding, her head was pounding. She did not need to hear this part, did not need to see this part. She had already imagined it, a thousand different times, a thousand different ways. She felt herself slipping back to it. The sickly yellow lights of the tunnel, the constant feeling of lurking danger. Clair hated tunnels, and always held her breath while driving through them. *"What if something happens while you're in there?"* she used to ask. *"You'd be trapped inside."*

Those words had haunted Jane, for months after the accident. The images ran roughshod through her mind, then and now: the blinding flare of headlights, the swerve of cars; the shriek of brakes, like Valkyries heralding doom. An SUV, slamming into Clair's bumper. Nowhere to go, nowhere to run. Clair's car swerving, tires running up the wall as it began to flip. The moment of impact. Glass catching the lights, a thousand tiny prisms exploding all around her.

"Jane? *Jane!*"

Jane snapped back. A different car, a car at rest. An expensive car, the smell of leather and perfume. Her mother's hand on her shoulder—no, not her mother. Close enough to her mother.

"I'm sorry," Mrs. Maxwell said. "I'm so sorry, I didn't mean to—"

Jane held up her hand. She took deep breaths, in through her nose, out through her mouth. The metallic taste of blood and fear stained her tongue.

A story, Mrs. Maxwell had said. It was worse than a story, though—it was the truth. No unexpected reversals to soften the blow, no happy endings to make everything all right. Clair was dead. It was never going to be okay.

Mrs. Maxwell rubbed Jane's shoulder. Motherly and comforting. "I'm not trying to upset you. It's just . . . when I realized that it was *you*, and not *her* . . . I thought that you should know. I tried to tell Jane to go back, to talk to you. She was feeling so guilty, and . . . and you deserved to know. That Amy didn't die alone. That someone was there for her, that in a way *you* were there for her."

Jane's phone buzzed. She dug it out of her pocket as Mrs. Maxwell withdrew her hand. It was just as well—Jane didn't know what she was supposed to say to Mrs. Maxwell right now. Not after . . . well, everything. She was still trying to process the idea that her double had *been* there, that she'd *seen* it. She couldn't deal with it right now. It was a relief, then, to swipe her phone awake, read the brief text that had come in.

Two words: *She's out.*

"I have to go," Jane said. She was already scrambling for the door latch when Mrs. Maxwell grabbed her arm.

"Jane . . . I know that I'm not really your mother, but can I give you a piece of advice?"

Jane shrugged. "Sure." She didn't care, either way. The door was open, and she already had one foot literally out the door.

"Please just try to remember: the woman upstairs right now . . . she's not your wife."

Not your wife. Jane flinched. "I know," she said. She peeled Mrs. Maxwell's grip off of her elbow, and slipped out of the car. She ducked her head, looking back in as she prepared to close the door. "But she's the only thing I have left anymore."

Mrs. Maxwell frowned. Jane pulled back, shutting the car door. Her own reflection replaced the view of her mother. Jane watched herself turn away.

It wasn't until she was punching the floor button that something Mrs. Maxwell said came back to her: that Amy didn't die alone. Jane frowned as the elevator lurched underneath her, yanking at the pit of her stomach. *No*, Jane thought, *she didn't. She died a week later, with me by her side.*

Jane brushed it off. Squared her shoulders, adjusted her glasses. It didn't matter, she told herself. A story of a story. There were bound to be mistakes. She looked at her phone, tapping out a quick reply. *I'm on my way.* That was all that mattered anymore.

Amy was waiting for her.

19

DAY TURNED TO NIGHT. NIGHT TRUDGED EVER ONWARD.
Jane was parked in a chair beside Amy's bed—a familiar post, a
familiar feeling. Dread coated the back of her throat as memories
assaulted her, but Jane fought against them. *Not this time*, she
told herself firmly. *Never again.*

She squeezed Amy's hand and Amy, still drugged out from
surgery and only occasionally brushing against consciousness,
squeezed back.

"She's incredibly lucky," the doctor had said, as she brought
them all up to speed while the rest of the medical staff got Amy
settled in her new room. "None of her major organs were affected,
and I'm optimistic that she'll make a full recovery, in time."

Everyone had made a big show of being relieved, but none
of them compared to Jane. She'd collapsed, a sob escaping her
chest as she fell to her knees. Only the dimmest awareness of her
surroundings kept Jane from kissing the germ-riddled hospital

floor. When the nurses had finally let them into the room, Jane had dragged a chair forward and stationed herself in the prime spot beside Amy, and she hadn't left since.

The two of them were alone now. The others had stayed for a while, waiting for Amy to wake up, but one by one they'd drifted off. Cal was the last to leave, his attention lingering on Jane as he stood in the open doorway. "Are you sure you'll be okay here?" he asked. He'd been trying to pry her away for over an hour—insisting that Amy would likely sleep all the way until morning.

"I'm not leaving," Jane had said. Over and over, until finally Cal had no choice but to accept it.

At six in the morning, the timer on Jane's phone started to chime. Her finger was already poised over the screen, ready and waiting to shut it up as soon as it began.

Amy's chest rose and fell with a deep, stirring breath. "Sounds like birds," she said. Actually, what she said was, at best, a half-mumbled version of those words, most of the letters dropped—but Jane knew what she'd meant. A wife knew.

"I suppose it does," Jane said as she tucked the phone into her back pocket. She stood up and brushed Amy's bangs aside. Amy still had her eyes shut, but there was a subtle shift in her face, an alertness as sound and smell and touch came back to her. Jane's chest felt like it was collapsing in on itself; this was the moment that she'd never gotten before. Last time. With Clair. This, right here: the slow process of watching someone come back to themselves. Jane had dreamed about it, wished for it—even broken down and *prayed* for it, though she'd given up religion years ago.

It had never come.

Amy licked at her lips, found them dry, made a face. "Water?"

"Of course."

There was an ugly, salmon-pink pitcher on a table nearby, which Jane had helped herself to at around 2:30. She poured a fresh glass now, into a disposable cup from the stack. Straws lay in a scattered pile beside them, and it took only a moment to unsheathe one and pop it into place. The soft *brrrk* of the straw cut the room as Jane bent it down, and she held it carefully to Amy's lips.

"Here you go, m'lady. The bartender made it special, just for you."

The twitch of Amy's cheek betrayed the hint of a smile. She took a long drink, during which time Jane relished every sign of life: the tuck of Amy's cheeks as she sucked in the water, the pulse fluttering in her neck, the twitch of her eyes behind her eyelids, the warmth of Amy's breath against Jane's knuckles. This moment: it was nothing like Jane had imagined, all those endless hours at Clair's bedside. It was so much better than that.

Amy shifted, pressure shoving at the straw as she pushed it away with her tongue. Jane took the water away, leaving it close in case it was needed again. She had to turn away to make sure that she didn't put it down on the remaining straws, and by the time she turned back, Amy's eyes were open.

They were trained right on Jane. Perhaps she'd had enough time to take in the rest of the room before Jane had turned back, perhaps not.

Jane forced a smile, newly self-conscious. "Hey," she said. "How are you feeling?"

Amy grimaced. "Is this where I tell you that it's not so bad, and you give me a platitude about staying positive?"

"Something like that," Jane said. "Unless you'd rather just tell me how you feel like shit."

"I feel like shit."

"I'm sorry."

Amy shook her head. Her eyelids were already drooping, and her voice went warm and mellow as she mumbled, "It's not your fault."

"It's sweet of you to lie."

"I'm not lying," Amy said. She opened her eyes only enough to narrow them, the way that Clair did whenever she was scolding someone. "I make my own choices, Jane. I followed you to the apartment, and I faced off against UltraViolet. I could have stayed out of it."

"But you wouldn't have." Tears pricked at Jane's dry eyes, hot manifestations of the guilt that had been eating her alive since they'd gotten back. She took off her glasses only long enough to brush them away. "Not with the way you feel about me."

"And don't you dare try to take that away from me," Amy said. "I own that. Those are *my* feelings. You didn't *make* me fall in love with you, like I was under the influence of some kind of potion. I did that all on my own."

Jane looked down. Her nails were chipped from the scramble, the only sign that *she'd* gotten into a fight. "I know," she said. "But . . . I still could have done something. I could have tried using my powers, it's just—"

"You're scared of them."

Jane made herself nod—there was no point in lying, not to Amy.

"It's okay," Amy said. "You wouldn't be the first person to get freaked out by the sudden appearance of superpowers."

"I think it's more than that."

The words came out in a whisper, though of course Amy heard them. Still. Jane bit her lip, nervous about her half-confession. She hadn't said a word about the whispers in City Hall, and didn't know if she could now, either.

The back of Amy's gloved hand brushed against Jane's.

"Jane . . . you're going to get a handle on this. Trust me. I believe in you."

"Thanks," Jane said, her voice small.

"Come on, stop beating yourself up. You didn't do this to us—that's on UltraViolet, you got that? Besides, look at me. I'm going to be okay."

Jane nodded again, though she still couldn't bring herself to look at Amy yet. It wasn't even the bandages, the scrapes that lined her face, the IV sticking out of her arm, the sunken look of her as she struggled back to health. All of that, Jane was used to. Clair had looked worse, and it hadn't mattered.

No, it was precisely what Amy was saying that made it so hard to look at her now. She *was* going to be fine. She would recover, in a way that Clair never had, never could. Jane twisted her wedding ring around her finger, her heart torn in a thousand different directions. The moment of Amy waking up had been wonderful, more wonderful than Jane could have ever imagined. It was what to do *now* that was difficult. What to do *now* that left Jane floundering in uncharted waters.

But Amy didn't deserve that turmoil. So Jane forced a smile, and forced herself to look up. "You're right," she said. The brave one. The healthy one. "You're absolutely right. You're going to be fine."

Jane would make sure of that, personally. Even if it broke her.

THEY TRANSFERRED AMY BACK TO HEADQUARTERS AS soon as it was safe to move her, to recuperate in a rejuve pod. The doctors wanted to keep her a while longer, but, well—there are benefits, being secret superheroes. People who owe you favors. You don't necessarily need to reveal your identity to leverage your assets. Amy was still bed-bound, still weak, but getting stronger every day. This, Jane held on to with both hands and all of her heart.

While the rest of the team was busy sweeping the city, trying to track down either their Jane or the location of UltraViolet's base of operations, Jane spent her time with Amy. Watching her sleep, helping her to the bathroom and back again, getting her food.

"You really don't need to stay with me 24/7," Amy said at one point, two or maybe three days later. It was hard to keep track of time, one hour flowing to the next and the next. Jane had just helped Amy back into her bed, the healing glow of the rejuve pod lending a bright sheen to her skin.

"I think you'll find it's closer to 22/7," Jane said. "I took two whole hours yesterday, to go back to my own quarters and shower."

"Oh, well. That makes all the difference."

Jane fluffed Amy's pillow before easing her against it. "Are you really going to complain about my excellent level of care and service?"

Amy smirked. "Wouldn't dream of it. Though, I will say, my toast was burned this morning."

"*That* was hardly my fault."

"How so?"

"I think Marie was futzing with the toaster yesterday. When I turned it on this morning, it greeted me in fluent Japanese."

Amy laughed, then grimaced, then grabbed her side.

"Sorry," Jane said.

"It's fine," Amy said, still wincing. "It's good to laugh . . . even if it hurts."

"And now you know why I stay here 24/7," Jane said. She picked up Amy's hand—still in her fingerless gloves, even now—and kissed it through the knitted fabric.

The day stretched on. Amy slept. Jane kept watch.

After a couple of hours, her timer chimed. Jane swiped it off, glancing at Amy to make sure it hadn't woken her. Jane's stomach rumbled, a Pavlovian response after all of this time, but Jane really didn't feel like eating.

She turned so that she could get to the top of her uniform, hanging off the back of the chair like a jacket. There was probably some gum in the pockets—she thought she remembered dropping a pack in there, a cheap little peppermint brand, full of crunchy breath fresheners. Jane rummaged in first one pocket and then, finding nothing, moved on to the next.

Her fingers brushed against a folded sheet of paper.

The memory of it came to her in a rush: retrieving Clair's journal from the nightstand, the paper fluttering down from somewhere pressed between the pages. Jane had stuffed it into her pocket without any further thought, and in the crisis of everything that had happened since, had forgotten it.

She held it now, her breath frozen in her chest. In the healing light of the rejuve pod, the paper seemed to have an ethereal glow, like a holy relic.

Clair's handwriting peeped out at her as she inched the paper open. Neat letters in rich black ink. Clair was the only person that Jane knew that still used cursive for anything other than a signature or the occasional check.

Jane shut her eyes, giving herself a minute. She didn't know if she was ready for this. She glanced up at Amy, suddenly self-conscious. It felt *wrong* to do this here, and so Jane got up and slipped out the door. She didn't stop walking until she was outside, the warm breeze teasing her hair.

She leaned against the side of the building. Blue glass chilled her back—there was little in the way of sunlight to reflect these days. Jane opened the note back up. Her eyes shifted back and forth, taking it in quickly. It was only two lines, neither of which made sense. *Lasers are just light*, it said, and then below that: *I believe in you.*

Jane snorted. *I believe in you.* Yeah, Amy had said that, too, and what good had their faith in Jane gotten them so far? Disappointment stung at Jane's heart. All that effort, all that sacrifice, and *this* is all they had to show for it? Briefly, she was tempted to crumple the note up and burn it—but no, she realized with a tug in her chest, she could never do *that*. Instead, she folded it carefully, and slid it into the back pocket of her jeans. Jane walked to the corner, her stomach churning with guilt. Past closed-down flower shops and newsstands, past a gas station packed with a snake of cars fueling up, just in case. Rumors of UltraViolet's weapon were spreading, however much the mayor's office tried to deny them, and grocery shelves were emptying faster than they could be restocked.

Jane was almost to the Beef-Up Burgers on the corner when her phone buzzed. She pulled it out, annoyed. Mrs. Maxwell and Allison had both been texting her once in a while, and Jane hadn't been able to bring herself to reply to either of them, even though she knew she should.

It *was* a text message, but not the one that Jane expected. Her eyes went wide as she read.

We found Jane, Cal's message said. *Meet me?*

THE STRETCH OF ROAD LOOKED DIFFERENT IN THE daylight, years later. Jane almost didn't recognize it, as Cal drove them in silence out of the city, beyond the suburbs, through the expanse of crumbling industry that had built the town up so long ago. She only caught on at all because she'd come back here once, when it was time to draw the origin story of the Heroes of Hope.

ChemWerks Industries. White letters, faded almost to the point of obscurity, ran just beneath the flat roofline of the old brick building. A scraggly field of knee-high brown grass stood as skeletal sentries between it and the sagging chain-link fence that ringed the perimeter.

Jane stared at the building in disbelief as Cal shut the engine off.

"*Here?*" she asked. "Really?"

Cal's blank stare revealed nothing. "What's wrong with here?" He was reaching over to unbuckle Jane's seatbelt for her, as if she was incapable of punching a red button on her own.

"Don't you recognize it?"

For one fleeting moment, she wondered if maybe things had happened differently here. If the origin story that she'd dreampt up for her imaginary heroes was somehow different from their real-life counterparts, despite the fact that everything else important had remained the same.

Cal shrugged. "There are only so many abandoned factories around here. It's a coincidence."

Jane snorted. "There are no coincidences in stories, Cal. Any writer can tell you that."

"This isn't a story, Jane."

"Could have fooled me," Jane muttered. But she got out of the car all the same. Jane's red uniform reflected in the black door of Cal's SUV. She paused for a moment, trapped by the sight of it. Framed in the window, she looked as though she belonged on the cover of a comic book.

Jane pulled herself away. Cal, dressed as Deltaman, was already trudging toward the building, gun drawn. His cape fluttered in the afternoon breeze, brushing the tall grass. They'd met up halfway to the factory, Cal tossing Jane a bag with her uniform in it. The others would be along as soon as they could, he'd said. Until then, they needed to hurry. They found an empty gas station for Jane to slip into the restroom and change, and then they were off.

They approached with caution, but the door was unlocked this time. The hinge was rusted off, busted open.

Deltaman led the way. A light strapped to his wrist illuminated empty corridors and decaying offices.

Not that Jane needed it. Her training had done more good than she realized, because an infrared haze superimposed itself over her vision in the blink of an eye. It was a shift that she didn't even need to consciously work for anymore, though she didn't know if she would *ever* get used to it. Most of the factory stretched out in pale shades of artificial blue and gray and green, while Deltman's body heat stood out in glaring orange/red/purple combinations. It was all rather psychedelic for Jane's tastes.

"Shouldn't we wait for the others?" Jane whispered.

Deltaman shook his head. "No time. My contact said he spotted Shadow Raptors hauling equipment out of here, just a few hours ago. If they're moving shop, then Jane's likely to be next, and we can't afford to lose her again."

"But you're *sure* they're on their way?"

"*Yes*, I'm sure. I texted them myself. They all replied. I promise, they'll be here. Now, please . . . can we just focus on finding Jane?"

Jane fell silent, cheeks flushing without understanding why. But then . . . this was probably hard for Cal, Jane realized. If any of what he'd said about the two of them was true . . . She watched his back, the stiffness of his shoulders, the nerves easy to read even for her.

Nobody was here.

"Cal," Jane hissed, but Deltaman held up his hand, a signal for quiet. Jane bit her lip, following him through the darkness, through the emptiness. Jane's heart pounded in her chest. This whole thing felt wrong. Like UltraViolet keeping the antidote right there, in City Hall. Like the way that she'd shown up in Jane's apartment, knowing somehow exactly what they were looking for.

They needed to get out of here. Every instinct told her that, and so she rushed forward again, trying to grab for Deltaman's shoulder, but then he was turning a corner, throwing open a door, and . . .

And there she was.

Jane Maxwell.

Jane stopped in the doorway, dumbfounded, as her vision switched back to normal. Her double was tied to a chair in the middle of the room, a bare bulb buzzing over her head. This other version of Jane had her hair thrown back in a ponytail, and her uniform was dirty and battered. Her body was slumped forward as if she was unconscious.

Deltaman rushed forward. "Jane!" he said, and the concern in his voice twisted Jane's heart like a knife.

"Cal, wait!"

She had no choice but to follow. A sense of *wrongness* pulled at Jane as they approached. She wanted to tell herself that it was nothing—after all, no traps were springing, were they? No Shadow Raptors bursting out of the darkness, no alarms blaring, no bullets piercing the air. And yet . . .

Deltaman was the first to reach Jane's double. He checked the slumped Jane's pulse, nodding at Jane to indicate that her duplicate was still alive and well. Jane crept up. Her stomach was twisting up on itself as she approached. Part of it was the paranoid feeling that had crept up the back of her neck since they'd first stepped out of Cal's SUV. Another was more basic than that. It was hard to look at her double, harder than she'd ever expected it to be. Which was weird to her, because she'd been living with this messed up, alternate-universe version of everyone else for a while now, and while she wasn't exactly *comfortable* with it all yet, it had at least taken on a sense of familiarity.

Nothing compared to this. Her own brown hair tied up in a hasty ponytail, her own prone form slumped in a chair. Her own uniform, a copy of the one that she was currently wearing, her own mask. Her own collarbone, visible where the neck of her uniform pulled back. Jane looked, tried not to look, looked again.

And then she went very cold.

"Wait!" Jane said, just as Deltaman was reaching to cut the ropes binding Jane's double in place. She grabbed his arm, stilling him.

Deltaman sighed. "Jane, we don't have time for this."

"No, but *look*." Jane pointed at the exposed length of neck on her double, the line where her collarbone jutted toward the base. The uniform had taken a beating, a rip exposing more of her skin than normal. "I broke my collarbone when I was nine, remember?"

"So?"

"So, it's never healed properly. See?"

Jane reached up, zipping down the top of her uniform's jacket just enough to pull the neckline over. The line of her bone was slightly jutted, a bump rising in the middle. Jane's finger ran along the knob, the place where two halves of her bones had fused together. But all the while, she was staring at the person slumped in the chair, her collarbone intact.

"This isn't me," Jane said. She reached over, pulling the mask off of the nearly perfect mimic of her own face. Jane crouched down for a better look, her heart twisting up in her chest. "Oh my god. It's Allison."

"No way," Deltaman said from behind her. "Jane, you're imagining things."

Jane shook her head. "No, I'm not." She looked up sharply, her attention flying to the edges of the room. The nervous flutter in her stomach leapt to her throat, unable to be ignored. "It's a trap," Jane said as she stood up. "It has to be. We've got to get out of here! We've got—"

But whatever else she was going to say died as she turned around. Jane froze in place, shocked into silence as she found herself staring at the barrel of a gun, so close to her face that she went cross-eyed looking at it.

Cal's gun.

In Cal's hand.

Past the weapon, up the straight shot of Cal's arm, his shadowed face seemed to have dropped the Deltaman persona, despite the fact that nothing had *technically* changed.

He heaved a weary sigh. The sigh was battle-worn and ancient beyond his years, as if the world was simply too much to be borne another moment. "I'm sorry, Jane. But you're not going anywhere."

Jane managed to shake her head, just once, side to side. "Oh, Cal. No."

The thing is, she should have seen this coming. Jane had written so many dramatic reversals, so many betrayals—how had she not seen it coming? Hadn't she said it herself, there are no coincidences in stories? Jane realized, suddenly, that they were not here by accident, that Cal had been the one to bring Jane here, that no one was coming to join them after all.

Panic flared in Jane's stomach, seizing her up. "Why?" she managed to ask, the only question that mattered anymore.

Cal smirked. "There's someone that wants to meet you."

Jane knew before she even turned around what she would find. Sure enough: Cal jerked his head, indicating something behind Jane. Jane's every muscle protested as she made herself move, first one foot and then the other, her body swiveling reluctantly to follow.

In the doorway, a shimmering purple blur shifted in and out of partial focus. UltraViolet strolled in with languid steps, the factory rippling around her like heat rising from a car's hood on a summer day. She began to slow-clap as she approached, a digitized laugh escaping her.

"Well done," UltraViolet said as she came to a stop in front of Jane. "You're not quite as stupid as I thought you were."

Jane forced herself to swallow, though her throat had gone completely dry. "You'll never get away with this."

It was a dumb line, meaningless really, but it was all Jane had at the moment. Panic danced freely through Jane's body, tempered only by a feeling of disconnect, a sense that what was happening around her couldn't possibly be real.

UltraViolet put her hand on her hip. "And there you had to go and ruin it. Oh well"—she shrugged—"it won't matter for long."

"Stay back!" Jane raised her hands defensively, flickers of light already bursting free of her fingertips. "Just stay back!"

"*Please*," UltraViolet sneered, "do you really think that your powers are going to intimidate *me*, of all people?"

"What's that supposed to mean?"

"Seriously? You haven't figured it out yet? God, no wonder you had to steal all your ideas from Clair."

UltraViolet strode forward, her steps wide and sure, as if she was invincible, as if nothing that Jane could think of would be of any threat to her.

Not that Jane was doing anything. She knew that she shouldn't just stand there. It was obvious that she shouldn't just stand there. Just standing there was exactly what Ultra-Violet wanted her to do, and yet: Jane couldn't get herself to move. Up close, there was something even more maddening about UltraViolet, some tangle that Jane couldn't quite unravel. Intellectually, she told herself to move. Demanded it, screamed it in her mind. But there was a larger force at work here, something holding her in place, something demanding an answer.

"Let me make this easy for you, then," UltraViolet said, her voice warbling as the distortion eased back, just a little. "Since it's obvious you'll never get there on your own."

Jane's breath caught in her chest. She did and didn't want to know, but it didn't matter what she wanted, anymore. UltraViolet was right in front of her now, their faces mere inches from each other, and the haze that forever surrounded her was shifting, the light and colors settling back into their proper place. With each new feature becoming clear, Jane's eyes widened in horrible recognition, as the last of UltraViolet's distortions faded away, leaving only a familiar face, smoky eyes and purple lips curled into a smirk of triumph.

A very familiar face.

Her own face.

"Hello, Jane," Jane Maxwell said to her, grinning that purple grin. "It's nice to see you again."

TWO YEARS AGO . . .

"*Ten* grand? Are you joking?"

Jane Maxwell smiled. She stabbed at her eighty-dollar salad, a blend of organically grown kale and avocado and a half-dozen other raw ingredients specially designed to contain high levels of antioxidants or whatever else the health craze of the year was. God, what she wouldn't give for a drive-thru burger about now.

"You have to consider the honor," Jane said.

"Honor doesn't pay my client's bills," Blue countered. Blue Hamilton—agent to the very best artists in Grand City—and Jane went way back, to the days just after Jane graduated from Sutton University with a degree in art history. "This painting is easily worth *five times* what you're offering."

"Today, yes. But I only want to display it for four years. Imagine what it will be worth after that."

"In four years," Blue said, "Knisley can paint two dozen more masterworks."

Jane set her fork down. "So? I'm offering you the chance to have your client's work positioned *directly behind* the mayor's desk. It will be in every picture of his office for the remainder of his term."

Blue shook her head, a tender smile softening her otherwise harsh features. Blue was tall and angled—all jawlines and collarbones—with a nose slightly too large for her face. When Blue was younger, she'd tried to hide herself behind traditional hairstyles and carefully applied makeup, but these days she embraced a "fuck all" attitude that Jane couldn't help but admire. Barefaced, her hair cut spiky-short and died a bubblegum pink that defied her name, it was a wonder to Jane that none of Blue's clients had painted her yet. There were so many wonderful angles and shadows to Blue. If Jane was still an artist . . .

Jane looked away, biting her lip.

"Look, Jane . . . I understand that you're excited to be in charge of this project. And I get that you're working on a strict budget. But if I start undervaluing my client's works just to help out a friend—"

"Forget it," Jane said. "You're right. I'm sorry for asking."

Blue reached over, resting her hand on Jane's and giving it a tiny squeeze. "You can always *ask*."

Jane slid her hand away. The café was spacious, the tables positioned so far apart that you could easily fit twice as many in the same space if this was any other establishment. The odds of anyone looking over at the two of them at that particular moment were slim, but Jane still found herself glancing around for prying eyes. She had a reputation for being standoffish, even cold, around her female friends, which she laughed off as just not liking to be touched. But it was more than that. Jane couldn't take the risk that one of these days she might let the hug last a little too long, that the look on her face might reveal more than she could afford.

In the café, though, no one was paying them any attention. Two waiters flitted like hummingbirds from one self-absorbed table to the next.

Blue sat back. She wasn't offended—she was never offended. Her phone buzzed, facedown on the table, and Jane watched as Blue flipped it over and read whatever had just come in. Her lips always parted, just a little, as she read.

"I'm sorry," Blue said, smiling, as she stood up from the table. "I'm afraid that I have to go. Can you . . . ?" She pointed at the remainder of their food. Most of it was still uneaten.

Jane nodded. "Yeah, I got it. You go ahead."

Blue's grin lit up the café. "Thanks. I owe you." She leaned in fast, gracing a kiss on Jane's cheek.

Jane sat there, still as a rock, trying to will the flush away from her face. She could actually do that sometimes, a skill that she always attributed to the mental discipline she'd acquired in the years spent mastering her superpowers.

Five minutes later she was walking down Forecastle Street, her head still buzzing with the effort of keeping her body in check. Her chest was warm. Jane took a deep breath. *Think about Cal*, she told herself firmly. Jane had finally broken down and started sleeping with him several months ago, just after her father had announced his candidacy for mayor. It would not do to have one of his two prominent daughters going so long without a boyfriend—it had been, God, what, six years since Jane had broken up with the only other man she'd tried to date? The press would have started asking questions, Jane was sure of it.

She was still trying to collect herself when an odd flash of light drew her attention. By now, she was three blocks away from the restaurant. The flash didn't seem to register with anyone else milling up and down the street, and maybe Jane wouldn't have paid attention to it, either, except that in her bizarre lifestyle, flashes tended to coincide with trouble. Light flashed again, from a nearby alley. Just ahead. Jane quickened her pace and ducked into the shadows between buildings.

The alley looked empty, but Jane knew better than to trust that. A buzz permeated the air. She kept the tickle of power in her fingertips, ready to use should worst come to worst—though she was hoping that it wouldn't, since her uniform was back at headquarters. Halfway down the alley, the buzz increased. It was vibrating the air so badly that Jane could almost *taste* it, bitter like blood on the back of her tongue. She inched forward, pointed heel to toe. She undid the button of her silk blazer, to allow for better movement of her arms.

Even still, the blast caught her off-guard. Jane yelled, light flaring involuntarily, as something collided with her back. She fell forward, pinned underneath the weight of another person. Training kicked in and, within moments, she managed to flip her would-be attacker off her. She scrambled up into a crouch, one arm spread ready, the other steadying herself against the pavement.

But she was not being attacked. In fact, the person that had collided with her was thoroughly down, sprawled face-first in a puddle; her brown hair spilled across the water, her red uniform stained with the deeper shades of blood.

The first trickle of recognition ran like a chill up Jane's spine. She scrambled forward, rolling the woman onto her back.

She was looking down at her own face.

Nausea roiled through Jane's gut. There was no mistaking it—this could not even be her sister, who everyone was always saying looked so much like Jane. Jane's mind raced, running down all the absurd possibilities: was it time travel, like last time? Some kind of cloning experiment? An alternate reality, bleeding through? Ordinary people may have scoffed at each of these options, but Jane's life had gotten distinctly *weird* ever since that fateful day at the factory when she was fifteen. At this point, she couldn't rule out anything.

Jane quickly checked the pulse of this . . . *other* Jane, whoever she was. She pressed her fingers against Other-Jane's neck, nearly jumping out of her skin when Other-Jane's eyes fluttered open. Other-Jane winced in obvious pain, which wasn't surprising— Jane could find at least three sources of blood from just a cursory glance. She blinked as her focus seemed to come back to her, her gaze locking in on Jane.

Not a single hint of surprise ran across her face. In fact, she smiled. "It worked," she whispered, raising her hand in triumph. A bulky cuff was strapped around her wrist, and Other-Jane's last expression before she passed out was something near to bliss.

Jane hastily pulled her phone out. She ripped off a piece of her suit's silk lining, pressing it against the gash on the side of Other-Jane's head as she dialed the Heroes' emergency number.

"THIS IS SO COOL," MARIE SAID.

She was sitting at the table of the command room, the wrist cuff Other-Jane had brought with her splayed open like a dismantled sandwich.

Jane's stomach growled. Dammit, she had definitely not eaten enough at her overpriced lunch. She drummed her fingers on the table. "Well, I'm glad that you're so fascinated," Jane said. "But what does it *do*?"

Marie shook her head. "I have no idea."

"Great."

"Hey, did I say I was giving up? I'll figure it out, you can bet your panties on that. I just don't know what it does *yet*."

"Yeah, and in the meantime—"

The doors hissed open. *"Welcome, Amy. Welcome, Devin."*

"Well?" Jane asked. She leaped to her feet so fast that the chair she'd been sitting in spun several rotations in her wake.

"She's in a rejuve pod," Devin said. "But . . . I'll be honest, Jane. I'm not convinced that she's going to make it."

Jane's world tilted hard underfoot. She had to steady herself against the edge of the table. *Don't panic yet*, Jane told herself, though her voice was dry as she asked, "What else?"

Amy hesitated. She was watching Jane as if Jane was a bird that she'd stumbled upon, and was afraid that one wrong move might frighten it off. "She's . . . definitely Jane Maxwell," Amy said finally. "But I don't think that she's *you*."

Marie glanced up from her work. "What kind of zen bullshit is that?"

Amy shrugged. "That's the best I can describe it. Her sense of identity screams Jane Maxwell. I dipped into a few of her memories, and she has Jane's life . . . pretty much. But there's something distinctly *off* about her. It doesn't feel like *our* Jane."

Jane nodded, taking this in. A cool wash of relief trickled down over her: so, not time travel, then. Which means that she was not destined to suffer this same fate, somewhere in her future. The impulse to smile crept up on Jane, but she managed to stamp it down.

Amy was watching her carefully. She was always doing that: studying Jane, as if she was constantly on the lookout for some sign or another. Jane didn't know what it was Amy thought she would find—a couple of times, Jane wondered if maybe Amy harbored some kind of feelings toward her, but she'd dismissed that possibility when they were teenagers. And anyway, in recent years, her watchfulness had taken on a *wary* turn, which frankly pissed Jane the hell off.

She had to get out of there.

"I'm going to check on her," Jane said, breezing past Devin and Amy, leaving Marie behind with her work.

It was hard to say what, exactly, drew Jane back to Other-Jane. It had started off as an excuse to leave the room, but as soon as she was in the corridor, she knew that she would follow through with it. An odd sense of fate settled over Jane as she walked. She saw herself as if from above: a long white corridor, snaking into the distance; a lone figure at the far end, a shadow trailing behind her like the train of a royal robe. Her powers still hadn't settled from earlier in the day. Her chest felt warm and bubbly, her head light, her fingers tingling as if they'd been pinched asleep. It wasn't good, Jane knew, to let her powers stay switched "on" for this long, but none of her usual routines had quieted them. Energy thrummed through her as she walked, her heartbeat seeming to echo against the walls.

Light was already snaking out from underneath the door as Jane approached Other-Jane's rejuvenation pod. Jane shielded her eyes as she let herself inside. Though none of the monitors for her vitals were displaying any warnings, Other-Jane was obviously flaring. The entire room was basked in the purest white light, not a single shadow left standing.

Jane rushed up to her side. It was only because they were also her own powers that she was able to squint through and see at all; anyone else would have been blinded. Other-Jane was shaking violently in her bed. Perspiration lined her skin, which had drained of all color. Her eyes were open, but her pupils were so small that they almost weren't there. They swiveled, pin-pricks searching the room, until they settled on Jane.

Other-Jane held up her hand. Jane grasped it, wrapping Other-Jane's clammy palm tightly in her own. "It's okay," Jane whispered. "It's okay, I'm here." She brushed sweat-soaked hair from Other-Jane's forehead.

There was no denying it: Other-Jane was dying. Oddly, Jane didn't feel anything about that. Now that she knew she wasn't watching her future, all fear of what was unfolding before her had vanished.

Other-Jane's lips parted. A faint creak escaped, like she was trying to say something. Her mouth gaped, open–shut, open–shut, but Jane rested her fingers across Other-Jane's lips.

"Shh. Don't speak."

Other-Jane jerked her head, but Jane pressed down harder, straight over Other-Jane's mouth. Jane's fingers curled tightly against Other-Jane's cold cheeks. Anger and power coursed through her, so bright that her mind cleared on its own.

"I *said*, 'Don't speak,'" Jane snapped. "God, you're already dying. Why make a fuss about it? Just let go."

Other-Jane's already wide eyes widened even farther. Empty, ghostly, just the faintest dot in the middle of a bloodshot sea of white. She jerked again—and again, Jane clamped down harder. Jane's own powers were raging so pure in her mind that it was like they'd started to whisper to her, *do it, do it, do it, do it*, and half of Jane's lip curled up in a grin.

She released Other-Jane's hand, and pinched Other-Jane's nose shut instead. She watched the shock and panic flare through those unnatural eyes. Other-Jane's hands flew at Jane, but her power was leeching out in so many different ways that the attack washed over Jane like water. Jane laughed, lapping up the light that was pouring off of Other-Jane. Other-Jane's nails scratched down Jane's arms, but Jane kept up a tight grip. A tongue tried to push against Jane's hand, teeth tried to wrench out enough to bite down, but nothing was working. No matter how much Other-Jane bucked or struggled, Jane quite literally had the upper hand. The light from Other-Jane soaked into Jane's skin, adding to the rush in her head. Jane felt it seep in, stoking her own powers.

She knew what she had to do.

"Shh, shh," Jane whispered to her again. "It's okay . . . I've got you." She grinned.

Other-Jane jerked underneath Jane's grip. Once, twice. Three. Weaker and weaker. Her nails dug less forcefully against Jane's arms, until finally they dropped away completely.

She was still.

Jane stepped back, spreading her arms. A flare of light, so strong that it seared red across her eyeballs, burst out of Other-Jane . . . and plunged into Jane's waiting embrace.

The force of it sent Jane staggering back. She hit the wall of the rejuvenation pod, knocking her head. She took several deep, gasping breaths, as the power of Other-Jane tore through her. For one awful second, she feared that she'd made a mistake, that the power was going to overwhelm her. That she'd flare bright and terrible, burning herself out. Her skin felt like it was on fire. Her head felt like it was splitting open. Jane cried out, collapsing to her knees, a wail echoing through her mind. She squeezed her eyes shut, though it didn't make any difference. She curled up on herself, waiting to die.

She didn't.

The pain cut itself off. The wailing stopped. Jane cautiously raised her head, waiting for it to start up again.

When a few moments passed and nothing happened, she stood up. Her muscles felt raw, like she'd spent a week straight in the gym. Like she'd grown three inches overnight, and now her skin was tight, too small against the frame of her body. She took one tentative step. When she didn't collapse, she let out a sigh of relief. She shut her eyes, grateful for her narrow escape. A piece of her mind shifted, the way she did when she needed night vision, and Jane frowned. She opened her eyes.

The world was aglow. A pale blue and purple haze filtered over her vision, colors popping odd and bright. Traces that she had never seen before now jumped out in brilliant blue. Jane stared, gawping for several minutes. She looked at everything: her hands, her shoes, the bed that Other-Jane's body still lay sprawled upon. She took out her wallet, just for something familiar, and froze as the security features of the bills glowed obvious and in her face. Jane stared at a fifty, twisting it this way and that, while a quiet understanding fell around her, like snow in the night. A smile twitched at the edges of her mouth.

Ultraviolet.

EIGHTEEN MONTHS AGO . . .

Jane slammed the gas. Tires spun, kicking white gravel high, as she backed up and spun the car around in her parents' driveway. Her mother, running out the front door, was framed in the rear view mirror as if it was a comics panel. Jane shifted, throwing the car into drive, and blasted past the guard posts at the entrance to the street. Her tires slipped as she turned sharply onto the road, then bit down against the pavement as Cal's car shot forward.

The island whipped past Jane's windows. She blared the air conditioning, despite the fact that it was freezing outside. Jane gulped down cold lungfuls, trying to steady herself. Her hands were shaking, but the car purred steadily underneath her fragile grip. The speedometer crept up—sixty-five, seventy . . . eighty.

An animal darted in front of her. Something large, maybe a deer growing brave in the absence of summer tourists. Brakes squealed, the animal bolted. Cal's car swerved, nearly spinning out as Jane jerked it to the side. It crashed into the tall grass beside the road, and Jane didn't even bother putting it in park as she leapt out of the door. She raced across the road into the dry grass, kneeled over, and upchucked the one slice of banana bread that she'd accepted from her mother.

What had she been *thinking*, taking Cal's car? She should have used the bike. A car was . . . God, Jane might not ever be able to get into another car again. She fell back, her ass smacking against frozen dirt, and buried her face in her hands as sobs wracked her body.

Didn't her mother understand? Jane *couldn't* go back there. She might never be able to go back there again, but certainly she couldn't do it to face . . . *that* Jane. Not after what she'd done.

She hadn't meant for it to go that far. In truth, it was supposed to have been easy. Fun, even. Jane thought back to two days earlier, a bitter laugh escaping her chest as she remembered the giddy anticipation that had coursed through her. She'd had it all planned out: an outfit that matched this lesser Jane, her hair loose, contacts swapped out for glasses. She'd purchased a prepaid phone from a street vendor, called Clair at work, arranged to meet up for lunch. Jane had walked through the streets of Grand City, familiar and yet somehow distinct, practically skipping down the sidewalk in her glee. She even bought Clair flowers. Clair had lit up at the sight of her, cradling the flowers and cooing over how sweet it was, what a nice surprise. "God, Jane," she'd said, "this is so great. Thank you."

Then she'd touched Jane's face.

It was a loving gesture. Her palm flat against Jane's cheek, her fingers threaded around Jane's ear and into the tangle of her hair. Jane was sure a kiss was going to follow, and her heart skipped a beat, but instead Clair had gone still. She stared at Jane, her lips slightly parted.

Clair leaped away from her. She *recoiled*. Horror and revulsion replaced the joy upon her face as she threw the flowers at Jane's chest. Jane scrambled to catch them, confused. If it had been *Amy*, well, okay, her powers would have easily explained the reaction . . . But *Clair*?

"Get away from me," Clair said. She said it softly, barely more than a whisper, but to Jane it might as well have been shouted from the rooftops. Rejection seared through her, hot as a branding iron.

"Clair, what are you talking about? It's *me*. It's—"

"Bullshit!"

Several people turned their heads, previously content to ignore them, drawn now by the spectacle.

Jane's cheeks burned. Both from shame at being called out, and embarrassment at this taking place publicly. Her power twitched, and Jane clenched her teeth with her effort to quell it. "Fine . . . I'm—I'm not Jane," she snarled. "But can we please find someplace a little quieter to have this conversation?"

Clair shook her head. She was backing away from Jane now, panic flooding her eyes. "No . . . I know what you've done. Oh God, I know what you've done."

"Clair—"

"No!" She turned and ran, shoving through a crowd of nosy spectators.

Jane threw the flowers aside. She gave chase, ignoring the shouts of alarm as she and Clair went racing down the sidewalks. Power and humiliation boiled through her. *Talk.* That was all Jane had wanted to do. Clair had information, some bizarre connection to Jane's own world that gave her insight into what was going to happen there, and *all Jane wanted* was to find out what this world's Jane was going to write in the next story arc of *Hopefuls.* That's *it.* That's *all she needed.*

But oh, no, Clair had to go and make it complicated. Had to run, triggering the hunter instinct that had been drilled into Jane from so many years spent chasing criminals down these very streets.

Clair fled to a nearby parking garage, found her car in record time. Jane had to jump aside to avoid being run over as Clair squealed past, the sound of her engine revving loudly against the surrounding concrete.

Looking back, Jane probably should have left it there, but what would happen when Clair got home? When she ran to her own Jane, telling her everything? Maybe this world's Jane wouldn't believe her, but Jane couldn't take that risk. Self-preservation guided her to the nearest car, and within moments she was barreling down the city streets.

She had almost caught up by the time they reached the tunnel. Jane surged forward, her car's front bumper connecting with Clair's rear one. And then . . . Clair must have panicked. Swerved when she should have used the brakes, or something, because the next thing Jane knew, the taillights were crawling up the wall beside her. They traced the line of the tunnel, all the way to the arched ceiling, where they seemed to hover for one endless second. Jane saw the gap between the tires and the ceiling, and then Clair's car slammed against the road with a sickening crunch.

"*Amy!*"

Jane was out of her car before she realized what she was doing. She leaped up, jumping across the tangled mess of Clair's wreck.

The driver's side door was crunched shut, but it didn't last long under a concentrated laser beam. Jane ripped the door off. She scrambled down. Clair was upside down, pinned between airbags and seat belts, her head smashed against the roof of the car. A pool of blood was already soaking into the fabric.

"Shit, shit, shit!" Jane said. "Clair, come on. Come on. I'm here, it's okay." She reached in, groping around for the seat belt release. Somewhere in the back of her mind was a warning about moving injured people, but Jane couldn't listen to it. She dragged Clair out of the car. Cradled Clair's head in her lap. Clair's eyes were slowly blinking, like she couldn't quite wake up. Jane brushed Clair's bangs aside.

"Why couldn't you have just listened to me?" Jane whispered. "It didn't have to come to this."

A muscle in Clair's face twitched, as if she was still trying to flinch away from Jane's touch. Even now, as Jane held her, bleeding in her lap. Even now, as she was dying. Even now.

Jane's hands curled into fists. A siren was wailing somewhere in the distance now—they didn't have long.

"Dammit, Clair. *Talk* to me. Tell me what you know. I *know* you have a connection to my world—I *know* you can predict what's going to happen there. I need you to tell me what you've learned, do you understand? Clair? *Clair!*"

It wasn't working. Clair's eyes had fallen shut now, and she was stubbornly making no more effort to open them back up.

"Fine," Jane snapped. "You want to do this the hard way? Let's do this the hard way."

Jane dug around in her pockets. Her fingers curled around a small disk—a prototype of a device she'd once hoped to use on this world's Jane, before she learned that Jane didn't have powers over here. Jane didn't know why she'd brought it with her. Maybe, on some level, she knew that it would always have to come to this.

A twinge of guilt stabbed Jane as she moved Clair off her lap. But . . . really, what difference did it make now? Clair was dying—and anyway, it's not like it mattered. This wasn't really *Amy*, after all, merely a cheap copy of her. Someone who didn't even possess a fraction of Amy's true power. There were probably hundreds—thousands?—of them out there, in the spread of parallel worlds. Just because Jane had only ever managed to figure out how to cross over to this one . . . that didn't make it any less likely.

She had to work quickly. The sirens were growing louder. A few people were coming over to gawp at the wreckage, but for the most part everyone crept their cars around it, wrapped up in their own concerns. Jane threw a temporary wall around them, warping the light so that anyone glancing over wouldn't see what was happening. She tore open the top of Clair's shirt and stuck the cold metal disk to the skin between her breasts. Tiny white electrodes were housed inside, which Jane hurriedly dragged out and spread to Clair's temples.

This, at least, got a little bit of Clair's dwindling attention. She blinked once or twice more, a frown marring her forehead. "What . . . ?" she started to ask, but that was as far as she was able to get.

Jane leaned over, planting a fast kiss on Clair's cheek. "Just remember that you did this to yourself," she whispered.

She pressed a button.

Clair flared. Her mouth and eyes flew open, her body jerked up, flopping against the asphalt like a fish. She coughed, blood spurting out of her mouth and spraying Jane in the face. A thin wail escaped her, though it fast trickled down into a moan, like a dying animal.

Jane slapped Clair's cheek. "Stop it! You have to focus, Clair. This isn't going to last long, not in your state. *Tell me what you know.*"

Clair's eyes flew wildly around the tunnel. "Where . . . ? What happ—?"

"UltraViolet," Jane said. She pinned Clair's shoulders down, and leaned over until there was nothing above Clair but Jane's own stern face. "What happens to UltraViolet? *Tell me!*"

"Ultra . . . ," Clair started. Her breath was coming so fast that it was difficult to hear her, her pulse beating so hard that veins were popping up all along her forehead. Clair's pupils were constricting. The device was drawing Clair's power to the surface all at once—dangerous, even deadly, for someone in a normal state, but with the extensive injuries that Clair had already suffered? It was a long shot, but it was Jane's *only* shot.

"Come on, you bitch," Jane snarled. "You're dying, just give it up. UltraViolet!"

Clair's gaze settled on Jane, her pupils dilating just a little in recognition. "UltraViolet," Clair managed to whisper. She stared, in what looked almost like a state of awe, at Jane.

And then she started to laugh. High and loud, her mirth barking out and echoing against the walls of the tunnel. Her teeth were shockingly white against the ribbons of blood seeped between them, the sharp red flick of her tongue.

Jane gripped Clair's shoulders harder, nails cutting through Clair's shirt. "Stop it!"

But Clair didn't stop. She laughed and laughed, laughed until she started to cough. Jane jerked back, and Clair turned herself partially toward the road, coughing out a pool of red. When Clair was finished she groaned, falling onto her back once more. She closed her eyes.

"Jane," Clair whispered.

The sirens were almost here. Shrieking as they plowed through the knot of traffic, splashing the walls red and blue.

"Fuck," Jane said. She yanked the device off Clair, electrodes popping, and hastily stuffed it back into her pocket. She drew the bubble of distorted light tighter around herself as EMTs raced to Clair's fallen body. Jane stole one last look back: Clair's face, Amy's face, looked almost peaceful as blue gloved hands strapped an oxygen mask over her nose and mouth. Jane's heart twisted, and she hastily turned away.

Nobody saw her leave.

JANE HAD RUN TO HER MOTHER IN PANIC, AND WHEN SHE did finally tell her, she told her in the desperate hope of confession. Granted, she . . . she'd skimmed over certain details. But you couldn't blame her for that. Jane had wanted a mother's forgiveness, had *needed* a mother's forgiveness.

Instead, she'd gotten a lecture. Mrs. Maxwell had gone all high and mighty, telling Jane about how she *needed* to go back and explain Clair's accident to that other Jane, about how she *needed* to stand up and do the right thing. Even if it was the last thing that Jane wanted to do—it was the *right* thing to do, and Captain Lumen always does the *right* thing.

This is when Jane had stormed to her feet. The bar stool that she'd been perched on went toppling back. She'd been managing to hold it together, staying remarkably controlled (given the circumstances), barely even raising her voice.

No longer.

"What if I don't *want* to do the right thing?" she shouted. "What if I'm *tired* of always being the pillar of moral fortitude?! Shit, don't I do *enough*? Don't I save enough lives? Do I *always* have to be the bigger person, too, in *every* aspect of my fucking life?"

Mrs. Maxwell set her coffee mug down so heavily on the counter that Jane jumped. "Um, yes? That's not only a large part of being an adult, that's what you signed up for when you put on that mask. You're not just a person anymore, Jane, you're not even really *you*—you're a *hero*. A symbol. You're supposed to represent everything that is good and honest and true in people. You're supposed to be *better*. Even when anyone else would want to quit, you turn around and fight the good fight. So that when the rest of us are tempted to give into our baser instincts, maybe we can remember everything that you stand for, and maybe we'll be able to find a piece of that inside of ourselves, too. So that we won't . . . We won't—"

Mrs. Maxwell broke off. She turned away, her hand pressed against her mouth as if she'd said too much.

Jane stared at the hunch of her mother's shoulders, too stunned to even feel anger.

A *hero*. A *symbol*. Not even really a *person*.

Jane knew that was how some people saw her, although she might not have ever put it quite so directly. But certainly the idea was there. It's what had been making her uniform slightly uncomfortable lately, like it didn't quite fit anymore. Not since Other-Jane. Not since her powers had expanded tenfold, her ability to manipulate the electromagnetic spectrum shooting up into and beyond the ultraviolet range. Not since she'd made the decision to seek out another parallel world, another Jane that would help her expand her powers even further.

But it was one thing to know that other people saw her like this—it was quite another to hear it coming from *her own mother.* Her *mother,* who had seen every ugly stage of Jane's childhood, heard every rebellious curse from her angsty teenage mouth. Her mother, who should have known better.

Jane's rage came rushing back to her, even stronger than when it had left. A burst of light coursed through her, and she narrowed it down to shatter her mother's coffee mug. It was one of Mrs. Maxwell's favorites, and Jane enjoyed the gasp of surprise as her mother turned and realized what Jane had done.

"You know what?" Jane said. She made sure to stand tall, her spine straight. Her hero pose. She pointed at her mother. "*Fuck you.* I *am* still a person, Mom. I *don't* always have to do what's right—and if that somehow makes it harder for you to maintain your *own* humanity, then you can kiss my fucking ass."

Mrs. Maxwell's eyes flew wide in shock. "Jane . . ."

Jane's hand snapped up, cutting her off. She spun on her heel. She was halfway to the front door before her mother seemed to realize what was going on.

"Jane, wait!"

She didn't wait.

"I'm sorry!" Mrs. Maxwell shouted, as Jane let a burst of light blast the front door off of its hinges. "I'm sorry! Jane, please! Come back—you're right, I—That wasn't even really about you, I just feel so guilty, I—"

Jane wasn't even listening. She yanked open the door of Cal's car, slamming it shut as the engine roared to life.

"*Jane!*"

But a spray of white gravel and a puff of exhaust were Jane's only parting remarks.

THREE WEEKS AGO . . .

It was a glorious explosion.

Jane and Cal watched it from the rooftop of the headquarters. A green arc of energy streaking like reverse lightning toward the sky. The blackening of the clouds, roiling thick across the city. The energy burned bright as it flashed back and forth from sky to ground, over and over again, until the whole city started to tremble. Cal steadied himself against one of the many satellite receivers that lined the roof of the headquarters, but Jane stood tall as she watched. She would not flinch away from this. She felt in her bones that this was the path she was meant to follow. As the energy reached its crescendo, pouring down into the building where Doctor Demolition had set up his device, a sense of peace settled thickly over Jane's shoulders.

Freedom, she thought, as every window of the building exploded all at once.

The blast was so bright that everyone else had to shield their eyes, but Jane saw it all. Glass and metal flying; girders ripped apart like toothpicks; flames billowing out, destroying everything in their wake. The building burst outward, taking several of its neighbors with it, singeing several more.

"My god," Cal whispered.

Jane reached out, patting his shoulder reassuringly. It had been a delicate balance, swaying Cal to her way of thinking. To get him to see these masks for the prisons that they really were. But she knew that she needed to secure his loyalty if she had any chance of dismantling the Heroes of Hope from the inside out, and so she'd stuck with it. Long days and longer, grueling nights.

It would be worth it. Jane knew this, as a stirring of hope rose in her chest. Smoke was billowing up from the blast site now, the familiar wails and screams of people running around madly down below. It was a sound she knew well, except this time, it was *Jane* who had caused it.

Correction: *UltraViolet* had caused it. For that was who she was now, or at least it would be very soon. Jane rolled the name around on her tongue, savoring it, as the first of the calls came in. The rest of the Heroes, reaching out in a panic. How had their plan failed? How had they not managed to reach the building in time? What were they going to *do*??

Jane muted her earpiece, laughing at them as she and Cal made their way down the tower. She zipped up the last piece of her familiar red uniform, the prison that she would soon be freeing herself from. Her plans were taking shape—she'd just finished her new uniform, rigged out with smoke bombs and lightning-generating gloves to disguise her powers—but she still had work to do: they had to capture Doctor Demolition, they had to worm out the admission of who he was really working for. Then Jane, as UltraViolet, would need to carefully set up her grand chess move, the one that would necessitate the capture of the parallel Jane. This was assuming that they could trigger what Jane believed to be the parallel Jane's latent superpowers, and assuming that she would prove capable of controlling and growing them. But *then* . . .

Jane took a deep breath. One step at a time, she told herself. It's the mantra that she'd been living by for more than a year now, ever since she'd made the decision to . . . retire.

One step at a time. There were so few left anymore:

Capture Doctor Demolition . . .

Extract the name . . .

And then . . .

Jane smiled. And then she could disappear.

NOW . . .

Jane didn't remember passing out, but the sharp tang of anesthetic brought her back to herself.

She jerked awake.

An all-powerful light filled her vision, washing everything the purest white. Jane blinked, letting her powers clear the sight before her. Shapes resolved themselves from the mist: concentric circles, one much larger than the other, like a wide-brimmed hat, or a stretched-open eye pinning Jane in place. A few more blinks, and the center turned into an egg, bulbous underneath a tented background.

No, not just bulbous—an actual bulb. So bright that it almost hurt, and trapped in a wide fixture which swayed just the smallest bit over Jane's head.

Panic sent her scrambling, but straps held her in place. Jane looked down. She was lashed to a . . . table? Bench? One of those tilted slabs, like a pushcart for people, that movies use to indicate the situation was about to get Serious.

Jane gulped, her mouth suddenly dry.

The rest of the room wasn't any more inspiring: it was the same place where they'd found Allison, apparently, because there she was, pinned beneath her own lamp, still unconscious and tied to a chair some distance away. Tables separated them, an assortment of nasty-looking instruments strewn across the surface.

Heavy footsteps sounded behind her. Cal came around. He'd changed out of his uniform, put on black jeans and a navy v-neck t-shirt that clung to his chest and biceps. He gave Jane a sympathetic look as he unclipped a walkie from his back pocket and raised it to his face. He pressed the button. "She's awake."

A subtle click preceded Jane's own voice coming through from somewhere else. "Excellent. I'll be right there."

"Cal," Jane said. She did not even try to keep the fear and pleading out of her voice. "Don't do this. Let me out."

Cal smirked as he clipped the walkie back into place. "Can't do that, Main Jane."

Jane winced at the use of her nickname. "Don't you dare call me that. Not if you're going to betray everything we ever had together."

"Ah, but that's the thing." Cal motioned between them. "We never had anything, did we? It was always *Amy* this, and *Amy* that. What?" he added, scoffing, "You think I didn't notice?"

"So because I wouldn't sleep with you, you're going to throw my life away?"

Cal rolled his eyes. "Don't be so dramatic. You never noticed me. Not in the way I wanted you to, no, but not any other way either. Admit it: I was always just taking up space with you."

"That's not true," Jane said. "I trusted you. I liked you. You trained me! We . . . God, Cal, we were friends. We've always been friends."

"The real Jane, yes." Cal smiled. "And more. So don't think for a minute that you have the power to come between us."

A laugh drifted in from the shadows. "Loyal, isn't he?" Ultra-Violet said, as she stepped forward. Her image was solid and whole, Jane's own face painted up with those purple lips and smoky eyes. Her hair was pulled back in a high ponytail, teased and curled so that it floated behind her.

Jane's stomach writhed. Given the options, she decided she preferred *not* being able to see what UltraViolet looked like. Jane said nothing as UltraViolet, in her skintight purple catsuit and stiletto heels, marched over and looped her arms around Cal's hips. Cal's arm was instantly around her, and he buried her face in an overly dramatic kiss. Jane nearly vomited in her mouth, just watching.

UltraViolet pulled away, raising her hands and shooing him back with her fingers. "Find something useful to do," she said, and to Jane's surprise, Cal turned and moved out of sight.

UltraViolet shook herself off, a tiny sneer crossing her face and then smoothing itself out. "Now"—she turned her attention to Jane, grinning—"shall we begin?"

Jane couldn't help it—she glanced nervously at the equipment spread around her. She had an unpleasant sensation of being in a dentist's office or a surgeon's operating room, pinned underneath the light. She felt ridiculous, suddenly, dressed up like a hero. Allison's words from their first dinner together came back to her, how she'd called the Heroes a bunch of trick-or-treaters. Jane never should have taken insult to it: it was true. She'd been prancing around the city pretending to do good, but really she was nothing more than a child playacting at being strong and brave.

And now she was going to die.

The idea struck her hard and fast, stealing her breath. Oh God, she was going to die. Trapped in a parallel world, where no one from her real life would ever find out what had happened to her.

"Please," she said. It hadn't worked on Cal, but fuck it, Jane had nothing to lose. "Please just let me go."

UltraViolet laughed. She pinched her chin, her finger tapping her cheek in a mockery of contemplation. "Hmm. How about . . . no?"

"What do you *want* from me?!"

The question came out more desperate than Jane intended. She'd written scenes like this—oh, so many scenes like this—and the hero always put on a brave face.

A single eyebrow arched up. "Your powers, of course," Ultra-Violet said, as if it was obvious. She motioned at the equipment around them. "Why would I go through all the effort to lure you here if I could have gotten what I wanted anywhere else? Do you have any idea how complicated it was, to stage a scenario where the Heroes would need to turn to *you* for help?"

Jane's stomach dropped, as if UltraViolet's words had punched her in the gut.

She'd been right. All this time, all these odd little coincidences, the perfect timing . . . She *knew* that UltraViolet was trying to manipulate her, and dammit, *she was right.*

Jane had never hated being right as much as she did in this moment.

But okay, okay, there was no time to panic. Somewhere, even now, Jane's mind was whirring. UltraViolet had turned her back, which made it marginally easier to think. Even if she was selecting some horrible tool from her horrible instrument tray, even if Jane's death was inching ever closer.

Tears pricked Jane's eyes. Dammit, what did she think she was going to be able to *do*? This wasn't a comic book. There was no rescue coming her way. There was no one tiny weakness that Jane could use to exploit UltraViolet. She didn't have a trick up her sleeve. She couldn't even get out of these *restraints*!

She was supposed to be a hero, but right now all Jane felt like was a fraud.

UltraViolet turned back. She had a metal disk in her hand, cold and clinical.

Jane shrieked as UltraViolet yanked open the neck of Jane's uniform.

UltraViolet rolled her eyes. "Pathetic," she muttered. She pulled the front of Jane's uniform open, just enough to slap the disk onto Jane's sternum. Two white electrodes were nestled inside, and UltraViolet strung them up to adhere to Jane's temples.

"You know," UltraViolet said, "there's a certain poetry in this."

Jane hesitated. The last thing she wanted to do was rise to UltraViolet's bait—but on the other hand, it could only work in Jane's favor to keep her talking.

At least, that's how it worked in comics. Who knew if the rules were the same here? But it was all Jane had to go on, all that she knew when it came to situations like this.

"How so?"

UltraViolet smiled, purple lips curling in self-satisfaction. "Let's just say that it'll be interesting to see if you handle this experience any better than Clair did."

Jane rolled her eyes. "You expect me to fall for that?"

"It's no joke. I've been to your world plenty."

"Oh, I know all about your little stint as a stalker," Jane said, and when UltraViolet glanced up, brow wrinkled, Jane added, "Your mom told me."

"Of *course* she did."

"Yeah. So if you think that you're going to shock me with this blinding revelation, think again. If anything, the story only makes you look sad and pathetic. Spying on us from a distance, sobbing over Clair's accident . . . running to *mommy* for comfort? But let me tell you something, bitch: you don't have the *right* to cry over Clair. You have *no idea* how amazing she was."

A smirk drew up the corner of UltraViolet's mouth. "No. I probably don't. But I'll tell you what I *do* know." She leaned in, so close that her breath was hot against Jane's cheek as she whispered, "That wasn't an accident."

The burst of light from Jane's hands was fast, and involuntary. She balled her fists, cutting it off, but the damage was done. UltraViolet stood back, a look of feigned innocence upon her face. She shrugged.

"Sorry," UltraViolet said, in a voice the exact opposite of sorry. She raised her hands in a what-can-you-do? gesture. "It's the truth."

"Don't you *dare* say something like that."

UltraViolet's lip jutted out in a mock-pout. "Aw. Did I hurt your feewings?"

"No," Jane said. "I just don't believe you."

"Why not? Why should I care? She wasn't *my* wife."

Another flash. "Shut up!" Jane shouted.

UltraViolet laughed. "I know. The truth hurts, doesn't it? But it's important that you know, Jane Maxwell. It is so important. I didn't just *witness* Clair's accident, sweetie. I made it. And then I dragged her out of it—"

"Shut up!"

"—and I *killed her*."

"*Shut up!*"

The room flooded. Blaring light and sound and gizmos switching on. The walkie-talkie that UltraViolet had been using blared, *SHUT UP! SHUT UP! SHUT UP!*, and a wordless shriek of rage bounded through the factory.

UltraViolet's grin lit up so bright that it may as well have been electric. "There it is," she said, her voice drowning in the noise as she reached forward and switched on the device sitting on Jane's chest.

LIGHT FLARED.

Jane, however, did not.

She wouldn't be able to explain what happened, certainly not at the time, nor for a long while after. What she knew is what she saw: UltraViolet's finger, pressing a button on the disk on Jane's chest. A flash of light, a burst of electrical energy. One of the wires that led to Jane's temple crossed the chain of her necklace, and this is where the spark began. The necklace glowed—Clair's ring glowed—and then the energy thrummed straight down to Jane's bones as it roared to life. It burst outward, a bubble of glowing red and purple and pink.

UltraViolet was thrown back. Cal, who'd been approaching again, his phone in hand, was thrown back. He had the harder landing, but then, he took the larger burst of energy. His body went flying, crashing into a set of shelves full of beakers and spare parts, everything falling and shattering underneath his weight.

Jane screamed, and the disk on her chest buzzed and burned.

Energy surged through her, enough to fry the restraints holding her in place. She threw them off, leaping up from the table and ripping the disk from her chest just as UltraViolet was staggering back to her feet.

The world around Jane was aglow. Jane had drawn this before, Captain Lumen's powers switched on so much that light seemed to ooze from everything, but never did she expect to actually see it. It was always written in the Hero Moments, the times when Captain Lumen had to dig deep, the moment when the tables would turn and you just *knew* that the enemy would be vanquished in the next few pages.

No pressure, or anything.

Before Jane knew what was happening, UltraViolet was barreling toward her. Jane leaped aside, but UltraViolet's nails raked down Jane's arm, and caught on the lacing of her sleeve. Her grip tightened, and Jane was yanked like an elastic snapping back. She slammed against the table, the light glaring in her face.

Jane's wince was more reflexive than anything else. If she was the proper Captain Lumen, she wouldn't have shut her eyes at all, knowing that she'd still be able to see even in the brightest glow.

But she wasn't, so she did. And in the meantime, the "proper" Captain Lumen—twisted now into a darker shade of herself—had bent down and retrieved the disk from where it had fallen to the floor.

There was no way in hell that Jane was ever letting that thing touch her again. Her knee flew up before she could think about it. It collided with UltraViolet's elbow, jostling her arm aside. Just enough for Jane to slip her own arm free, and punch UltraViolet in the ribs.

UltraViolet cried out. She'd been favoring that side ever since she was thrown back, and the pain of it was enough of a distraction to weaken her grip on Jane. Jane slipped out, slithering off of the table and landing in a crouch.

"Shouldn't have had Cal teach me quite so well," Jane said, as she stood back up.

UltraViolet snorted. "Learn this." She reared back and kicked the table hard at Jane.

It collided with Jane just above her hips. She staggered back, and in this opening, a flash of condensed light shot in Jane's direction, straight for her heart.

Instinct threw Jane's hand up. She knew that it would do her no good, and she flinched, anticipating the impact.

A soft tickle brushed her palm, like a feather across her skin. Jane lowered her hand and stared at it, pink and unblemished.

She looked up. UltraViolet was watching her with matching bewilderment.

Jane threw her own laser beam in UltraViolet's direction, and UltraViolet reached up, almost lazily, like catching a baseball in a glove. The light struck UltraViolet's palm, dissipating as soon as it landed.

UltraViolet's mouth twisted. "Guess we'll have to do this the old-fashioned way," she said. She whipped a knife from an unseen sheath, the blade glinting as she turned it in Jane's direction.

Jane was running before she realized that was her plan. Around the equipment, over a table, through a door. Jane blinked, shifting her vision in the sudden darkness. The door led way to a staggeringly enormous room, the ceiling so far above her that it was difficult to see. Huge vats filled most of the space, glowing in infrared, a conveyor belt snaking between them. Ladders and catwalks provided access up above, but there was no way that Jane would have time to climb up before UltraViolet caught her. She needed someplace to hide, and fast.

She darted between the vats. With luck, the heat signatures being generated by whatever chemicals were cooking up inside would mask her from UltraViolet's vision. They glowed so bright in infrared that it was certainly distracting for *Jane*, and she switched her vision back to normal as she considered her next move.

Footsteps echoed among the burbling of the chemicals, the groan of the pipes.

"Really, Jane?" UltraViolet called. Her voice boomed through the open room. "Aren't we a little old for hide-and-seek?"

Jane said nothing. She inched her way along the edge of the

vats, mindful of every shaky breath, every heartbeat slamming against her ribs. If she could just find a way out of here . . .

Oh, but then what? UltraViolet could likely track her, no matter where Jane went. Even returning to her own world wouldn't keep her safe—experience alone had taught her that.

As if sensing her thought process, UltraViolet laughed. "You know, this really is pointless. Where are you going to go? There's no one to help you this time. You're all on your own. Poor little Jane, always alone now. No Clair. No Amy. Not even *Cal*—and trust me, he's a pitiful substitute to begin with."

Jane shut her eyes. *No*, she told herself. *Do not let her get to you. You have to find a way out of here. That's all that matters right now.*

Jane craned her neck. She blinked, temporarily switching her infrared back on. There seemed to be a door in the far corner. There: a solid plan—well, part of one, at any rate.

UltraViolet's footsteps drew closer. Jane scrambled back, retracing her steps. Okay, fine—she could get to the door some other way. They circled the same vat for a few seconds before UltraViolet paused. Jane stopped, too. Shit, was UltraViolet listening, as well? Had Jane been too fast, in her movements? Too loud with her breathing?

"I have to say, I really don't know what Amy sees in you," UltraViolet said after a moment.

Jane shut her eyes in relief. Taunting, she could handle.

"She loves you, you know."

Was it Jane's imagination, or did a tinge of sadness mar Ultra-Violet's otherwise booming voice? But then it was gone—Jane could *hear* the smirk as UltraViolet continued:

"And you love her. Though I'm sure you're denying that to yourself, even now. But *I know*, Jane Maxwell. I've seen that look a thousand times."

Jane gritted her teeth. *Don't react. Don't react, don't react, don't react.*

She took another step around the vats.

"What do you suppose *Clair* would think, though?"

Jane froze. *Don't. React.*

"I mean, I know she's dead. So I suppose that nothing you

do can technically be called cheating anymore. But *really*, Jane. Are you *that* desperate for a lay these days, that you'd desecrate the memory of your wife by sleeping with a cheap copy of her?"

A burst of adrenaline shot through Jane. For a second, there was nothing but the pounding of her feet, the thunder of blood in her ears. "She's not a cheap copy!" Jane shouted, as she rounded the vat.

UltraViolet wasn't there.

Jane scrambled to a halt. A faint shimmer rippled the darkness, and in an instant Jane remembered her own comics: Captain Lumen could refract light around him, essentially turning himself invisible. Jane blinked, and the infrared glow of an orange fist coming at her filled her vision.

She ducked. The fist went flying over her head, and Jane wasted no time—she swung her own punch sideways, connecting once again with the tender flesh of UltraViolet's injury.

UltraViolet cried out, collapsing to her side. Jane stood up, glaring down at the heat signature of her double.

"I can still see you, you bitch," Jane said. She kicked at Ultra-Violet, but UltraViolet rolled out of the way.

"Shit," Jane heard UltraViolet mutter. But in an instant the infrared glow was fading, refracting until there was nothing left to see in either range.

Jane stood in the middle of the factory, surrounded by vats but feeling utterly exposed.

And yet, that didn't matter anymore. UltraViolet had been retreating as she cloaked herself, and now Jane knew one thing for certain: there was no way she was letting that monster escape.

"What's wrong?" Jane called into the darkness. "Can't handle a fair fight?"

There was no answer. Jane strained her ears, and peered all around, but neither footsteps nor the faint shimmer of Ultra-Violet's refraction were anywhere to be found.

"Goddammit," Jane muttered. She glanced to the side—a ladder rose up along one of the vats, like a rose trellis on a garden wall. Jane scrambled up it, heading for the catwalks. If she could get a higher vantage point, out from the forest of the vats, perhaps she'd have an easier time spotting UltraViolet.

The grating of the catwalk rattled underneath her. Jane tried not to think about how long it was since the last time this place had undergone a safety inspection, as she toed along the narrow pathway. She told herself not to look down as she walked. Jane gripped the railing. She counted her footsteps, until she felt that she was probably in the middle of the room, and only then did she stop, only then did she allow herself to look out over the sea of bubbling vats.

Pain shot through Jane's thigh. Jane cried out, twisting, her fingers colliding with the hilt of a blade as she clutched at her injury. She barely had time to process it, though—pain, blade, blood—before a fist that she couldn't see connected with the underside of her chin, and sent her sprawling onto her back.

UltraViolet shimmered back into sight above her. "You're right," she said. "I don't like a fair fight."

She lunged for the blade in Jane's leg. Jane kicked up, hooking UltraViolet in the gut as she grabbed UltraViolet's arms. It was a move that Cal had just taught her, in their last training session. She had never quite gotten the hang of it, but it worked now. Maybe UltraViolet had never mastered it, either. Jane watched in satisfaction as UltraViolet was flipped over Jane, coming to land with a *bang* and a rattle on the catwalk beyond Jane's head.

There was no time to gloat. Jane hauled herself up, grinding her teeth together to keep from screaming in agony. She was maybe halfway to her feet when an arm wrapped around her neck, dragging her backward. Jane elbowed at UltraViolet, but it didn't work. She tried to pull on UltraViolet's arm, which was pressing down on Jane's windpipe, but it didn't work. Tried shoving them both back, but it didn't work.

She reached for the knife in her leg. It was a stretch, pinned back as she was, struggling to keep her footing, struggling to keep from passing out. Jane's fingers knocked against the hilt, sending a fresh wave of pain and nausea roiling through her.

The blade felt just as bad ripping out as it had plunging in. Jane gasped, or tried to, her chest burning as her lungs sucked in nothing. She threw her arm up, not even caring at this point what the knife hit.

It sunk into flesh, not her own. UltraViolet howled as her grip on Jane released, and Jane staggered forward, catching herself on the railing. Jane gulped down air, but she did not have time for the sweet relief it gave her. She spun, just in time to grab UltraViolet's wrist. The knife was free again, clutched and aimed at Jane. The force of UltraViolet's rage shoved Jane backward, until the railing dug into her spine. Jane leaned back, the knife and UltraViolet's face both leering over her. Blood dripped from the blade, splashing against Jane's cheek.

Jane had never been great at arm wrestling. Her muscles were screaming at her from the effort of holding back the blade at her face. For one heart-stopping moment they failed, and the blade surged another inch or two closer before Jane was able to catch hold again.

She was going to lose this struggle if she didn't do something. Jane jerked to the side—she released the grip with one of her hands, just long enough to reach out and flick a laser beam at the numerous pipes that littered the air above them.

Sparks flew, and metal screamed and groaned. A pipe swung down, forcing UltraViolet to leap back in order to avoid being clobbered. Jane ran as best as she could, ignoring the pain in her leg. Blood spurted out of the wound with every step, seeping between Jane's fingers as she tried to hold herself together. The grating hissed underfoot, acid burning into the metal of the catwalk. Just a little farther, and she'd reach another door, above the one she'd spotted earlier. Beneath her, liquid from the pipe was pooling into the vats, which burbled and sent up great belches of steam.

The shriek of metal burst through the factory. Jane's stomach lurched as the catwalk disappeared from underfoot. Apparently, she had given UltraViolet an idea: the catwalk swung down, the support cables above flapping like handkerchiefs being waved at a parade. Jane fell, forward and down, her hands scrambling for something to grab on to.

She managed to hook part of the grating. Her fingers screamed at her, as her weight caught against them. She crashed into the catwalk, both her and the metal swinging ominously.

UltraViolet's laugh billowed throughout the room.

If Jane was stronger, better trained, perhaps she would have been able to hold on longer. Perhaps, even, she would have been able to catch her footing against the grating; scale the hanging catwalk, scramble her way back up to stable ground.

She wasn't, though.

Her fingers slipped, first one and then another in a cascading sequence of doom. Jane screamed as she fell. She landed—hard—on one of the conveyor belts, the whole thing shuddering on impact.

How long did she lie there? It was impossible to tell. The world compressed and blurred, her head spinning, her whole body aching. On some level she knew that this wasn't over, that UltraViolet was still loose in the factory, was quite possibly coming for her right now. That she needed to get up, needed to fight back, needed to find the resolve to *keep going*, but these thoughts were crowded out by another, so large that it overwhelmed the rest:

Being a superhero *sucked*.

The conveyor belt jerked beneath her, jolting Jane out of her self-pity. Gears groaned from lack of use, and the belt stuttered in fits and spurts as it began to trudge forward.

Jane blinked, trying to clear her head. She dragged herself onto her elbows, her eyes immediately widening in terror. The belt was drawing her forward, toward a giant spigot hanging off one of the vats. When the factory was still in operation, this line must have brought in canisters to be filled, because now great spurts of liquid were shooting at intervals onto the conveyor belt, melting through metal and rubber. Yet still, it soldiered on. Jane was jerked forward, once and then again. She rolled to her side, leaping from the conveyor as a spray of chemicals flew over her head.

Her leg collapsed as she hit the floor. Jane tried to roll with it, though it wasn't as graceful as it appeared in her head. She reached beneath the armor of her uniform and ripped off a piece of the base layer, wrapping her thigh in a crude bandage.

Good enough. She dragged herself back to her feet.

UltraViolet stood in the middle of the room. She had her

hands on her hips, as if nothing in the world could possibly touch her. The vats stood as tall sentries around her, still churning from the mess that Jane had made above.

"Nice work," UltraViolet called. "I have to admit, I couldn't have planned it better myself. The city is going to *love* it when it comes out that Captain Lumen sabotaged this place."

"I didn't sab—"

"Well, maybe you didn't get the formula quite right, no. But then, you weren't *trying*." UltraViolet grinned. "*I*, on the other hand . . . well, let's just say I've made sure your hard work won't go to waste."

Jane didn't have time to ask, even if she'd wanted to. With a lazy flick of UltraViolet's wrist, a beam shot from her fingertips. It struck a trail of green liquid, oozing across the floor, and instantly ignited the end of it. Fire licked up the line, following it back, until it had completely encircled one of the vats like a brazier. Panic coursed through Jane, as the line crept from one vat to the next to the next, each one lighting up in turn.

"Enjoy the show!" UltraViolet called. She blew Jane a kiss, then whirled and raced off into the darkness.

FLAME BILLOWED UP, PERILOUSLY CLOSE TO JANE. SHE
flinched back as she darted between the vats. They were already
wheezing and hissing and groaning, and as Jane leaped up the
stairs to a lower platform, the pressure gauges of the control
panels teetered toward the red.

"Fuck!" Jane shouted. She ran her hands over her head, grabbing her ponytail. She had absolutely no idea what to do. What
could she do? She wasn't an engineer, or a firefighter, or even a
proper *superhero*. She had no powers to control flame or water
or time. Her heart skittered as nervously as the needle on the
gauge.

There was no way that she could handle this on her own, that
was for sure. Jane glanced around, not knowing what she was
looking for. She needed help, but the only person around to help
her was . . .

Allison. Her heat signature glowed through the wall, shifting as if she was finally beginning to wake.

Shit, it was better than nothing.

Jane raced through the door. A glance to the side of the room confirmed that Cal was gone, probably dragged out by Ultra-Violet while Jane was distracted—but she didn't have time for that. Jane looked over; sure enough, Allison was just starting to lift her head.

"What . . . ?" she muttered, as she squinted into the darkness around her. "Hello? Who's there?"

"Allison!" Jane ran toward her, this woman that wasn't her sister.

Allison took *one look* in Jane's direction, and instantly groaned. "Oh, no. Not *you*." She glanced down at herself. "Wait a second . . . Why the fuck am I dressed like *you*?"

Jane rocked to a halt. She had reached the edge of the pool of light that poured down over Allison—enough for Allison to see the iconic red of her uniform, but still obscuring Jane's face.

For now. One more step, and there would be no more secret between them.

This world's Jane clearly didn't want her sister to know. But then, this world's Jane had also turned into UltraViolet, so maybe it was time for Jane to stop worrying about whether or not she was "messing up" her double's life.

"Because," Jane said, as she stepped forward, "UltraViolet needed a body double."

Was it wrong to enjoy this moment, just a tiny bit? Jane had always liked drawing these moments. One panel with Captain Lumen hidden from view, just a few hints of her true identity visible to the readers. A slim diagonal line to divide the panels, and now here she is again, stepping out into the light. Everything behind her is drawn in dark blues and grays, all the color and vibrancy reserved for the hero shot, the moment of truth revealed. Jane would position her panels at the top corner, filling the rest of the page with a reaction shot of Allison. The room in shadow around her, a silhouette of Jane's own back visible along the side. Allison's face, brighter and filled with greater detail than the rest of the scene.

Her face narrowed into a withering stare. "Get me out of this."

Jane's mouth twisted up. Okay, so some things don't quite live up to expectations. Still: Jane hurried over to Allison. Without a word, she reached out and aimed a laser beam at the ropes, cutting through each layer with caution.

Allison was only about half-free when she sprang to her feet. Her legs were still tied up, but her arms—her arms swung wide and loose, as she pulled one back and then brought it forward.

She decked Jane square in the jaw.

Jane staggered back, clutching her face. "*What was that for?!*"

"How many times?" Allison shouted. "Huh? How many times were you out there, putting yourself at risk, and you didn't even have the decency to let us *worry* about you? God! I just . . . I can't *believe* you. I can't believe you'd just *lie* to us like that!"

"Hey!" Jane said. She held up a finger. "First of all . . . okay, that's kind of a weird point to get hung up on, but whatever—Listen, I'm not your fucking sister, okay? So whatever it is you're actually pissy about, can you just stuff it long enough to help me contact the Heroes?"

"What are you *talking* about?"

Jane hesitated. Allison was staring at her as if she was crazy, which . . . yeah, Jane couldn't really blame her for that. She didn't even know why she'd brought up her real identity, rather than playing along to this world's Jane. It wasn't planned. Jane could only begin to rationalize it as not wanting to get caught up in old arguments she didn't understand. Right now, she needed Allison's trust and cooperation, and if there was one thing that Jane had learned about the Maxwell girls in her time here, it was that Jane was the last person that Allison would trust in a crisis.

So there it was.

"I'm not Jane Maxwell," Jane said finally. "I mean—I *am*, but I'm not the Jane Maxwell that you know. I've been brought here from a parallel world, because the Heroes needed my help. *Your* Jane Maxwell, your sister . . . well, *she's* UltraViolet."

"UltraViolet," Allison said. Her voice was as level as her stare, as she studied Jane.

Jane nodded. "I'm afraid so. And as much as I wish I could help you process all this, we really don't have the time. I need you to go and get the rest of the Heroes for me. Something's wrong with the factory, I mean"—Jane's voice pitched up, nervous laughter cracking her words—"I literally think it's going to explode, and—and I can't do it on my own. I need help."

Allison glanced at the ropes, still caught around her legs. "Cut these."

Jane stepped forward, doing as she was told. When she stood back up, she regarded Allison warily. "So . . . you'll help me? You'll go find the Heroes?"

"No, you idiot," Allison said. She kicked the last of her ropes aside, stepping out of the tangle that had held her in place. "I'm going to stop the explosion."

Jane's mouth gaped several times in rapid succession. Allison was already striding off, her copy of Jane's ponytail bouncing as if waving goodbye.

"Right," Jane said a moment later, after she'd jogged to catch up. "Um, so just to clarify: when you say that you're going to stop the explosion—"

"Yeah?"

"Well, just—what did you mean by that?"

"I mean I'm going to find out what's wrong, and fix it. Save your sorry ass, and the city."

"Yeah, okay, I got that, but . . . *how*, exactly?"

"Wow, you really *don't* know anything about me, do you?" Allison asked.

"No." Jane shrugged. "Sorry, but . . . no."

"Not that I'm saying I believe your 'parallel worlds' story, but what—is the me over there some kind of wet noodle or something?"

Jane hesitated. There really didn't seem to be any good way to break this.

"There, um . . . there *is* no 'you' from my world," she said finally. "Our mom had a miscarriage before you would have been born."

Allison paused—just long enough to cut Jane a sidelong look. Jane was expecting her to take this rather hard. *Jane* certainly would have taken it rather hard, or at least she assumed so. What must it be like, Jane wondered, to learn that there's a world out there in which you never existed? Would it cause a crisis of confidence, like maybe you were never "supposed" to have been born? Would it make you doubt yourself? Make you question your place in your own universe? Wonder if your family and friends would have been better, worse, different, without you among them?

But all Allison did was quirk an eyebrow.

"In that case," she said, "prepare to be amazed."

JANE WAS AMAZED.

They raced back in as the pressure gauge was breaching into the red zone. Pipes wheezed with the effort of holding back steam. Canisters bulged ominously. Sweat had built up on a large tank in the corner, like a glass of lemonade on a hot summer day. The water dripped onto the cement floor, pooling outward, and Jane and Allison dodged flames and leaped across snaking puddles as they ran for the control console.

The metal grating rattled underneath them. They vaulted up the stairs two at a time, and ran across the platform until they were right above a smaller vat. One glance down, and Allison's face paled. "Okay, not good."

"What's wrong?"

"My sister is what's wrong!" Allison said. She ran over to the vat, ducking down to read a gauge near the lip. "Shit. I never should have tutored her ass in tenth-grade chemistry."

Jane jumped as a loud *ping!* split the room, a valve breaking off of a pipe somewhere far overhead. Hissing followed, loud enough for Jane to have to shout. "Okay, well, I didn't *have* a tutor, so can we pretend like I'm a complete idiot here?"

Allison ran for a control console, on a platform just beside the tanks. "Mixing chemicals bad. Heat worse. Factory about to go *kerblooey!*" God, she even did the little hand motions, her fingers spreading in a mock explosion.

"Yeah, maybe don't need to dumb it down quite *that* much!"

"Do you really need the fucking science?" Allison snapped, as she tapped furiously on the console. Light flickered behind the controls, just barely enough power to see by. Her face went still, only the subtle shift of her throat as she swallowed. "Or should I just give you numbers? We have four minutes until this whole factory goes up, and I cannot even begin to predict the contamination if these chemicals hit the river."

Jane's stomach pitched. "Sorry I asked."

If Allison had a witty retort to this, she held her tongue. She pried an access panel off of the control console, her face twisted up in concentration as she wrenched away rusted metal. The panel clanged to the floor, and Allison began to rip out bundles of cable, searching for something that Jane couldn't even begin to understand.

Jane shook her head. "Where did you *learn* all this?"

"That's classified," Allison said. At first Jane thought she was joking, but there wasn't a single hint of sarcasm or mirth upon Allison's face. Allison spared a fast glance. "Or did you think I live in D.C. because my husband is a lawyer or something?"

Jane flushed. She hadn't given the matter much conscious thought, but now she realized that's the exact assumption she'd had.

Allison snorted under her breath. Her attention was fixed on the console again, but she spared enough to mutter "typical" as she stripped a piece of heavy wiring. Several inches of twisted cable were now exposed, and Allison hurriedly worked to unbraid them.

"What can I do?" Jane asked.

Allison brushed the sweat off her forehead. She set the cable down and began to fish around in the guts of the console. "Unless your powers are good at putting out fires? Shut up and let me work."

Jane bit her lip. Inside the console was a mess of circuit boards and more cabling. As much as she hated it, Allison was right, there was nothing that Jane could do *besides* shut up. She stood back, trying to give Allison some room. At least the flames hadn't reached their corner yet, though the room itself was heating up rapidly. Sweat ran rivulets down Jane's skin.

A dull prickle raised the hairs on the back of Jane's neck. She looked up. She hadn't heard anything, but *something* had caught Jane's attention. Maybe instinct, or maybe something just on the edge of her hearing—maybe just paranoia, the adrenaline pumping through her veins with no place to go. She blinked, shifting her vision. No heat signatures lurked in the corners, but still Jane's skin wouldn't stop crawling. Her eyes swept the entire room, but there was nothing, nothing, nothing—

Something. A blur of movement, and then a Shadow Raptor—cold-blooded, dammit—was leaping from the darkness right above them.

It landed on the console before Jane could react. Metal *crunched* and sparks flew, and Allison shouted "Jane!" as she ducked, just in time to avoid the Shadow Raptor's swinging tail.

Panic jumped in Jane's veins as her powers kicked into gear. She struck the Shadow Raptor with a laser beam, a tightly focused tunnel of light boring straight into the flesh of its leg. The thing howled, whipping its tail as it turned toward Jane.

She ran, and it followed. "Keep working!" Jane called back, hoping that Allison could hear her over the groaning of the pipes, the roar of the flames, the rattle of the grating as the Shadow Raptor barreled after her. "I've got this!"

She sure as shit hoped that she'd got this.

The shadow of a Shadow Raptor loomed large on the cement floor in front of Jane. She ducked, and the whistle of talons sliced the air over her head. The talons hit the floor, gouging deep grooves as they scrambled to catch themselves. Jane reached out, firing another laser beam—this time at its toes, hoping to destabilize the creature.

It worked . . . sort of. The Shadow Raptor wailed and leaped aside, and then aside again—it would have been funny, under other circumstances, making this massive beast leap and dance about like a monkey on parade. But then the next leap was straight forward, right at Jane, claws and teeth and daggers all bared in her direction.

Jane flashed a burst of light as she feinted, hoping to disorient the creature. The Shadow Raptor flew past her, and for a split second Jane thought she was safe. But then its tail swung wide, catching Jane in the ribs. She went flying, an action figure hurled across the room in a fit of rage.

She hit a set of pipes with a sickening *crunch*. Metal clattered to the floor, and steam poured out thickly overhead. Jane wheezed, muttering to herself as she pushed back to her feet. Her boot caught a segment of pipe, nearly tripping her, so she did not see at first that the Shadow Raptor went lunging for Allison.

A crash brought Jane back to reality. The Shadow Raptor had landed back on the console—Allison, mercifully, must have ducked again, as she was now crouched on the ground nearby. The Shadow Raptor's tail swung repeatedly over her head, keeping her pinned.

"Oh no you don't, you fucker," Allison said. She grabbed the panel that she'd pried off of the console, and before Jane could even think to stop her, she'd leaped up, timed between the swing of the Shadow Raptor's tail.

Allison drove the corner of the panel into the Shadow Raptor's flesh.

The Shadow Raptor wailed. The frenzy of its tail increased, and Allison only narrowly avoided being tossed aside like Jane had been.

Jane ran up. The Shadow Raptor was still on top of the console, and Jane took a deep breath. The piece of pipe that had fallen to the floor was tight in her hands, and she pulled it back like a baseball bat.

There was only one thing that Jane missed about the summer she'd spent at the ball field with her dad, the year she'd thought she wanted to be an athlete. Jane didn't have the best timing, or coordination, and she wasn't crazy about running—but dammit, she could swing that bat *hard*, and when it did manage to connect with the ball, it was the best feeling in the world.

A Shadow Raptor was much larger than a baseball, and Jane was a lot stronger than she'd been as a kid. The pipe hit the creature's side, the force of it nearly knocking *Jane* back as well. But it was enough. The Shadow Raptor teetered, limbs whirling as it tried to catch its balance.

It never did.

Jane grabbed Allison, both of them ducking for cover as the splash of chemicals crashed up onto the platform, like the front seats at an aquarium show. Steam billowed up around them, heat burning the chemicals off faster than they could eat through the metal. By the time Jane and Allison peeped up a moment later, all that was left of the Shadow Raptor was one last flick of its tail, disappearing beneath the hissing mist of the chemicals.

Allison ran back to the console. "Brace yourself!" she shouted, as she slammed down on a control.

An alarm blared overhead. All around the room, heavy lids crashed down onto open tanks. The spit of some kind of sprinkler system kicked in, and Jane gasped as it soaked her and Allison in something not-quite water.

The whole factory flushed. The gurgle of pipes, the glug of tanks emptying, filled the building. Jane turned, and sure enough, the fires were going out, and the heat of the larger tanks was retreating into evacuation pipes buried in the floor. Jane stared and stared, blinking back the artificial rain.

"What did you *do*?"

"Exactly what I said I would do," Allison said, as she approached. "Triggered the factory's old safety protocols. Saved your sorry ass, and the city." She glanced over, raising an eyebrow. Hair was plastered to her forehead, droplets careening in rivers past her eyes. "Congratulations, Captain. It's over."

A swell of relief bubbled up in Jane's chest and burst, dying as fast as it began. Her eyes widened. "No, it's not," she said, turning toward Allison. "UltraViolet is still out there."

23

JANE BLINKED, AS A PANEL OF NOTHING BUT MARIE'S GRANITE FIST SWUNG FAST IN HER DIRECTION.

It wasn't supposed to go like this.

Jane had raced back to headquarters in a fit of panic, barely thinking. Her phone was gone, her civilian clothes were gone, and she couldn't get a hold of the Heroes. She was already imagining the worst: the building up in flames, an epic battle sprawling across the heart of downtown. UltraViolet on a rampage, bent on destruction. Amy, trapped inside as flames licked up the walls of her rejuve pod. Oh God, if anything had happened, if anything was *happening*—

But the building was fine. The city was fine. Jane burst in through the doors and there was Marie, perched on a couch with a gadget spread across her lap. She had looked up, quizzical, as Jane raced inside.

"That was fast," Marie had said.

Jane had stumbled to a halt. The *lack* of any apparent emergency, combined with Marie's nonsensical statement, had thrown her for such a loop that Jane couldn't even think anymore. "Huh?"

This is when Marie's face had gone stony. She set the gadget down. Stood up, slowly and deliberately.

"You don't know what I'm talking about, do you?" Marie asked.

Jane shook her head.

This is when life turned into a comic page, and Jane's story skipped forward.

Now the world came back to her in bits and pieces. The coppery tang of blood on her tongue. The cold floor beneath her cheek. Words floating through the air, disconnected from time and place and purpose:

"—*supposed to do with her?*"

"*We keep her.*"

"*What, like she's just another prisoner? We can't simply throw her in there, as if she's—*"

"*We can, and we will. She made her choice.*"

Pain in her temple, kicking back to life. Jane groaned, and clutched at her head.

Red leather. She was wearing her uniform. Jane squinted through the crack of her eyelids, staring at the lacing that ran along the arm of her suit. Beyond it was a wash of muddy blue and glowing white, figures shifting in the haze.

Memories slid into place. A terrible, fun-house version of Jane's own face, done in purple. Shadow Raptor talons cutting next to her head. Allison's fist, colliding with Jane's jaw. Marie's fist, stony as a statue, barreling forward—

"Why does everyone keep punching me in the face today?!"

The question exploded out of Jane as she pushed herself up. She was still holding her head, which spun for a moment as her world swayed like the contents of an unsteady cereal bowl. Bile crept up the back of Jane's throat, and she swallowed it back down with bitterness.

A bitterness that matched Marie's tone as she spoke next. "Oh, I don't know, *UltraViolet*. Why don't you tell me?"

Jane looked up. She found herself, quite suddenly, inside one of the cells of the Vault, as if the whole thing had just sprung up around her. She could practically see the scribbles as the last of the guidelines melded into the drawing, colors madly shaded in around her. A panel seemed to trap her in place: the Heroes, gathered just beyond the glass of her cell. They stood with hands on hips, or arms crossed sternly over chests. Their arrangement, the tilt of their bodies, the jut of their chins, was a perfect cover shot for the newest season of a hip superhero show.

All Jane could do was shake her head. "What are you talking about? I'm—"

"Don't deny it," Tony said. He was one of the hands-on-hips, and he made one threatening step closer, the better to tower over Jane. "Jane and Cal told us all about how you ambushed them in the factory."

"How *could* you?" Keisha asked. Both her voice and her face were twisted up with anguish. "After everything we've been through?"

"Does the team mean *nothing* to you?" Devin added.

Jane groaned, as it suddenly all made sense; UltraViolet must have gotten here first, spun a lie to convince the others. She scrambled to her feet. "No no no, guys, listen: you're right, your Jane is UltraViolet, and you have every reason to be pissed—but I'm *not her*, okay? I'm the Jane that you dragged into all this! The Jane that *you* saw is UltraViolet! She only told you that to keep me from stopping her—to keep *you* from stopping her!"

Jane saw how this landed, or rather, how it *didn't*. Her words bounced off of the Heroes' righteous faces as if their expressions were steel.

"Nice try," Marie said. "It's a clever ploy, I'll grant you, but you're forgetting that it's not just your word against hers. Cal—"

"Is *working with her!*"

"Oh, please," Marie said.

"It's true! I swear it! I just—*gah*, forget it." Jane ran her hands over the top of her head, tugging at her ponytail in frustration. She turned away, and then turned back. "Okay, okay, here, wait, you know what? Just go get Amy. Please. One touch from her, and you'll know I'm telling you the truth. That's all I'm asking."

The team looked at each other, considering this. Unspoken arguments played back and forth between their faces.

God, they didn't have time for this. Jane didn't care about dignity anymore—she clasped her hands together in front of her, as if in prayer. "*Please.* You can't risk me being right about this."

"It's not unreasonable . . . ," Keisha said.

Marie heaved a weary sigh. "Fine," she said. "Whatever." She moved over to a screen embedded in the wall, and tapped it to wake it up. Another tap for the command she wanted. "Hey, Amy?"

Silence answered her.

Jane's stomach tightened. They all waited, seconds piling up with alarming speed. How long would it reasonably take Amy, to hear Marie's voice and respond?

Marie tapped the screen again. "Amy?"

"Shit," Devin muttered.

"Check the access logs," Tony said.

"Yeah, like I didn't think of that." She was already moving, swiping and tapping the screen as she brought up a long, scrolling list. Blue light washed Marie's face as she read, her jaw setting hard as stone.

"Tell me," Jane said, and when the team stayed silent, reading over Marie's shoulder, Jane slammed her fist against the glass that separated them. "Tell me!"

"Amy left the building," Keisha said. She paused, just long enough for dread to shoot through Jane's veins. "With Jane."

"You idiots!" Jane slammed her fist against the glass again. "I told you! I fucking *told* you! You have to let me out—she's up to something terrible, I *know* it. Come on. Come on!"

"It's not that simple," Marie snapped. "Okay? Look, what you're saying is ridiculous. I mean, Jane being evil is bad enough, but . . . but Cal, too?"

The screen beside them flashed on. "Oh, let's be honest, that part isn't hard to accept," Allison said.

For the first time, a tiny flicker of hope sparked in Jane's heart. On the screen, Allison's image was framed by a room crammed with tech, and she looked up beyond the camera with something like awe on her face as she took in her surroundings.

Unfortunately, she and Jane seemed to be the only ones encouraged by this turn of events.

The rest of the team exploded.

"*Allison?*"

"What the fuck are you doing here?"

"How did you even—?"

"Get out of my tech room!"

"No," Allison said, answering Marie. She flashed a badge at the camera. "Agent Maxwell, from ARRO. And listen, while the rest of you have been playing Liar Liar, I've been taking stock of your supplies. Nice toys, by the way—*love* the free-range quantum calibrator. But!" She held up a finger, as she lifted whatever tablet or phone was recording her. "According to this, you're supposed to keep the field destabilizers that you stole off Dark Atom over here, yeah?" She motioned over her shoulder with her thumb.

Marie scowled. "Yeah . . . ?"

Allison swiveled out of the way. The wall behind her was lit up, racks standing empty.

Marie jerked in front of the screen, cutting off Jane's view. "*Where are they*, you bitch?"

"Jane already told you," Allison said, her voice laced with contempt. "My psycho sister and her stooge of a boyfriend have made off with everything they need to build a breach between worlds, and *you assholes* let them waltz right out the door. So I suggest you stop arguing, let this Jane out, and get your spandexed asses in gear before it's too late." She scoffed, the sound of it echoing through the Vault. "I mean, are you people supposed to be Heroes, or what?"

THIS TIME, THEY TOOK THE VAN.

Jane's stomach was jittering around as much as her knee, as she sat in the back across from Allison.

Allison ignored her. She'd taken the time to change while the rest of the Heroes had suited up, and now she looked like something out of a SEAL-team action movie: black outfit loaded down with fully stocked weapon holsters, pockets carrying who knows what kind of tools and additional firepower. Her hair was tied back into a severe bun, her face steady as she studied a blueprint of some type displayed on a tablet resting on her knees.

"Thank you," Jane said after a few minutes of silence. They were alone in the back of the van. Pixie Beats and Granite Girl, in the cabin, were driving, while Windforce and Rip-Shift scouted up ahead to get some sense of what might be lying in wait for them.

Allison shook her head. "Don't thank me."

"But you got them moving." Jane reached up, pulling the chain with Clair's wedding band out from beneath her uniform. She held it tight, pressed against her heart. "Time can be crucial, and . . . you got them moving. So thank you."

Allison glanced up. She studied Jane in silence for a moment—the necklace in her fist, the expression on her face. Jane thought, perhaps, that Allison might say something, but she didn't. She turned back to the blueprints, as if Jane hadn't spoken at all.

"Can I ask you something?" Jane said.

Allison shrugged. "If you must."

"If you're this much of a badass, why didn't you just rescue your dad yourself, when he was being held hostage in City Hall? Why wait for us to do it for you?"

"Orders," Allison said. She tapped something on the tablet, enlarging a portion of the blueprint. "We weren't allowed to touch him."

"What, and that stopped you?"

Allison cut a glare at Jane. "*Yes*, that stopped me. Some of us have *responsibilities*, Jane. Some of us work for a sanctioned organization, with rules and a strict chain of command. I can't just go in guns-blazing and expect to show up for work tomorrow as if nothing happened."

"You could, if you were a Hero."

Allison snorted softly, as she returned to her work. "Oh, please."

"I mean it," Jane said. "You could join us."

Allison said nothing.

Jane sighed. She turned, instinct making her want to look out the window, except that there were no windows to look out. All that surrounded her were computers and guns, and none of that was exactly comforting. She tucked her necklace away and stuffed her hands under her legs, sitting on them to keep them still. Her uniform was still singed around the edges, scuff marks running down the pants.

"So what's different now?" Jane asked.

"I'm sorry?"

"You're acting now. What's different?"

"Nothing," Allison said. She looked up, looked Jane dead in the face. "If it was up to me, none of you would be involved in this operation at all. But my bosses feel differently. They order me to stay out of your way, I stay out of your way. They order me to cooperate with you, I cooperate with you. My feelings on the subject are irrelevant. So, you see," she added, turning away, "there really is no reason to thank me."

Jane frowned. Her impulse was to argue, though right now she found herself quite devoid of words. It didn't matter, though—the van was slowing, and Allison glanced up, checking something on the computers as she tucked her tablet away.

"We're here," she said.

Jane took a sharp breath as her stomach clenched. She checked her mask, still secure on her face. She tried to tell herself that this wasn't anything worse than she'd already dealt with, that this time she even had the whole team on her side, plus Allison. That they were going into this one armed to the teeth, ready and raring for battle. That she'd managed to hold her own earlier— and okay, so UltraViolet was injured, but it's not like there had been much time for UltraViolet to heal herself since then, right? This shouldn't be anywhere near as nerve-racking as all *that* was. If she could survive *that* . . .

There was only one problem with her reasoning:

Amy wasn't in danger last time.

The van shifted, probably Pixie Beats and Granite Girl getting out of the front. Allison got up, making one last check of her holsters as the back doors swung outward.

A figure all in black filled the open view.

"Hello, ladies," Doctor Demolition said with a grin. He raised his hand, a triggering device with a big red button held tight in his fist. "Lovely evening for some fireworks, isn't it?"

His thumb crashed against the button.

The van erupted.

24

FOR THE FIRST TIME IN JANE'S LIFE, SHE UNDERSTOOD THE TERM "BONE-JARRING."

The van burst upward, lifting Jane and Allison as easily as flipping an omelet. Dry heat covered their skin with searing kisses. Jane didn't even see Rip-Shift's rip until she was falling through it headfirst, a shimmering line that disappeared from her sight as quickly as it had appeared.

She tumbled onto the concrete sidewalk, maybe a dozen yards from the van. Allison spilled out beside her, both of them hitting the ground and rolling, coughing and gasping as the smoke that had fallen through the rip with them dissipated harmlessly in the open air. The van crashed, somewhere nearby; a sickening, shrieking crunch of metal and glass that sent Jane straight back to her nightmares of the tunnel all over again.

Someone slapped her firmly on the shoulder.

"Up," Allison said. It wasn't a suggestion.

Jane groaned, but she reached out, knowing that Allison would grab tight and help haul Jane to her feet. The world was still spinning around her—probably around Allison, too, by the way she shifted her footing—but they were still alive, and that was all that mattered for now. Still in the fight.

Night had fallen during the drive. They were standing in a plaza, spotlights flooding the space so that it was lit up like an arena. Jane took a second to crane her neck back, trying to orient herself—and promptly froze, staring at the bronze letters secured above her.

She didn't need to read them. She would recognize them anywhere.

Grand City Museum of Fine Arts.

A crash brought her back to herself. Allison had already run off, heading back into the thick of the fight, which was now spilling onto the street in front of the museum. Doctor Demolition had crawled into the sculpture that stood beside the entrance steps, laughing at the Heroes' reluctance to destroy it simply to get to him. Jane's heart warmed; she'd seen more than enough superhero movies where there was not even the slightest consideration for property damage.

Doctor Demolition, however, did not hold the arts in as high of esteem. In addition to the myriad of blinking lights that ringed the sculpture itself, waiting to go off, tiny explosions were bursting all throughout the plaza. Chunks of dirt and cement flew through the air, and a haze was beginning to sting at Jane's eyes as she raced forward.

A square of paving stone exploded in front of Jane. She leaped back, narrowly avoiding the debris.

"Ah!" Doctor Demolition called, temporarily secure in his nest of metal and fine art. "Captain Lumen! So glad you didn't die just now. We have a special present planned for you."

With a flick of his wrist, a mechanical whirring filled the air. Vibrations met her boots, and Jane glanced down in time to see what looked like metal cockroaches burst out from the gaps between paving stones. They wriggled, and leaped into the air—all of them vaulting straight in Jane's direction.

A gust of wind swept in just as Jane began to scream. It burst up from the ground, tossing Jane high. She flipped over from the force of it, turning just in time to see the cockroach devices collide in the space where Jane had been and burst into a glorious explosion, a tidy little ball of flame worthy of a comics page.

The wind cut out from underneath her.

Jane screamed again, starting to fall—and then, all of a sudden, a miniaturized Pixie Beats was cutting through the air like a bullet, expanding out to full size just long enough to wrap her arms around Jane. The impact sent them flying sideways, hooking Jane as if she was being yanked off stage by one of those comically long canes. "Hold tight!" Pixie Beats shouted, and the world ballooned out around them.

That's how it felt, anyway.

It took Jane almost the entire arc of Pixie Beats's trajectory to work out that she had actually reduced Jane to the size of a mouse. Wrapped tightly in Pixie Beats's arms, Jane's entire structure had shrunk down alongside her, until they were both falling harmlessly to the ground. They landed with the softest bump, and Jane didn't even have time to boggle at the scale of the world before Pixie Beats was letting her go, and she was springing back to full size once more.

Pixie Beats was already back on her feet. She nodded down at Jane. "Might be best if you let us handle this," she said, and she did not wait for a response before spinning and springing back toward the action.

The *whoop-whoop* of a siren announced the arrival of the GCPD. Five squad cars careened onto the scene. Their doors flew open, spilling guns and officers.

Rip-Shift held up his hand, stilling the cops—for now. He stood near the base of the sculpture, glowering up through his mirrored sunglasses. He had to be trying to figure out an angle that he could slice a rip beneath Doctor Demolition, but the layout of the sculpture, twisting around his body, wasn't providing much help. Too far in one direction, and Rip-Shift risked setting off the bombs. Too far in another, and he'd accidentally cut off part of the sculpture itself.

"Give it up, Doctor!" Rip-Shift said. "You'll never get away with it. You never do."

Doctor Demolition grinned. Light from the patrol cars splashed over his face in alternating red and blue. "Don't need to 'get away with it' this time, though, do I? Just need to keep you goody-two-shoes busy. And believe me," he added, pulling a small detonator box out of his pocket, "that I can do."

Jane braced herself for an explosion as he pressed the button.

But none came. The cops and the Heroes exchanged glances, as if trying to corroborate between themselves that the plaza was, indeed, still intact.

"Two buses," Doctor Demolition said. He held up his fingers, wiggling first one and then the other, as if there was any doubt how to count that high. "Each on their normal routes, somewhere in the heart of Grand City. If they stop driving, they blow. If you attempt to disarm them, they blow. If you so much as open the doors . . . they blow."

"You asshole!" Pixie Beats shouted. "You're fucked up, you know that?"

Doctor Demolition laughed as he threw his arms wide. "That is the general idea!"

One of the cops jumped forward, his gun trained into the heart of the statue. "Stand down!"

"No, don't!" Rip-Shift said. "Seriously, Ted . . . leave it to us."

"Can't do that, sir," the cop—Ted?—said. "This man poses a clear and present danger to the city, and it's my *duty* to—"

"It's your *duty* to shut the fuck up and not screw this over for everyone," Rip-Shift snapped. "We're *handling* this."

Ted shook his head. He hadn't so much as looked away from Doctor Demolition, not for an instant. "Put down your weapons, and step away from the statue!"

Doctor Demolition laughed.

"This is your last warning!" Ted called.

"Ted—!"

Ted fired.

It wasn't possible for Jane to watch the bullet's journey, but it certainly felt like she could. Time hung, suspended, a slow progression of panels that track the bullet, first with a side view and then slowly coming around to ride on its tail as beyond it, Doctor Demolition throws himself out of the way.

One last panel: the bullet, piercing through the protective casing on one of the bombs strapped to the sculpture's arms. The slightest tint of orange-red fills the background, before the whole thing explodes in a terrifying fireball. *Kaboom!*

Jane gasped. Someone grabbed her roughly by the arm, throwing her down as twisted bits of sculpture flew like javelins through the air. She hit the paving stones and curled her arms over her head, wincing as the sounds pierced the night. The shriek of metal and the roar of fire, the shouts and insults hurtling at Ted, the crackle of radios, the arguments sizzling between the Heroes and the cops.

By the time Jane got to her feet, Ted was already cuffed and being hauled away by Windforce. Heat from the fire pummeled the plaza. Allison had her badge out, directing the cops. Jane heard words like "cordon off" and "innocents" and "fuckfaces." Jane smirked as they glowered in Allison's direction, but ultimately, what was there for them to do, but obey?

Pixie Beats jogged over. "Hey. You okay?"

"Yeah," Jane said.

"Good," Pixie Beats said. "Because we're going to need your help, once we get inside. Windforce and Rip-Shift are going with the cops to try to rescue the passengers out of the buses, now that . . . well, now that the remote's been destroyed."

Jane's mouth soured. She tried not to look, but couldn't help it—a charred lump sat beneath the flaming sculpture (what was left of it, anyway), and Jane forcibly shoved the thought away, of what and who that probably was. Used to be.

Vertigo washed over her, and Jane had to pause for a moment, to duck her head between her knees.

Pixie Beats patted her back, but Granite Girl's voice, coming close a moment later, wasn't as sympathetic.

"Not as *tidy* as your comics, is it?"

"Oh, give her a break," Pixie Beats said. "You weren't any better, in the beginning."

"No, I wasn't." Granite Girl smacked Jane's shoulder, and Jane glared up at her stony face. "But guess what, newb? It doesn't get easier. So you take a deep breath, and you put on your big-girl panties, because this night's just getting started. Now, come on," she said, turning toward the entrance of the museum. "We've got a job to do. Just try not to get yourself killed, all right?"

JANE REMEMBERED HER FIRST VISIT TO THE GRAND CITY Museum of Fine Arts. Ten years old, a Girl Scout trip into the city. Her troop leader had the girls partner up for the day; the instructions weren't even fully out of her mouth when Jane and Clair linked hands, ready to go. The day was perfect—until it was time to leave, and Jane turned around, and suddenly she couldn't find Clair.

It was one of those childhood traumas, where the world feels like it's about to end even though there was never any real danger after all. It turns out that Clair had raced off for a last-minute trip to the bathroom before they piled into their chaperon's car, and in the commotion of all those giggling girls, Jane hadn't heard Clair say it. But Jane would never forget the panic, standing there as the lobby emptied out, crying wordlessly while the chaperons spread out in search of their lost charge. Halfway through, the lights snapped off automatically, the museum closing down for the night, and Jane had screamed in shock. It was the scream that Clair heard, which made her come running back.

More than twenty years later, the same dread clung to Jane as she and Allison and Pixie Beats and Granite Girl stepped into the lobby. It looked the same: shut down, the only light pouring in from the lamps outside, the glow of the emergency exit lights. The lobby was cavernous, at least as large as it had been when Jane was a child. And it was so *quiet*. Even their breaths were subdued, as if they'd entered a sacred space.

"You're sure they're inside?" Pixie Beats asked in a whisper.

Granite Girl nodded, wordless. She held up a tablet, the tracking device for Amy clearly blinking over the blip of the museum.

"Okay," Pixie Beats said. She shrank down, looking like nothing more than a flower petal blowing across the floor of the lobby.

"Should we spread out?" Allison asked. "Assume a standard search perimeter?"

"We don't *have* a standard search perimeter," Granite Girl said.

Allison sighed. "No, of course you don't."

"Hey," Jane cut in, "it works for us, okay? Besides—"

She froze. A beam of laser light, invisible to everyone but her, had cut through the lobby and trained itself in the middle of Allison's forehead.

"Get down!" Jane shouted, as she launched herself at Allison. The crack of a bullet cut through the open lobby as they hit the ground.

Allison threw Jane off of her. The three of them scrambled for cover as another shot broke the glass door of the gift shop beside them. They cowered behind a thick marble bench, heads clustered at the base like kittens vying for the prime suckling spot on their mother.

"Can anyone see where it's coming from?" Allison asked, and Granite Girl shook her head.

"I didn't see a thing!"

"They're using an infrared laser sight," Jane said. She looked over her shoulder and watched, her throat closing up, as the beam of light danced on the walls behind them, seeking them out. "Cal showed me one, when we were training. He said—"

"Real military sniper rifles don't create little red dots, like in the movies," came a voice from the ceiling. The loudspeaker amplified every tiny breath in Cal's voice as he sighed, and continued. "I should have realized you'd be able to see them anyway."

"Cal, you bastard!" Granite Girl said. "When I find you, I'm going to rip your fucking head off!"

Allison clamped her hand over Granite Girl's mouth. "*Not. Helping.*"

Cal's laugh boomed through the PA system. "Oh, Granite Girl. What would the public think of you now? Death threats? Those are hardly the words of a Hero, are they?"

Granite Girl wrestled with Allison's arm, but it was Jane that spoke next.

"You're right . . . that wasn't very heroic. But she's better than that, and so are you. I don't think you really want to turn a gun on your friends, Cal."

Allison shot Jane a look like, *You really think that's going to work?*, but all Jane could do was shrug in a way that said, *It's worth a try.*

"Whatever," Allison muttered.

The PA system clicked back on. "You're absolutely right, Jane." A smile curled his voice. "Maybe you should come out, and prove how much you believe in me."

Jane shut her eyes. "Shit."

Granite Girl wrenched Allison's hand away from her mouth. "It's not a terrible idea," Granite Girl whispered.

"What? He's going to *kill* me."

"Like she said," Allison said, "not a terrible idea."

Jane scrunched her face at Allison. Allison scrunched hers back.

Granite Girl snapped her fingers between them, the scrape of stone grating to Jane's ears. "Ladies, focus. No, listen: Jane can keep Cal busy, right? Play this stupid banter game with him. Go out there if you have to—you'll see the shot coming, you can dodge it. Allison and I will make our way to the security office."

"And if I *don't* see it coming?"

Granite Girl shrugged. "You will."

"Thanks," Jane said. "That's a big help."

"Shut up," Allison said. "She's right, it's worth a try. If we can get in there, we can track him on the cameras."

"Yeah, and then Jane lures him into a prearranged area, somewhere secure, and we'll activate a lockdown around him. Easy-peasy."

Jane looked from Allison to Granite Girl and back again. "This is a *terrible* idea."

Allison clapped a hand on Jane's shoulder. "You're only saying that because you're the one that needs to put yourself in the line of fire," she said. "But you know what?"

"What?"

"I don't care."

Allison shoved Jane, hard enough to roll her out into the open space of the lobby.

Jane gasped. She threw her arm out, stopping herself, and scrambled up just as a bullet bit deep into the marble floor by her head. Granite Girl and Allison had already moved, using the distraction to avoid becoming targets themselves. Jane blinked, and saw their heat signatures cowering behind the admissions desk.

The laser sight skittered up Jane's body.

Jane jumped to the side, twisting out of the way. Another crack, and this time the whole glass window of the gift shop came shattering down.

"Goddammit, Cal!" Jane shouted, as she ran for cover. She threw herself beside the main staircase, sliding in next to a potted plant. The leaves burst as another bullet tore through their branches.

Jane shut her eyes. She counted to a rapid ten, trying to will her heart back down from the stratosphere.

The PA system clicked on. "Yeah, I may have been lying earlier."

Jane bit down on her first response, the impulse to dish his taunting right back at him. Instead, she turned toward the staircase, shifting her vision until she could see through the marble. She craned her eyes around, looking for heat signatures.

And there he was. Up in the corner of the lobby, crouched low and stable. He looked like he was leaning against something, probably a banister of some type that he had the sniper rifle resting on.

Jane tapped her earpiece. "He's in the northwest corner. Near the ceiling."

"On it," Granite Girl said. *"We're almost to security. Just keep him distracted a little while longer."*

"Right, sure," Jane whispered to herself. "Like it's that easy."

She'd have to make it easy.

"You were right, you know," Jane called. "What you said, earlier: that I never paid attention to you, that you didn't matter to me. That was wrong, Cal. You were a good friend. You always were. I want you to know that I'm sorry."

Silence. Jane stole another peek in infrared—Cal wasn't moving, though whether it was because he was trained on Jane's position and just waiting for her to appear, or whether her words had actually made some kind of impact, it was impossible to say.

"Cal? Did you hear me?"

"Oh, I can hear you. It's just not going to make a difference."

Cal's voice seemed to come from everywhere, echoing down like the word of God. Jane couldn't help but feel like maybe he was telling her some deeper truth: it wasn't going to make a difference. None of what they were doing was going to make a difference. UltraViolet had so far managed to outmaneuver them at every turn, making them dance to her tune as if they were amateurs. Why would this time be any different?

Jane shook her doubts off. They had no time for doubts.

"*All right, we see him,*" Granite Girl said in Jane's earpiece, and not a moment too soon. "*Jane? If you can lure him down the hall to your left, we should be able to seal him in between some emergency doors.*"

Jane tapped her earpiece. "I'll do my best."

She only hoped it would be enough. Jane reviewed the layout of the building in her head, trying to figure out the best way forward, any viable means of escape. Her stomach gave a restless flutter, and Jane frowned because it was right, she was stalling. Jane took a few quick breaths. *Okay, okay*, she thought to herself. *Three . . . two . . . one.*

"All right, tough guy," Jane called. She shut her eyes, just for a moment, gathering strength. "If you think you're so badass . . . come and get me."

She threw one hand up, casting a glorious burst of light throughout the lobby, and tore off down the hall.

25

PAINTINGS STARED DOWN IN JUDGMENT AT HER.

Jane couldn't blame them. It was one thing to feel brave while caught up in the adrenaline of combat; it was quite another to stand in the middle of a darkened gallery, waiting for an attack that she both was and wasn't hoping would come.

Jane turned in place. She was looking for heat signatures, laser sights, anything that might give her some indication of when and where Cal was coming from. So far—nothing. Even Granite Girl and Allison had lost track of him, in the gaps between security camera coverage. All that she could picture were the dark hallways stretching out from the gallery, the rooms stacked together to shepherd patrons from one exhibit to the next to the next.

And still, they hadn't found UltraViolet or Amy yet. Jane tried not to worry, but it was impossible. What kind of dastardly scheme was UltraViolet putting in motion, even now, as Jane stood in the gallery as bait for Cal? Had she managed to get the larger version of Doctor Demolition's weapon working? The only small comfort Jane could take is at least if *that* was true, it wouldn't detonate in the same building UltraViolet herself was in—but that wasn't as reassuring as it should have been. UltraViolet could leave, after all. Or maybe she'd never even been here in the first place. Maybe she'd found some way to fool the Heroes' methods of detection. Or maybe she *had* been here, but was already gone—maybe she'd set up the weapon, tied Amy to it like in the old comics, and booked it to safer ground. Maybe it was going to blow, any second now, and take all of them with it. Maybe—

A ceiling panel crashed to the floor, so close that the edge of it grazed Jane's back. She didn't even have time to scream before a figure tumbled down after it, catching her shoulders and sending her into a face-plant.

Her training kicked in. Jane caught herself, marble floor smacking hard into her palms, one elbow knocking against the ground. Her foot darted out without thinking, as Jane twisted to see exactly who and where she was kicking at. She aimed for Cal's legs, hoping to unbalance him, but he stepped back out of her reach.

Good enough—Jane scrambled to her feet, running hard for a door marked "Employees Only." She tore through it as Cal lunged for her, but Jane twisted aside just in time to avoid being snared.

She turned around, her heart pounding high in her chest. Cal kept advancing, as Jane scurried back. In the darker corridor, he looked somehow larger than he really was; he'd fill an entire panel, his shoulders buckling the framing lines, his face full of heavy strokes. Jane's feet stumbled over themselves, counting steps—four, five, six—at seven, her fingers brushed over the beginning of an open door, and Jane leaped back, skipping right over steps eight and nine. Green *EXIT* light spilled across her face.

"*Now!*"

A low *slam!* filled the corridor—but not the one that Jane had been counting on. Not the emergency doors, shutting safe between Jane and Cal. Jane blinked in the sudden darkness, the whole building now plunged into the pit of night.

Cal's grin glowed a wicked orange in infrared. Like the devil himself. "Whoops," Cal said. "Looks like *someone* sabotaged the security systems before you arrived." He flicked on a light strapped to his wrist and raised it up until it caught his face from below, a child telling ghost stories. "Boo."

He lashed forward.

The next instant was a jumble, faster than Jane could scream. She saw Pixie Beats expanding rapidly, crouched on Cal's shoulder—she must have been clinging to his collar, Jane had written that trick before—and she saw Cal spill forward from the sudden weight. Pixie Beats leaped away, bouncing off the wall behind her, as Cal turned his fall into a roll. He found his footing again right in front of Jane, and Jane, acting on impulse, shot off a quick laser beam at his leg.

Cal roared. Jane saw his jacket pull back, the holster of his gun.

A flash of light as Jane feinted to the side. The deafening explosion of Cal's gun, so much louder in an enclosed space. The heat of the bullet buried itself in the wall beside Jane. Jane's throat dried. Pixie Beats leaped forward, landing in a quick handstand on Cal's hunched back. The gun clattered from his hands as he caught his weight, palms splayed on the polished floor, and Jane kicked the gun to send it spinning into the darkness. Pixie Beats landed lightly beside Jane; she grabbed Jane by the waist, and Jane let out a yelp as her feet left the floor. The world spun, warped like a bad acid trip as Jane's size reduced and ballooned again. Pixie Beats had thrown her over Cal, shrinking her just long enough to pitch her like a baseball. Jane landed hard on the floor as Cal was leaping up, intent on Pixie Beats. Pixie Beats spun a kick at his head, but Cal was prepared for that—he shoved at her leg, using a block maneuver to keep her spin going, farther than she'd intended, and he used his free arm to throw a punch for her now-exposed midsection.

Jane gave a sympathetic wince as Pixie Beats flew back, off-balanced and clutching at her kidneys. Pixie Beats shrank, retreating, but Jane did not give Cal even an instant to regain his own footing. She tried to surprise him. He had taught her a fantastic punch-punch-kick combo, and Jane could see the maneuver in her head: how she'd surprise him, his lessons come back to bite him in the ass. The shock exploding across his face, captured in a close-up.

Turns out that life wasn't quite as neat as a comic, and Cal's military training was better than Jane's makeshift sessions. Her first punch was deflected, and Cal used Jane's own momentum against her as he threw her to the nearest wall.

The sound of a gun broke through the hall. Jane's heart leaped, sure that Cal had managed to retrieve his somewhere in the chaos, sure that she was going to die.

Instead, mad footfalls crashed toward Jane. Thunderous as stone.

Cal booked it out of there, as Granite Girl and Allison came tearing through.

"Don't just stand there!" Allison said, as she grabbed Jane by the collar. "Run!"

They ran. All four of them, racing down the halls of the museum. Darkness was cut only by the swath of flashlights, catching signs and the polished posts of velvet ropes.

When they reached a T-junction, Jane pointed left. "You guys keep following him. I'm going to swing around, try to cut him off."

"Right," Pixie Beats said. She and Granite Girl took off, but Allison stayed put.

"I'm not leaving you," she said.

"Fine."

Jane veered to the right. She didn't have time to argue. She was tracking Cal through the walls as best as she could, though it was mostly her familiarity with the museum that made her confident she'd be able to cut off his escape. She ran past one exhibit and then another. Past the stairs, and then the entrance to the auditorium. Up ahead . . . Jane tried to keep her eyes away from the next room, because the next room was the gallery that they'd reserved for their wedding, but memory drew her gaze. Just for an instant.

Heat signatures glowed through the walls. Jane scrambled,

her boots squeaking like a basketball court as she slid against the polished floor. She came to a halt in front of the open door, and her infrared vision switched off as she gaped through the doorway.

Amy.

"Amy!"

"No, don't!" Allison grabbed Jane just as Jane began to plunge into the gallery.

"Let go of me!"

"No, but *look*."

Jane looked.

It wasn't easy, to force her eyes on anything but Amy. Amy, who was lashed to an ornate chair in the far end of the gallery, pinned beneath a spotlight like the focal point of the whole exhibit. Amy, a tangle of electronic devices spread at her feet, another encircling her head like a crown. A trail of wires strung down from her temples; they clustered at a silver disk sealed over her heart, gathered there like the stems of roses held fast in a suitor's hand. The same disk that UltraViolet had used on Jane back at the factory. The same one, supposedly, that had been used on Clair after her accident.

Amy stared at Jane, and Jane stared at Amy. Amy's mouth was gagged, but her eyes were pleading.

"*Look*," Allison urged again, and this time Jane tore her gaze away.

She looked.

The gallery was littered with laser beams. Invisible to anyone else, so high frequency that even Jane could barely see them. They cut an intricate lattice between Jane and Amy, wound tight as a net.

"How—?" Jane started, but Allison jerked her chin toward the walls. Black boxes clung in tight knots along the wainscoting, the crown molding, the floorboards.

"I recognize a trip-beam explosive when I see one," Allison said. "We can't approach."

UltraViolet's voice echoed through the gallery. "You should listen to her, Jane. Our teachers always did say she was the smart one."

She stood up. She must have been working on something behind Amy's chair, and Jane had been so focused on the horror in front of her that she hadn't seen UltraViolet, any more than she'd seen the laser beams. Jane's head spun now, looking at her. UltraViolet had changed into Jane's own clothes, the ones that she'd left in Cal's SUV when they'd headed for the factory, what seemed like a lifetime ago. It was beyond weird, watching "herself" as she checked her watch.

"I have to admit," UltraViolet said, "you got here faster than I expected. The team actually *believed* you?"

"I have an honest face."

"Why, thank you." UltraViolet touched her own cheek. "I like to think so."

"Too bad you don't live up to it," Allison said.

UltraViolet's lips twisted in distaste. "Ugh. Why did you have to bring *her*, though? She's no fun at all."

"You want fun?" Allison asked. She snapped her gun up, steady in her hands. "I'll show you fun."

"Allison!"

Jane grabbed Allison's wrist. The barrel of Allison's gun hovered in front of them, barely an inch from the closest laser.

UltraViolet laughed. "Yeah, maybe not the smartest move, sister dear. These things are *everywhere* in here, trust me. And since you can't see them . . . you wouldn't want to risk me falling over and crossing one of them, now, would you? I mean . . . shit, what would the agency think? You might tarnish that golden reputation of yours."

"Not if they don't know I'm here."

Jane's hand went cold.

A glint sparkled in the corner of UltraViolet's eye. "Why, *Allison*! How naughty of you. I'm impressed."

"But . . . ," Jane said. "You told me—"

"I *know* what I told you. But someone has to stop my sister, before she can hurt any more people." She tightened her grip on her gun. "She almost killed our *father*. I won't let anyone else suffer at her hands."

"Oh, please," UltraViolet said. "You say that like it's supposed to mean something. The bastard had it coming."

"Shut up!" Allison said. "Just shut up, or I swear I'll drop you right here!"

UltraViolet rolled her eyes. Still, her hands went up, in a mock I-surrender pose, before she dramatically drew a zipper motion across her lips.

She went back to work.

Jane wrenched Allison's hands down, and the gun with it. "Are you *crazy*? She's right, this place is rigged to go up a thousand times over. You can't just shoot her if you don't know where she's going to fall. And anyway, how's that going to help Amy? We have to find some way to—"

"*Jane?*" came a voice in Jane's earpiece. "*Allison? Where are you guys? I thought you were going to cut off Cal's escape!*"

Jane's stomach twisted up.

"Shit," Jane muttered. She'd forgotten all about Cal.

Allison glanced back at UltraViolet, then craned her neck toward the door. She leaned over, just enough to whisper, "I'm going to head back, get the others."

A tiny nod was the most Jane could manage.

"Not so fast," UltraViolet said, just as Allison was beginning to turn. She pressed a button on a laptop that everything was plugged in to like a central node, and another set of laser beams sprang to life—cutting off access to the door. "You didn't think it would be that easy, did you? As if I haven't been preparing for this. I know *everything* that you two clowns can think up, you know. I'm ready for them all."

"*Jane?*" Pixie Beats tried again. "*Jane?*" Granite Girl added. "*Dammit, Jane, can you hear us?*"

"Don't answer," Allison whispered. She looked pointedly at UltraViolet, as if Jane needed to be reminded that, regardless of how little attention she appeared to be paying to them, she was actually listening to everything Jane and Allison said.

"But—"

"No. We're on our own."

Jane shut her eyes. A childish reaction—if I can't see it, it can't see me—but one that Jane retreated to without shame. Maybe at the end of our lives, we all circle back to the beginning again.

No, Jane told herself firmly. This wasn't the end—she would not *let* it be the end.

She opened her eyes, and nearly staggered back from the sight that awaited her. The gallery was full to the brim with rippling waves of color, a thousand hues, going all different directions. It was like . . .

Well, that was the problem—it wasn't *like* anything Jane had ever seen before. Like cascading soap bubbles, and rainbows if rainbows came out to dance, and the ocean at sunset, and trippy sixties animation, and the way that laughter would look if you could give it a shape. Bubbles constantly bloomed and became ripples, one after the next and the next and the next, colliding with walls and statues, passing *through* walls and statues. Jane stared and stared, turning in place to take it all in.

"Jane?" Allison asked softly, in the hope of not drawing Ultra-Violet's attention. "Jane, are you okay?"

Jane made herself nod. She turned back, and had to bite down to keep from bursting out laughing. Bubbles were blooming out of Allison's head, encircling her like deep-sea diving helmets and then growing to cartoonish proportions. No—not her head. Her *ear*. Or, more accurately, the earpiece hidden inside.

It hit Jane all at once, then, what she was seeing: wireless signals. Her previous success in this range had been tiny bursts, instinctive explosions that had grazed against the frequency without really allowing her full access, much like her uncontrolled bursts of light. Intentional manipulation would require a more delicate touch, to be able to see what she was doing, to be able to watch the signals bounce around her.

But . . . *could* she? It's true that her powers didn't feel threatening at the moment, but that could change in a heartbeat.

It was a risk that Jane would just have to take. She looked hurriedly to the bombs littering the walls, but of course they were static, with vine-like cords trailing from them to gather in a nest at UltraViolet's laptop. Jane frowned; she knew it couldn't be that easy. On the other hand, that did also mean that UltraViolet wouldn't be able to trigger the detonations remotely either, so Jane supposed that, at least, was good to know.

Okay, but there had to be something else that Jane could do. The laptop?—but no, that, too, was lashed to an outlet in the wall, undisturbed by the wifi floating over and through it. Jane bit her lip, looking again to Allison.

The earpiece just kept transmitting, wave after wave of signal as it kept in touch with the others.

Maybe that was the key, then.

After all, UltraViolet couldn't overhear something, if she couldn't *hear* it.

Jane took a steadying breath. *It's okay*, she told herself. *You're in charge this time.* She let her powers fill her up, until she was nearly drowning in them. Focus, focus. Her own earpiece was throwing out waves around her, too, and it was these that Jane concentrated on, nudging them just a little bit this way and that.

A squeal tore out of the earpieces. Allison cringed, doubling over as she grabbed at her head. "What the—?"

"*Sorry*," Jane said, or at least *a* voice—Jane's words, distorted as they were carried out in the wireless waves. The sounds were tumbling back into her own earpiece, too, and so she heard just how terrible she sounded, all eighties-speak-and-spell. "*Sorry, I'm not . . . this is really hard, okay?*"

Allison turned, her eyes widening as they settled on Jane.

Meanwhile, Granite Girl's voice came fast in Jane's ear. "*Jane? Jane, is that you?*"

"*Hope so*," Jane "said." "*Is everyone okay out there?*"

"*We're fine*," Granite Girl said, "*though Cal got away. Where are you?*"

"*With UltraViolet. Listen, we don't have much time: the room is littered with infrared trip lasers. I need Pixie Beats to sneak in here and disable them.*"

"*Problem*," Pixie Beats said. "*I don't know shit about disarming explosives.*"

"*I do*," Granite Girl said. "*Bring me. Jane, what are we working with, here? How many bombs?*"

Jane winced. Pain flared through her head from focusing so hard. "*Too many. Hooked to a laptop. Please hurry. Lasers aren't to the floor, should be enough space to walk beneath.*"

"*How much space are we talking?*"

Jane glanced at the emitters just above the baseboards, and saw Allison do the same.

"*Maybe two inches?*" Jane said. She looked to Allison, who gave a subtle nod.

In the earpiece, nothing but silence.

Panic fluttered at the edges of Jane's mind.

"*Guys?*"

"*It's fine,*" Granite Girl said pointedly. "*Don't worry about it. We're on our way. Keep UltraViolet busy in the meantime. The last thing we need is for her to realize what's happening.*"

"*On it.*"

Jane and Allison exchanged a look.

Allison cleared her throat.

"You don't have to do this, Jane."

Jane frowned, confused—until she realized that Allison wasn't talking to her, but rather to UltraViolet.

UltraViolet glanced up. She was working on something just beside her laptop, a box made of crude sheet metal, wires sticking up like pins splaying open a dissected frog.

"Of course I don't," UltraViolet said. "But I'm still going to."

"Janie, please. Listen to me, okay? This isn't *you*."

UltraViolet laughed. "Actually, sister dear, I think if you stop to think about it, you'll realize this is *exactly* me. Come on. You can't tell me you never saw something like this coming."

"My sister becoming a supervillain?" Allison said, a fractured laugh tinting her voice. "Yeah, no—I admit, we've had our differences, and I can't say you've ever been my favorite person. But no. I never saw this coming. Do you even realize how many people are going to die, when you set that thing off?"

UltraViolet looked up, eyes alight with amusement. "Oh good lord, you still think this is about what blew up Woolfolk Tower? Sister dear, we are *way* past that old plan."

"I don't believe you," Allison said. "There's no way you've found something worse than that."

A flicker of irritation crossed UltraViolet's face. "The fact that you can't picture it just means that you have a poor imagination, but that's hardly my problem. You, on the other hand . . ."

UltraViolet turned to Jane.

"I admit that I underestimated *your* imagination. Here I thought you were just a useless scribbler, but you worked out the connection between Amy and Clair. I suppose I should thank you. I *was* just going to content myself with stealing your powers—but why steal just one Jane Maxwell's powers, when the whole *multiverse* can be my oyster?" She motioned at her laptop, a triumphant grin already spreading from cheek to cheek. "All I need to do is push this button, and your precious Amy will act as a compass, leading me to any universe I want—there should be no limit to the number of Janes I can capture. Think about it: the *power* I could achieve!" UltraViolet's face went soft. "I'm going to be like a *god*."

"You're delusional," Jane said.

UltraViolet rolled her eyes. "Says the woman still pining after her dead wife. Face it, Jane, she's gone. This?" UltraViolet stepped over and grabbed a chunk of Amy's hair—she jerked Amy's head back so that the whites of her eyes flashed. "Is not her. It will never *be* her."

Amy whimpered.

"Stop it!" Jane shouted.

UltraViolet pouted down at Amy, ignoring Jane. "Aw. What's wrong, sweetie? I thought you *liked* having your hair pulled." UltraViolet snorted. She released her hold, throwing Amy's head forward again. Turned back to Jane. "So you see, there really is no reason for you to risk your life to save her. Not that your efforts will do any good. You'll never stop me, you and your 'friends.' You know that I was the only thing holding that team together, right? Without me . . . what good are they, really?"

Jane stole a subtle glance. Several feet away, a tiny flutter of color was making its way across the surface of the floor.

"They're Heroes," Jane said, and now, finally, she understood what that meant. Watching Pixie Beats and Granite Girl, running on hope across what would be a vast wasteland from their tiny perspective, charging into unknown danger, so frail and small in the face of something so terrifying. They had not even questioned Jane, when she told them her plan.

"Oh, *yes*, how foolish of me," UltraViolet said. She crossed her arms, and sneered. "*Heroes.* Let me tell you something about being a hero, Jane: it's not worth it. Oh, you can hold evil at bay for a day, a year, a decade—it doesn't matter. You'll suffer through battle after battle, you'll watch good people die, you'll tell yourself that it's worth it, but in the end . . . someone like me will always come along. You can't *stop* us all. It just takes one victory, and then all of your hard work will be for nothing. Why fight it? Evil will triumph, sooner or later. It's a mathematical inevitability."

"That's where you're wrong."

"Trust me, I'm not. I've been in this gig a hell of a lot longer than you; I know what I'm talking about."

"You may have played the part of a hero," Jane said, "but you clearly never understood it. A *real* hero knows that it's not about a tally of victories and losses. It's not even about 'holding evil at bay,' not really. At the end of the day, there's only one thing that truly counts for anything, and it's not something that can ever be defeated. And you don't even know what it is, do you?"

UltraViolet gave an exaggerated sigh. "Let me guess: *love?*"

"Love is great," Jane said. "But no. What love does, is help us remember what's important. It doesn't *define* what's important."

"Okay, seriously, can we just skip to the end?"

"What matters is doing the right thing."

UltraViolet raised an eyebrow. "That's *it?*"

"That's *everything*," Jane said. "And that's why evil will never triumph—not forever, anyway. Because no matter how bad things get, no matter how bleak the future looks, there will always be people who will do the right thing. In the face of all odds. Even if no one will ever know they've done it, even if there is no hope of recognition for their actions—*someone* will make the right call."

"Will they, now?" UltraViolet smiled. "We'll see about that."

UltraViolet put her foot on top of a wireframe box, something that had been sitting in the jumble of equipment. She dragged it out with the toe of her shoe and then, keeping a steady eye on Jane the entire time, kicked it to the side.

The box scraped across the floor. Jane's heart leaped to her throat—if it hit the laser beams . . .

But it didn't. UltraViolet had shoved it with just enough force, her timing perfect. The box slid to a halt: right before the beams . . . and directly over where Pixie Beats and Granite Girl had just crossed into the open space surrounding UltraViolet and Amy.

UltraViolet stomped on a switch on the floor. A thin cord connected it to the box, and Jane watched in horror as a net of laser beams snapped to life around Pixie Beats and Granite Girl. Only this time, a series of LED lights sprang up alongside them, leaving no room for anyone to mistake what had happened.

"No!"

UltraViolet rolled her eyes. "Jane, Jane . . . You think I wouldn't have thought of that? You think I wasn't listening in to the wifi, while you schemed over the earpieces? Face it: you have no idea what you're up against. I *know* this team. I *know* what they're capable of—and what they're not. Speaking of . . ." Ultra-Violet walked over to the laser cage that she'd constructed. She crouched over Pixie Beats and Granite Girl, grinning down at them like they were animals in a pet shop. "Oh my, Keisha. That does look uncomfortably small, even for you. How long do you think you can keep that up, exactly? Especially while holding Marie the same size."

A faint whisper breezed through the gallery.

UltraViolet cupped her hand around her ear. "What's that? I'm sorry, your voice is a little *small*." She laughed.

Pixie Beats's voice came through Jane's earpiece next. "I *said*, 'As long as it takes, you bitch.'"

"Keisha!" UltraViolet gasped. She sat back, her hand at her chest in feigned shock. "Such *language*."

"Let them go!" Jane said.

"Or *what*?" UltraViolet stood and spun around, glowering at Jane. "Tell me, *Captain Lumen*, what exactly are you going to do to stop me? Hmm? Because I don't see a lot of options for you right now! Do you?"

Jane swallowed. No, she didn't, though she wasn't inclined to admit that.

A *bing!* broke the silence, cheerful as an egg timer. UltraViolet looked over at her laptop, a grin spreading across her face. "Ah! And we're ready. Ladies," she said, "as fun as this has been, I'm afraid my hour is at hand."

UltraViolet took an exaggerated bow, twirling her hand out beside her with a flourish.

She walked over to the laptop, now filled with green ready lights. A single button hovered in the middle, the cursor already positioned over it.

Amy screamed through her gag. She jerked at the bonds of her chair, desperate to get away.

"No, don't!" Jane shouted. "Just *stop*! UltraViolet—*Jane!* Think about what you're doing."

UltraViolet clutched her heart. "Oh! Is this where you finally convince me that I'm a good person, underneath it all? Remind me of my humanity? Get me to see the error of my wicked ways? I know! Maybe I should adopt a puppy! That would make everything all better, wouldn't it?"

"No," Jane said. "I know you're too far gone for that."

UltraViolet blinked. "Well *that's* surprisingly sensible of you."

"All I'm saying, is that there has to be another way for you to achieve your goals—without using Amy. Okay? Please. I know that you don't really want to hurt her."

"*Do* you?" UltraViolet sneered. "And how do you know this? Because you looked into my heart, and knew that I've been in love with her all this time? Grow up, woman. This isn't a fairy tale."

Jane shook her head. "I didn't look into your heart. You looked into my face."

"Excuse me?"

"In the factory. You said you knew I was in love with her, because you recognized that look. But how could you? Unless you've seen it before. You've spent your whole life burying it, Jane, but you can't deny it anymore. Not to me. You're Jane Maxwell," Jane said, but it wasn't her double that she was looking at anymore. Instinctively, Jane's eyes had drawn toward the chair, seeking out Clair's face. God, it was just the same. Jane's expression softened. "She's Amy Sinclair. And if there's one constant in all this vast stretch of parallel worlds, it's that we will *always* love her. No matter what."

Amy's eyes welled up, alongside Jane's heart.

UltraViolet cleared her throat. "That's really touching, Jane. Truly. I had no idea I was capable of such poetry." She threw her arms wide. "Very well! I repent!"

Jane ripped her attention away, a puzzled frown scrunching her eyebrows. "Really?"

UltraViolet's face convulsed as she fell into a messy snort of laughter. She pointed at Jane, then shook her head. "No. Nice try, though." Her hand hovered over the laptop, finger poised. "But it's too late for that."

She struck the key and the lights flickered off and on, searing the vivid white of UltraViolet's Cheshire-cat grin across Jane's eyes.

"Let the Spectral Wars begin."

REALITY SPLIT ITSELF, DIVIDING INTO NEAT LITTLE squares, moments frozen in time. Jane, trying to lunge forward despite the net of laser beams, only Allison's desperate grip holding her back; Jane's face is contorted in a thousand shades of pain, heavy shadows lending depth and detail to her features. UltraViolet, head thrown back in riotous, triumphant laughter. The contrast in her panel is so sharp that she appears nearly in black-and-white, lending her a creepy, inhuman vibe. There's a tight shot, low to the floor, the explosion of color in Pixie Beats's uniform played against the dull gray of Granite Girl's stony skin. Their hands are gripped together, and Pixie Beats's face is lined with sweat, the effort of holding both of them so small finally beginning to show.

All of these are smaller pieces, scattered at angles like fallen photographs around the larger horror. A distance shot of the gallery, the details obscured by shadow. The light spilling over Amy draws the eye toward the center.

Her powers are not light-based, so her flare does not blind those who look upon her. Reality split itself, people's truths revealed and mirrored back to them. For Jane, it was her comics: a full spread of her failure, laid out in perfect detail. Look at what she had done. Look at what she had allowed to happen.

Then the moment passed, the initial shockwave of Amy's flare bursting past Jane, expanding out through the rest of the museum. The world sprang back to life. The scream that was already tearing itself from Jane's throat, and Allison shouting at her to stay back; UltraViolet's cackles as they rose to the ceiling and crashed back down on Jane. Amy had her eyes squeezed shut, her jaw clamped tightly behind the duct tape across her mouth, her whole body tensed as if trying to hold herself together just a little while longer.

UltraViolet hopped eagerly from foot to foot as she watched readings pour into the laptop. Her fingers danced together, tapping excitedly in front of her lips.

Jane sagged back against Allison, defeated. They had failed. After everything—all the near misses, all the hurt and heartbreak, all the strength that it had taken to keep fighting . . . Okay, so there were plenty of times Jane had felt she was going to *die*; she had never considered, though, that it might not *work*. The Heroes didn't fail, not when it really mattered. Yet here they were.

"No," Jane mumbled. She pushed herself back to her feet. No, that wasn't how this worked. They were Jane's *stories*. There was always another way out. There was always *something*. If only these damned lasers weren't in the way, if only . . .

The image of Clair's note rushed back to her, two lines scrawled in haste: *Lasers are just light. I believe in you.*

Lasers are just light.

Jane looked over. The whole world seemed to slow, the chaos of the gallery retreating to the background. The explosives blinked on the walls, perfectly synced with each other. Their beams cut a thick network back and forth between Jane and Amy, invisible to everyone else, but just another light to Jane.

Lasers are just light.

UltraViolet was turning now, gathering up one of the wrist cuffs. A pale glow washed over her hand as she set it on the table, and she strung a cord to plug it into the laptop.

Lasers are just light.

Pixie Beats fell to her knees. Granite Girl shrieked, barely keeping hold. The light of their cage clashed with the vibrant colors of Pixie Beats's uniform. Their size slipped, just for a moment, just a hair's breadth, before Pixie Beats was able to catch it.

Lasers are just light.

Beside her, Allison had raised her gun again. She shouted at UltraViolet, her words lost in the haze of Jane's perceptions. UltraViolet turned, quirked up an eyebrow, *Would you really shoot your sister?* It was a question mirrored in Allison's own face, uncertain even as her fingers gripped against the trigger.

UltraViolet raised her hand. A beam cut through the network of lasers, high enough in frequency that even Jane couldn't see it. She only saw the result, like everyone else: the barrel of Allison's gun melting, useless as putty.

Jane's breath escaped her. Her mouth hung open, the last puff hovering at her lips.

Lasers are just light.

Time caught up with Jane. Allison threw her gun to the floor, swearing loudly.

Jane gripped Allison's sleeve. "I'm going in there."

Allison snorted. "Yeah, that would be nice." She stomped down on the gun, just for some way to express her frustration. UltraViolet had already turned away, eagerly tapping commands into her laptop.

"No, Allison . . . I'm serious. I can do it. If I redirect the light in just the right way, I can trick the sensors into thinking that the beams are unbroken. I'll pass right through them."

"Are you *crazy*? That will never work!"

"Lasers are just light," Jane said. She turned, looking Allison straight in the face. "I control light."

Allison shook her head. "It's too risky. If you're off by even a fraction of—"

"I won't be."

Allison sighed. "Jane—"

"*No.* Listen to me: I know that you don't trust your real sister, and you have every reason not to. I'm not her. I can do it."

"*Guys!*" Granite Girl's voice came screaming into their earpieces. "*Guys, whatever you're going to do, please do it fast!*"

Jane turned back toward the lasers. "I can do it," she repeated. If she said it enough, would that make it true?

She shut her eyes. "Lasers are just light," she whispered.

Allison's hand rested on Jane's shoulder. "Good luck . . . Captain Lumen."

Jane nodded. She opened her eyes, focusing on each tiny beam crossing in front of her. Fuck, there were so many of them.

I believe in you.

Jane stepped into the light.

ULTRAVIOLET COULD DO NOTHING BUT STARE. THE DEVICE was still in her hand, the cord that linked it back to the computer hanging as low as her open mouth.

So you think you know everything we can come up with, huh? Jane thought. Power coursed through her, and yet . . . it did not overwhelm her. Jane felt it, the pull of it, the strength of it—it *could* have been overwhelming.

It wasn't. Clair's faith in Jane had lodged itself in her own heart, and Jane did not fear it anymore. The gallery had taken on a soft-glow effect, as time and light and distance seemed to meld into one pliable form. The laser beams passed straight through Jane, a faint tickle against her skin, like raindrops.

A gurgle escaped UltraViolet. Genuine terror seemed to flit about the corners of her eyes.

It was this complete and utter bafflement that let Jane get the first punch in.

She had barely finished crossing the laser grid. Her arm swung up, her fist connecting with the underside of Ultra-Violet's jaw. Jane had to be careful—she did not want to knock UltraViolet so far off her feet that she fell into the lasers around them.

UltraViolet staggered back, dropping the device and catching herself against the table. It was all the opening that Jane needed—she lunged to the side, making an effort to stomp on the switch trapping Pixie Beats and Granite Girl, but not quite fast *enough*. The punch must have stirred UltraViolet back to her senses, because now she clawed at Jane, yanking back on her ponytail.

With such tight quarters to work with, their scuffle was cramped and nasty: nails and knees, stomping and pulling. It was a good thing that Cal wasn't there, because Jane was quite sure that he'd be able to read perversion into the experience. Jane made for UltraViolet's eyes with her thumbs, just as UltraViolet grabbed at Jane's throat.

It wasn't clear, in the end, which one of them ended up stepping on the switch. One moment they were struggling against each other, locked in a vicious cage fight. The next, Pixie Beats and Granite Girl were full sized beside them, their bodies practically knocking Jane and UltraViolet down.

Granite Girl wasted no time. Jane managed to hold UltraViolet back with a hard punch to her throat, as Granite Girl made a beeline for the laptop. Pixie Beats was still down, crouched on all fours, taking steadying breaths. Jane didn't have time to worry about her, though, because now UltraViolet had twisted around, hooking Jane's feet and sweeping them out from underneath her.

Jane hit the ground, hard, just as the network of lasers shut down.

"We're clear!" Granite Girl called, for the benefit of those without the ability to see lasers.

Jane scrambled to her feet. Allison was already charging toward them, hellbent on UltraViolet. A split-second decision: did UltraViolet turn and try to get the lasers back up, or did she deal with the more immediate threats in front of her?

She grabbed Jane, all but throwing her in Allison's path.

Jane collided with Allison, who immediately used a block to knock her sideways. Jane's momentum carried her straight past Allison, and she crashed into the floor.

That's when the Shadow Raptors appeared.

One, and then two, and then three, leaping over her—then another two, bursting in through a staff entrance tucked into the corner.

Jane's impulse was to cry out to alert the others, but it wasn't needed. They were already engaged, almost as soon as the Shadow Raptors appeared. Pixie Beats was leaping and whirling, her limbs a perfect arc of grace and power as they struck each of the Shadow Raptors' vulnerable parts in turn; she wasn't shrinking—probably recovering her strength, though you'd never know it just to look at her. Granite Girl was still typing madly on the laptop, pausing only long enough to snap the neck of any Shadow Raptor foolish enough to approach her— she barely even looked up, though a sickening *crunch* filled the gallery each time one of them tried. None of them seemed to be attacking Allison for now, though Allison had her hands full: she and UltraViolet were entrenched in deep combat, the sisters wailing on each other with a lifetime of repressed resentment. Jane winced as a laser beam cut right past Allison's head.

Jane was so busy watching that she did not see the Shadow Raptor approach her from behind. It was only the widening of Amy's eyes, desperately tracking Jane, that alerted her to the danger.

Jane rolled fast to the side, as an obsidian dagger struck the gallery's marble tile. She reached out, drilling a laser beam straight for the Shadow Raptor's face—it struck one of its eyes, the Shadow Raptor wailing and jerking its head aside.

Another lunged at Jane from behind. She raced to her feet, twisting away just before it was able to grab her. It blocked her laser beam, bouncing it off of its daggers as the creature protected its face.

A mad scramble of dodges and attacks. Jane was trapped on the defensive, the Shadow Raptors boxing her in so that she had no choice but to shuffle backwards toward the rest of the fighting. Shouts and crunches met her from behind—once, she even had to duck, as a Shadow Raptor went flying over her head, no doubt thrown across the gallery by Granite Girl. That one did at least catch the leg of one of her own Shadow Raptors, allowing Jane to get a solid bore into its opposing hip. She did finally manage to down one—the one that she'd half-blinded, its wild swings not even remotely close to hitting her—but doing that, unfortunately, opened up a huge vulnerability to her left side.

She saw the opening, too late to do anything about it. Saw herself from the outside, frozen as she stood over the body of the half-blinded Shadow Raptor. Her body is twisted as she begins to turn around. She's shadowed by the approaching attack, the whites of her eyes popping against the darker shading on her face. In the next panel, nothing but the vicious curves of the Shadow Raptor's talons, the glint of its horrible teeth.

Jane ducked. It wouldn't help, but her muscles didn't care. She threw her hands over her head, cowering like a little girl. She did not see, then, the Shadow Raptor as it veered off course, thrown to the side by the collision of Allison's running leap. Only the sound of their crash made her look up. Allison had a garrote wire out, already wrapped tightly around the Shadow Raptor's throat. Spurts of blood traced the wire, as the force of it cut lines into its scaled skin.

It was the last Shadow Raptor. Jane leaped up, a swell of triumph making her cocky.

Cold steel found her neck. A voice, rough like cheek stubble, nuzzled against her ear. "Miss me?"

Cal.

Fear turned Jane's blood to ice. Her heroism abandoned her, bolting for warmer climates.

Cal stood at her back, one hand meat-hooking her arm, the other holding the knife. He raised his voice, as he called over her shoulder, "Everybody stop!"

Everybody turned. Everybody stopped.

Allison released her grip, and the Shadow Raptor's head landed with a wet *splunk* against the floor. Granite Girl raised her hands from the keyboard, holding them open and nonthreatening as she took a step back. Pixie Beats landed midtwirl, falling to her knees as she rolled out of her aborted maneuver. She knelt on the floor, her back held straight and proud; height had never been the master of her, and the lack of it never diminished her importance, or the impact of her stage presence.

The sound of UltraViolet's clapping cut through the gallery like lightning.

"Oh, very good, very good," she said, as she scampered up toward Jane and Cal. "Yes, *well done*."

Cal's chest puffed against Jane's back. "Thanks."

"Shut up, I wasn't talking to *you*," UltraViolet said with a dismissive wave of her hand. She grinned at Jane, pinching her cheek like a fussy old aunt. "Has anyone ever told you that you make such a *good* little piece of leverage?"

She laughed, not waiting for a response.

"That's right everyone, give it up! Wouldn't want to risk your teammate, now, would you?"

UltraViolet strolled over to the table. Brushing Granite Girl aside, she picked up the wrist cuff and began to strap it on.

Panic rose in Jane's throat. She tried to catch the eyes of the rest of the Heroes, but somehow nobody was willing. With Cal's breath heavy at her neck, there was little that any of them could do. Now, look: UltraViolet adjusting settings on the wrist cuff, inching ever closer to her ultimate victory, and *nobody was doing anything.*

Always—*always*—UltraViolet kept getting the upper hand, but why? It couldn't be that evil was inherently stronger than good; Jane would never accept that. And it couldn't be that Ultra-Violet was smarter than Jane, because they had the same brain to work with. The same childhood, the same heart. Hell, they even had the same superpowers. The only real difference, when it came to these face-offs anyway, was the costume.

Maybe . . . maybe it was time to take a page out of UltraViolet's book.

Just a little one.

Jane straightened her spine. "Hey, Cal," she said, loud enough for UltraViolet to hear, "I finally learned what the big fight with Jane's mom was about. Turns out, it had nothing to do with you after all."

"Shut up," Cal hissed in her ear.

But, as Jane had hoped, it caught UltraViolet's attention. She looked up from her work, the tiniest wrinkle between her brow.

That's right, Jane thought. *Come on.*

"You?" UltraViolet asked. "Why would it have been about *you*?"

Cal laughed. "It wouldn't. Of course it wouldn't. I don't know why she said that."

UltraViolet's eyes narrowed. "Don't lie to me."

"I'm not," Cal said. So plain, so sincere. "Babe. She's trying to mess with your head. You know how it goes."

Jane forced a laugh, hoping it sounded more cocky than it felt. "What's the matter? Didn't you tell her? Well, no—I suppose that isn't the kind of thing you'd want to admit out loud."

"Tell me *what*?"

"Nothing!" Cal said.

"On the other hand, you told me, and it wasn't even *my* mom."

"Shut up," Cal said again. His blade shifted, just enough to leave the smallest paper cut against her neck. "No one asked you."

UltraViolet raised her hand. "*I'm* asking."

Jane felt Cal catch his breath. UltraViolet's cold stare had narrowed itself on Cal, her hand poised and ready to strike. Tiny flashes, like paparazzi cameras, lit her fingertips. The effort of holding herself back was clearly visible in the tension of her jaw.

Perfect, Jane thought.

"Let her go," UltraViolet said. She kept her voice slow, steady. She raised her chin. "Let her *speak*."

For a moment, it wasn't clear what Cal was going to do. Jane could practically *hear* the gears of his brain turning, as he struggled to determine how best to weasel out of this one.

"Babe—" he said, but a narrow beam of light caught his knuckle. Just enough.

Cal hissed as he yanked his hand back. In the distraction, Jane darted out from underneath his grasp. An angry red burn marred his hand when he took it out of his mouth, where he'd sucked at the pain.

He shook it at the wrist, as if drying it off. "That wasn't necessary."

"I decide what's necessary," UltraViolet said. She kept her arm raised in Cal's direction, but her attention turned to Jane. "Talk."

"Is *now* really the time for this?" Cal asked.

"*Talk!*"

The slightest hesitation, as Jane glanced at Cal. Then, all in a rush: "Cal slept with your mom."

UltraViolet's head whipped back to Cal with the explosive force of a bomb. "You *what*?!"

"Babe, it's not—!"

"Don't 'babe' me! You slept with my *mom*, you disgusting piece of shit!"

"I didn't!"

"*Liar!*"

A burst of blistering light and uncoordinated radio waves exploded out of UltraViolet, a heat that brushed Jane's cheek like a sunburn. Everyone else went scrambling, blocking their eyes and diving for cover. Even Amy, still struggling to hold on, squeezed her eyes shut and turned away. The light was omnipresent, stripping away every shadow, purging every hiding spot.

Only Jane could see what happened next.

The brunt of UltraViolet's rage struck Cal straight in the chest. Shock forced his eyes open, despite the searing light. His body went rigid, each muscle snapping to attention. His lips parted, just slightly, half a breath stolen from the chaos.

He fell. Cal's body toppled like a toy soldier, bouncing once before landing facedown on the marble floor. Dead? It was impossible to say from here—Jane couldn't take the time to check on him even if she'd wanted to.

The flare had staggered UltraViolet. Veins in her temples bulged from the effort of holding it in, but the light kept spilling over, a flood that couldn't be stopped. She knelt on the gallery floor, clutching her head as she fought to regain control of herself.

A silhouette of Jane draped across UltraViolet like a cape, the only shadow in the room.

UltraViolet raised her shaky head. Her sneer turned into a wince as Jane towered over her.

"Go on, then," UltraViolet said, biting out her words. "Kill me. Take what's yours."

Jane crouched down in front of UltraViolet. "*That's* what you think I'm doing?"

"Of course it is," UltraViolet said. She boggled up at Jane, like this was obvious. "You're *Jane Maxwell*. This is what you've always wanted, isn't it? Power? Revenge?"

Jane's heart twisted. *There, but for the grace of Clair* . . . Without thought, Jane ran the back of her fingers across UltraViolet's cheek.

"You really don't get it, do you?" Jane said. She tipped Ultra-Violet's chin up. "Jane: I already *had* what I wanted—and you took her away from me. But if you think I'm going to let myself become you, in some futile effort to exact vengeance for something that can never be undone . . . then you really don't know me at all."

Jane stood back up. UltraViolet's eyes, wide and wild, tracked her movement.

"Then . . . what are you going to do?"

"This," Jane said. She wheeled her arm back and hooked UltraViolet's chin with a sharp uppercut.

The force of it threw UltraViolet back. Across the room, landing in a slide, slamming against the wall. UltraViolet's flare flicked off, the world plunging back into shadows and shading.

"That's for Clair," Jane said, as she strode over toward Ultra-Violet's crumpled form. "And this is for Grand City."

Jane threw her arms wide, all of her fingers spread. Power surged through her as UltraViolet began to look up. Lasers leaped from the trip-beam explosives, and Jane ripped them toward her. UltraViolet threw herself to her feet, but nothing is faster than light.

And the light belonged to Jane.

It snapped together in front of UltraViolet, knitting itself into a prison cell. Beams bent and hugged a tight net around Ultra-Violet's body, spooling from the base and ignoring the laws of physics as they danced to Jane's will. The intensity glared brightly in Jane's vision, burning lines between them that only she and UltraViolet could see.

UltraViolet barely managed to stop in time. Her hands were thrown in front of her, as if they'd literally caught her against the net. She glared at Jane. "This isn't over, Jane."

"I think it is," Jane said, as the rest of the team rushed back to stand tall beside her.

UltraViolet's eyes flicked to each of the other faces, in turn, as if searching out the weakest link. They settled, finally, on the laptop she'd been using earlier, the one that all of the trip sensors were hooked in to.

"Don't even think about it," Granite Girl said. She raised her fist, a solid block of granite, and held it over the laptop. "I'll smash this thing in a heartbeat, and then who will let you out, hmm?"

UltraViolet sneered. "What makes you think I need someone to?" She jerked her chin at Jane. "I can just walk out of here, the way she did."

"Yeah . . . I really don't think you can," Granite Girl said. She glanced sideways at Jane, something halfway between respect and awe tucked in the corners of her eyes.

Jane watched as UltraViolet regarded the spread of lasers in front of her, weighing her options. How much risk was she willing to take, exactly? What was she willing to lose?

UltraViolet's fingers curled in, one at a time. She lowered her hand.

A low moan from beside them jolted Jane's heart.

"Amy!"

"Jane, no!" Granite Girl said, but too late. Jane had raced the small distance between them; her fingers brushed against Amy's cheek.

Such a minor point of contact. She wasn't even trying to touch Amy, not specifically, but it happened just the same, a moment frozen in time: Jane, finding the corner of the duct tape that gagged Amy's mouth. A single spark of contact. That was all it took.

A deafening *crack!* split the gallery. Jane was thrown back, limp as a discarded cape, a piece of duct tape pinched in her grip. She crashed into a vase on a pedestal, toppling both. The vase shattered into a thousand pieces, and Jane landed hard on top of the shards.

Ringing drove all thought from her mind. Her head spun as she picked it up, and drew herself unsteadily to her elbows. The world wavered. Distantly, there was the sound of people shouting, and through a blur, Jane could see legs running as people scrambled from one point to another.

A pair of steady hands yanked Jane back to her feet. Time tumbled on.

"Are you okay?" Allison asked, still holding fast to Jane, but Jane couldn't even begin to answer. Wind was kicking up the gallery, racing in tight circles like it was the Indy 500. Sparks crackled out from Amy's chair, sending paintings crashing to the ground. The crack of frames sounded like bones breaking.

"What's happening?" Jane called over the tempest.

Allison shook her head. "I don't know!"

"I do!" Granite Girl said. She hunched over the laptop, typing madly. Hair whipped across her cheeks, and she ripped it back. Her face went stony as she turned to Jane. "*You* did exactly what you weren't supposed to do! Your touch provided the machine with the emotional resonance that it needed to lock on to. Clair's connection to Amy wasn't born out of nothing—it was that they both loved the same person. Now the machine is reaching out into the multiverse, and it's pulling along that thread. And any second now—"

Another *crack!*, and a rumble of thunder shook the museum.

A figure appeared in front of them, half-formed, like mist.

And then another.

And another.

Another.

Jane turned. The gallery was filling up fast, like patrons crammed in on free admission day. The figures swept through as if they were ghosts. Going about their day. Eating, walking, punching . . . sketching.

So many of them were sketching.

A cold prickle ran up Jane's spine. ". . . Marie?"

"Shit," Granite Girl said, turning back toward the laptop. "Shit, shit, shit!"

"They're . . . they're all me," Jane said. Her mouth went dry, and she tried to swallow, to regain some moisture. "*Why are they all me?*"

"I don't know!"

The sound of laughter drifted in, like litter washing up to ruin a perfect day at the beach.

UltraViolet was watching from her prison of lasers. Her lip stuck out in an exaggerated pout.

"Oh, dear," UltraViolet said. "Did someone forget to tell you? I reconfigured one of your toys to act as a resonance magnet."

Granite Girl's eyes widened. "You didn't."

UltraViolet smiled. "I did."

"Are you *insane*?" Granite Girl said. "You can't just yank that much matter from one universe into another! The imbalance would—"

"Trigger an implosion, and destroy us all? Yeah, I worked that out, thanks. Call it my fallback plan. If I can't have ultimate power . . ." She shrugged. "It's better than prison."

"Jane," Allison said, "you can't be serious."

UltraViolet smirked. "Can't I?"

Amy screamed.

"Shut it down!" Jane shouted, her heart pounding so hard that it felt like it would rip from her chest. *Not again, not again, not again*, went the song in her veins as she ran over to the laptop. "Marie, seriously, who cares? Just—just shut it down!"

"We can't! It's a self-sustaining process! As long as Amy remains linked into the machine—"

"Then get her out of there!"

UltraViolet chuckled. "I wouldn't do that, if I were you."

"Like I'm going to listen to you," Jane said. She shoved her way forward, past Granite Girl and the laptop—but a stony hand grabbed her elbow.

Granite Girl looked up. "Jane. If we take her out without closing down the flare, the shock to her system will kill her."

"Leaving her in there will kill her!"

"Not if she absorbs someone's essence."

"I don't—" Jane started, but then she did. Flashes of her own comics went flying through her head, panels enlarged and plastered smack-dab in front of her. Mindsight in a cramped cell, Dark Atom looming large over her as he tries to induce a flare. An issue with a glimpse into the future, a vision that haunted the team for months: Mindsight overtaken by the personality of a madman. The downside of Mindsight's powers, the one aspect of her powers that Clair had always insisted *had* to be true.

Jane jerked back, as if she'd been physically shocked. "No . . . no! That's the same as killing her!"

"Not technically," Granite Girl said. "She'd still be alive. And, I mean, we don't know . . . maybe there would be a way to bring her own personality back to the surface. At least we'd have *options*!" Granite Girl added, raising her voice as Jane began to protest. "Which is more than we have right now."

Jane shook her head. "No. No, I won't let you do it."

"Jane—"

"I said no!"

"Then the whole universe is going to collapse!" Granite Girl said. "Because I don't see any other way of stopping this process. And then she'll be dead anyway, just like the rest of us."

Pixie Beats's hand rested on Jane's back. "We all knew the risks when we put on these uniforms, Jane."

"Oh, for fuck's sake," Allison said, "if we have a way to stop this, then stop talking and just *do* it!"

Not again, not again.

Jane's fists clenched hard at her sides. A flash of light burst out from her, strong enough to send everyone staggering back.

"*I said no!*"

"But I'm saying yes."

Jane froze.

The voice that had spoken was soft, barely registering above the wind that still howled around the edges of the gallery. It strained with the effort of speaking, as if her throat was dry. And yet, Jane would recognize that voice anywhere, in any state. She heard it with every beat of her heart.

She made herself turn around.

"Amy?"

Jane ran over, stopping just short of the chair. She got down on her knees. Amy's head was slumped forward, but her eyes were clear, and fixed on Jane as Jane looked up at her.

"Amy, you can't."

"I *can*," Amy said, wincing. "And I will. Under one condition."

Condition. A strangled laugh escaped Jane as she made herself ask, "What's that?"

"That you let me use Clair's ring."

Jane could barely breathe, for the sudden constriction of her chest. "What?"

Amy gave a shaky smile. "Hey, if you've got to be subsumed by another personality, it might as well be your own."

"It's not your own, though," Jane said. She reached up, cupping Amy's cheek—damn the risks of contact, and anyway, how much worse could things get? Their foreheads dipped, leaning against each other. "Amy," Jane whispered. "I'm sorry, but you're not Clair. If you take her ring, you're going to die."

Amy nodded, her head brushing against Jane's. "I know. But I've been listening the whole time. I'm going to die anyway. At least this way, something good can come out of it."

"Don't say that. Please, please don't say that. There's got to be another way."

"There isn't," Amy said as she drew back. "I know that. You know that. Please, Jane. Just let me fix this for you. Let me be your Clair."

Jane's chest seared, as if her heart was cleaved in two. She couldn't look at Amy's face anymore, Clair's face anymore. Instinctively, her fingers found the chain around her neck. The links were warm from being against Jane's skin.

"Please," Amy whispered, and Jane had to shut her eyes. "Jane . . . you know this is all I've ever wanted."

Jane nodded. Tears cut hot tracks down her cheeks as she made herself look back up. "I know."

"Then don't argue with me."

Amy's wrist was still bound to the chair, but she stretched her hand out, fingers spread.

Her hand was shaking.

Clair's hand had shaken, too, on their wedding day, out of nerves and joy and disbelief that this was finally happening, that this was finally *allowed* to happen. They stood there, exactly where they were right now: beneath the display lights, against a blank wall as if their love was a piece of art. This gallery had been reserved private, just a handful of family and friends allowed in— a perk of Clair's new promotion. History and beauty surrounded them, a special exhibit that Clair had curated herself. It had a wholly different theme presented to the public, but they knew the truth of it. Clair had watched Jane slide the ring on her finger, as if she was trying to remember every last detail. Jane had sketched it for her, later, and the drawing hung framed in their bedroom.

Jane dug the ring out from underneath her uniform. Her neck felt empty as she pulled the chain over her head. For so long, Clair's ring had hung there, tucked safely beside Jane's heart. Her fingers fumbled with the clasp—she had never opened it, not once, not since stringing the ring into place.

She opened it now. The ring slid off, landing in Jane's open palm.

Clair. The prospect was as impossible as a dream. It *was* a dream, in fact, the only dream. The one that Jane had kept having, in her weakest and most vulnerable moments—that there was some way to fix this, that everything would somehow be okay. She'd never expected it to actually be *possible*.

Jane's throat closed up. She held the ring, poised at the tip of Amy's finger.

It felt wrong, trading one for the other. The hero for the wife. Even if it was what Amy wanted, even if it meant saving the universe from imploding, even if it meant *Clair*.

"I don't want you to go," Jane whispered.

Amy's face softened. She leaned forward, and Jane barely contained a sob as Amy's kiss grazed the top of Jane's head—a blessing, permission . . . forgiveness. "It's okay," Amy said, her breath hot in Jane's hair. "It's okay, I promise."

Jane pulled back. She forced on her bravest face as she made herself meet Amy's eyes directly.

"You *really* want me to do this?"

Amy nodded, even as tears cut down her face. All around them, half-formed Janes were pressing in thick, as if sensing their imminent fate. "I do," Amy whispered. The faintest smile tugged at her lips.

Jane shot forward, kissing Amy hard. "Know that I love you," Jane whispered against her lips. "Every version of you. And thank you."

"You're welcome . . . wife."

Jane slid the ring into place.

Her lips locked with Amy's. The ring was probably enough, but Jane would be damned if she took any chances. She opened her heart to Amy and let Clair tumble out: every late night spent laughing instead of sleeping, every afternoon they spent baking cookies together, every stress they'd ever helped each other bear, every quiet evening side by side on the couch, every morning that Clair had woken Jane up. Days and weeks and years, piled together, and she let Amy have them all. Amy's empathy was like stepping through a warm waterfall. It engulfed Jane in a deluge: Clair's smile, her sigh, her laugh as she scolded Jane, her voice humming under her breath while she did the dishes. The way that she'd look back over her shoulder, a smile quirking her lips as she spotted Jane. *Clair.*

The wind died around them. The gallery fell into silence. Jane sat back, and she didn't need to look around to see that the figures that had been fading into existence had disappeared like the dreams that they were.

It must have worked then, but Jane didn't dare accept it—not yet. Amy . . . Clair . . . whoever she was now, was slumped over, eyes closed, chest rising and falling in a steady rhythm.

Jane held her breath. She reached out, brushing back the woman's hair.

Eyes blinked open. Slowly, cautiously. They looked down at the body they belonged to, the bindings still holding it in place. They raised up, and took in a sense of the room.

They settled on Jane.

Clair's eyes.

A smile quirked her lips.

"Ja—" Clair started to say, but Jane's kiss cut her off.

Guilt and loss and mixed feelings would find them both later and be dealt with, but for now there was nothing but this: Jane had finally gotten her moment. And it was *everything*. It was tears and laughter and kisses and relief as giddy as a drug straight to the veins. It was a thousand things said overlapping at once, and it was all the things that they didn't need to say sitting between them. It was every Christmas, every birthday. It was the one single thing that should never have happened, happening. It was Jane's heart bursting, healing, bursting again, an endless loop as she wrapped her arms around Clair—*Clair*—and held her as tightly as she could, and swore that she would never, ever, let go again.

The sound of a door opening cut through the gallery.

"All right, UltraViolet!" Windforce said, his voice booming into the room. "Prepare to—! Oh."

"Aw, shit," Rip-Shift said, his footsteps coming in next. "What did we miss?"

Jane and Clair broke apart, laughing. Jane took the technological crown off the top of Clair's head and tossed it aside. They let the rest of the team sort out the cleanup—transferring Ultra-Violet, notifying the mayor, checking on Cal . . .

Cal was gone. He must have woken up and escaped in the chaos, and though the Heroes broke up to do a quick search of the building, there was no sign of him. Jane tried not to worry too much. After all, he didn't have superpowers, and without UltraViolet to pull the strings for him, how much harm could he really *do*?

Besides, at the moment, nothing could dampen Jane's mood. She grinned from ear to ear as she helped Clair outside. During cleanup, Keisha had run out and tucked a car behind the building, away from the mob of press that had gathered at the main entrance.

"It's a good ending," Jane said now, Clair's gloved hand wrapped tight around Jane's for support.

Clair shook her head. She settled into the seat, then reached out to brush Jane's cheek with the back of her fingers. A flood of emotion passed between them, unchecked and bursting with gratitude. "There's where you're wrong," Clair said. She smiled. "It's not an ending, Jane . . . it's a new beginning."

27

A CITY SKYLINE, RENDERED IN MUTED WATERCOLORS. THE sky above takes up most of the panel, swirling clouds of purple-gray with streaks of red flashing like lightning. Dark lines capture the silhouette of a caped hero flying in from the distance, too far away to make out any details.

"New project?" Clair asked.

Jane shrugged. She was leaning on her elbows on her drawing table, her fingernails ring-stained with ink and paints, her hair tied in a messy bun on the back of her head. Clair's hand rested against Jane's shoulders, and Jane closed her eyes as a kiss landed atop her head.

Nearly six months had gone by, and not a second passed that Jane was not grateful. Every day was like Valentine's Day, their anniversary, Clair's birthday, all wrapped up into one. *"You know that you have to stop buying me flowers one of these days, right?"* Clair had asked once, about a week in.

"I don't have to do anything of the sort," Jane said, wrapping Clair's waist in a hug.

The flowers *had* tapered off since then—somewhat—but the sentiment hadn't wavered. Not for a single instant.

Clair's hand moved up from Jane's shoulder to her head, brushing back the loose hairs that had fallen free of Jane's bun.

"Don't you think it's a little . . . meta?" Clair asked. "A superhero writing about superheroes?"

Jane turned around in her chair, grinning. "I can't help it. It's what I do."

Clair smirked. She glanced out the window. The skeleton of the new Woolfolk Tower could just be seen over the treeline of Regent Park.

It had taken a long time to decide, and a lot of soul-searching, but eventually the two of them had opted to stay in the Grand City of the Heroes' world. Well, it kind of made sense: Clair was dead in their own universe, Jane was unemployed—not to mention the superpowers that both of them now possessed, and the large gap in the team if they left *on top* of Cal's disappearance. Jane had, at least, taken the time to return home for a few days, long enough to try to explain things to her mother. Her mother, who had listened as patiently as she possibly could, though Jane knew that she already had one finger on the speed dial of her phone under the table, ready to call Jane's grief counselor.

"I'll prove it to you," Jane had said, and she knew that her mother was rolling her eyes as Jane got up, crossed the apartment, opened her bedroom door. But all of Ms. Holloway's doubts had flown out of the room the minute Clair stepped through, arms thrown wide for a hug.

They visited every few months, now. Hopping universes long enough for a Sunday dinner—well, more or less. Time dilation, and all that.

"Do you like it, though?" Jane asked now. She gestured behind her, at the spread of paintings and sketches littering her work surface. Brand-new heroes, brand-new adventures. A fictional city, ready to be saved.

Clair leaned over, taking her time as she examined them. Her fingerless gloves—nothing from Amy's collection, all of them bought to Clair's own tastes—bore yellow lightning bolts across the back, and Jane smiled at them as she waited for Clair to finish assessing Jane's work.

"It's good," Clair said finally.

"Really?"

Clair nodded. "Really. I like Atomita the best."

"I knew you would," Jane said, grinning.

Clair gave Jane's shoulder a playful swat. "Remind me which of us is the empath, again?"

Jane's grin widened. She waggled her eyebrows. "Oh, that would be you, my dear. No doubt."

A flush tinged Clair's cheeks as she turned away. "I should get to work."

"What's the rush?" Jane asked, as she hooked Clair's waist.

Clair stuck her tongue out. Jane leaped up from her chair, catching it in a sloppy kiss.

"Ugh, gross," Clair said as she pulled away, but her voice was light and amused. She nodded at Jane's drawing table. "Anyway, do you have a publisher in mind yet?"

Jane shrugged. "Dunno. There's no QZero here."

"You could start one," Clair said as she moved to the door. "Publish the little voices. Make your mark. Goodness knows we have the money in this reality."

"Save the world through comics?"

Clair's laugh filtered back through the open doorway. "There are worse ideas, Jane Maxwell."

THIRTY MILES OUTSIDE OF GRAND CITY, A SHITTY LITTLE BAR FACES THE SUNSET WITH DEFIANCE.

It used to be a diner, and before that, it was a train car. It sits on a stretch of track not connected to anything, its wheels cemented in place like maybe if they weren't, the whole thing would go racing off into that sunset in search of greater things.

Lou Gaines knows the feeling, though it's money and not cement that ties her down. Or lack thereof, which, isn't that the kicker? When she thinks about what her life could be like . . .

But it's best not to go down that road. She's seen that road, in the form of her brother, and while it looks pretty at the time, in the end it'll only bite you in the ass. So here she is: no money, no options. Wiping down tables and mixing drinks and fending off wandering hands. Still, it's not all bad. Or at least that's what she tells herself, to keep from going crazy.

She's wiping down the counter at the bar when the man walks in. He's not one of her usuals, which in and of itself makes him interesting. He's wearing dark jeans, and an expensive t-shirt from some popular sporting-goods company, which Lou recognizes but can't ever remember what it's called. Lou has never understood why some people spend fifty bucks or more on a tee, which in her mind is something to be worn until you can't wear it no more, then used for rags until they disintegrate. No point in shelling out good money for something like that.

The man stands in the open door for a minute. A baseball cap obscures his face, though he doesn't need to bother—with the sun going down, everyone stepping into the bar is backlit like they're a Jesus painting.

Lou ignores him. Her boss is always telling her to greet people when they come in. ("A pretty girl smiling at customers can't hurt business," he says, though if that's what he wants Lou for, he picked the wrong woman. "Then hire a pretty girl," Lou tells him, and then he gets mad and protests, like Lou cares if he thinks she's pretty.) She goes back to working on her counter.

A few minutes later the man walks over. He sits down at the bar, almost but not quite directly across from where Lou is working.

"Can I get you somethin'?" Lou asks.

The man takes off his cap, and rests it on the counter beside him. He's shockingly handsome, like he just stepped out of a billboard. "Can I just have some water?" he asks. "I don't have any money."

Lou raises her eyebrow at his outfit, but she keeps her mouth shut. Someone wants water, hell, they got plenty of water. She turns away from him, as the TV on the back wall switches from commercials to what tries to pass for news these days. Lou glances at the ticker along the bottom. DELTAMAN STILL AT

LARGE | MAYOR MAXWELL: CITY IS "SAFEST IT'S EVER
BEEN" | PROTESTORS GATHER AT—

"Here you go," Lou says, as she returns with the glass. "Fair
warning, though: our water is nasty as shit."

"That doesn't matter." The man is staring over Lou's head,
fixed on the TV. He takes a drink without even looking.

Lou doesn't know what he finds so interesting. It's the same
crap that it's been every day for the past couple of weeks. The
Heroes fight a baddie, the Heroes defeat a baddie. People come
on to argue about whether the city *needs* people "like them,"
whether they're doing more harm than good, whether their presence is the reason for all of these increased attacks, blah blah, cut
to the next song please. She's disappointed in the guy's interest;
he seemed better than that.

Though, probably, it was just his chin. He has a heroic chin,
Lou decides.

She goes back to wiping down the counter.

"If people only knew," the man says.

Lou looks up to find that he's staring right at her. He points
at the TV, glass still in his hand, just his finger extended at the
screen.

"Knew what?"

"What they were really like. All of this pointless debate would
die in an instant."

Lou glances over her shoulder. "You mean the Heroes?" she
asks. "Or just . . . Enhanced?"

It's the new word that everyone's using. Lou doesn't like
it. Enhanced means more, enhanced means that someone's got
something that other people would want. Lou's cousin's new
iPhone is *enhanced*. Chocolate cake is *enhanced* by a splash of
blackberry brandy. Powers are nothing to be jealous of.

The man doesn't say anything at first. Lou fears that she's gone
too far, said the wrong thing somehow. But he smiles, eventually,
and takes another drink of the shit-water.

"Just the Heroes," he says, as he wipes his mouth with the
back of his wrist.

Lou laughs. It's relief, mostly, though she plays it off. "You're
fulla shit."

"Oh?" He's not offended, she can tell by his tone. Probably, he thinks she's flirting, but she's not.

Lou shrugs. "Acting like you know them."

"Maybe I do."

"Sure," Lou says. She's not going to argue—what's the point?—but she doesn't have to listen, either. She turns her back on him, heading for the dishwashing sink in the corner. Technically, it's Carlo's job, but he's been skiffing off work every day for a week now, and Lou hasn't said nothing cause it's not really her business, though it pisses her right off. She turns on the tap, and the faucet spits twice, pipes rattling, before it pukes water all over the glasses in the sink.

Just the same, though . . . what if it's true? If he actually does know them. *Someone* probably has to, after all, though what are the odds of that someone ending up in her bar, on her shift?

Probably not great, Lou tells herself. Probably one of those big numbers, like the odds of an asteroid crashing into Earth, or Lou getting struck by lightning, or winning the lottery. Though one of those has already happened.

She finds herself leaning on the bar across from him. Her chin is cupped in her hand, and the towel that she's been using is thrown over one shoulder.

"Okay," she says. "So tell me what they're like."

The man smiles. He's got the kind of teeth that Lou never sees around these parts. City teeth. Dental-insurance teeth.

They remind her, uncomfortably, of a wolf.

It occurs to Lou now that the two of them are alone. That the last of her dayside regulars has shuffled off to start his graveyard shift, that the next wave won't be coming in for another half hour or so. She hears her momma's voice in her head, the fear that Henrietta Gaines tried hard to instill in her children. The man is a lot larger than Lou is, she notices this now.

Except Lou isn't afraid. She has a shotgun tucked under the counter, which she hides behind bottles of Tabasco sauce when her boss is around. She doesn't actually need the gun, anyway, but it seems like something a normal girl would do, when faced with a shitty job in a shitty bar in a shitty town. It keeps people from asking questions that she doesn't want to answer.

"Oh, I think you already know what they're like," the man says. He reaches into his pocket and Lou straightens up—is he going for a knife?—but all he draws out is a folded scrap of paper. It's a printout from a news website.

The man has folded it so that mostly all you see is the photo that accompanies the article. Lou recognizes the picture—she has a copy of it herself, tucked into the front cover of a book in her bedroom. It's a blurry shot from her brother's arrest. You can't really see his face, and because he was under eighteen, and because of "the nature of his crime" (their words), his identity was mercifully kept from the press. The shot isn't really of *him*, anyway, so much as the three people standing in front of him as he's hauled away. Captain Lumen, Granite Girl, Windforce.

That paper scares her more than anything else that's happened so far.

"What's this?" she asks, playing it cool. She motions at it like it's nothing, like it means nothing. Though she probably hasn't looked at it long enough, she realizes, too late.

"This," he says, stabbing the paper against the bar with his finger, "is why you're going to help me. I have need of someone with your particular skill set."

Lou gives a nervous laugh. It doesn't convince either of them. "Bartending?"

"Sure," he says with a smirk. "Bartending."

He raises his glass to his lips. The amber of his beer catches the light, and the drink leaves behind a faint mustache that he wipes off with his hand. He sets the glass down pointedly between them.

Lou stares at it. It feels as if the world has begun to spin, like the bar actually *has* taken off from its tracks, bouncing and bumping over uneven terrain. She clutches the bar to steady herself.

She did not pour him that beer.

It's the same glass that she gave him, though, exactly the same one—Lou recognizes the faded logo on the front, a drawing of an eagle, the dark scratch like a lightning bolt across its face.

She looks up. Meets his eyes.

He *knows*.

She *knows*.

The man takes another drink. Puts it back down. "Here's the deal: you help me out, and I guarantee that I can get your brother out of prison. For good."

Lou goes cold. She doesn't like being manipulated, not one bit. She doesn't like any of it: not her secrets, somehow in the hands of this wacko, not his smile that she'd thought looked so cute at first, not the way that he's just been able to come sauntering in here and turn Lou's life upside down on a whim. If he was anyone else, Lou would not hesitate to tell him exactly where to stuff it.

But.

On the other hand.

Her brother.

The man grabs a napkin, and a pen left behind on the bar. "Tell you what," he says, as he jots something down quick. "You give it some thought. Let me know when you decide."

He slides the napkin across to her. Lou reads it in an instant: *Cal Goodman*, it says, with a phone number scrawled beneath that.

He stands up, taking the glass with him. "After all . . . ," he says, and then he pauses to drain the last of his beer. The glass *clunks* against the bar like a heavy door slamming shut. He looks straight at her, flashing another one of his grins. "It's not like I'm going anywhere."

TO BE CONTINUED...

PHOTO BY CORIE KELLEY

ABOUT THE AUTHOR

If JENN GOTT could have any power in the world, it would be superjumps. Lacking that, she fills her days writing stories about people with extraordinary abilities and tragic pasts. Her weaknesses are parallel worlds, time travel, and girl heroes. She lives in New England with her equally nerdy husband and their spoiled snuggle-cat.

🌐 jenngott.com
🐦 @gottwords
✉ jenn@jenngott.com

Sign up for the latest news and updates at:
jenngott.com/newsletter

CPSIA information can be obtained
at www.ICGtesting.com
Printed in the USA
LVHW112254230419
615338LV00002B/123/P